UNLOCKING THE ITALIAN DOC'S HEART

KATE HARDY

SAVING THE SINGLE DAD DOC

LOUISA HEATON

MILLS & BOON

First Published in Great Britain 2018
by Mills & Boon, an imprint of HarperCollins*Publishers*
1 London Bridge Street, London, SE1 9GF

Unlocking the Italian Doc's Heart © 2018 by Pamela Brooks

Saving the Single Dad Doc © 2018 by Louisa Heaton

ISBN: 978-0-263-93358-1

UNLOCKING THE ITALIAN DOC'S HEART

KATE HARDY

MILLS & BOON

To my much-loved editor Sheila,
with especial thanks for her patience. xx

CHAPTER ONE

'JENNA HARRIS—JUST the person I was looking for.' Robert Jones, the head of paediatrics, walked over to Jenna with a man she'd never seen before. 'Jenna, this is Lorenzo Conti, our new senior registrar. He's rostered on to the Paediatric Assessment Unit with you today, so I wondered if you'd mind settling him in?'

'Sure,' Jenna said. She held out her hand to Lorenzo. 'Welcome to the children's department at Muswell Hill Memorial Hospital, Dr Conti.'

'Thank you, Dr Harris,' he said, smiling back. His handshake was firm without being over-pushy, Jenna noticed; she liked that. 'Call me Renzo.'

His voice, with that slight Italian accent, was like melted chocolate. Add those expressive dark eyes, hair that flopped slightly over his forehead and that killer smile, and he'd have all the women in the hospital falling at his feet. And Jenna was horribly aware that her skin was tingling where he was touching her.

Oh, for pity's sake. This was totally inappropriate. Lorenzo Conti was her new colleague. She'd only just met him and he might already be involved with someone. Even if he wasn't, Jenna had promised herself that she was going to focus on her career and make up the ground she'd lost when she'd taken a year's career break. Right now, she really wasn't interested in starting a relationship with anyone; Danny's refusal to support her decision and the ultimatum he'd given her had put her off the idea of sharing her life with anyone else. Ever.

Though she didn't regret the choice she'd made. If she could go back to that moment, knowing what she did now, she'd still make exactly that same choice. The only thing she regretted was her poor judgement. How had she not seen Danny for what he was, earlier? How had she let herself be blinded by all that charm?

'Renzo,' she said, ignoring the fact she felt very slightly flustered. 'I'm Jenna.'

'Jenna,' he said, inclining his head slightly.

She was pretty sure the temperature in the room hadn't suddenly increased by five degrees, though it felt like it.

Oh, honestly. She needed to pull herself together. Now. Be professional, capable and polite, the way she'd normally be with a new member of the team. This pull of attraction towards Lorenzo Conti was something she'd just have to ignore, because it was going nowhere.

'Shall we?' She gestured to the door, and he released her hand.

'In the PAU, we see children who've been referred to us by their family doctor or by the Emergency Department,' she explained as she ushered him through to the assessment area.

'We had a similar system when I worked at the London Victoria,' he said.

'So coming here to Muswell Hill is a promotion for you?' she asked.

'Something like that.'

Though that clearly wasn't the whole story, because it was as if the shutters had just gone down behind his eyes. Whatever had just made him back away from her was none of her business. Time to back off. She smiled and said, 'Let me introduce you to Laney, our triage nurse in the PAU this morning. Laney, this is Dr Conti, our new senior reg.'

'Call me Renzo,' he said, shaking Laney's hand, and Jenna felt ever so slightly better that Laney seemed to be just as flustered by Lorenzo Conti as she'd been.

Their first case was a little girl who'd been eating an orange and stuffed a pip up her nose.

'OK for me to take this one, Renzo?' Jenna asked.

'Sure.'

'Mrs Peters, if you'd like to come this way, I'll examine Callie,' she said with a smile, and ushered the young woman and her daughter through to one of the cubicles.

Renzo could hear Jenna talking, all calm and reassuring with the mum; he liked her bedside manner very much. She was straightforward, explaining things easily in layman's terms without frightening either the child or the parent, so she'd be good to work with. And he liked what he'd seen of the rest of the team so far.

Making a fresh start here at Muswell Hill Memorial Hospital had definitely been a good idea.

'We see lots of small children who've stuffed something they shouldn't up their nose,' Jenna said, 'and I want to avoid putting Callie through a general anaesthetic and an operation if we can.'

Clearly she'd just looked up Callie's nose with a penlight torch, because then Lorenzo heard her say, 'I can see the pip very clearly, but because it's hard and round I can't put a crocodile clip up Callie's nose to grab it. I can't ask her to blow her nose, either, as she's too little to be able to blow it with the force she'd need to get the pip out, so I'm going to need your help with this. Is that OK?'

'Yes, of course. Just tell me what I need to do,' Mrs Peters said.

'I'm going to lay Callie down on the bed with her head on the pillow and block the nostril that hasn't got the orange pip in it. Then I'm going to ask you to blow into her mouth, and it should make the pip pop straight out. It doesn't always work, and I wouldn't ever advise you to try doing this at home if she does this again,' Jenna warned, 'because it's much safer to do it in hospital where we can act straight away if it doesn't work. But if it does work, that means we don't have to worry about an operation.'

There was a pause while Lorenzo assumed that Jenna was following through the actions she'd just described.

'Yay, it's out!' Jenna said. 'Well done for being so brave, Callie. And thank you, Mrs Peters.'

'That pip's got green bogeys on it,' he heard a high-pitched voice say. 'Yuck!'

Renzo didn't hear the rest of the conversation as he was busy with his own first patient, but he was pretty sure it would involve a special sticker for her patient and a reassuring smile for the mum. Just as he would've done, had he been the doctor treating young Callie.

Professionally, on first impressions he liked Jenna a lot. But he wasn't going to act on the pull of attraction he felt towards her. He'd learned the hard way not to risk his heart again. He'd lost too much, last time. His marriage, his daughter and his belief in love.

'I need both of you for the next case,' Laney said when Jenna and Lorenzo emerged from seeing their last patients. 'Billy Jackson is three. He fell on the stairs an hour ago and cut his forehead.'

Badly enough to need stitches rather than glueing the cut together, Lorenzo assumed, or Laney wouldn't have asked for them both to see the boy.

'Let's go and have a look at you and sort out that cut, Billy,' Lorenzo said with a smile when they went out to see the little boy.

Billy looked anxious and shielded the cut with his hand. 'I don't want to. It hurts.'

'I promise you we'll try our best to stop it hurting,' Lorenzo said, crouching down to the little boy's level. 'Do you like cars?'

Billy nodded solemnly and clutched his mother's hand.

'So do I. Tell you what, while I'm looking at your

poorly head, do you want to look through all my pictures of cars and see which one is your favourite?'

Again, Billy nodded.

'That's great. I'm Dr Renzo, and this is Dr Jenna. And I promise we're going to make your head feel much less sore.' He took a pack of cards from his pocket and handed them to Billy, straightened up and looked at the little boy's mum. 'Are you OK, Mrs Jackson?'

She gave him a rueful smile. 'Just about. There was an awful lot of blood. That's why I brought him into the emergency department—and they sent us up to you.'

'Head wounds always bleed a lot, and they always look much more scary than they really are,' Lorenzo said, to reassure her.

'Do you know how Billy banged his head?' Jenna asked.

'He tripped while he was going upstairs and he banged his head on one of the treads,' Mrs Jackson said.

'We see lots of children who've done exactly that,' Jenna said reassuringly. 'Was he unconscious at all after he banged his head, or has he seemed woozy since then or wanted to go to sleep?'

'No. He started crying the moment it happened.'

'Probably from the fright he gave himself, as well as the pain of the cut,' Jenna said. 'But it's good that he wasn't unconscious or woozy—that means he probably doesn't have concussion. I know it must've been a real worry for you but, as Renzo said, it's a lot less serious than it looks. Would you like to sit on the bed with Billy while we take a look at his cut and do a couple of tests?'

Between them, Lorenzo and Jenna took a closer look at the cut—a long gash, though thankfully it didn't have jagged edges—and then they checked his pupils and his reaction to light.

'I'm happy that we're looking at a straightforward cut rather than concussion or anything to worry about,' Lorenzo said. 'It's quite a big cut, so we're going to need to put stitches in. But I promise it's not going to hurt, Billy. I'm going to put some magic cream on your head so you won't feel anything when I mend your cut, and before that I'm going to ask Dr Jenna to help you to breathe in some gas and air. It's a bit like the stuff you get in a balloon when you've been to a party.'

'A balloon?' Billy's eyes went round with amazement. 'Will I go up in the air?'

Jenna clearly heard the slight panic in his voice because she said, 'No, sweetie, I promise you won't. You'll still be sitting there right next to Mummy.'

'And meanwhile you have a job to do,' Lorenzo said, gesturing to the cards Billy was holding. 'Have a look through these cars and tell me which one is your favourite.'

Jenna administered the gas and air, and Lorenzo put anaesthetic gel on the wound.

'Can you feel me touching your head?' Lorenzo asked.

'No-o,' Billy said, sounding surprised.

'That's good. Now, tell me about the cars you like best,' Lorenzo said.

While Billy held his mum's hand very tightly and looked through the car pictures, exclaiming every so often about one he liked, Lorenzo closed the wound with six neat, careful stitches.

'The good news is that the stitches are dissolvable, so you won't have to come and have them taken out again,' Jenna said to Mrs Jackson. 'I'll run you through how to care for the wound and I'll give you a leaflet as well, because obviously right now you're worried sick about Billy and it's hard to concentrate and remember things when you're worried. Basically you need to keep the area dry for the next two days, but you can wash it quickly with soap and water and pat it dry after that. If the wound opens up or looks red and swollen, or there's any kind of discharge, bring him straight back.'

'Thank you. I will,' Mrs Jackson said.

'So which one's your favourite out of the ones you liked, Billy?' Lorenzo asked when he'd finished the last suture.

'This one.' Billy handed him a card with a picture of a red sports car.

'Good choice. That's my favourite, too.'

'Because it's red?' the little boy guessed.

'Because it's Italian, like me,' Lorenzo said with a smile.

Billy's eyes widened. 'Have you got a real car like that?'

Lorenzo chuckled. 'I wish! Maybe one day.'

'I want a car like that when I'm all growed up,' Billy said.

'That sounds like a good plan,' Lorenzo said. He took a glittery sticker from his pocket with the words 'I was THIS brave' emblazoned across it. 'And I'm giving you a special sticker so you can show everyone else how brave you were today.'

'Thank you,' Billy said. With a shy look at his mother first, he handed the rest of the cards back to Lorenzo.

'Thank you,' Lorenzo said. He smiled at Mrs Jackson. 'Try not to worry. I know Jenna's taken you through what to look out for, but if you're concerned at all come back and see us.'

'I will,' she said. 'Thank you so much for what you've done for Billy.'

'Pleasure,' Lorenzo said. 'Take the stairs a bit more slowly from now on, Billy, OK?'

The little boy nodded.

'Nice work,' Jenna said when Billy and his mother had gone. 'So you use car pictures to distract little boys?'

'Not just boys. Girls like cars, too,' Lorenzo said. 'But I have a backup set of cards with puppies and kittens, to distract the kids who don't like cars.'

'Know your patient, hmm?' Jenna asked.

'Something like that.'

She glanced at her watch. 'It's almost lunchtime. Are you already spoken for?'

Lorenzo felt his eyes widen. Was she asking him out? He didn't have a problem with a woman taking the lead and asking a man out—but, considering they'd only just met, this was too fast for his liking. And he wasn't in the market for dating anyway.

'For lunch, that is,' she added swiftly. 'As this is your first day, if you don't already have plans, then you're very welcome to come to the canteen with me if you'd like some company and someone to show you where things are.'

Not a date, then: a colleague simply being kind and offering to show him around his new place of work. He could manage that. 'Thanks. That'd be nice.'

'Don't thank me just yet,' she warned.

'Why?' he asked, confused. 'Is the food not very nice here?'

'It's nothing to do with the food,' she said. 'Actually, I'll buy your lunch as I have a proposition for you.'

Lorenzo was pretty sure that it was just a turn of phrase, but the word 'proposition' put all sorts of inappropriate ideas in his head. Jenna Harris was gorgeous as well as being bubbly, with her mop of blonde curls that she wore pulled back in a scrunchie on the ward, wide blue eyes and ready smile. He liked the way she'd been with their patients and their parents: kind, clear and sympathetic.

But, after what had happened with Georgia and Florence, he wasn't up for falling in love again and getting his heart well and truly trampled on. This was his new start, and he intended to focus on his job, not his personal life.

'Proposition,' he said carefully.

'I'll explain over lunch. Meet you back here after your next patient?' she asked.

'OK,' he said.

At the canteen, Lorenzo chose a sandwich, fruit and coffee, and Jenna did the same.

'You really don't have to buy me lunch,' he said while they queued to pay.

'Oh, but I do,' she corrected, 'because I want you to feel ever so slightly beholden to me.'

So she was being manipulative? That was pretty much how Georgia had been with him. Except Jenna was being up front about it instead of hiding secrets. Well, he'd try to keep an open mind and listen to what she had to say before he made any judgements.

Once they'd sat down, he asked, 'So what's the proposition?'

Her eyes widened. 'Hang on, aren't we supposed to be doing all the usual pleasantries first? Like, where did you train, what made you pick paediatrics, does your family live near, that sort of thing?'

He shrugged. 'OK. I trained in London, I picked paediatrics because it was my favourite rotation when I was training; my parents, brother and sister all live in East London at the moment but my parents are thinking of moving back to their roots in Lake Garda when my father retires; and I'm single.' Most importantly, he added, 'And I'm not looking for a partner.' He'd had completely the wrong idea about his marriage, thinking that he and Georgia were happy. But things hadn't been what they'd seemed; he'd lived a lie for nearly two years before Georgia had finally cracked and told him the truth about Florence. Though he kept that particular black hole behind high walls and barbed wire. 'You?'

'I trained here in Muswell Hill, and I chose paediatrics for the same reason as you—I like kids and I really love making them better. My parents and my sister all live in London, about half an hour away from me; and I'm also single and not looking for a partner.' She smiled. 'Which means that you and I can be friends.'

'Is this part of the proposition?' he checked.

She laughed. 'Absolutely not. But we're a close-knit team on our ward and we do a lot of things together. Team nights out for pizza and ten-pin bowling, cinema, picnics on the beach in summer—that sort of thing. It's kind of like having an extended family. Partners and kids come along to half the stuff and it's lovely.'

A family. The thing he'd once had—and lost. And how he missed it. But he knew he was lucky to have what he had: a large extended Italian family who loved him. Wanting more was just greedy.

He shook himself. Jenna didn't know about his past, and she didn't need to know. Besides, she'd clearly meant to reassure him that he'd picked a really nice place to work. 'Sounds good,' he said, forcing himself to keep his tone light.

She raised her coffee mug at him. 'Welcome to the team. I think you're going to love it here as much as I do.'

He hoped so, too, but he'd reserve judgement until he'd been here a while. 'And the proposition?'

'I'm on the ward's fundraising committee. A week on Saturday, we're holding a six-hour danceathon to raise money for new toys for the ward,' she explained. 'People pay a fixed sum to enter, and they can be sponsored either for a flat fee or for each hour they stay on the dance floor.'

Now he understood what the proposition was. 'You want me to be one of the dancers?'

'If you're not on duty, then yes, please.'

Which would be an easy let-out for him. Except she'd know pretty quickly that he wasn't telling the truth, and he didn't want to start his professional life here with a lie. He'd had enough of lies.

'I'm off duty.'

'Good.' She smiled. 'It should be easy for you. Aren't all Italian men meant to be wonderful dancers?'

'That,' he said, 'is a sweeping generalisation. And I'm afraid I'll have to disappoint you, because I have two left feet.'

'So do half the people who are coming along on the day. It really doesn't matter what you look like or how badly you dance, as long as you raise some money for the toys. It's going to be fun,' she said. 'And you'll get to hear Maybe Baby play.'

'Who are Maybe Baby?' he asked.

'They're pretty much the hospital's house band—they play at a lot of weddings and special occasions,' Jenna explained. 'Half of them are from the Maternity ward—Anton on guitar and Gilly on bass—and from our department there's Keely on vocals and Martin on drums. They're fantastic.'

'They're playing for the whole six hours?'

'Probably for about half of it,' she said. 'Nathan, one of the porters in the Emergency Department, is a DJ when he's not working here, so he's doing the other half of the music for us. We're holding the danceathon in the local high school's sports hall; one of the local pubs is running a bar for us and donating the profits from the night, and a few of the parents of children we've treated heard what we're doing and offered to sort out the food for us. Plus we've sweet-talked a few local businesses into donating raffle prizes, everything from nice toiletries to chocolates to vouchers towards a meal.'

Lorenzo had the strongest feeling that she was downplaying her own role in this. Clearly it was something she'd been deeply involved in, something close to her heart.

'I'm more than happy to sponsor someone,' he said, 'and maybe take tickets on the door or help run your raffle stall. But I'm afraid it's a no to the dancing.'

'It's a shame I can't talk you into it, because it'll be fun,' she said, 'but I'll take the offer of manning a stall, for however much time you can spare. Thank you.'

'Are you dancing?' he asked, suddenly curious.

'Absolutely. You'd never get me running or struggling to lift stuff in the gym, because that doesn't appeal to me in the slightest,' she said, 'but I do a couple of dance classes a week and I walk my neighbour's dog at weekends. That's my preferred way of keeping fit.'

He should back off. It was none of his business. And he wasn't supposed to start being interested in someone else. This was *work*. But he couldn't stop the question coming out. 'What sort of dance classes?'

'Salsa on Tuesdays and Latin ballroom dancing on Thursdays. I'm not elegant enough to do the waltz or the foxtrot,' she explained, 'but I love dancing the samba and the cha-cha-cha.'

The fun and bouncy stuff. That didn't surprise him. From what he'd seen of her so far, that summed up Jenna Harris very neatly. 'So was the danceathon your idea?'

'Guilty as charged.' She raised an eyebrow. 'But everyone else on the committee said it sounded like a lot of fun, or we wouldn't have done it.'

'OK. Count me in for helping on a stall,' he said. And then his mouth ran away with him. He was supposed to be keeping things professional and slightly distant, not putting himself in a position where he'd see more of her. But the words came out anyway. 'I can help set up, too, if you like.'

'Thank you.' She smiled at him. 'And maybe I can talk you into just one dance.'

'Maybe. No promises,' he warned.

'Sure.' Her smile broadened, which told him she had every intention of breaking down his resistance.

Well, she had no chance there. His intentions were stronger still: to keep a professional distance between himself and Jenna. Yes, she was attractive and he liked her very much—but he wasn't risking his heart again. As far as he was concerned, they were strictly colleagues.

'I guess we ought to get back,' he said. 'Thank you for lunch.'

'My pleasure. And thank you for agreeing to help with the danceathon.'

'Prego,' he said, inclining his head. 'You're welcome.'

'If only you'd joined us a month ago. I bet you could've charmed a ton of money out of everyone who walked through the hospital doors by smiling at them and speaking in Italian. You would've been our secret weapon.' She looked at him with narrowed eyes. 'Would you be good at general knowledge, by any chance?'

'I'm reasonable,' he said.

'You're polite, so I'm guessing you're understating your talents because you don't want to boast about how good you are. Right. That settles it. I'm co-opting you onto our departmental quiz team, too.'

'You,' he said, 'are scary. All that sweet, sweet smile, baby-blue eyes and butter-wouldn't-melt expression— but you've got everyone organised and agreeing to things before they even have time to blink, haven't you?'

'Jenna the hustler—that's me,' she said, looking totally unrepentant. 'If I could actually play pool, I'd make gazillions out of unwary punters and we'd have the best-equipped paediatric department in the country.'

He couldn't help laughing. Even though he wanted to keep her at a distance, her warmth, her charm and her sheer chutzpah were irresistible. He would've liked to find something about her that wiped out that pull of attraction. But even her bossiness had a charm to it. She was *nice*. He'd have to rely on the determination that had got him through the miserable months when his marriage imploded, and keep things professional between them. 'I have a feeling you're going to get a ton of money out of your danceathon. And I bet you'll drive a hard bargain with a toy shop afterwards.'

'Cost price, that's what I'm after,' she said. 'So if you know someone with contacts to a wholesaler or a toy shop, I'm all ears.'

'Sorry. I can't help with that one.'

'That's OK. You're helping me set up, you're manning a stall for a bit, and you agreed to one dance. That'll do nicely.'

Lorenzo was pretty sure he hadn't actually agreed to one dance. But he was equally sure that Jenna wasn't going to let him get away with it. 'Let's get back to the ward,' he said. Where he'd be able to focus on work, and have the space to damp down the unexpected feelings that were threatening to turn him upside down.

CHAPTER TWO

'OH, NOW, THAT smells fabulous,' Jenna said, walking into the kitchen and hugging her twin. 'Tell me that's your lasagne cooking in the oven, Lu.'

'It is.' Lucy hugged her back. 'It'll be ready in twenty minutes. Grab a glass of wine. Will's in the living room with his nose in a book. How was your day?'

'Fine.' Jenna poured herself half a glass of wine. 'The new senior reg started today.'

'What's he or she like?'

'He's nice. Robert asked me to look after him in the PAU today.'

Lucy smiled. 'Because you, my dear sister, are brilliant at tucking new people under your wing.'

'Because I had a good example to follow in the best primary school teacher ever,' Jenna pointed out, and lifted her glass in a toast. 'So how was your day?'

'Fine. Ava spent the whole day chatting.'

Jenna grinned. 'That's because she takes after her aunt.'

'Strictly speaking—' Lucy began.

'I'm her *aunt*,' Jenna said firmly. 'Lu, we've been through this enough times. In every way, Ava is your and Will's daughter. All I did was lend you my womb for a few months—which I know you would have done for me if our situations had been the other way round.'

'Of course I would.' Lucy bit her lip. 'Though the egg was yours, too.'

'And, as we're identical twins, that means our genes are the same, so my egg is exactly the same as yours would've been,' Jenna reminded her. 'As far as I'm concerned, Ava's biologically yours, as well as legally and morally.'

Their friends and family—apart from one notable exception—had all been supportive about the surrogate pregnancy, but Jenna knew Lucy felt guilty about it. And usually Lucy's doubts came to the surface when someone had upset her on the subject. 'Has someone said something to you?' she asked gently.

'No—well, yes,' Lucy admitted.

'I hope you told them to walk a mile in your shoes and learn a few facts before they give you any more of their uninformed opinions.'

Lucy winced. 'It's my fault. The subject of surrogacy came up at toddler group. I should've just kept my mouth shut.'

'You have nothing to be ashamed of. If anything, your story might actually help someone who's struggling with the same issues you went through, and could see that there might just be a light for them, too, at the end of the tunnel.' Jenna sighed. 'But we seem to live in an age where everyone thinks their opinion is more valid than anyone else's, and they don't consider anyone else's feelings before they open their mouths.' Someone had clearly hectored her sister on the subject of surrogate babies. Jenna would've quite liked a serious chat with whoever had been so thoughtless, so she could put them very straight on the subject— and then shake them very hard until their teeth rattled.

'I guess.'

Jenna frowned. 'Lu, you know Ava's *yours*.' Had Lucy not been in a serious car crash which had ruptured her womb and damaged both her ovaries, five years ago, she wouldn't have needed an emergency hysterectomy at the age of twenty-seven, putting an end to any hope of having her own children naturally.

'I know.'

Jenna's frown deepened. 'Please tell me whoever it was didn't say something as vile as Danny did.'

'No-o.'

Which meant they had and Lucy didn't want to admit it. Jenna put her glass on the worktop and hugged her twin. 'Listen to me, you numpty. I love Will dearly, but purely as a brother. I don't fancy him and I never have. He doesn't fancy me, either. He'd drive me absolutely crackers if I had to live with him and all his vague professor stuff—just as I'd drive him crackers by bossing him around and organising him down to the last second instead of letting him get away with it, the way you do. And I love you more than anyone else in the world, Lu. I offered to be your surrogate because I was the one person who could actually make things right again after the adoption agency turned you and

Will down. I hated seeing you with a broken heart and I desperately wanted to be able to help you. Just as you would've done, if it had been me in your shoes. And you already know all that, Lu, so I don't know why I need to tell you again.'

Lucy swallowed hard. 'I know.'

'So please don't listen to some over-opinionated, thoughtless woman who clearly doesn't have a clue what it's like to be in that situation or care how she makes other people feel.'

Lucy swallowed hard. 'But I do feel guilty, Jen. If it wasn't for me, you'd be married to Danny by now.'

'And we'd probably be divorced,' Jenna pointed out dryly. 'Marrying him would've been a huge mistake.'

Lucy frowned. 'Would it? Because I worry that you're lonely.'

'I don't need a partner to have a fulfilling life,' Jenna said firmly. She wasn't going to admit to her twin in a million years that yes, sometimes she did feel lonely, when she woke at three in the morning and couldn't sleep. 'And I definitely don't need a partner who's going to issue ultimatums every time I suggest something that doesn't fit in with his world view. Any man who asks me to choose between him and you is going to lose—every single time.' She sang a snatch from the old song 'Sisters', just to emphasise the point, and hugged Lucy again. 'Danny lacked compassion. If anything, you did me a favour, because his reaction to the surrogacy is what made me finally realise that he saw everything in terms of financial cost.'

'But being our surrogate lost you your relationship.'

'Which wouldn't have worked in the long run, believe me. I don't want to be with someone who puts a price on everything and can't see any value if it can't be counted in cash. That isn't how I see things, and that kind of attitude makes me really unhappy. Marrying Danny would've been a disaster.'

'With the IVF treatment and the pregnancy, it cost you a year out of your career,' Lucy persisted.

'Which I can make up.'

'And it hit your earnings.'

That had been one of Danny's biggest arguments, and Jenna had despised him for it. Some things were way, way more important than money. Like her sister's happiness. Family. *Love.* 'I really don't care about the money, Lu. I had savings, and you and Will helped out with my rent. We managed just fine. It isn't an issue.'

'You've got an answer for everything, haven't you?' Lucy asked with a sigh.

'Yup. So, oh, best sister in the world, try to stop worrying about it and let me go and take a peek at my gorgeous niece—and I promise not to wake her.'

'I love you,' Lucy said.

'I love you, too,' Jenna said with a smile.

She tiptoed upstairs and crept into the nursery; Ava was fast asleep in her cot, with her hands thrown back over her head, looking totally angelic. Although Jenna had given birth to the baby, she'd always considered Ava as being Lucy's, not hers. And the love she felt for Ava wasn't that of a mother: it was that of a doting aunt. Which was just how it should be, in her view.

'Sleep tight, my beautiful niece,' she whispered, and tiptoed out of the nursery.

Back down in the kitchen, Will had joined Lucy and greeted Jenna with a hug.

'Perfect timing,' Lucy said with a smile, and served up.

Jenna took one mouthful and sighed in bliss. 'You really do make the best lasagne in the world.'

'And at least I know you're going to eat properly when you have dinner with us on Monday nights,' Lucy said.

'I *do* eat properly,' Jenna protested.

'Not when you're really busy on the ward, you don't. You grab a chocolate bar or a bowl of cereal.'

Jenna grinned. 'You do exactly the same when you're up to your eyes in baseline assessments in the first three weeks of the new school year and Will's forgotten the time and that it was his turn to cook that night.'

'I don't forget the time,' Will protested.

The sisters looked at him and laughed. 'Oh, you do, honey,' Lucy said, and leaned over to kiss him. 'Half the time you live in the first century, not the twenty-first.'

'It's my job,' Will said. 'And I'll join Lu in nagging you about eating properly, too, Jen.'

'Oh, give me a break!' But Jenna was laughing, knowing that her brother-in-law meant well. 'Now the new senior reg has started, it should be a bit less frantic on the ward.'

'So what's the new doctor like?' Will asked.

'He's good with kids. He has two packs of cards in his pockets as distractions—one with cars and one with puppies. It came in handy today when we had a toddler who slipped on the stairs and banged his head badly enough to need stitches,' Jenna said.

'Cars,' Will said dryly, 'shouldn't be gender specific.'

'Agreed, and Renzo isn't sexist. He says that girls also like cars.' Jenna smiled. 'But that might be because he's Italian and he loves fast cars and thinks everyone else does, too. He and little Billy—the lad who needed stitches—were practically drooling over this sports car.'

'I'd be drooling over that, too. Except we wouldn't be able to fit a baby seat in it,' Will said.

'Italian,' Lucy said thoughtfully.

'No, no and no,' Jenna said, knowing exactly what was going through her twin's mind. *Tall, dark and gorgeous.* Which pretty much summed up Lorenzo Conti. She definitely wasn't going to tell Lucy that he was single, because she knew her sister would go straight into matchmaker mode. 'But he did agree to help at the danceathon.'

'That's good. Though I still feel guilty about not being able to make it,' Lucy said.

'You have Will's niece's wedding in Edinburgh. And Will's parents need some catch-up time with Ava,' Jenna reminded her. 'You both gave me a massive donation and a raffle prize, so you've more than done your bit.'

'We wanted to help,' Will said.

'And you have. A lot,' Jenna said. 'So how's your day been, Will?'

'Full of deciphering illegible student handwriting—I swear it's twice as bad on exam papers,' Will said with a groan.

'Ah, the joys of May,' Jenna teased, laughing; she knew how much her brother-in-law loved his job and he adored his students—just as they adored him.

It was the perfect family evening, and Jenna was thoroughly relaxed by the time she got home. Though she couldn't quite get Lorenzo Conti out of her head. He'd been very adamant about being single and not looking for a partner; it sounded to her as if someone had really hurt him. Or maybe he'd lost someone to illness or an accident and didn't want to risk his heart again because the loss had hurt him too much. Not that it was any of her business. And she absolutely wasn't interested in anything other than a professional relationship with her new colleague. After Danny, as far as she was concerned, love was completely off limits. She didn't trust her judgement any more, not after she'd got it so badly wrong with him. She had a family she adored and a job that fulfilled her. She was lucky. Wanting to have the same kind of closeness with someone that Lucy had with Will, and a baby of her own—that would just be greedy.

Jenna's first patient in clinic the next morning, eight-year-old Maddie Loveday, was a puzzle.

'It started six weeks ago,' Maddie's mum said.

'She'd been at football club and came home with really red cheeks. It looked a bit like windburn, but it seemed a bit odd because it's not that cold and windy at the end of April. Then she went down with a really nasty virus. It hit the whole family and even I was in bed for three days with it.'

A rash and a virus. Two things that were really hard to narrow down, and half the time there wasn't an effective treatment and you just had to wait it out. Jenna smiled and waited for Mrs Loveday to continue.

'The rash didn't go away and it spread down her arms and legs. She said her legs hurt, she had pains in her tummy, and it hurt to swallow.' Mrs Loveday grimaced. 'Then she was really down and a bit weepy—which just isn't my Maddie. I took her to the doctor.'

'What did your GP say?' Jenna asked.

'He thought it might be allergic eczema, but my youngest has eczema and I'm really careful with laundry detergent and conditioner. Maddie's never had any kind of reaction to food, and that rash didn't look like any eczema I've ever seen.' Mrs Loveday sighed. 'I think he referred Maddie here just to shut me up.'

Seeing that she was close to tears, Jenna put a reassuring hand on her arm. 'Mrs Loveday, when our mums tell us that their kids aren't right, we listen. You're the experts on your kids, so you know when there's something wrong. It's our job to listen and help you.'

'Thank you.' Mrs Loveday swallowed hard. 'I know you can't believe everything you read on the

Internet, but I wondered if the rash was some kind of autoimmune thing.'

'That's a possibility,' Jenna said. 'Rashes have lots of different causes and they can be really tricky to diagnose. And you're absolutely right not to believe everything you read on the Internet, because there are a lot of scaremongering stories out there.' She turned to the little girl. 'Maddie, is it OK if I examine you?'

Maddie nodded.

Jenna looked at the rash. Coupled with the pain in Maddie's legs and tummy, and her difficulty in swallowing, the rash could well be a sign of an autoimmune problem, but Jenna wasn't sure quite which one. 'I've not seen a rash like this before,' she said. 'I think you're right, Mrs Loveday, and it's very likely an autoimmune disease. Do you mind if I have a quick discussion with one of my more senior colleagues?'

'As long as you can find out what's wrong with Maddie and make her better, then do whatever you need to,' Mrs Loveday said.

Jenna headed for the offices. None of the consultants was around, but Lorenzo was in his office. Given that he was her senior and had three or four years' more experience than she did, there was a chance that he'd seen a condition like Maddie's before. She rapped on his office door. 'Renzo, have you got a minute, please?'

'Sure,' he said.

'How are you on autoimmune diseases?'

'I've treated a few in my time,' he said. 'What are you looking at?'

'I'm not entirely sure.' She filled him in on Maddie Loveday's medical history and symptoms. 'I can see you're busy, so I'm sorry to ask, but I'm a bit stuck. I don't suppose I could borrow you to come and have a look at her, could I?'

'Sure,' he said, to her relief, and saved the file he was working on.

After Jenna had introduced him to the Lovedays, Lorenzo examined Maddie's skin. 'Mrs Loveday, has anyone talked to you about juvenile dermatomyositis or JDM?' he asked.

Mrs Loveday looked surprised. 'No. The GP just sent me here.'

'It's pretty rare, with about three in a million children being affected, and girls are twice as likely as boys to have it,' Lorenzo said. 'Basically "dermatomyositis" means inflammation of the skin and muscles, and from what Jenna's already told me and what I can see here, it looks to me as if that's what's happening to Maddie.'

'What causes it?' Mrs Loveday asked.

'We don't actually know,' Lorenzo said. 'Jenna told me about Maddie's virus, and in the cases we know of there was a virus involved.'

'So how long does it last? Will it ever go away? Is she going to get worse?' Mrs Loveday asked.

'Sometimes a child has one episode of JDM that lasts for a couple of years and then goes away for ever; sometimes it comes back again after a few years of remission; and sometimes it doesn't go away at all and needs managing for the rest of the child's life,' Lorenzo said. 'I'm sorry to be so vague, but the way the condition develops really varies. What I can promise is that we'll sort out some treatment so Maddie can live her life just as if she hasn't got JDM.'

'So what does this JDM do?' Mrs Loveday asked.

'It makes the muscles weaker and causes pain, so that's why Maddie's talked about her legs hurting and having tummy pains,' Lorenzo said. 'The inflammation tends to affect the large muscles around the hips and shoulders, so that means it's harder for Maddie to walk, climb the stairs, get up from the floor or lift her arms. And it'll make you tired, Maddie.'

The little girl nodded. 'Since I got the rash and tummy pains, I can't run as fast when I play football, and I'm really tired by the end of the match.'

'So how do you treat it?' Mrs Loveday asked.

'Medication and physiotherapy. I'd like to admit her to the ward for now,' Lorenzo said. 'Maddie might need to stay for a couple of weeks so we can get her condition under control—we can give her some medication to help, but there will be other treatments as well. We'll start with steroids at first and that'll really help with her muscles and her skin.'

Mrs Loveday looked shocked. 'Steroids? Isn't that the stuff bodybuilders use?'

'No, these are corticosteroids,' Jenna explained. 'They're naturally produced by the body, too, and we use them to bring down inflammation—that will stop Maddie's muscles hurting and it will also sort out the rash.'

'We'll also need to do some tests, including an EMG,' Lorenzo said. 'That's a special scan which

shows us the electrical activities in your muscles—
and I promise it doesn't hurt, Maddie.'

'Good,' the little girl said. 'Because I really, really
hurt right now and I hate feeling like this every day. I
just want to play football.'

'We'll make it stop hurting,' Jenna promised.

'We have physiotherapists here who can teach you
some exercises, Maddie, to make your muscles work
better,' Lorenzo said.

'They'll make you work hard,' Jenna added, 'but
they'll make it fun. You can come along, too, Mrs
Loveday, and learn how to do the exercises at home
with Maddie.'

'Will they be like the exercises I do at football?'
Maddie asked.

'Possibly,' Jenna said.

'Because I don't want to stop playing football. I
want to be a footballer when I grow up and be captain
of the women's team for England. I won't have to stop
playing, will I?' she asked, looking miserable at the
thought of giving up the sport she clearly loved more
than anything else.

'Definitely not,' Lorenzo said. 'And I know it's
horrible feeling so ill, but I reckon you timed getting
ill just right—the football season's over, so it means
you won't miss out on matches over the summer.'

'But there's football training camp in August. Will
I be better for that?' Maddie asked.

'Right now, we don't know how you're going to
respond to the treatment and if we'll need to change

your medication, but we'll do our best to make you well enough for the camp,' Jenna said.

'Once we've got the rash and the pain under control with the steroids,' Lorenzo said, 'you might need some other medication, Maddie. We'll see how things go, but you might need to have methotrexate injections once a week—the nurse should be able to do that at your family doctor's surgery, so you won't have to come back to hospital for it—and an anti-sickness medication.'

'Steroids sometimes affect your bone density— that means how strong your bones are—so we'll also need to give you special calcium and vitamin D supplements,' Jenna said.

'And, once you're responding to the treatment, we'll decrease the steroids gradually,' Lorenzo explained. 'If you do have a flare-up in the future, then we'll know which drugs work best for you and we can make sure you get the right ones to treat any future episodes.'

'You'll need to make sure you use plenty of sun cream and wear a hat in the summer,' Jenna added.

'Coach always makes us put sun cream on before training,' Maddie said.

'That's good. So we'll admit you to the ward now,' Lorenzo said, 'and try and get you all ready for football camp. Once you're home, we'll see you every few months to see how you're getting on and if we need to change your medication at all.'

Once Jenna had got one of the nurses to settle Maddie on the ward, she arranged the tests that Lorenzo had recommended. The EMG confirmed

Lorenzo's diagnosis; and she noticed that he gave up his lunch break to sit and chat to the little girl about football.

Lorenzo Conti was definitely one of the good guys.

She liked the way he worked, reassuring both their patients and their parents; and with him she really felt part of a team. It felt as if she'd worked with him for years, rather than only a couple of days. Which was crazy. She couldn't have that kind of rapport with him so soon.

In their afternoon break, she caught him just as he was heading for the staff room. 'I owe you cake for helping me with Maddie,' she said.

'You really don't. I was just doing my job, the same as you,' he said with a smile.

'You taught me something new today and I appreciate that, plus I happen to know you didn't have a lunch break—you spent it talking to Maddie about football,' she pointed out.

He shrugged. 'Maddie was fretting and I wanted to help her settle in to the ward. We had a fabulous argument about whether Italian football players were better than English ones, and that really cheered her up.'

Jenna could just imagine. Lorenzo had worked out the best way to take the little girl's mind off her illness and played his part with gusto. He was the kind of colleague it was a joy to work with. 'I just want to say thank you—I didn't want you to think I'm taking you for granted,' she said.

There was an odd expression on his face, but for so briefly that she thought she might have imagined it.

'I know you're not taking me for granted. We're colleagues. I'm just doing my job,' Lorenzo said. 'You really don't need to buy me cake.'

Then a really nasty thought hit her. Did he think that she was coming on to him? But she wasn't. 'I'd make the same offer to any of my colleagues who helped me like that,' she said. 'Regardless of gender or age.' And she hoped he'd follow through with the rest: regardless of marital status, because it was a platonic offer rather than a come-on.

'It's fine,' he said.

'Well, thanks. I really did appreciate your help,' she said. 'I thought Maddie might have some kind of rheumatology issue, but I haven't come across JDM before.'

'To be fair, I've only seen one case, and I wasn't the lead doctor in the case,' Lorenzo said.

'I'll look it up in my books tonight after salsa class.' She smiled. 'Which is a double-win situation for me, because it means I can find out what I need to know for Maddie's treatment, and revise for my paediatrics exams.'

Lorenzo stared at her. 'You're, what, three or four years younger than me?'

'I'm thirty-two.'

'Three years, then. I'm surprised you're not through all your exams already.'

'That's because I took a year's sabbatical,' she said.

'Sabbatical?'

His voice was soft and gentle, and Jenna almost confided in him about why she'd taken time off work. Then Danny's voice echoed in her head: *'You're going to be a surrogate mum for your sister? That's the most stupid idea I've ever heard. What about your career? How can you throw all that away just for a kid that you're not even keeping?'*

She didn't think Lorenzo was anything like Danny, but the situation wasn't exactly the easiest to explain. She didn't want him thinking that either she was a saint—because she was far from that—or the naive idiot Danny had called her when she'd refused to give in to his haranguing. 'Life throws up unexpected stuff, sometimes,' she said with a smile, fudging the issue.

Lorenzo had seen Jenna work with their patients. He knew she was competent, and also she was confident enough to admit when something was outside her experience, as Maddie had been today—so he didn't think she'd taken a year off because she'd been struggling with her work and needed to think about her future. So why had she taken a year's sabbatical? Had it been a career break to have a baby, perhaps?

Though, in his experience, when his colleagues had children, they tended to talk about them. Jenna hadn't said a word about having children of her own.

Maybe she'd had a child, then lost it.

He knew how that felt, and he didn't talk about it. He could understand why someone just wouldn't want the constant reminders of the empty spaces in their lives. So he wasn't going to push her about it.

Besides, she'd hit the nail on the head about his own situation. Unexpected stuff. In his case, it had been something he'd been too naive and stupid to work out for himself. That his wife had cheated on him with her ex, and the little girl he'd believed was his was actually another man's daughter. 'Very true,' he said. 'Life can be unexpected.' And sometimes it took you a while to pick yourself up and dust yourself off again. 'If you want anyone to test you on stuff before the exams, give me a yell.'

'Thanks. That's kind.' She smiled at him, and he had to damp down the urge to lace his fingers through hers and suggest something more personal than simply exam revision.

This was ridiculous. They'd both said that they weren't in the market for a relationship. After Georgia, he'd lost his capacity to trust.

Yet something about Jenna Harris drew him. Her warmth, her verve, her kindness.

He was going to have to be careful about this. Really careful.

Because he really didn't want to risk his heart again.

CHAPTER THREE

BY THE END of Lorenzo's first two weeks at Muswell Hill Memorial, he'd completely settled in to his new role. As Jenna had told him on the first day, the team on the ward was good to work with, and they were like a family. He'd already been to a team pizza night out, a weekend game of football in the park, and joined the ward's quiz team—and the danceathon was happening at the weekend. It felt as if he'd been working at Muswell Hill for months rather than a matter of a few days.

The only thing he needed to deal with now was his inappropriate feelings towards Jenna.

Every time his hand brushed against hers at work, he felt a tingle all the way down his arm. When she smiled, it made his heart feel as if it had just skipped a beat. And this was crazy. He didn't want to get involved and he knew that she didn't, either.

He really didn't understand why he was reacting to her in this way. It would be easier if she'd turned out to be a gossip, or an ambition-driven bitch who trampled on her colleagues to get a promotion—the kind of person he wouldn't want to be within a mile of. But she was warm, sweet, great with their patients and parents, and he'd seen her patiently explaining something to one of the junior doctors.

And he had to admit he was attracted to her. Physically as well as intellectually. The problem was, he'd been here before with Georgia. He'd fallen in love with someone he thought loved him back—and she'd let him down in the worst possible way. He'd pretty much come to terms with the fact that Georgia had left him for someone else; although it had hurt, he could understand that if you loved someone that much it just took you over and you couldn't help your feelings. But taking their daughter away had hurt him more deeply than anything he'd ever known. He had no intention of risking that sort of pain again.

Besides, for someone as nice as Jenna to be single and adamant that she wasn't looking for a relationship, he'd guess that she'd been let down by someone in the past. Something to do with her year off work, perhaps. Not that he could be intrusive and ask.

So he'd have to keep his feelings under control. Remind himself that relationships weren't for him, and he was Jenna's colleague. Maybe they could become friends—but he wasn't sure he could even handle that.

Strictly professional was the order of the day.

On Saturday afternoon, Lorenzo walked to the local high school and signed in, then followed the signs to the sports hall. Jenna was already there. He noticed that her hair was caught back in a scrunchie, the way it was at work, and he wondered what it would be like if she took the scrunchie out. Would her hair fall over her shoulders in wild curls?

Worst of all, he found himself wondering what her hair would look like spread over his pillow...

Oh, for pity's sake. This was a charity danceathon. This wasn't the time or the place to start fantasising about Jenna Harris. She was off limits and they had work to do. He shook himself mentally, then went over to her. 'Reporting for duty, as promised,' he said with a smile. 'What do you need me to do?'

Jenna looked up at Lorenzo and her heart skipped a beat. Instead of the formal shirt, tie and dark trousers he always wore on the ward beneath his white coat, he was wearing jeans and a T-shirt. It made him look younger and more approachable; and she was horrified to find that she was actually reaching out to put her hand on his arm.

Absolutely not.

This wasn't the deal. He was helping out. He was here as a new colleague and nothing more. She needed to keep this strictly professional.

She shook herself. 'Hi. Thanks for coming to help.' He'd asked her what she wanted him to do. Her head was suddenly full of all sorts of inappropriate phrases. She managed to get a grip on herself—just—and said, 'There's a table over there with all the raffle prizes on it. If you wouldn't mind taping raffle ticket numbers to the prizes, and then folding the rest of the raffle tickets for the box, that would be great.' She handed him a book of raffle tickets and a roll of sticky tape; her fingers brushed against his and a shiver ran down her spine.

Was it her imagination, or had his eyes just widened slightly?

Or was she reading too much into it?

This really wasn't the time or the place.

Tickets, she reminded herself sharply. 'We're just using the ones on the right-hand side of the ticket page that end in a zero to stick on the prizes, but all the left-hand tickets go in the box, folded so you can't see the number.'

'Which means there's a one in ten chance of winning a prize. That sounds reasonable,' he said, and went off to sort out the raffle table.

Nathan from the Emergency Department was helping the members of Maybe Baby to set up the stage and wire up the sound system ready for the sound check; the local pub was setting up the bar to one side of the hall; and a stream of parents of their former patients came over to her to check where she wanted the food set out.

All the time, Jenna was incredibly aware of Lorenzo's presence. This was crazy. The last thing she needed in her life right now was any kind of complication. She was busy at work and with her studies, and she liked her life just as it was.

Yet a little voice kept echoing in her head. *What if...?*

What if she could have what Lucy had? Someone who loved her and a family of her own?

She shoved the thought away. Apart from anything else, she had the strongest feeling that Lorenzo had been hurt in the past—hence his insistence on not wanting a relationship. And, given the way her judgement had let her down so badly over Danny, how could she be sure that she wouldn't be making just as much of a mistake with Lorenzo?

She was just going to have to ignore that little voice and listen to her common sense instead.

Once Lorenzo had sorted out the raffle tickets, he joined another team in setting out chairs for the people who'd just come to watch the dancing or who needed a break from the dance floor.

'It's really good of you to do this,' Jenna said, coming over to him. 'I feel a bit guilty, roping you in to help when you've been working at the hospital for barely a couple of weeks.'

'It's fine. I wasn't doing anything special at the weekend anyway—plus it's a nice way to get to know the team outside work,' he pointed out.

'It's still appreciated,' she said.

He had to muster every gram of professionalism when she smiled at him. What on earth was the matter with him? It was anatomically impossible for your heart to do a somersault, so feeling that it had just happened was utterly ridiculous. He needed to get a grip.

'Is there anything else you need me to do?' he asked.

She shook her head. 'I'm just handing out the cash

floats to the hospital-run stalls, and then I'm going to change into my dancing shoes.'

'Then I'll do my best to sell raffle tickets,' Lorenzo said.

When the danceathon started, Lorenzo was surprised to discover just how good the band was. Keely, one of the senior nurses in their department, had a beautiful voice and could easily have made a career out of singing. Nathan, one of the porters in the Emergency Department, was the DJ who did an hour's slot between each set the band played; and, in between sorting out the music, the band and the DJ all joined in with the dancing.

'You've done more than your fair share on the raffle, Renzo. I'll take over while you take a break. Go and have a dance,' Laney, one of the nurses on their ward, said with a smile, taking the box of tickets and the cash box from him.

It looked as if he didn't have much choice, even though dancing really wasn't his thing. He stood on the edge of the dance floor, moving awkwardly to the music and wondering how long he'd have to be there before he could justifiably go back to the raffle table, and then Jenna was there beside him.

'Hey. You've finally come to join us on the dance floor?' she asked.

'Laney bullied me into it. I did warn you that not all Italian men could dance and I have two left feet,' he said with a rueful smile.

'Everyone can dance. You just need someone to

show you how,' she said with a grin. 'This is salsa, and it's fun.'

No, it wasn't. He felt like a fish out of water. 'Can't I just move my feet any old how?' he asked plaintively.

She smiled. 'Not to salsa, but I promise the steps aren't so bad. Stand opposite me, and I'll show you. I'll slow it down for you so we do it at half the speed until you get the hang of it. This is the first step they teach you in class—the side basic.'

He stood opposite her, knowing he was just about to make a colossal idiot of himself.

'Now, you're going to mirror everything I do,' she said.

Mirror everything.

He noticed that she'd changed more than just her shoes, as she'd suggested earlier: the faded jeans and ancient T-shirt she'd worn while setting things up had been replaced by black trousers and a strappy top. And her shoes were clearly proper dance shoes, red and glittery. Somehow he wasn't surprised that Jenna had chosen such a bright, sparkly colour. They went perfectly with her personality.

'Stand with your left leg bent, and keep your right leg straight,' she instructed. 'Shift your weight to your right leg.'

Just the same as she was when she gave instructions at work, he noticed: clear, concise and making things easy to follow.

He really liked that about her; yet, at the same time, he was wary. He didn't think she was the sort to hurt other people; but then again he'd believed that about

Georgia, and how wrong he'd been there. He'd kept all his relationships strictly platonic, ever since, to make sure he wouldn't get hurt again. But Jenna tempted him more than anyone he'd ever met. Her warmth, her sweetness…

Yet he was pretty sure that she, too, had been hurt in the past. The way she'd avoided talking about her sabbatical was a big clue.

Maybe they could help each other.

Or maybe they'd just make things worse and he should just leave it.

He shook himself, realising that she'd spoken to him. 'Sorry. I missed that. Would you mind running through it again?'

'Sure. Take a step to the left with your left leg,' she said, 'rock back so your weight's on your right leg again, and close your feet. The beat's one, two, three-and-hold.'

Mirroring what she did, he managed to do it without tripping over.

'Now repeat it the other way,' she said. Again, she talked him through it and slowed it down so he could follow.

'Brilliant. Now we put them both together—in dancing everything's a count of eight. So it's one, two, three, hold, five, six, seven, hold.'

He couldn't quite follow her arm movements, but he managed the feet, and she seemed pleased.

'Perfect,' she said. 'We'll make a dancer of you yet. There's a back-and-forward one as well.'

Which sounded a bit too much for his confidence level. 'Let's just leave it at the side one,' he said.

'No problem. We'll stick to the side basic,' she said with a smile. 'Ready?'

He counted the beats. One, two, three, hold... And then somehow he was dancing with her. Really dancing, not just moving randomly and hoping he didn't look too much of an idiot on the dance floor. She was right: it *was* fun. He couldn't remember the last time he'd enjoyed himself so much.

Jenna had taken the scrunchie out of her hair, too, so her curls were free and wild; she was laughing and her blue eyes were sparkling, and she looked utterly beautiful—like a Pre-Raphaelite goddess. He hadn't felt this kind of pull towards someone since he'd first started dating Georgia.

The thought was enough to haul him up short and he missed the beat, stumbled and stopped.

'Are you OK?' Jenna asked.

'Sure.' He smiled at her, not wanting to tell her what was really wrong. 'I've just got two left feet, that's all.'

She smiled back. 'A couple of the guys at our salsa class just couldn't work out which feet to move, so our teacher got them to wear a band on each wrist—lemon for left and red for right—to give them a visual cue, and it really helped.' She shrugged. 'Though I guess this isn't really the place for it.'

She slowed her movements down and talked him through the steps until he was moving confidently again. Jenna was just the same outside work as she was on the ward, kind and considerate without making a big deal of things; Lorenzo really liked that about her.

He danced with her to the rest of the song, then said,

'It's time for me to go and sell raffle tickets among the crowd.'

Her glance said very clearly that she knew he was chickening out of the dancing; he wondered if she realised why, and that it was her nearness rather than the actual dancing that spooked him.

Did she feel the same pull towards him that he felt towards her? And, if so, what were they going to do about it? Could he take a risk with her?

Even though Lorenzo was officially walking round the seated audience, sweet-talking them into buying more raffle tickets, he still couldn't take his eyes off Jenna. She was dancing a much faster and more complicated salsa with three or four people he guessed might be from her class, because they were keeping up with her and doing all the dipping and swaying and turns—things he was very glad she hadn't suggested that he tried doing, because they were way above his pay grade.

The way she moved was stunning, all sinuous and sensual. He wanted to walk over there, dance with her and then kiss her until they were both dizzy. Which would be a really stupid thing to do. He worked with Jenna, and they'd agreed to be colleagues and friends. Anything else would just lead to heartache.

He concentrated on selling the raffle tickets until all the prizes had been won, then took Jenna a glass of water.

'Thanks, that's so kind of you.' She drank all the water in one go, and then smiled at him.

And how crazy was it that his heart felt as if it had just done a backward somersault?

He managed to pull himself together. Just. 'All the prizes have been won, so Laney and I are going to count up the money; and she said we need to take off the float.'

'The float was ten pounds. Thank you. There's a box under the table with bags for the coins and rubber bands for the notes, plus a big padded bag to put the whole lot in,' she said.

Clearly Jenna had done this sort of thing before, he thought, because she was perfectly organised.

As if his thoughts had shown on his face, she added, 'With my sister being a teacher, I've helped out at a lot of school events in my time and counted up a lot of takings, so I know the most efficient way to deal with the money afterwards.'

'Got you,' he said.

Between them, he and Laney totted up the takings and wrote them on the outside of the padded bag. And, when Maybe Baby had played the last song of the danceathon, Keely called Jenna on to the stage to round up the evening.

'Thank you, everyone, for coming tonight,' Jenna said. 'And I'd like to thank everyone who's helped at a stall, donated a prize, sponsored a dancer, danced here on the floor tonight or come along for support and bought things. Thank you to all the parents and local businesses who've helped us with food and drink and prizes. We'll total everything up over the weekend and I'll make sure how much we've raised is posted on the ward's website and social media page. And thank you, too, on behalf of our patients, because the toys your money's going to buy will help them settle on the ward and distract them from some of their worries. That really makes a difference and it means that treatment is less stressful for them. Thank you—all of you.'

There was a round of applause, and then the clearing away started. Everyone worked together, moving tables, chairs and the few bits of unsold stock. The band and the DJ cleared away the sound systems and their equipment, and then Jenna wielded a mop and bucket to make sure that the school's sports hall was left spotless.

'Thanks, everyone,' she said when it was all done. 'I've really appreciated your help tonight.'

'Can I give you a hand taking that home?' Lorenzo asked, gesturing to the box that contained all the proceeds from the night.

'I'm definitely not walking about with all this money. I've booked a taxi,' she said. 'You're very welcome to a lift, if you're on my way home.'

This was his get-out, Lorenzo thought. Even if they were going in the same direction, he could say no.

'Actually, come along anyway. I owe you a drink for giving up most of your day and all of your evening,' she added.

'It was my pleasure. You don't owe me anything,' he said. But then his mouth seemed to be working to a different script to the one in his head, and he heard himself saying, 'Though I'll wait with you until the taxi arrives. I know you're perfectly capable of looking after yourself, but you've got tonight's takings with you.'

'And you're right—I'd rather not be on my own with that sort of money,' she said. 'Thank you.'

It was only a few minutes' wait; and then somehow he found himself seeing Jenna home in the taxi anyway.

'Come in for a glass of wine,' she said.

And his mouth was really on a roll, because instead of making a polite excuse he found himself agreeing.

She ushered him into the kitchen and put the box from the danceathon on one of the worktops. 'What would you prefer—red or white?'

'Whatever's open,' he said.

She peered into the fridge. 'Rosé.' She paused. 'Is that OK?'

'It's fine,' he said.

She poured two glasses and handed him one before lifting her own in a toast. 'Cheers, and thank you again for your help.'

'My pleasure.' He took a sip of the wine.

Clearly he'd made a face, because she asked, 'It's too sweet for you, isn't it?'

'It's fine,' he fibbed.

'You said most of your family lives in Italy.' She bit her lip. 'Please don't tell me they have a vineyard.'

'I'm afraid they do,' he said.

'And they've won awards for their wine?' she guessed.

He nodded. 'Bardolino *chiaretto*.'

'That's red, right?'

'Red's the most famous Bardolino wine. But

chiaretto is rosé,' he said. Light, not too sweet, and perfect for summer evenings.

'Sorry, I'm afraid this isn't award-winning stuff. Though it's very drinkable in summer.'

It was way too sweet for his taste, but he wasn't going to make her feel bad. 'It's fine.'

'Given that there were really only snacks at the danceathon, I ought to offer you a very late dinner,' she said, 'but I'm afraid all I have in my fridge is some salad, plus some ready-made pasta sauce and some dried pasta in the cupboard. And, especially as you're Italian and you're used to proper home-made pasta, I'm not sure I dare offer you that.'

Her kitchen didn't look like a cook's kitchen. It looked more like the kind of place where she sat and chatted with friends, over coffee and cakes that she'd bought from the local bakery rather than made herself. There was a cork board on the wall with lots of leaflets pinned to it; dozens of photographs were held to the fridge with magnets, and he'd just bet the mantelpiece in her living room was crammed to bursting with photographs in frames.

'You've been literally rushed off your feet for the last six hours, not to mention setting up and clearing away again. I don't expect you to make dinner for me.' This was his perfect cue to go home.

Common sense said that he should go home. Now.

But part of him really wanted to stay. To get to know Jenna better.

He found himself saying, 'But I could cook for you, if you like.'

She blinked. 'Hang on. You're offering to cook for me?'

'I can't dance,' he said, 'but cooking's in my skillset.'

'That's one up on me,' she said. 'My family always teases me that I could burn water. Lucy—my sister—insists on cooking for me on Monday nights so she knows I eat one proper meal a week.' She looked at him and frowned. 'You said your family owns a vineyard. Do they own a restaurant as well?'

'Um, yes. Two or three. And a couple of hotels.'

She groaned. 'Then I am never, *ever* offering to cook for you.'

He laughed. 'Just because my cousin happens to be a Michelin-starred chef, it doesn't mean we're all that standard.'

She looked at him. 'Your cousin seriously has a Michelin star?'

'Yes. But Matteo's very down to earth,' Lorenzo protested. 'He just likes good, fresh food that's cooked well and presented well.'

She raised an eyebrow. 'I bet none of your family dares cook for him.'

'He's a chef, not a critic. If a meal is cooked for him with love, he'll eat it and smile, even if it's absolutely terrible.' Lorenzo grinned. 'Though the next morning whoever cooked it will get a quiet private lesson on how to make it better in future. Little tiny tweaks that you can remember easily and make a huge difference to how edible the finished dish is. Matteo's one of the good guys.' He smiled. 'And he taught me to make great pasta sauce from just about anything.'

'Well, if you really want to see what you can do with an almost empty fridge, be my guest.' She spread her hands. 'But don't say I didn't warn you.'

'Let's have a look at what's there.' At her gesture of permission, he looked in her fridge. There was some olive oil margarine, cheese, some spring onions and tomatoes that were past their best, half a bag of tired-looking spinach, and a bulb of garlic that had started sprouting. Not brilliant, but he could work with it. And he wasn't going to use the jar of sauce, either.

'Do you have any fresh chilli?' he asked, though he was pretty sure he already knew the answer.

'Nope.' She rummaged in a cupboard. 'How about chilli flakes? I've never actually opened them. Lu probably bought them for me. Oh, wait…'

Lorenzo had to smother a grin as she checked the sell-by date and gave a visible sigh of relief. 'It's OK. They're still in date.'

'Good. All I need now is a sharp knife and a chopping board, a grater, the pasta—oh, and two pans, please.'

A bit more rummaging in the cupboard, and she produced the dried pasta, a chopping board, a grater and two pans. 'The knife's in the drawer next to the sink. Don't you need the jar of sauce?'

'No,' he said with a smile. He put the kettle on to boil water for the pasta. 'We've got about ten minutes until dinner,' he said, once he'd poured the water over the pasta. 'Sit down and relax.' He grimaced.

'Sorry. I didn't mean to be bossy and take over. It's your kitchen.'

'It's fine,' she said. 'It's nice having my own personal chef.'

And actually it felt good to cook for someone again. He'd loved making pasta sauce for Florence, helping her feed herself and smiling as she smeared tomato sauce round her face and asked for more. *'Mato, Dada!'*

While the pasta bubbled away, he chopped the tomatoes, spring onions and garlic, added them to the pan with the margarine and sautéed them, then added the chilli flakes and the spinach to let the leaves wilt. Finally he grated the cheese.

Jenna had set the table while he was cooking; Lorenzo tested the pasta, then drained it and divided it between the two large pasta bowls she'd got ready, added the sauce, and sprinkled the cheese on top. 'Here we are.'

She took a mouthful and her eyes widened with pleasure, the way Florence's used to. 'I know what was in my fridge and I had no idea anyone could make anything from that lot, even Lu—and she loves cooking. This is seriously impressive. Did you ever think of being a chef, like your cousin?'

'No. I always wanted to be a doctor,' he said.

'Are either of your parents doctors?' she asked.

He shook his head. 'Dad's an architect and Mum works at the local nursery school. How about yours?'

'Dad's a GP and Mum's his practice nurse,' she said.

'Medicine runs in the family, then. So is your sister a medic, too?'

'No. Lucy is a primary school deputy head—one of the youngest to have the role,' she said, clearly very proud of her sister. 'What about you? Do you have brothers or sisters?'

'One of each—my brother's an architect, like my dad, and my sister's a florist. I'm the oldest.'

'Me, too,' she said with a smile. 'So does your cousin who's the chef live in London, too?'

'Verona,' Lorenzo explained. 'Most of my family live somewhere between the city and one of the towns on the southern end of Lake Garda, either working in the family vineyard or at the hotels or restaurants. My dad was the odd one out; he was always fascinated by buildings and he wanted to be an architect. Because he's the baby of the family, everyone supported him. They were really proud of him when he got a top job in London, even though it meant moving here and he wouldn't see much of everyone. Though obviously it's better nowadays with phones and video calls, and flights are so easy. We always spent the summer holidays at the vineyard when I was growing up and even during my student years, picking grapes and helping with the harvest. We'd take a boat out on the lake and have picnics after the day's work was done, and watch the sun set over the mountains.'

'That sounds idyllic,' she said.

'It was. Lake Garda's the most beautiful place on earth,' he said. 'Italy's my second home.'

'It sounds as if your family's close,' she said.

'They are.' Though he was the only one in his family who'd messed up his marriage. Both his brother and sister were happily married with a three-year-old each—exactly as he thought he'd be at this stage.

How wrong he'd been.

He looked at her. 'And, from the photographs on your fridge, so is yours.'

She smiled. 'We are.' She got up to take one of the photographs and handed it to him. 'That's Lucy, my brother-in-law Will, and their baby Ava. They would've been at the danceathon today—but Will's niece was getting married this afternoon, so they're up in Edinburgh for the weekend.'

He looked at the photograph and then back to her. 'Would I be right in saying Lucy's your identical twin?'

'Uh-huh. But I'm the oldest by a whole three minutes.' She smiled. 'And I'm a very doting aunt. What about you? Do you have any nieces and nephews?'

'Yes.' *And, for eighteen months, I had a daughter. Except it was all a lie.* He shook himself. 'One of each. Riccardo has a little girl, Emily, and Chiara has a little boy, Jack. They're both three.' A couple of months older than Florence. 'And they both go to the nursery school where my mum works.'

'Oh, that's lovely.'

'It means they both settled in really quickly, because Nonna was there to make it familiar,' he said with a smile.

'Just like Lu takes Ava to Dad's surgery for vaccinations because Granny can always make Ava laugh and take her mind off the sting of the needle,' Jenna said.

There was something wistful in her face, quickly hidden again. But it felt too intrusive to ask.

He made polite conversation about food until they'd finished dinner.

'I'm sorry, I can't offer you pudding,' she said.

'That's fine. I'll wash up.'

She shook her head. 'You cooked, so I'll deal with the washing up.'

And now it really was his cue to leave. 'I guess I'd better let you get on. I'll see you at work on Monday, then.'

'Thank you for dinner,' she said.

He spread his hands. 'Hey, you provided the ingredients. I just cooked.'

'Half that stuff was well past its best and you still produced something amazing,' she pointed out.

'I like cooking. It relaxes me,' he said. And then curiosity got the better of him. 'What would you have done if I hadn't cooked?'

'Probably poured myself a bowl of cereal,' she admitted. 'Which is why Lu nags me.'

'I'd nag my sister, too, if she did that sort of thing,' he said. 'Actually, I nag her about breakfast all the time, because she's always up so early for the flower markets and she claims she doesn't have time to eat. Chiara would live on coffee if I didn't nag her.'

She smiled at him. 'Bossy oldest sibling, hmm?'

He laughed. 'And do you boss Lucy about?'

'Sometimes,' she admitted.

'There you are, then. Takes one to know one.'

She grinned. 'Bet I'm bossier than you.'

'You're definitely more of a hustler than me,' he said with a grin. 'Seriously, though, thanks for today. I really enjoyed it.' And he was surprised by how much fun it had been.

'And I really appreciate you giving up your time to help,' she said.

He accidentally brushed against her as she walked with him to her front door, and it sent a tingle right through him. It tipped him off balance to the point where he said, 'Maybe, if you're not busy tomorrow, I could take you out for lunch.'

Her eyes widened. 'That's very nice of you to ask me, and I'm flattered,' she said carefully, 'but I'm afraid I'm focusing solely on my exams right now. I'm not looking for a relationship.'

'Neither am I.' He blew out a breath. 'I'm sorry. I don't know why I just asked you out.' Honesty compelled him to add, 'There's just something about you that—I don't know. Draws me, I suppose.' And he wanted to move on, past the loneliness. He had a feeling that Jenna could be the one to help him do that.

Her face shuttered. 'I don't do relationships.'

Someone had obviously really, really hurt her. Time to back off. 'Then please forget I said anything. I'll let you get on.' He smiled at her. 'Goodnight, Jenna. See you at work on Monday.'

'Goodnight, Renzo. See you at work,' she said.

And he left before he could do something really stupid. Like giving in to the temptation to lean forward and kiss her.

CHAPTER FOUR

'AM I DOING the wrong thing, Charlie, turning Renzo down for a proper date?' Jenna asked, the next morning, as she was playing ball with her neighbour's dog in the park. 'I mean, I've known him for a couple of weeks. I've worked with him and I've seen for myself that he's great with patients, he's great with their parents, and he's really good with the junior staff on the ward, teaching them without making them feel stupid. He fits in well on team nights out. Plus he gave up all that time to help out at the danceathon yesterday. He's one of the good guys. I like him a lot. And he's drop-dead gorgeous. Half the women at the hospital would fall at his feet.'

The dog barked, and Jenna threw the tennis ball for him.

He retrieved it, scampered back and dropped it at her feet.

'But I haven't been asked out by anyone since— well, since Danny. And I got it so badly wrong with him. I thought we were getting on just fine. I thought we were happy. I thought he was going to ask me to marry him, and I was going to say yes. And then the adoption agency turned Lu down. It broke her heart. Of course I was going to offer to carry a baby for her. I wanted to make things right for her again.' She sighed. 'And Danny made it into something disgusting. Once he realised I really don't care about money, he accused me of fancying Will, and carrying the baby for Lu meant I was getting what I really wanted, having Will's baby. And it just wasn't true. I love Will dearly, but not in *that* way. He doesn't make my heart beat faster when he smiles. The room doesn't feel different when he walks in.'

Charlie tipped his head on one side, as if to say, 'Does the room feel different when Renzo walks in?'

That wasn't a question Jenna wanted to answer. Not right now. She threw the ball. 'I don't know if I can trust my judgement again, after Danny. I was so wrong about him. What if I've got it wrong about Renzo, too, and he's going to be just as disapproving and judgemental about the surrogacy?'

Charlie retrieved the tennis ball and deposited it at her feet.

'I know what Lu would say. He's a nice guy, so give him the benefit of the doubt. Talk to him.'

Charlie barked, as if agreeing.

'But it's not the easiest thing to talk about. What do I say? *Hey, before we start dating, just so you know, I was a surrogate mum for my twin sister's baby.*' She grimaced. 'It's not exactly the kind of thing you can just drop casually into a conversation, is it?'

Charlie cocked his head on one side, clearly waiting for her to throw the ball again.

Jenna threw it as hard as she could, and watched the dog run after it and bound back to her, his tail a blur. 'He asked me to have lunch with him. I said no. But I could call him, see if he's still free. Maybe we could go out as friends. See if we like each other enough to take it a step further. And if that does happen, then I'll work out how to tell him about Ava.'

Charlie brought the ball back and waited patiently for her to throw it.

'I guess I just need to take life one step at a time instead of trying to plan it all in advance,' she said, and threw the ball. When the dog brought it back, she ruffled his fur and said, 'OK, sweetie. That's it for this morning. We need to get you back home to Evelyn.'

Charlie barked, as if to say, 'Just one more throw.'

How could she resist those adorable brown eyes?

Lorenzo's eyes were brown and adorable, too...

'How feeble am I, Charlie?' she asked ruefully, and threw the ball one last time. Then she made a fuss of the dog, stuffed the tennis ball in her coat pocket, clipped his lead back onto his collar and walked him back through the park to their street.

When she got back to her own house, she stared at her mobile phone. Lorenzo had given her his phone number before the danceathon, in case of emergency. Should she call him? Ask if his offer of lunch still stood?

It would be a risk. Opening herself up to rejection again.

But part of her knew she needed to move on from

the past. Move on from the hurt Danny had caused her. And maybe Lorenzo was the one who could help her? Maybe she was the one who could help Lorenzo move on, too, from whatever had happened in his own past that put shadows in his eyes every so often?

There was only one way to find out.

She took a deep breath and called his number.

'Jenna,' he said when he answered. 'I wasn't expecting you to call me.'

'About yesterday,' she said. 'I was rude, and I apologise.'

'No, you were honest, and that's absolutely fine.'

'The thing is… I was wondering if you're still free for lunch? Because we could…' Her throat dried. 'Have lunch. As friends.' Oh, why was it so hard to get the words out? She sounded like an inarticulate teenager.

'Lunch as friends would be nice.'

'Not a date,' she checked.

'Not a date,' he agreed. 'Didn't you say you walk your neighbour's dog at weekends?'

'Yes, but I've already done that this morning.'

'Then we could meet at the tube station at, say, twelve,' he said.

'Twelve it is,' she said. 'See you there.'

And she ended the call before she could change her mind and make a fool of herself.

At twelve—after changing her mind half a dozen times about what she was going to wear, going from pretty dress to smart trousers to jeans and back again—Jenna met Lorenzo at the tube station. And her heart actually skipped a beat when she saw him in the distance and he smiled and raised his hand to tell her he'd seen her.

This could be really dangerous to her peace of mind. She hadn't reacted to anyone like this since Danny. But she knew she needed to put the past behind her. This was the first step.

'How was your dog-walk?' Lorenzo asked when she reached him.

'Half of it was playing ball in the park, so Charlie—that's the dog—did most of the work, running to fetch it and bring it back to me,' she said with a smile. 'But I think I've worn him out for Evelyn—my neighbour—so he'll sleep for most of the afternoon now.'

'It's nice of you to walk him for her.'

'It's not just me. I have a rota with four of my neighbours,' she explained. 'I do weekends, because I don't have children or any urgent calls on my time if I'm not at work, and the others do either the morning or evening walks during the week. We're all really happy to do it, because it means Evelyn doesn't have to give up her dog now her arthritis has made her too frail to walk him properly herself—that would've broken her heart. Plus we all get to enjoy having a part-time dog without worrying or feeling guilty about having to leave him alone at home all day while we're at work. And it's a really good excuse for us to be able to keep an eye on Evelyn and make sure she's all right, without stripping her of her dignity or her independence.'

'It sounds like a nice community.'

'It is,' she agreed. Everyone had kept an eye out for

her, too, when she'd been pregnant with Ava. Not that she was ready to tell Lorenzo about that. Not just yet.

'So what made you change your mind?' he asked.

'About lunch? I was hungry.'

He simply looked at her, and she grimaced. 'OK. What you said last night—when you said there was something about me...' She stumbled over the words. 'Maybe there's something about you that draws me, too. But I have to be honest. This whole thing scares me. I wasn't looking for a relationship.'

'You're not alone,' he said. 'I wasn't looking for a relationship, either. And this scares me as much as I think it scares you.'

She took a deep breath. 'I'm guessing someone hurt you. And I'm not going to push you to talk about it.'

He nodded. 'I'm guessing someone hurt you, too. And I'm also guessing that what you just said means you don't want to talk about it, either.'

'Correct.' She wasn't ready to tell him about Ava, but she could tell him about Danny. 'Bare bones—I picked the wrong guy and he gave me an ultimatum. It was an easy choice. But I was pretty shocked he'd taken that attitude. He wasn't the man I thought I'd fallen in love with, so I don't trust my judgement any more.'

Ultimatum. Maybe he'd got it wrong about her possibly taking a sabbatical for a pregnancy and then losing a baby, Lorenzo thought. But what kind of man would give an ultimatum to a woman like Jenna? OK, so he didn't know her that well, and she could have a massive character flaw—but he didn't think so. Her ex sounded like a control freak.

To reassure her, Lorenzo said, 'Just so you know, I don't do ultimatums.' And, because she'd shared a confidence, he felt he ought to do the same. Not the whole messy story, but enough for her to know that he too had picked the wrong one for him. 'My ex-wife,' he said, 'left me for the love of her life.' Which he'd thought was him. How wrong he'd been. He didn't want to tell Jenna the rest of it—he didn't want to face the kind of pity that had soured his shifts at the London Victoria—but maybe this way she wouldn't feel so alone.

And it felt strangely healing to say it out loud: that Georgia had left him for the man she really loved. That she'd married him without really meaning her vows. That she hadn't loved him as much as he'd loved her.

'So we've both made mistakes,' she said. 'And learned from them.' She looked at him, her eyes very blue. 'So. No pity.'

'No pity,' he agreed.

'And we'll see how things go,' she said. 'No promises.'

'That sounds good to me. Where would you like to go for lunch?'

'That depends. I was thinking,' she said, 'maybe we could do something after lunch, too.'

He smiled. 'I'd like that. Do you have something particular in mind?'

'Yes. But I need to ask you first—seeing as your

dad's an architect, does that mean you love buildings or they bore you to tears?' she asked.

'I love them,' he said.

She looked pleased. 'I was hoping you'd say that. How would you like to go and visit the ruins of a Roman bath house that are usually hidden from view?'

He blinked at her. 'A Roman bath house? Hang on. My family's Italian, and I've spent most of my life in London. How come I've never heard of this Roman bath house before?'

She wrinkled her nose. 'It's in the basement of a building, and I don't think it's had very much publicity. But they do tours. I could see if I can book us tickets for this afternoon, if you like.'

'I'd like that.'

She grabbed her phone and found the website, then went through to the ticket-booking section. 'We're in luck—they have spaces in the two o'clock tour today, which means we have time for lunch first. Monument's our nearest Tube station, though we're getting in at Moorgate and it's only a few minutes' walk from there.'

'Walking sounds fine,' he said, and she booked the tickets.

'How much do I owe you for my ticket?' he asked. 'Or can I buy us both lunch on the grounds that you bought the tickets?'

'Lunch would be nice,' she said. 'I've no idea where, though. Do you happen to know that bit of the city very well?'

'Not really. I know South Bank better, and obviously Victoria because I worked there for years,' he said. 'So either we need to look up a few reviews while we're on the train, or we have a wander round when we get there and find somewhere with a menu we like the look of.'

'My vote's for wandering round,' she said promptly.

'Mine, too.'

It was too noisy on the train to chat much on the way in, but once they'd got to Moorgate and were walking through the city, it was easy to talk.

'That's amazing,' he said, gesturing up to the enormous white column looming above the streets in front of them. 'I know it's daft, considering how famous it is, but I've never actually seen the Monument for myself. I had no idea it was that tall or the gold urn at the top was so bright.'

'I've been this close to it before, but never actually climbed it,' Jenna admitted. 'The views from the platform at the top are meant to be amazing.'

'Maybe,' he said, 'we could do that some time.'

'We could make a list of the touristy things we'd like to do in London but we've never actually done because we live here and take it all for granted,' she suggested.

'Great idea. Let's start the list over lunch,' he said.

They wandered round the streets, looking at the menus in the windows of all the restaurants.

'This one looks good,' he said.

Jenna checked the dessert menu, and smiled with pleasure. 'Salted caramel profiteroles—my favourite. Oh, yes. I agree. Let's go here.'

'Do you always read menus backwards?' he asked.

'Yup. If I love all the puddings, then I'll choose a

restrained main course. If I'm not that fussed about the puddings, then I'll have a larger main instead,' she said.

'That works for me, too,' he said.

Once they were settled at their table, Jenna ordered smoked salmon fishcakes with a green salad, and Lorenzo chose ale-glazed chicken with mashed potato, green beans and heirloom tomatoes. And both of them ordered profiteroles.

The food was good, but the salted caramel profiteroles were outstanding.

'Utterly gorgeous,' Jenna said after her last mouthful. 'This was an excellent idea.'

After Florence had been born, Georgia had become really fussy about food, convinced that she needed to lose weight when she was perfectly fine as she was. It was a really nice change to have lunch with someone who enjoyed what they ate, Lorenzo thought. True, Jenna had asked the waitress to swap the sweet potato fries for a green salad, but her order had been made with the profiteroles in mind. For her it was about balance rather than self-sacrifice.

With Georgia, after Florence's birth, nothing had seemed to be right. He'd tried to be patient, and he'd talked in confidence to an obstetrician friend about the possibility of postnatal depression and how to help her. And all the time he'd had no idea what was wrong. She wouldn't tell him, and he hadn't been able to reassure her that whatever it was he would be there and they could work it out together.

When she'd finally told him about Scott, everything had fallen into place.

He'd felt so betrayed. She'd cheated on him and she'd married him without really loving him. It had taken him quite a while to come to terms with that.

Finding out that Florence wasn't his daughter had been hard, but he could've dealt with that. He'd fallen in love with the baby the second that he'd first held her. Even if he'd had a rough day at work, going home would make things all right in his world because he knew she'd beam at him the moment he walked in the door, holding her chubby arms up to him in a demand to be picked up. 'Dada' had even been her first word. He'd adored her, and she'd loved him all the way back. Finding out that he wasn't actually her biological father had made no difference to his feelings about Florence. She was still *his* daughter, in his eyes.

And losing her had made him feel as if he'd been dropped down a deep, dark well.

He'd tried to tell himself that Georgia was doing the right thing, making a family with Scott—her ex and Florence's natural father. And of course there could be no room for Lorenzo in that family. It would be way too confusing for the little girl, not knowing who to call 'daddy': the man who'd brought her up for the first eighteen months of her life, or the man who was her biological father and now lived with her mother. Plus Georgia and Scott had moved to Birmingham, too far for Lorenzo to drop in to see Florence after work on a weekday.

Lorenzo just hoped that Scott really *had* changed.

That he wasn't going to drift back into his old ways and end up back in prison. That he'd be a proper father to Florence, loving her and protecting her from any hurt, splashing about in a swimming pool with her and telling her bedtime stories—the kind of father Lorenzo had been to her.

His parents, too, had been desperately hurt at losing one of their three grandchildren. But Georgia had insisted on a clean break. A break that had left Lorenzo with nothing. No closure.

There had been no chance for him to fight Georgia for custody, because the DNA test proved that Florence wasn't his. Plus his name wasn't on the birth certificate: Georgia had said she'd get it changed once they were married, but she hadn't got round to it. Probably because she'd always guessed that he wasn't Florence's father—Florence had Scott's grey eyes and red hair rather than Lorenzo's dark eyes and hair—and Lorenzo had tried to tell himself that at least Georgia had been honest in that respect and hadn't lied on the birth certificate.

But, oh, how he missed his little girl. How he missed being a dad. How he missed the closeness of living with a family.

'Are you OK?' Jenna asked as they reached Billingsgate.

He forced himself to smile. The wreckage of his life wasn't Jenna's fault, and he didn't want to dump his feelings on her. 'Sure. I was just wool-gathering. Sorry.'

'No problem. We're meant to meet the tour guide

just here,' she said, indicating a very plain and modern-looking building.

Once the group was gathered together, the guide led them inside the building and down a flight of steps to the basement. And there in the centre of the floor was the base of a Roman bath house, with a hypocaust system and arches showing where the furnaces once were.

The guide talked them through the different areas of the bath house.

'So the caldarium was the bit like a modern sauna, the tepidarium was the largest room where they had all the treatments in a nice warm area, including having hairs plucked out, and the frigidarium was the bit where they closed their pores in a freezing bath—well, in this case, there wasn't room to build a plunge pool, so the bathers dipped into the water tank at the end of the frigidarium,' Jenna said.

'All that oil being scraped off with strigils, and bits of hair everywhere—can you imagine how vile the floor of the tepidarium would be at the end of the day?' Lorenzo asked with a grin.

'Ah, but as the rich young man who was being scraped off and depilated, you wouldn't care—because you wouldn't be the one to clean it up,' she retorted, laughing.

'It's strange. In Italy, you're used to the ancient buildings being scattered around the city on full view,' Lorenzo said. 'You've got the Arena in Verona, then all the buildings of the Forum and the Colosseum in

Rome. I thought in London all that was left of the Roman settlement was a bit of the old boundary wall.'

'There are quite a few more bits of wall left than you'd think there are; it's just that a lot of them are hidden away underneath or inside newer buildings,' Jenna said. 'The Roman settlement here was totally deserted after the Romans left, and everything just collapsed in on itself. It wasn't rediscovered for years—or, rather, it was just ignored until the ground was cleared and new footings were dug and then the remains were rediscovered. There's an amphitheatre under the Guildhall, there's a temple of Mithras that ended up being moved so people could see the ruins properly, and there's a Roman ditch and pavement in the crypt at St Bride's church, just off Fleet Street. Oh, and there's another Roman pavement in the crypt at All Hallows, next to the Tower of London.'

Lorenzo was impressed by her knowledge. 'How do you know all this stuff, Jenna?'

'That's the thing about having a nerdy history professor for a brother-in-law,' she said with a smile. 'Will's specialist subject is Roman Britain, and he does quite a few field trips with his students. Before he plans a new field trip, Lucy and I get to do a trial run with him. So I've been to every fort on Hadrian's Wall and walked quite a lot of the route, too. And I'm pretty sure Will's actually worked out a walk so you can see every bit of the old Roman wall here in London. I can ask him, if you'd like to do that.'

'So you've obviously been here before?'

'With Will and Lucy,' she confirmed. 'So I know the

floor here has tesserae but it wasn't an actual mosaic floor—say, like the amazing ones at the palace in Fishbourne—and archaeologists are never really going to be able to prove whether this was a private house or an inn, because what we can see of the ruins is bounded by the Thames on one side and the roadway on another and there isn't quite enough evidence to say either way.'

'Fair point,' he said. 'So you bonded with your brother-in-law over history?'

She nodded. 'I really thought about becoming a forensic archaeologist, when I was in my teens. But then I did work experience on a dig in Northumbria, the summer I was waiting for my exam results, and I realised that as an archaeologist I was going to spend a lot of my working life kneeling in mud under a leaking tarpaulin in the rain. That wasn't what I wanted. So I switched to living patients rather than dead ones.' She smiled. 'But whenever I go on a city break, the first place I check out is the museum. Luckily Lu feels the same way that I do about history—that's how she met Will.'

'In a museum?'

'Planning a trip on Roman London for her Year Six class,' Jenna explained. 'A friend of a friend suggested that she talked to Will. So they met at the British Museum one Saturday morning for an hour's chat, and they were still there at closing time. Six months later, I was walking down the aisle behind her, carrying Lu's train and holding her bouquet at the aisle while she and Will plighted their troth.'

'That's nice,' Lorenzo said, meaning it. His own

siblings were happily married, and it was good to hear of relationships that had worked. Not everyone's was a failure, the way his had been.

'Everyone likes Will. He's a sweetie. Though he does like doing the vague professor thing, which drives me crazy.' She rolled her eyes. 'Lu has to tell him they're meeting friends an hour before they really are meeting up, otherwise they'd always be late.'

'Is your twin like you?' Lorenzo asked.

'Organised and a hustler? Put it this way, she's the deputy head at her primary school. So among other things she needs to be incredibly organised, juggle budgets and support the PTA in fundraising.' Jenna wrinkled her nose. 'But I think she's nicer than I am—plus she can cook.'

Cooking was optional, in Lorenzo's view. As for nice: the more he talked to Jenna, the more he liked her.

Was she the one who could teach him to trust again?

When their tour was over, they headed back out into the sunshine.

'I happen to know somewhere else really nice just round the corner from here,' Jenna said. 'You said you didn't know this bit of the city. Shall we do some exploring?'

'Sure.'

She took him round the corner to what looked like a church—until he noticed that it was roofless, there was ivy growing over the walls and there was no glass in the windows.

The plaque on the wall told him that the church of St Dunstan's in the East was rebuilt by Wren after the

Great Fire of London; it was bombed in the Blitz but Wren's tower remained and the church area was made into a garden.

'So just over there we have all the hustle and bustle of the City of London,' Lorenzo said. 'And here it's just peace and calm, full of flowers and bees.'

'Amazing, isn't it?' Jenna said. 'I came here with Will and Lu, too. She used it as inspiration when they started building the sensory garden at her school.'

'I can see why,' Lorenzo said.

There were several wooden benches arranged around the small bubbling foundation in the centre of the church floor. They sat on one of the spare benches and watched the bees hovering over the flowers of the shrubs planted in the garden.

'The perfect English summer day,' Jenna said.

'Maybe there was a garden here in Roman times, too,' Lorenzo said. 'Just round the corner from the bath house.'

'A walled one, to help shelter from the cold in winter,' she said. 'No wonder they needed the underfloor heating in that Roman house. I still can't imagine how cold it must've been back then for the Thames to freeze over.'

'Especially on a warm summer day like this one,' Lorenzo agreed.

As they left the church grounds, their hands accidentally brushed against each other again. Lorenzo gave in to the impulse to let his fingers link with Jenna's. She didn't pull away, and they walked in silence back towards the Monument, hand in hand. Oddly, this felt *right*.

'Maybe,' he suggested, 'we could walk by the river for a bit.'

'I'd like that,' she said. 'From here, we could walk down to Tower Bridge, then head over the river to the South Bank.'

'That'd be good.'

He held her hand all the way along the side of the Thames and across the bridge. And somehow they were still holding hands by the time they got to the South Bank. There were street entertainers, stalls selling everything from jewellery and crafts through to books and prints. Children were darting in and out of the fountain installations, laughing. Something he'd enjoyed doing with Florence, as soon as she was old enough to toddle. He'd lifted her over the walls of water and she'd giggled and clapped her hands. *'Uv oo, Dada.'*

Gone.

All gone.

Something had put the sadness back in Lorenzo's face, Jenna thought. What was it about the South Bank that had made him feel that way? She loved the vibrancy of the area, the street entertainers and the art installations. And she'd always loved the fountains.

On impulse, she tugged at his hand. 'Come on. Let's get to the other side of the fountain rooms. The one who gets wettest buys the drinks.'

At that, the shadow seemed to clear from his face. 'OK. You're on.'

Lorenzo was the first to get sprayed by the fountain when a mini wall of water sprang up unexpectedly.

Jenna, halfway across the installation and still completely dry, grinned. 'Oh, dear. Poor Renzo. You are so buying those drinks.'

'Don't bet on it,' he teased back.

She was just about to be smug and step out onto the other side of the installation when she realised she'd misjudged her timing—and was promptly soaked by the largest wall of water popping up.

Lorenzo strolled across when the water had died down again. 'You were saying, Dr Harris?'

'All right, so the drinks are on me,' she said, giving a mock pained sigh. 'Do you want beer, wine or coffee?'

'Actually, the smoothies over there look good,' he said, indicating one of the stalls.

'Smoothies it is, then,' she said with a smile.

Once she'd bought their smoothies, they sat on one of the benches overlooking the Thames, watching the light playing on the water and looking over at the buildings on the North Bank, from the glass and steel constructions of the buildings in the City of London through to the towering dome of St Paul's. She felt Lorenzo shift slightly next to her, and then his arm slid round her shoulders.

They'd held hands. This was the next logical step. If she pulled away, she knew without having to ask that he'd respect her boundaries and give her space.

The problem was, she didn't want to pull away.

So she shifted slightly, too, moving closer to him. And in response his arm tightened slightly round her.

It was so easy to be with Lorenzo. Jenna didn't feel that she had to chatter to fill the space. It was fine just sitting together in the sunshine, sipping smoothies and watching the world go by. She couldn't remember the last time she'd done something like this, and it made her ache.

When they walked to the Tube station, their arms were still wrapped round each other. Lorenzo held her hand on the train and all the way back to her flat.

Butterflies were doing a stampede in her stomach, a mixture of excitement and fear.

What now?

She turned to him, intending to kiss him on the cheek and thank him for a lovely day. And somehow she missed and her mouth brushed against his. Her lips tingled where they touched his, and the tingle ran all the way down to the base of her spine.

Knowing she shouldn't be doing this, she did it again. And this time his arms wrapped round her and he deepened the kiss.

Kissing like a teenager on her front doorstep.

How long had it been since she'd done something like this? Years and years and years.

She pulled back slightly and looked him straight in the eye. 'Sorry. That wasn't supposed to happen.'

'No need to apologise.' He rested his palm lightly against her cheek and stroked the pad of his thumb over her lower lip. 'But it did happen. So what now?'

'We both said we weren't in a place where we

wanted a relationship,' she reminded him. 'That we'd just see how things go.'

'True,' he said. 'But this thing between us—somehow I don't think this is going to be easy to ignore.'

'Also true,' she said. 'But you and I—I think we both come with baggage.'

'Stuff that's been hard to deal with, and just as hard to talk about.' He looked at her. 'So we'll be kind to each other. No pressure. No promises. Just enjoy each other's company.'

Friends, but with the possibility of more. Not rushing into things. 'Taking it slowly,' she said, 'sounds good.'

He leaned forward and kissed her again. This time it was very deliberate and it made her knees feel as if they'd melted.

'See you tomorrow,' he said.

'Tomorrow,' she echoed.

And Monday suddenly looked as if it was going to be very bright indeed.

CHAPTER FIVE

AT WORK THE next day, Jenna and Lorenzo were both busy in the PAU. It seemed to be Jenna's day for sorting out fractures: a girl who'd fallen over roller-skating and put her hands out to save herself, ending up with a greenstick fracture of her arm; a boy who'd fallen off the monkey bars in the playground and fractured his elbow; and a toddler who'd fallen over while running around at playgroup and ended up with a spiral fracture of his tibia.

'Got time for lunch before your next clinic?' Lorenzo asked as they headed out to the staff kitchen.

'Lunch would be great. I could really do with some coffee,' Jenna said feelingly. 'It's been one of those mornings.'

'Rough cases?' he asked.

'Fractures, fractures and more fractures,' she said.

'Don't tell me. Greenstick ulnar fractures?'

She grimaced. 'One, plus a spiral tibia—though the one that worries me is the lad who fell off the monkey bars.'

'Supracondylar fracture?' Lorenzo asked.

Breaking an arm just above the elbow was one of the most common fractures in children, so it was a fair guess. 'No. This one was actually on the joint. I had to send him up for surgery.'

Lorenzo winced. 'Poor lad. Was it a simple fracture or has he injured the growth plate as well?'

'Right now, I don't know. We'll need to keep an eye on him,' she said. 'How about you? How was your morning?'

'Full of small children with rashes, along with mums who were in a bit of a panic,' he said. 'Thankfully none of them turned out to be septicaemia. I've put one toddler on a food exclusion diet, though, to see if it helps with her eczema. Her mum's already using non-bio washing powder and being careful with detergents and toiletries, so we agreed to look at foods, and we're following up in a fortnight.'

'Starting with dairy?' she asked.

He nodded. 'The usual suspects. I gave the mum a list of substitutes—she was already clued up about caring for sore, itchy skin and she's using the right emollients.'

'It's tough for parents, isn't it?'

'Yes.'

There was another shadow in his face, quickly masked, and Jenna was starting to wonder. She knew that his wife had left him for someone else, but she had a feeling there was more to it than that—just as there was to her situation with Danny. Had they maybe lost a child, first, and the only way his ex had been able to cope was to find someone else, someone who hadn't shared the pain with her and reminded her of the loss every time she saw him? In which case, working on the paediatric ward must be so difficult for him—or maybe he was such a dedicated doctor precisely because he knew how it felt to have a sick child and he wanted to spare other people going through the same pain.

Though asking him straight out felt much too intrusive. Until he was ready to talk to her, she wouldn't pry. Especially because she wasn't enough of a hypocrite to expect him to open up about his past without admitting to her own.

Awkwardly, she changed the subject. 'I'm ordering toys this weekend. I have a wish-list going round the ward for suggestions so, if you have any strong views on what we need, make sure you grab the list.'

'I will.' He smiled at her. 'Can I take you out to dinner tonight?'

'Sorry. Mondays are my evening with Lucy, Will and Ava.'

'Tomorrow?'

She shook her head. 'Tuesday is salsa class.' She smiled back. 'You could come to salsa class with me, if you like, and we could grab something to eat afterwards.'

'Thanks for the offer, but my two left feet are already wincing at the idea of more salsa. Wednesday's the team ten-pin bowling night out,' he said.

'And Thursday is my ballroom class. So maybe we can do something on Friday?' she suggested.

'Friday it is,' he agreed.

When they walked through the reception area back

towards the ward, Jenna noticed there was a table with a bake sale in aid of dementia patients.

'Hang on a sec,' she said, and browsed the table for a couple of minutes before buying a coffee and walnut cake.

'Is that for the ward kitchen?' he asked.

'No, it's for my sister tonight. Coffee and walnut cake is her absolute favourite.'

'Then I'll buy some cake for the ward kitchen,' he said, and chose a lemon drizzle cake.

'I would've pegged you as a chocolate cake fiend,' she said.

'Pretty much any cake will do,' he said, 'but lemon drizzle cake has always been my favourite. My mother puts limoncello in hers.'

'Would that be limoncello made by your family, from your own lemon orchard?' she asked.

'Actually, yes, it would.' He laughed. 'We're terribly clichéd. Wine, lemons—the only thing we don't grow right now is olives, though I think one of my cousins is eyeing up a grove or two and thinking about branching out. Pun most definitely not intended,' he added with a grin.

'It's nice that you're kind of the bedrock of the local economy,' she said. 'Lu's very keen on all the slow food stuff.'

'Good food is always worth paying attention to,' he said.

'You sound like my twin,' she said with a smile. Lorenzo and Lucy would get on really well, she was sure. But she wasn't ready to introduce him to her family just yet. They'd agreed to take it slowly and see where things took them. And that suited her just fine.

That evening, Jenna skilfully used cake to deflect Lucy's questions about the danceathon, and turned the conversation to the wedding in Scotland. She knew if she admitted that she was seeing Lorenzo, Lucy would insist on meeting him, checking him out to make sure he wasn't another Danny. And then the grilling would begin—for both of them. She wasn't ready to talk, yet, even to her twin.

Yes, she'd like to be as happy and Lucy and Will were. But where did you find somebody to love, somebody who'd love you all the way back? In your thirties, anyone you met had baggage. Cracks in their heart from previous relationships. Could she and Lorenzo heal each other's hearts, or would their new relationship fall through those cracks?

On Wednesday night, Lorenzo and Jenna were both at the ward's ten-pin bowling night out, though they were on different teams and didn't get much chance to talk to each other. But on Thursday evening Lorenzo was browsing through the local 'what's on' website and spotted something he liked the look of: Screen under the Stars. He really liked the idea of seeing a film outdoors.

Even though he knew Jenna was at her dance class, he sent her a text, knowing she'd pick it up at some point later that evening.

Pop-up cinema in the park tomorrow evening. Weather forecast good. Shall we?

As he'd hoped, she texted back after her class.

Love to. What's the film?

Dirty Dancing.

Excellent choice :) What time?

Meet you at your place at seven?

Perfect.

They were both too busy even to grab a cup of coffee together, the next day. But at seven that evening, he rang her doorbell.

'What's that?' she asked, nodding at the large bag he was carrying.

'A fleecy blanket,' he said. 'It'll be cold when the sun goes down, even though it's June.'

'Good thinking,' she said. 'Shall I go and dig out my fold-up picnic chairs?'

'No need,' he said with a smile, 'because our tickets are the VIP ones that include chairs.'

'Excellent organisation on your part, Dr Conti,' she said, and slid her arm round his waist. 'And, because you bought the tickets, I'm buying the drinks and nibbles.'

'Fine by me,' he said.

They walked to the park together, queued up so their tickets could be scanned from his phone, bought drinks and popcorn, and then went to find their chairs.

'I really love this film,' Jenna said with a smile.

'So Patrick Swayze's your ideal man?' he asked.

'Dancing like that? You bet!' She wrinkled her nose. 'Though really it's the way he sticks up for Baby at the end that I like most. It's important for your partner to fight your corner.'

'Rather than giving you an ultimatum.' The words were out before he could stop them, and he winced. 'Sorry.'

'No, you're right.' She sighed. 'Danny didn't agree with me taking a sabbatical.' She looked torn, as if she wanted to tell him more but something was holding her back.

She'd told him that she didn't trust her own judgement any more. So he simply took her hand. 'I'm assuming you had a good reason. It's a shame he didn't support you.'

'He said it was career suicide. That I could never make up the lost money and promotions.' She dragged in a breath. 'But some things are more important than money.'

Was this time she'd taken to have a child—and perhaps lost the baby and Danny hadn't been there for her? Though he could hardly ask.

'From what I see, you're a well-respected member of the team. He was wrong about a sabbatical being career suicide. Doctors do it all the time. Some to work for

Doctors Without Borders, others take parental leave, others need to look after a sick relative for a while. Life happens. You didn't make the wrong choice.'

'Thank you,' she said.

Her ex sounded incredibly selfish. No wonder she didn't trust her judgement, if she'd fallen in love with someone like that. 'No problem,' he said softly.

Lorenzo held her hand all the way through the film and just enjoyed the movie.

As the sun finished setting, he noticed that Jenna was shivering slightly, so he tucked the blanket round her and went to fetch hot chocolate and hot dogs to warm them up.

'Thank you,' she said, and kissed him lightly. 'It's nice to have someone make a fuss of me.'

Clearly her ex hadn't done that, and he knew what it felt like to choose the wrong partner. But he didn't want to talk about that, either, so he just smiled. 'My pleasure.'

There was something special about watching a film under the stars, and Lorenzo enjoyed every second of it.

'So would you do a lift like that one in your ballroom class?' he asked as they walked back to her place after the movie had ended.

'I guess some choreographers might put it into a show dance,' she said, 'but to be honest we don't tend to do lifts when we go through routines or learn new steps. I'm not in the advanced class.'

'The way you were dancing at the danceathon looked pretty advanced to me.'

She shook her head. 'Those were really just easy basics. If you put a few of them together in a combination, the routine looks a lot more flashy and complicated than it really is.'

Back at her flat, he kissed her goodnight on the doorstep. 'Can I see you tomorrow?' he asked. 'I could cook dinner for you.'

She looked pleased by the idea. 'Thanks. I'd like that.'

'Good. Is there anything you don't eat?'

'I like everything,' she said. 'Except maybe not lasagne, because my sister's lasagne is the best in the world—and, yes, I know your cousin has a Michelin star, but I still stand by my opinion and I reckon her lasagne could hold its own against his.'

For a moment, he wondered if she was going to suggest meeting her family. But this was still very early days. He wasn't sure he was ready for her to meet his family yet, either. 'Fair enough.' He kissed her again, then told her his address. 'Is seven o'clock OK?'

'That's fine. See you then. And thank you again for a really lovely evening.'

'My pleasure.' He stole a last kiss. 'See you tomorrow.'

'I think I've made the right decision, Charlie,' Jenna told the dog when they went to the park the next morning. 'Lorenzo's really lovely—and yes, he does make the room feel different when he walks in.' She ruffled the dog's fur. 'But we're taking it slowly, just getting to know each other. I know I have to tell him about Ava, but…' She wrinkled her nose. 'Maybe not just yet.'

Once she'd delivered Charlie back home and made Evelyn a cup of tea, she headed to the shops to find something nice to take with her that evening. She browsed in the local chocolatier's and found something she hoped would be perfect, then bought a couple of bottles of wine from the posher shelves at the supermarket. After giving Charlie his second, shorter walk of the day, she went home to shower, wash her hair and change into a dress.

At seven precisely, she stood on Lorenzo's doorstep and rang the bell.

He answered immediately. 'Hello.'

He was wearing a smart casual shirt and chinos, and looked utterly edible. Her pulse speeded up a notch.

Though he'd invited her for dinner and she couldn't actually smell anything cooking…

The doubts must've shown in her face, because he said, 'I've done all the prep for dinner, but it takes just ten minutes to cook, and I've cheated with the bread and bought the sort you just heat through in the oven—because my bread-making is on about a par with my dancing.'

Jenna liked his honesty. Danny would've bluffed his way through it and made out that he'd been slaving away in the kitchen all day. Danny liked to impress; 'my girlfriend, the doctor' brought him kudos, in his eyes, whereas 'my girlfriend, the surrogate mum' most definitely hadn't.

She pushed the thought away and smiled. 'You're still one up on me, because I can burn water, remember?'

'Hmm.'

Lorenzo kissed her hello, and even though it was a relatively chaste kiss it still made her knees go weak. She hadn't felt like this about anyone since she was a teenager, and it was scary and exciting at the same time.

'I forgot to ask you if I should bring red or white wine, so I played it safe.' She handed him a bottle of each.

'You really didn't need to do that.'

'Yes, I did—it's my contribution to tonight. Oh. And this.' She handed him a box of *gianduja*. 'Though it kind of feels a bit cheeky, giving Italian chocolates to an Italian.'

'Not at all. These are my absolute favourites. *Mille grazie*. Thank you very much.'

Oh, she loved it when he spoke Italian. So *sexy*.

He kissed her again. 'I hope you don't mind eating in the kitchen, but I don't have a separate dining room.'

'It's fine,' she said. 'And I get to watch you cook, so it counts as dinner and a show, right?'

He laughed. 'Now you've said that, I can definitely do you a show. I have a whole range of terrible jokes, half of which were taught to me by seven-year-olds.'

She laughed back. 'I bet they're very similar to the ones that some seven-year-old patients taught me. Which means they're really terrible.'

'Let's see. Why did the bicycle lean against the wall?' he asked.

She grinned. 'Because it was two-tyred. Actually, that's one of my favourites.' She paused. 'I have one for you. Knock, knock.'

'Who's there?'

'Cows go.'

'Cows go who?' he asked.

'No, silly. Cows go moo.'

He groaned. 'That's absolutely awful!' Then his gorgeous brown eyes crinkled at the corners and her knees went weak again. 'I'll remember that, next time I have a patient who's scared of needles and needs distracting. Thank you.' He ushered her into the kitchen. 'Can I get you a drink?'

'Yes, please. Whatever's open,' she said.

He took a bottle from the fridge, poured her a glass, and gestured to her to sit at the table.

'This is really nice,' she said after the first sip. 'I assume it's a Conti family wine?'

'Yes. It's the *chiaretto*. Actually, I helped pick the grapes for this particular vintage.'

'There aren't many people who can say that about the wine they drink,' she said.

There were two chopping boards on the worktop next to the cooker, one with a pile of chopped vegetables and one with a pile of what looked like chopped scallops. There were a couple of saucepans on the hob, a jug of stock and a couple of bowls with ingredients in.

'Are you hungry? Is it OK for me to start cooking?' he asked.

'Sounds perfect,' she said with a smile. 'I would ask

if there was anything I can do, but it's probably safer for me to sit here and let you do the magical stuff.'

'No problem.' He glanced at his watch, then poured boiling water over the pasta; next, he switched on the oven and put the bread in to heat through; and finally he heated butter and began to sauté the chopped garlic and onions. Within two minutes, the kitchen smelled heavenly. Lorenzo was a very deft cook, but Jenna had already seen the way he'd worked in her own kitchen, so she knew what to expect.

'So is this one of your cousin's recipes?' she asked.

'It's the family version,' he said. 'The one Matteo would cook in his restaurant is a bit more complicated, plus he'd do all the flashy plating with pretty dabs of sauce. Which, by the way, you won't get from me.'

'That's fine. I already know from what you did in my kitchen that you're a good cook. You don't need to pretty up the food on my behalf,' she said. She watched Lorenzo sauté the chopped courgettes and scallops; then he added stock, saffron and sun-dried tomatoes.

'That smells amazing,' she said.

'It's one of my favourite sauces,' he said.

He checked his watch, then added a spoonful of crème fraîche to the sauce. Then he drained the pasta, mixed in the sauce and divided it between two bowls, took the bread from the oven, and served up.

'I've never seen pasta like this before,' she said, looking at the short, fat, ridged tubes. 'Lucy likes messing about with different pasta shapes, but even she hasn't cooked me this before.'

'It's *pacchieri*,' he said. 'The shape and the ridges mean it holds the sauce better.'

'Right.' She took a mouthful. 'Wow. This tastes even better than it smells.'

'Thank you—but you saw for yourself, it really wasn't that difficult to make. All you do is follow a recipe, just like you follow the procedures for treating a medical condition.'

'Nope, not convinced,' she said. 'This is wonderful. Between you and Lucy, I've eaten really well this week.'

'What, no bowls of cereal for dinner?' he teased.

'Twice, this week,' she said. 'After salsa and ballroom class. But I'll have you know it's seriously good granola, and I added blueberries and banana and Greek yoghurt—so it was pretty healthy.'

'I'll teach you a couple of easy recipes,' he said.

'Thanks for the offer, but Lu's already tried and failed. I'm much better at appreciating food than cooking it, and I'm happy to stay that way,' she said.

'Fair enough.'

After they'd finished the pasta, he cleared their empty plates away and brought over a bowl of strawberries, then a plate of shortbread and a tub of premium vanilla ice cream.

'The strawberries look nice,' she said.

'I've done them the Italian way, sliced thickly and marinated in balsamic vinegar, sugar and black pepper for thirty minutes at room temperature.'

She raised an eyebrow. 'Black pepper, with strawberries? Seriously?'

'Seriously. It brings out the flavour. Give it a try.'

She did. 'You're right. It really brings out the flavour. And that shortbread is fantastic. If you make some of that for the ward kitchen, you'll have everyone worshipping you.'

He laughed. 'It's not *that* difficult to make. Maybe we can cook some together, at some point.'

'Maybe,' she said, her tone making it clear that she was volunteering for washing-up duties rather than actual cooking.

When they'd finished, he said, 'Shall we have our coffee in the living room?'

'That'd be nice. Is there anything I can do to help?'

'No, it's fine. But thank you for the offer.'

'Can I at least wash up?'

He shook his head. 'I have a dishwasher. No need.'

He did at least let her carry her own mug of coffee into the living room. It was very plain, with a sofa, a state-of-the-art audio-visual system, and a large bookcase. But there were masses of framed photographs on the mantelpiece, just as there were on her own.

'May I?' she asked, gesturing to the photographs.

'Sure.'

She put her mug down on the coffee table and went to take a closer look. There was a graduation photograph of him with an older couple who were clearly his parents, plus wedding and christening photographs.

'My brother, Riccardo, and sister-in-law, Helen, on their wedding day,' he said as she picked up the frames one by one, 'and with their daughter Emily on her christening day. And my sister, Chiara, and her husband, Mark, on their wedding day, and with their son Jack at his christening.'

They looked a warm, close family, she thought.

The photo she really liked was the family portrait of them all in front of a Christmas tree with an elderly golden retriever.

'That's such a gorgeous photo,' she said.

'My parents are at the stage of life where it's almost impossible to get them something for Christmas, so we get together and do a family portrait for them every year,' he explained.

'Including the dog.'

'Suki's part of the family,' he said simply. 'That's obviously last year's family photo. And actually it's lovely seeing Emily and Jack change every year, from babes in arms, to toddlers, to how they are now.'

Again, there was sudden sadness in his face, as if he was remembering something painful. She knew about his ex, but she was growing more and more convinced that he'd also lost a young child and that was why his ex had found consolation elsewhere—but she really didn't want to trample on a sore spot by asking him.

'It's lovely seeing children grow up,' she agreed instead. 'Lu gets an official portrait done of Ava every three months, and I've got all mine in a special album.'

'I have one of those, too,' he said. 'It's one of the perks of being an uncle—well, aunt, in your case.'

It was slightly more complicated, in her case. But

she still hadn't found the right way to explain to him about Ava.

They curled up together on his sofa, just enjoying each other's company. But then Lorenzo stroked her cheek. 'Jenna.'

She turned to face him. 'Yes?'

He leaned forward and brushed his lips lightly against hers. Asking, rather than demanding; and she found herself kissing him back, sliding her arms round his neck and letting him deepen the kiss.

'I know this is maybe rushing things,' Lorenzo said, his voice low and husky, 'but you're irresistible—and right now I want to do more than just kiss you.'

Desire surged through her. 'I feel the same,' she admitted.

'Then maybe we should just go with our feelings,' he said softly.

This was it. Decision time. She knew if she said no, he'd give her space and take it more slowly.

But actually, she didn't want to take it slowly any more. She wanted Lorenzo. All of him.

'That,' she said, 'is a very good idea.'

He smiled, and she let him draw her to her feet and lead her to his bedroom.

Afterwards, curled up in bed with him, she said, 'I guess I shouldn't overstay my welcome. I ought to head for home.'

'You don't have to go. Stay tonight, if you like.' He paused. 'Though I'm due at my parents' tomorrow. Every other Sunday we all gather there.'

So he was a real family man. That was reassuring. Danny hadn't been close to his family, and he hadn't been that keen on coming to Harris family gatherings, either.

'I know we said we'd take it slowly, but you'd be very welcome to come with me tomorrow,' he said.

She scoffed. 'That's not quite what your face is saying.'

He stole a kiss. 'I'm not doing you down. My family would adore you.'

'Mine would really like you, too,' she admitted. 'Lu's already asked me to bring you over for dinner.'

'It just feels too early to…' He tailed off.

'To let everyone else in just yet,' she finished. That was exactly how she felt. 'My family would interrogate you horribly.'

'Try growing up in an Italian family where everyone wants to know everything and there's this weird osmosis where you tell one person and then everyone seems to know it simultaneously,' he said. 'My family would interrogate you horribly, too.'

'So shall we just keep this between you and me, for now?' she asked.

'I think that would be a good idea.'

She nodded. 'I'll go home tonight.'

'You don't have to go,' he said, keeping his arms wrapped round her. 'This is comfortable.'

'But you're busy tomorrow—plus I need to be back at my place before nine so I can walk Charlie.'

He lifted one shoulder in a half-shrug. 'That's not a problem. We're both used to waking up early for work.

And I have a washer-dryer, so I can put your clothes through the washing machine tonight.'

'Actually, I changed before I came out, so maybe if I can just wash my underwear and it'll dry overnight in your bathroom?' she suggested.

'That's fine. I'll show you where my laundry stuff is.' He stole another kiss. 'And I'll make us hot chocolate while you're sorting out your washing.'

Lorenzo really was lovely, she thought, warm and sweet and kind. So very different from Danny, thinking of others instead of putting himself first, middle and last.

But she still hadn't told Lorenzo the truth about Ava.

She really had to find the right words. And soon.

The next morning, Jenna woke to find Lorenzo curled round her. It made her feel warm and safe and cherished, and part of her wanted to stay right where she was for the rest of the day. But that wasn't the deal. He needed to go to see his family, and she needed to get up and walk Charlie for Evelyn.

She wriggled round to face him and woke him with a kiss. 'Good morning,' she said softly.

'Good morning.' He stroked her face. 'I'm glad you stayed.'

'Me, too.'

'What's the time?' he asked.

'Half-past seven.'

'And you have to go right now?'

She nodded. 'Sorry.'

He kissed the tip of her nose. 'Help yourself to

whatever you need in the bathroom. There are fresh towels in the airing cupboard. And I'll make coffee and breakfast.'

'You really don't have to make me breakfast.'

He raised an eyebrow. 'You're seriously turning down a bacon sandwich and good coffee, on a Sunday morning?'

'Ah. In that case, thank you, I'll happily stay for breakfast,' she said with a smile.

Her underwear had dried overnight; she showered and dressed swiftly.

'Perfect timing,' Lorenzo said, and handed her a plate holding what turned to be the best bacon sandwich she'd ever eaten in her life.

'Thank you, this is fabulous.'

'My pleasure.'

He wouldn't let her do the washing up. 'It's fine. It'll go in the dishwasher. Besides, if you're late, Evelyn will worry about you, and that isn't fair.'

'That's true. Thank you.'

'I'll see you at work tomorrow,' he said, and kissed her lightly.

'Enjoy your family day,' she said.

'Enjoy your day, too.'

CHAPTER SIX

ON FRIDAY NIGHT, Lorenzo stayed over at Jenna's and joined her in taking Charlie for a walk on Saturday morning.

'He's gorgeous. A big fluffy teddy bear of a dog,' he said, ruffling the dog's fur.

'He's a cockapoo—a cross between a cocker spaniel and a poodle,' Jenna explained. 'And he's got such a sweet nature. I think he'd make a fabulous therapy dog, but obviously Evelyn wouldn't be able to manage taking him round to schools or nursing homes or what have you.'

Charlie was on his best behaviour, walking nicely beside them rather than pulling, and sitting nicely while waiting for Jenna and Lorenzo to throw the tennis ball for him in turn.

'He's a great dog,' Lorenzo said.

'Have you ever thought about having a dog of your own?' she asked.

He shook his head. 'Not with the hours I work. I'd have to leave the dog home alone for too long.'

'Me, too,' she said. 'I grew up with dogs, so I miss

having one around and it's nice to be able to help Evelyn with him.'

With Georgia working part time, Lorenzo had thought about getting a dog. His family had always had a dog while he was growing up and he had wanted the same opportunities for Florence. Especially as Florence had always made a beeline for Suki, his parents' golden retriever, whenever they had been at his parents' house. He'd been about to suggest it when Georgia had dropped the bombshell about Florence not being his, and that she was leaving him to make a new life with Florence's natural father.

She'd moved away and left him to pick up the pieces of his own life—selling the house, which had taken months and months, and giving Georgia her share through his lawyer; sorting out all the paperwork for the divorce; facing all the pity and the conversations that stopped suddenly when he walked into the staff kitchen at work; and seeing the sorrow in his mother's eyes every time she looked at him, because she clearly realised how deeply all this had hurt him and hated the fact she couldn't fix it for him.

Lorenzo had struggled on for more than a year. He'd actually been at the point of asking his parents if they'd look after a dog for him during the day, because going back to that empty house with all the memories had made him so lonely and miserable. And then finally the house had sold and then the job had come up at Muswell Hill Memorial Hospital. The same job he'd always loved, but with new colleagues who didn't know his past and wouldn't look at him with pity. He'd jumped at the chance.

He knew he ought to tell Jenna about Florence. He didn't think she was the pitying sort, but he didn't want to take the risk that it would change the way she saw him. He liked the fact that she saw him for himself.

'Let's play ball with him,' he said, and held his hand out for the tennis ball.

Once they'd tired Charlie out and had a cup of tea with Evelyn, they spent a lazy day together, enjoying the food stalls and choosing fresh produce for dinner at Borough Market. 'Would I be right in thinking that you don't have a griddle pan?' he asked.

Jenna just laughed. 'You're lucky I have even normal pans, let alone fancy ones. Are you quite sure I can't tempt you to a bowl of hand-poured granola with hand-chopped fruit and hand-spooned Greek yoghurt tonight?'

He laughed back, enjoying her sense of humour. 'So that'd be a no if I asked if you had specialist pasta cutters, too.'

She gestured to the stalls. 'That's what this place is for. So people don't have to buy flashy gadgets they use once and then the things sit gathering dust in their kitchen cupboards. It's much, much easier and quicker to buy ready-prepped food from someone who knows what they're doing with the gadgets.'

'Remind me not to buy you a spiraliser instead of a bunch of flowers,' he teased back. 'I'll bake the salmon tonight rather than grilling it, then. I could cook it with a pesto crust.'

'Are you quite sure you don't want to be an award-winning chef like your cousin?' she asked.

'I just like cooking,' he said. And it was good to cook for someone else, to share the pleasure of food rather than sit at a table with only a medical journal for company.

Sunday morning dawned bright and sunny.

'After we've walked Charlie,' Lorenzo said, 'how do you fancy going to the seaside?'

'That would be perfect,' Jenna said. 'It's ages since I've been for a paddle in the sea.'

Once they'd tired out the energetic cockapoo, he drove them down to Brighton. It was a long while since Lorenzo had been to the seaside, too, and he'd even made excuses to avoid Italy for the last year or so, because being with his big, happy, extended family was too painful a reminder of what he'd lost. But the sunshine, the sound of the waves swishing across the pebbles on the beach, and the scent of salt and vinegar from the fish and chip stands brightened his mood.

Better still, he was with Jenna. Being with her felt like being bathed in sunshine.

'So are you a funfair person?' she asked.

He had been. Florence had laughed and clapped her hands as he'd taken her on the carousel, holding her safely in front of him on the painted wooden horse. 'Dada! Horsey!' He'd loved taking her to the swings and slides at the park.

'Lorenzo?' she asked softly, squeezing his hand.

'I…' He took a deep breath. This would be good

for him. It might exorcise a ghost, maybe. 'Let's give it a go.'

As if she'd guessed that he was finding this hard, she held his hand without comment, not pushing him to talk but making it clear she was there for him. They started at one end of the pier and did every single thrill ride until they were out at the other end.

'Better?' she asked softly.

'Better,' he confirmed, and kissed her. 'Thank you.'

'Any time.' But that wasn't pity in her eyes. It was sympathy. And he liked the fact that she hadn't pushed him and asked: that she was waiting until he was ready to explain. 'Fish and chips are on me.'

'I'll take you up on that.' He stole another kiss.

They were halfway to the nearest fish and chip shop when they heard a scream and saw a small child sprawled on the pavement next to a lamp-post. The mum looked worried and the baby in the pram started wailing.

'I'm a doctor. Can I do anything to help?' Jenna asked, going over to them.

'I…' The woman raked a hand through her hair.

'Cuddle the baby,' Jenna said, 'and we'll look after your little girl—we're both doctors. I'm Jenna and this is Lorenzo.'

'I'm Sally. And my daughter's Daisy.' Gratefully, Sally scooped up the baby and began rocking him against her shoulder.

'Daisy.' Jenna gently picked up the little girl. 'Where does it hurt, sweetheart?' she asked.

'I bumped my head,' the little girl sobbed. 'And my knee. I want Mummy.'

'Mummy's here,' Sally said. 'The nice lady's a doctor and she'll make you better.'

'Can I have a look at your bumped head?' Jenna asked.

The little girl gave a shy nod.

'You'll definitely have a bit of a bump there tomorrow,' Jenna said, and took a small first-aid kit from her bag. 'I'm going to wipe your knee and put a plaster on it. While I'm doing that, can you sing me a song?'

In response, Daisy sobbed.

'You can help me sing a song, if you like,' Lorenzo said. 'Do you know "Old MacDonald Had a Farm"?'

'Ye-es,' she said, sounding slightly doubtful.

'Let's sing it together, and you can choose what animals we sing about,' Lorenzo said.

Jenna gave him a grateful smile. While Lorenzo distracted the little girl with 'Old MacDonald'—getting her to do the animal noises and a very loud 'ee-I-ee-I-oh'—she cleaned up the cut and put a sticking plaster on it.

'It's a non-allergenic plaster,' she told Sally. 'As she had a bump on her head, I just want to check her pupils, if that's OK with you?'

At Sally's nod, she took a penlight from her bag. 'Daisy, your singing is beautiful. Can you keep singing with Lorenzo while I shine a little light in your eyes?'

'Yes,' Daisy said, this time sounding less unsure.

'Equal and reactive,' Jenna said when she'd checked Daisy's pupils. 'Which is a very good thing.'

'What's happened?' A man carrying wrapped parcels from the fish and chip shop came hurrying over.

'Daddy!' Daisy said, and burst into tears.

'Daisy fell and bumped her head. These nice people are doctors—they're helping,' Sally said.

'Thank you,' he said. But then he looked worried as Sally's words sank in. 'Bumped her head? Do we need to take her to hospital?'

Jenna shook her head. 'Just keep an eye on her for now. Children often go to sleep after a bump on the head, but keep a check on her and make sure you can wake her. If you can't wake her, or say by the end of the afternoon she tells you she has a headache, she feels sick or she's still sleepy, take her straight in to the emergency department and tell them when she bumped her head and what her symptoms are.'

'Thank you,' Sally said, still rocking the baby, whose wailing had turned to soft, huffing sobs. 'Both of you. That was so kind of you to help.'

'It's what anyone would do,' Jenna said with a smile. 'Take care of yourself.'

'You're really good with children,' Lorenzo said as they walked on.

Jenna rolled her eyes. 'I hope so, or I'd be a bit rubbish at my job.'

'No, I mean you have that warmth about you. Kids respond to you.'

'They respond to you, too,' she said. 'And it's not just your packs of cards and terrible jokes.'

Tell her.

She hadn't been judgemental when he'd told her the bare bones about Georgia. And that definitely hadn't been pity in her eyes.

Could he tell her?

If he opened up to her, would it change things?

Stupid question. Of course it would change things. But maybe she could help him move on. It still wouldn't be closure, but Jenna would have a different perspective on the situation, not having been involved. She might help him see a way through.

'Let's go and sit down,' he said.

'Sure.' As if she guessed that he wanted to tell her something monumental, she didn't try to chatter; she simply held his hand and waited while he found a relatively quiet spot on the beach.

Tell her.

He took a deep breath. The words felt as if they would stick in his throat, but he forced them out. 'I used to be a dad.'

She didn't leap in with questions. But she held his hand very tightly, just letting him know that she was there.

He braved a glance. There was only concern for him in her face. Gentleness, warmth, kindness.

He stared at the sea. Now he'd made up his mind to talk, why wouldn't the words come?

'You don't have to talk if you don't want to,' she said. 'But, if it helps, I'm not going to judge you—

and everything that you say to me will be strictly in confidence.'

Funny, he hadn't even considered that. He already knew that that Jenna wasn't a gossip. 'Thank you.' He was silent for what felt like minutes, though it was probably only a few seconds. And then he swallowed hard. 'I met Georgia at a party—she was a nurse in the emergency department at the London Victoria, where we both worked. We started dating, and I fell for her. She was funny and sweet and smart. We'd been together for about six months when she told me she was pregnant.' He continued staring out to sea. 'The baby wasn't planned, but it didn't matter. We were going to be a family. I loved her and thought that she loved me. I asked her to marry me and she said yes.'

Now he'd actually started talking, the words spilled out in a rush. 'What I didn't know was that Georgia had an on-again, off-again relationship with a guy she'd gone to school with. Scott had fallen in with a bad crowd in his teens and started taking cars for joyriding. He'd been in court for it a couple of times; but it went from there to petty theft and then burglary. He was caught and sent to prison for a few months. Georgia broke up with him because he broke his promise to her to go straight, and that was the night she met me. When he was released from prison, he asked to see her. She told him it was over, but I guess they had a moment for old times' sake. Because he thought it was over between them for good, in his eyes there wasn't any point in trying to go straight, so he ended up back with his old crowd. He was arrested for burglary and sent back to prison—this time for two years. And I suppose Georgia panicked when she realised she was pregnant.'

'Because she looked at the timing and couldn't be sure if the baby was yours or his, and he would still be in prison when the baby was born?' Jenna guessed.

Lorenzo nodded. 'She talked it over with her family. They all liked me and they persuaded her I'd be a much better dad to the baby and a better partner for her than Scott would.' He grimaced. 'I should've seen all the clues and worked it out for myself, but I didn't. I just took everything she said at face value. She said she didn't want to get married until after the baby was born, because she didn't want to be pregnant in her wedding dress. I know it's sexist of me, but I put it down to pregnancy hormones.'

'It was a reasonable guess,' Jenna said.

He sighed. 'I didn't push her because I didn't want to pressurise her. I tried to be understanding. But, because we weren't married when she had Florence, she didn't put my name on Florence's birth certificate. She said it didn't feel right to do that when we weren't married, and she'd get it changed as soon as we got married—but then she just didn't get round to it. Again maybe I was sexist, but I assumed some of it was post-pregnancy hormones and some of it was because it just isn't that easy to adjust to having a baby. I talked to a colleague to see how I could make things better, in case she had post-natal depression.'

Jenna squeezed his hand. 'That's not sexist, it's thoughtful. Putting yourself in her shoes and actually considering that things might not be OK for her.'

'It didn't ever occur to me that there was someone else. That she snapped at me all the time because I wasn't the one she wanted around, and that made her feel guilty and snap at me even more. I tried to be a decent, supportive husband and a good father.' And that was the rub. Maybe he hadn't been a great husband, but he knew he'd been a good dad. 'I fell in love with Florence, the moment I first held her,' Lorenzo said softly. 'She was my little girl.' He looked away again. 'And then, when Florence was eighteen months old, Scott was released from prison. He came round, saying that his mum had told him about the baby and he'd worked out the dates and knew Florence was his. This time, he really would go straight, for his daughter's sake. He wanted to be a family with them.' He blew out a breath.

'Scott was the love of Georgia's life, and he told her what she wanted to hear. To be honest, once I'd seen his picture, it was pretty obvious that Florence was Scott's daughter. They both had the same red hair and grey eyes—and you and I both know that dark hair and dark eyes are dominant, genetically speaking. I assumed that maybe red hair ran in Georgia's family, plus Georgia had grey eyes. But, the second I saw Scott, I could see that Florence was his.' His face tightened. 'Georgia did a DNA test without telling me, and the results proved beyond all doubt that Scott was Florence's father.'

'That's…' Jenna shook her head, as if unable to find the right words. 'I'm so sorry you had to go through that.'

'Me, too,' he said softly. 'I couldn't contest Georgia

for custody, because my name had never been on Florence's birth certificate and she had absolute proof that Florence wasn't my child. Bringing her up as my daughter for eighteen months counted for nothing. Georgia and Scott moved away, and she said it would've been too confusing to keep me in Florence's life.'

'But so many blended families manage to deal with having more than one mother or father. Surely it wouldn't have been that difficult?' Jenna asked.

'That wasn't the way Georgia saw it.'

'Does Georgia at least let you know that Florence is OK?' Jenna asked. 'Does she send you photos, so you can see Florence growing up?'

'No. She insisted on a clean break as part of the divorce settlement.' And that was the bit that hurt the most. He could just about handle the fact that he hadn't been Mr Right for Georgia, that she'd cheated on him with the man she really loved, but losing his daughter felt like being flayed alive. 'I hope for Florence's sake that Scott really has turned his life around and he's a good father to her.' He raked a hand through his hair. 'I did go to see her parents, but they said Georgia was their daughter so they had to stand by her wishes and support her. Obviously that didn't help me, but I understand where they were coming from.' He grimaced. 'Short of hiring a private detective, I have no way of knowing how Florence is getting on.' And how he hated that. 'She'll be three in a few weeks' time. And I won't even be able to wish her a happy birthday.'

She squeezed his hand. 'That's hard. I'm so sorry.'

'I don't want pity, Jenna.'

'I'm not offering pity,' she said. 'I'm sad that you've been so hurt, and to be honest I'm pretty angry on your behalf that Georgia didn't try to find a better compromise. Why didn't she tell you when she did the pregnancy test that she'd met up with Scott again and she wasn't sure if the baby was his or yours?'

'Maybe she was scared that I'd walk away as soon as she told me she'd cheated on me, so she'd end up being alone and would find it hard to cope with the baby,' Lorenzo said with a sigh. 'When she realised she was pregnant, Scott had already been taken into custody and the evidence against him was watertight. And she didn't actually know whether the baby was mine.'

'It was a difficult situation for both of you.'

'I wouldn't have walked away from her. Yes, of course it hurt that she slept with her ex, but we could've got past that. I would've supported her. I'm not...'

'Not like my ex,' she supplied. 'You're one of the good guys. And I'm sorry you got hurt like that.'

He shrugged. 'I guess at least she didn't lie on the birth certificate.' But that was a very small consolation.

'I don't know what to say,' she said. 'There isn't anything I can do to make it better. But thank you for trusting me.'

'Thank you for listening.'

This time she wrapped her arms round him. 'This isn't out of pity. It's a hug, because sometimes that's better than words.'

He hugged her back. She was right. This was what he needed most at this precise moment.

They stayed there for a while, just holding each

other, and then she said, 'I also have a very English answer for right this very second. A cup of tea.'

He couldn't help smiling. 'That,' he said, 'would be good.'

'With scones. Warm ones.'

'Jam or cream first?' he asked.

She spread her hands. 'I can never decide, so I split mine between the two.'

Funny how just being with her made his heart feel lighter. Her solution of a cream tea really did make him feel better. As did the fact she asked him to stay when he drove them home, that evening. If he'd gone back to his own place, he would have lain awake and brooded. Instead, he fell asleep in Jenna's arms, feeling lighter of spirit than he had since Georgia left. There would always be a Florence-shaped hole in his life. But right now Jenna had made him feel so much less alone.

CHAPTER SEVEN

'I TOLD YOU you were fussing over nothing, Mum,' Cameron said.

'Nope, she was dead right to bring you in to see us,' Jenna corrected the teenager. 'I'd much rather see you now than in three weeks' time when you're in major pain. And a parent's intuition should never be underestimated.'

'Mum *does* fuss, though,' he said in a stage whisper.

'I do,' Mrs Blake admitted. 'Probably more than the average mum, because he's my only one.'

'Actually, given all the mums I've met in my career, I'd say most mums worry just as much as you do—it's perfectly normal,' Jenna said with a smile. 'I can give you a leaflet on Henoch-Schönlein purpura if you like, so you don't have to think back to our conversation today and worry that you can't remember it all.'

'Yes, please,' Mrs Blake said. 'I don't want to miss any important signs if he gets worse.'

Cameron rolled his eyes. 'Mum, I'm going to get a drink from the vending machine. See you in reception.'

'He's hitting the independent years, then,' Jenna said as she signed into the computer system and printed off the leaflet.

'Tell me about it,' Mrs Blake said wryly. 'Everything I do or say is wrong.'

'For what it's worth, you did the right thing bringing him in. We know what's wrong; if he gets any worse we can give him the steroids to sort out the stomach pain, so he's not distracted in his exams.' She gestured to the computer. 'I'll just need to take you over to the office where we have the printer to grab this, if that's OK.'

'It's fine. And thank you for being so calm and reassuring.' Mrs Blake followed Jenna over to the offices in the department. 'Cam's right, though. I do fuss too much. We couldn't have children naturally, and we had to admit defeat after four cycles of IVF. Luckily a very, very kind woman acted as our surrogate, and because of her we have Cam. I still can't thank her enough for what she did for us.'

It was just what Jenna had done for her sister, so she understood completely from both sides of the situation—how her sister had felt as a woman who was desperate for a baby, and how she'd felt as a surrogate who'd really wanted to help make things better in someone else's world. She squeezed Mrs Blake's shoulder. 'Knowing that you love him to bits and worry about him would be enough thanks for your surrogate, believe me. You carry a baby for someone else because you know how much that child is wanted and just how much he or she will be loved.'

* * *

That sounded really personal, Lorenzo thought, looking up from the notes he was writing in the office next door to where Jenna was talking to her patient's mum.

Or maybe he was overthinking it. From what he knew about surrogacy, surrogate mothers tended to have children of their own already, and he knew Jenna was single and childless. Maybe she had a close friend who'd acted as a surrogate, so she was talking from her friend's perspective. Though asking her would make it sound as if he'd been deliberately listening in instead of catching the tail end of a conversation and being curious; he didn't want her to think he was snooping, so he left it.

But then the question of surrogate mothers came up in the staff kitchen, a couple of days later, when some of the staff were chatting about a programme they'd seen on the television, the night before.

'I can't believe that storyline on the soap last night about the surrogate mum,' Keely said. 'If Jenna's been watching it, she'll be frothing at the mouth.'

Why on earth would Jenna be upset by a soap storyline about surrogacy? Lorenzo wondered.

Then he remembered the conversation he'd partly overheard. Had he been right in guessing that maybe one of Jenna's closest friends had acted as a surrogate?

'That's so horrible, with those poor people having a legal fight with the surrogate to keep their baby, and they'd already paid her all that money,' Keely continued.

'What I hate about it is that it's nothing like real life,'

Sanjeev, one of the junior doctors, said. 'In the UK, you can't pay someone to be a surrogate mum for you. You're only allowed to pay their expenses.'

'Exactly. You know what you're going into when you're a surrogate,' Keely said. 'You're prepared right from the start that you're carrying a baby for someone else, so they're obviously doing it for dramatic purposes.'

'But if you were desperate for a baby and you couldn't adopt, and you were thinking about finding a surrogate, watching that storyline would put you right off,' Laney added. 'You'd be worried sick that it'd all go wrong, when in real life the agencies are really careful about putting the right people together. I really wish these dramas would get their facts right instead of twisting them to suit the plot—and I know they put that notice up at the end of the show with a helpline number to call if you're affected by any of the events in the programme, but it's too late by then. They've already planted the doubts and given them time to fester.'

'The woman who gives birth is the legal parent, and she can't agree to a parental order until the baby's six weeks old,' Sanjeev said. 'Plus there are all sorts of conditions about getting a parental order in the first place.'

Lorenzo knew about parental orders first-hand. His lawyer had broken the bad news to him. 'You have to be in a stable long-term relationship, one of you has to be biologically related to the child, and the child has to be living with you.' None of which had applied to him where Florence was concerned, and he'd had no rights whatsoever. He hadn't even been able to ask for access, because Georgia had proved that Florence wasn't his biological daughter. Bringing her up for eighteen months and being there for her mother during her pregnancy counted for nothing in the court's eyes.

Even so, everyone here seemed really well versed in the legal side of surrogacy—much more so than in the paediatric department at his last hospital. It was the sort of thing that the maternity unit staff would be more likely to know more about, especially if there was a specialist IVF unit attached to the department; so why did the paediatric department here know so much about it? Did someone here in the department have first-hand experience, maybe?

And again, he wondered, why had Jenna's name in particular cropped up?

Did it have anything to do with the sabbatical she'd mentioned, but never actually said what she'd done on her time away from her job? And Jenna had said that her ex had disapproved of a decision she'd made. Would that have been the decision to act as someone's surrogate and have a baby for them?

As a theory, it all hung together.

But she hadn't chosen to confide in him.

It was none of his business.

He should just leave it.

But it nagged at him for the rest of the week. That half-heard conversation with a patient's parent and the chatter in the ward kitchen... Perhaps he was adding two and two and making five. But somehow he didn't think he was. The answer he kept coming back to was that Jenna had had a surrogate baby.

The thought twisted deep in his gut, reminding him of how Georgia had lied to him about Florence. Why would Jenna not tell him about something like this?

Maybe he was being oversensitive and overreacting because it was getting so close to Florence's third birthday, and he knew from seeing his niece and nephew just how much he was missing out on; but it unsettled him enough for him to bring up the subject casually when he went out to dinner with Jenna on Saturday night.

'Keely and Sanjeev were talking about that soap storyline, the other day,' he said. 'The one about the surrogate mum.'

'Oh?' Her voice was perfectly neutral, as if he was talking about something as anodyne as the price of bananas.

Part of him knew he ought to change the subject. But part of him was hurt that he'd opened up to her and she was still completely closed off from him. Was she keeping a big secret from him, the way that Georgia had?

'Never mind. Forget I said anything.' He looked away.

Jenna had known for a while that she needed to tell Lorenzo about Ava. Especially because he'd told her about Florence.

But the words had stuck in her throat, along with

the memory of how scathing Danny had been. And the accusation Danny had thrown at her when she'd refused to give in to his ultimatum—untrue, unfair and totally unjustified.

She didn't think that Lorenzo would take the same approach. But what if he did? What if she'd made the same mistake all over again? She'd got Danny totally wrong. Who was to say she hadn't got Lorenzo wrong, too?

But she couldn't put this off any more. Not really. It was time to tell him. She took a deep breath. 'You told me about Florence. So I guess I ought to tell you about Ava.'

'Ava?' he asked. 'Your niece?'

She nodded. 'She's why I took that year's sabbatical.' And now for the hard bit. 'I was a surrogate mum for my sister, because she couldn't have a child of her own.'

She was almost afraid to look into his face, just in case she saw the same disapproval she'd faced from Danny. But she made herself do it. She had to look twice, because she wasn't quite sure what she was seeing.

'You took a year out of your life because you were being your twin's surrogate mum?' he asked. And then he said something she wasn't expecting. 'That's the most amazing, selfless thing I've ever heard.'

'You don't think I was stupid? Naive and...' The words choked her.

He reached across the table and squeezed her hand. 'No, I don't. That's the most incredible gift to give anyone—a child. Why would you think I'd judge you like th—?' He stopped. 'Your ex, right?'

She nodded. 'I know you're not him, but...'

'But, thanks to him, you've lost faith in your own judgement and you don't trust yourself or anyone else. I get that. Jenna, we all make mistakes—I've certainly made enough of them—but I'm telling you now that what you did for Lucy wasn't one of them. It was a brave, kind and selfless thing to do.' His fingers tightened round hers. 'You don't have to say anything more. You don't owe me any explanations.'

He didn't think the same way Danny had.

He actually approved of what she had done. He thought she'd done the right thing.

And that gave her the courage to carry on. 'I'm sorry. I shouldn't have judged you. Or expected you to react the same way Danny did.'

'It's fine. If it makes you feel any better,' he said, 'I was feeling worried that you might be keeping a secret from me, the way Georgia did. Though now I know with you it's the other way round—you were giving a baby, not taking one away.'

'I kind of understand why Georgia did what she did, even though I would have handled the situation very differently,' Jenna said. 'I would never have taken a baby away from anyone.'

'Wasn't it hard to hand the baby over, though, when she was born?' Lorenzo asked. 'You'd carried her for nine months. Bonded with her.'

'She was always Lucy's baby, not mine,' Jenna said. 'Yes, of course I felt that rush of love that you hear mums talking about when Ava was born. But I'm also a doctor. I knew what the hormones were doing to my body, and right from the start I thought of Ava as my sister's baby. She's my niece, and she's a joy to have in my life. I love being her aunt and spending time with her, seeing my sister's little girl growing up and exploring the world—and I see Lucy in her all the time.' Though she'd caught herself since feeling all wistful and wondering what it would be like to have a baby of her own and a partner to share that love with.

'So how come…?' Lorenzo stopped. 'Sorry. I don't mean to grill you. You don't owe me any answers.'

'And you're not judging me,' Jenna said.

'No. Not at all. Though I'll listen if you want to tell me. And everything you tell me,' he said, echoing what she'd said to him on the beach, 'will be strictly in confidence.'

She knew he'd chosen those words deliberately—to give her courage, the same way she'd tried to give him courage to talk. 'Can we… Just not here?' she asked.

'Sure. Go to the bathroom or something and I'll sort everything out here.'

'Sorry. I ruined dinner.' She bit her lip.

'You didn't ruin anything. It's fine. I'll make us an omelette or something back at mine if you want to eat later, or we can grab a kebab on the way somewhere.'

'Thank you.' She really appreciated how kind he was being. She would never have believed he could be so understanding about the situation. Though she knew it was wrong to let Danny's behaviour colour her judgement of all men.

She went to the bathroom and splashed water on her face, then joined Lorenzo by the reception area.

'Let's go,' he said, and took her hand.

They walked by the river until they found an empty bench, then sat down. Lorenzo simply waited until she was ready to talk, not pressuring her.

She took a deep breath. 'When we were twenty-seven, Lucy was in a serious car crash,' she began. 'She was driving up to York to spend the weekend with her best friend from university, having a fitting for her bridesmaid's dress—but she never got there. A lorry hit her on the motorway and her car was pretty much squished. She had serious internal injuries, with a ruptured womb—her ovaries were damaged, too, and they couldn't stop her bleeding in Theatre. It was a choice of giving her a hysterectomy or losing her completely. So obviously Will, as her next of kin, opted for hysterectomy. And we were all there, too, to support him—me, Mum and Dad.'

'A hysterectomy is a horrible thing to happen when you're that young,' Lorenzo said. 'It takes away a lot of your choices.'

Jenna nodded. 'Lucy and Will had planned to start trying for a family, the following summer. She was devastated, Renzo, when she realised that couldn't ever happen. But she got over the operation and recovered from her injuries, and then she and Will applied to be put on the register for adoption.' She grimaced. 'Except the authorities turned her down. Will's fifteen years older than Lucy, and the authorities decided that meant he was too old to be a dad.' She shook her head in disgust. 'I hate the fact that some faceless bureaucrat could take away their dreams like that, for such a ridiculous reason, because it was obvious to the rest of the world that Lucy and Will would both be brilliant parents.' Anger at the injustice flooded through her. 'Lucy and Will appealed against the decision but, even with the social worker's help, they lost the case.' She shrugged. 'So then it hit me. I was the one with the answer—I could be Lucy's surrogate and carry a baby for them.'

'That's an amazing thing to do for someone,' Lorenzo said. 'To give them their dreams.'

'She's my twin. She would've done the same for me.'

'It's still amazing.'

'It was an arrangement between me and Lucy, and we opted for IVF. The IVF team prefers surrogate mums to finish having their own family first, before they carry a baby for anyone else—because of course there are always risks with a pregnancy, and we didn't know whether I'd even be able to carry a baby to term. But we argued that we were a special case,' Jenna said. 'Because I'm Lucy's identical twin, this would mean we'd be having a baby who was genetically the same as her own would have been. The IVF team insisted that we had counselling first, but it was all fine. We used Will's sperm and my egg. Our family and friends were supportive—well, nearly all of them were.' She looked at him. 'The only problem was Danny, my ex.'

'Why didn't he want you to do it? Did he want you to have a baby with him first?'

'No. It wasn't that at all. He couldn't see that

I was making the world all right again for Lucy.'
Her lip curled. 'He saw it in terms of losing all my
promotion prospects at work, the sheer cost of the IVF
treatment—even though Lucy and Will paid for that, he
still thought of it as money—and the amount of salary
I'd be losing by taking a year's sabbatical.'

Lorenzo winced. 'That's an appalling way to look
at things.'

'You're telling me. And, when I argued that none of
that was important,' she said, 'he said he'd end things
between us if I went ahead. I was so angry, I told him
I didn't want to be with someone like him anyway.'
Bile rose in her throat. 'Then he accused me of wanting
Will and said this was the only way I'd get to have
Will's baby.'

Lorenzo stared at her. 'You're kidding.'

'Sadly not.' She gave a hollow laugh. 'This was
the man I'd actually been considering marrying. But I
don't want to be with anyone who has no compassion
and sees everything in terms of money, and who turns
spiteful if you disagree with him. So I walked away.'

'Good. Because he sounds like a totally selfish idiot
and he wasn't good enough for you.'

Jenna rather liked the fact that Lorenzo was fighting
her corner. 'Thank you for—well, for understanding
why I did it.'

'You're amazing.'

'I love my sister. And, as I said, Ava was always hers.
Lucy was there every step of the way, from holding my
hand in the clinic when the eggs were harvested, and
later when the embryos were transferred and during

the thirty-minute waiting time afterwards, through to taking the pregnancy test, every single scan, and the birth itself. Lucy was the first person to hold Ava after she was born, the person who cut the umbilical cord, the person who did the first feed with the milk that I'd expressed. As far as I'm concerned, she's Ava's mum—biologically, morally and legally.' She grimaced. 'I know it's a bit complicated, but they're my family and I love them. Ava's eighteen months old right now. When she's old enough to understand, we'll explain to her that her birth was a little bit complicated—but my egg was genetically identical to Lucy's, so her mum is still her mum and her dad is still her dad, and nothing has changed apart from the fact that her mum borrowed my womb so Ava could grow.'

'Eighteen months old. The same age Florence was when I last saw her.' His eyes were sad. 'It's a lovely age.'

'It is. She chatters a lot. And she loves dancing and messy play and making cookies—obviously the baking bit is with her mum rather than with me, but if I'm off duty I get to go swimming with her and Lucy, and it's just magical watching her grow up.' She smiled. 'And the best bit is seeing my twin so happy and fulfilled. With the life she always wanted—the life she deserves.'

Lorenzo put his arms round her. 'Someone very wise once said to me that sometimes this works better than words.'

'It does.' And knowing that this time she'd picked one of the good guys—one who was as far from Danny as you could get—was like a weight lifted from her shoulders. She held him close. 'So now you know.'

'And I'm sorry,' he said. 'I guess what happened with Georgia has made me a bit paranoid. I thought you were keeping some deep, dark secret.'

'I kind of was,' she said. 'And I'm sorry, too. I know you're nothing like Danny, but I was so scared you'd judge me. Especially because you lost Florence, and I didn't want you thinking that I'd just blithely had a baby and given her away. Ava was never mine to start with.' She smiled. 'I might be a tiny bit biased, but she is the most gorgeous niece.'

'You're not the first who hasn't wanted to tell me about a baby,' Lorenzo said. 'My little sister didn't want to tell me she's expecting—but I guessed when she was helping me clear up after Sunday lunch and she was gagging at the kitchen smells.' He grimaced. 'She didn't want to tell me because she felt as if she was rubbing it in. I told her not to be so daft—and I'd better be the first person she asks to babysit.'

Jenna pulled back slightly. 'Has anyone ever told you how nice you are?'

He laughed. 'You're nice, too. You're a hustler and you're bossy—but there's a sweetness about you. Not cloying and sickly, but lovely. You make the world feel as if it's certainly full of sunshine.'

'That's how you make me feel, too,' she said.

'That,' he said, 'sounds almost like a declaration of intent.'

She wasn't ready to say the three little words. But she was ready to think them. 'Maybe,' she said instead, 'you'd like to meet my sister? And actually you'd get to meet the whole family, because we're close and they'll refuse to be left out.'

'I'd like that,' he said. 'And maybe you'd like to meet my family, too. It's large, Italian and noisy—and close, like yours sounds.'

She nodded. 'Let's call them.'

'We'll call them now,' he said, 'and then we'll get some food.'

CHAPTER EIGHT

PREDICTABLY, BOTH FAMILIES jumped at the chance to meet. So, the following Saturday morning, Lorenzo met Jenna at her flat, carrying wine and flowers.

'You really don't need to bring anything just for lunch with my family,' she said.

'Yes, I do,' he corrected. But part of him felt ridiculously nervous. Would Jenna's family like him? In a way, meeting them would be like the most important job interview he'd ever had.

Once they'd taken Charlie for his run in the park, Lorenzo and Jenna caught the Tube to Lucy's house.

'Lucy's obviously my twin, this is Will, and Ava, my mum, Rosie, and my dad, Greg,' Jenna said, introducing them swiftly. 'Everyone, this is Lorenzo Conti.'

'Please call me Renzo. And it's lovely to meet you,' Lorenzo said, shaking Will's and Greg's hands, kissing Rosie and Lucy on the cheek, and smiling at little Ava—who went all shy on him and clung to her father. 'Lucy, thank you so much for inviting me to lunch.' He handed her the flowers and wine.

'My pleasure—and thank you for these,' Lucy said,

smiling back. She glanced at the label. 'Conti? Is that as in your family?'

'It's from my family's vineyard,' he explained.

'And Renzo helped pick the grapes for that particular vintage,' Jenna chimed in.

'That's impressive,' Lucy said. 'Come and help me put the flowers in water, and you can tell me how you like your coffee.'

In other words, he was in for a grilling. He glanced at Jenna, who just spread her hands and smiled. Well, if it was OK with her, it was OK with him.

'I know Jenna's told you about Ava,' Lucy said, when they were in the kitchen and she was putting the flowers in a vase.

'Your sister,' Lorenzo said, 'is an amazing woman.'

'I'm glad you realise how special she is.'

'I do, and I'm not Danny,' he said, though he was pretty sure that Lucy would know her twin had told him about her ex.

'Danny!' Lucy grimaced. 'The less said about him, the better.'

'Agreed,' he said. 'And you obviously already know she's meeting my family tomorrow.'

'That means it's serious, for Jen.'

'And for me,' he said softly. 'I really want this to work.'

'Me, too. She deserves someone who'll be good to her.'

'That would be me,' he said. 'And I assume she told you everything about me?'

Lucy nodded. 'I'm sorry you've been through

something so hard. Even the idea of not being able to see my daught—' She caught her breath. 'Well. Are you sure you're okay with Ava being around?'

'Apart from the fact that my entire working life is spent with children,' Lorenzo said, 'I have a niece and nephew I adore who are almost the same age as Florence. I've been looking forward to meeting Ava. But thank you for asking. I appreciate it.'

'It can't be easy for you. I know how bad it felt when I was told about the hysterectomy. Will and I were planning to try for a baby, the following summer. And when the adoption people turned us down...'

He could see the tears sparkling in Lucy's eyes. 'But Jenna was there.'

'And she gave me the most precious gift of all.' She blinked the tears away.

'Let's change the subject to something that's not going to make you cry,' Lorenzo said. 'Something smells very good. What can I do to help?'

'Just tell me how you like your coffee.'

'White, no sugar, please.'

'That's easy—the same as the rest of us. I'll bring it out in a second. Now go and chat to the others.' Lucy shooed him out of the kitchen.

It was surprisingly easy to fit in with Jenna's family, Lorenzo found. He enjoyed talking history with Will and medicine with Greg and Rosie; and he could see for himself how close Jenna was to Ava. They clearly adored each other, as aunt and niece, and Jenna was right at the heart of her family. Jenna Harris was a woman who would never betray the man she loved or take his child away.

But there was still a tinge of sadness in his heart. Jenna was very much part of Ava's life, whereas he was completely blocked out of Florence's. He shook himself mentally. Today was about getting to know her family, not fretting about his past.

Finally he ended up on the floor with Ava, helping her make a tower of bricks she could knock down and then patiently reading a series of board books she brought over to him from the lowest bookshelf.

'Ezzo 'tory,' Ava said imperiously for the fourth time, toddling over and thrusting another book at him. 'Ezzo 'tory, *peese*.'

'Hey, missy, he's already read you three stories. Enough, now. His coffee will get cold,' Lucy said.

'I really don't mind,' Lorenzo said with a smile. He'd always loved reading to Florence, his nephew Jack and his niece Emily; and he was charmed by the way Ava had pronounced his name when she'd asked for a story. *Ezzo*. His family would love that, too. 'I think your sister will tell you, on the ward, you take your coffee at whatever temperature you can get it.'

'I know, I know, it's a medic thing. Mum and Dad say the same. Even so.' Lucy scooped Ava into her arms and kissed her. 'How about Daddy reads you the duck story? Then it's time for lunch.'

'Unch,' Ava said, and clapped her hands. 'Dada 'tory. Duck!'

'They're gorgeous at this age,' Lorenzo said. Ava was the same age Florence had been when he'd last seen her; and at the same stage, starting to put words together and making tiny sentences. He loved this and feeling part of the family, even at the same time as it squeezed his heart with a reminder of what he'd lost.

Lucy lived up to her reputation as a great cook, because lunch was fabulous—roast chicken with all the trimmings, followed by strawberries and home-made caramel ice cream.

'I didn't dare make lasagne for you, especially when Jenna told me that not only are you Italian, your cousin is a Michelin-starred chef who taught you to cook,' Lucy said. 'In fact, I was a bit worried about even cooking you roast chicken.'

He laughed. 'Apart from the fact that this was amazing—and, yes, I did notice that you put fresh tarragon and butter under the chicken skin—I have it on good authority that you make the best lasagne in the world, and I'm very much looking forward to sampling it.'

'Perhaps the next time we have a meal together,' Lucy said.

'The time after,' he corrected, 'because next time it's my turn to cook.'

'As long as it's that scallop and pasta thing,' Jenna said. 'It's amazing.'

Lorenzo couldn't help being amused. 'It does have a proper name, you know.'

'Scallop and pasta thing sounds good enough to me,' Lucy said with a grin. 'Be kind. Jen burns water, remember.'

'And offers people her special granola for dinner,' Lorenzo teased, and everyone laughed.

Will patiently helped Ava with her meal; and when they'd all finished eating Lorenzo shared the washing-up duties with Will before they all took Ava to the park.

Ava insisted on holding hands with Lorenzo and Jenna, and wanted Lorenzo to push her on the swings.

'You're a natural with children,' Lucy said.

And how he missed his little girl. 'I like kids.'

As if she'd guessed what he wasn't saying, Lucy said gently, 'Maybe when Florence is older she'll come looking for you.'

'If she does, I'll welcome her with open arms,' Lorenzo said. 'Biology has nothing to do with being a parent.'

'I'm glad you feel that way. Not everyone does.'

Lorenzo knew exactly what Lucy was telling him. 'Danny needs to take another look at his priorities.'

'Danny had better keep a million miles away from my sister, or I'll take him to pieces with a rusty spoon,' Lucy countered.

'I can assure you that you won't need a rusty spoon for me,' Lorenzo told her.

'Good.'

'Ava's adorable.'

Lucy grinned. 'I won't argue with that.'

'And so,' he said, 'is your sister.'

'I won't argue with that, either.' She patted his arm. 'I reckon you'll do, Renzo.'

'Glad to hear it.' He smiled, and continued pushing Ava until she'd had enough of the swings.

* * *

'I like him,' Rosie said, keeping her voice low, when they were back at the house and Will and Lorenzo were settling Ava in her cot for a nap.

'He's definitely a family man. And I notice he puts other people first. That's a good thing,' Greg agreed.

'Will said he likes him, too. So you can tell Renzo he has four yeses from us,' Lucy said with a grin.

Jenna rolled her eyes. 'This isn't a TV talent show, you know.'

'We know. But you knew we were going to check him out when you brought him to meet us. And he gets extra points for the way he played with Ava and read her those stories,' Lucy said. 'You picked the right one this time, Jen.'

'But I haven't met his family yet,' Jenna said. That could possibly be a sticking point. Bearing in mind how much Georgia had hurt him, no doubt they'd be very protective of him.

'They'll love you,' Rosie told her, patting her shoulder.

'They'll see the way you both look at each other and they'll adore you,' Lucy added. 'Just as we noticed the way you look at each other.'

'We don't look at each other like anything,' Jenna protested.

'Oh, you do, love,' Rosie said gently. 'And that's a good thing.'

Later that evening, Lorenzo and Jenna walked back to her flat with their arms wrapped round each other.

'I like your family,' Lorenzo said. 'A lot.'

'Good. They liked you, too.' Jenna took a deep breath. 'One hurdle down, one to go.'

'You'll probably get a grilling from Chiara,' he warned.

'Like you did from Lucy?'

He smiled. 'That's what siblings are for. And I didn't mind. I knew she did it because she loves you and she's worried about you. Which is exactly why you won't mind getting a grilling from Chi.'

On Sunday, after they'd taken Charlie for a run in the park, Jenna picked up some fresh flowers to go with the chocolates she'd bought earlier in the week. 'I'm so not taking wine to a family who owns a vineyard,' she said. 'And, actually, maybe the flowers are a mistake, given that your sister is a florist.'

'No, it's not. Stop worrying.' Lorenzo kissed her. 'They'll love you.'

'Didn't you worry about meeting my family?'

He squeezed her hand. 'Of course I was worried. I wanted them to like me.'

'Exactly. And Italians are even more protective of their family than the English.'

'They'll know immediately that you're not like Georgia. They won't give you a hard time,' he reassured her, clearly working out what she was worried about.

Jenna wasn't so sure; but, when they arrived at Lorenzo's parents' house, the warmth of their welcome melted her worries away.

'Jenna, this is my mother, Luisa, and my father,

Enrico,' Lorenzo said. 'My sister, Chiara, my brother-in-law, Mark, and their son, Jack; and my brother, Riccardo, my sister-in-law, Helen, and their daughter, Emily. Everyone, this is Jenna Harris.'

'Pleased to meet you,' she said, and handed the flowers and chocolates to Lorenzo's mum.

'How lovely—*grazie, bella*,' Luisa said, and hugged her.

'I didn't bring wine because—well, the vineyard, and Renzo absolutely hates the wine I buy,' she said. 'Sorry if that seems rude.'

'It's not rude at all, *bella*. You didn't have to bring anything, just yourself. Welcome to our house,' Enrico said, and hugged her warmly.

After that, Jenna lost track of who was saying what because everyone was talking at once, and she lost count of all the hugs, too.

The Contis were clearly a very tactile family. And she liked that.

'I'll put the flowers in water, Mamma,' Chiara said. 'Come with me, Jenna, and I can get you a glass of wine. The men can go and light the barbecue.'

In other words, Jenna thought, this was her turn to be grilled, just as her own sister had grilled Lorenzo yesterday.

'Good choice of blooms,' Chiara said as she put the flowers in water.

'Bringing flowers to a florist…' Jenna winced. 'I knew it was stupid. Sorry.'

'You brought the flowers to a florist's mother, if we're being picky. Mamma loves flowers, and I'm not in the least bit territorial,' Chiara said with a smile. 'Now, wine. Red, white, rosé?'

'Whatever's open,' Jenna said politely.

'*Chiaretto*, then.'

'The wine your family won an award for.'

'Lorenzo's told you a lot about us?' Chiara paused. 'Did he tell you…?'

'About Florence?' Jenna nodded. 'That was so hard for him. And I assume he's told you about Ava.'

'What you did for your sister was amazing,' Chiara said softly. 'The most precious gift you could ever give someone.'

'I love my sister and I was the one person who could make her world right.' Jenna shrugged. 'Anyone would've done the same in my shoes.'

'Not everyone.' Chiara looked closely at her. 'You have a good heart, and I think you'll be good for Renzo.'

'Just as I think he's good for me. So are you hoping for a girl, this time round?' Jenna asked.

Chiara's eyes widened. 'Renzo told you about the baby?'

Ouch. Jenna didn't want to drop Lorenzo in it, so she fibbed slightly. 'Just that he was about to be an uncle again. But I remember what the early days are like. Plus I noticed you didn't have a glass of wine and Helen did.'

'Ah.' Chiara smiled. 'I couldn't *not* tell him about the baby, because I didn't want to leave him out. But I felt bad about the timing.'

'Because it's near Florence's birthday?' Jenna asked.

Lorenzo hadn't actually said when it was, but she knew it was soon, and guessed that he'd find that day hard.

'Yes. We all miss her. And it's such a shame Georgia wouldn't let her daughter share our family. Jack and Emily are around the same age as Florence, and they all played so nicely together. We were good for her, and she was good for us.' Chiara sighed. 'But Georgia didn't see it that way, and she broke Renzo's heart.'

And Jenna hoped that she could mend it again.

'He looks happier than I've seen him in a long time. That's a good thing,' Chiara said. 'Now, let's join the others in the garden.'

The men were all fussing over the barbecue.

'They're all pretending to be Matteo,' Luisa said with a grin. 'Even Mark.'

Chiara rolled her eyes. 'Men and grilling things over a fire. It brings out the caveman in them.'

'Is there anything I can do to help?' Jenna asked.

'All the salads are done,' Helen said, 'and it's just a matter of putting the lemon and rosemary potatoes in the oven when Ric gives me the nod.'

'Let's leave them to it and play with the children,' Luisa suggested.

Jenna, used to being very hands-on with Ava, thoroughly enjoyed building a castle with Jack and Emily, taught them a song she'd learned the day she went with Lucy and Ava to toddler music class, and then sat reading a story to them with both children seated happily on her lap.

She glanced up to see Lorenzo looking down at her, a wistful expression on his face. Was he thinking of

Florence? He barely mentioned her, but Jenna knew he was nearly always thinking of the little girl he'd lost. She wished she could do something practical to help, but Georgia was the only one who could change things. And even if Jenna by some means managed to contact her, she didn't think Georgia would listen.

'Everything OK?' she asked.

'Everything's fine. We're ready for lunch,' he said.

'We'll finish reading, and then we'll be there,' she promised, and duly finished reading the story.

The large trestle table in the middle of the garden was laden with bowls of salad, a plate with large slices of tomato interleaved with slices of mozzarella and avocado, chargrilled vegetables, grilled chicken, skewers of tuna and salmon that had been marinated in olive oil and herbs, and the lemon and rosemary potatoes Helen had mentioned earlier.

Jenna ended up sitting opposite Lorenzo and between the children. And how easy it was to feel part of this large, noisy family, she thought as she chatted with everyone, helped the children with their food and poured a glass of water for Chiara.

The meal was followed by grilled peaches, and the best tiramisu she'd ever eaten.

'Luisa is an excellent cook,' Enrico said, 'but you need to go to Verona. My nephew Matteo—now his food is really amazing.'

'Yes, Lorenzo, you must take Jenna to the vineyard and to see Nonno and Nonna,' Luisa added.

Lorenzo spread his hands. 'There's the small matter of work, Mamma. We're both busy at the hospital.'

'You get annual leave,' Luisa said. 'And I know you're planning to go out there later in the summer. Make it sooner and take Jenna with you. There's plenty of room at the villa.'

Lorenzo looked helplessly at Jenna, and she smiled at him. 'I've heard a lot about the vineyard and Matteo's food,' she said.

'Then it's settled. I'll text Nonna now and tell her to expect you both,' Luisa said.

Later that evening, as they walked back to Lorenzo's flat from the tube station, he slid his arm round her shoulders. 'I'm sorry. My family's a bit full on.'

'I liked them,' Jenna said. 'A lot.'

'And they loved you. I had eight texts from them while we were on the train,' he said. *'Eight.'*

'Well, it's good that they approve.' She grinned. 'My lot gave you four yeses. Five, if you include Ava.'

'That's good.' He wrinkled his nose. 'Eight texts. That includes one from Nonna, and one from Nonno, and they're not even good at texting! They want you to go out to Verona with me.' He looked awkward. 'I know my parents suggested it, but how would you feel about going to meet the rest of my family in Italy?'

'That'd be nice. I've never been to Verona or Lake Garda,' she said. But she remembered Lorenzo saying that it was his second home; clearly he loved the place.

'Maybe we could make a long weekend of it. Stay one night in Verona with dinner at Matteo's restaurant, one night at the vineyard, and one night just to ourselves by the lake?' he suggested.

'That sounds perfect,' she said. She stole a kiss. 'It

sounds to me as if both our families think that this is a good idea—you and me, I mean.'

'So it's worth taking the risk.'

'It's worth taking the risk,' she agreed. 'Maybe we can sort out the off-duty rota tomorrow.'

'That,' he said, 'would save me from a gazillion nagging texts from my mum. And my sister. And Nonna.'

'Done,' she said with a smile.

CHAPTER NINE

A COUPLE OF weeks later, Lorenzo and Jenna headed for Verona. And, even though he was looking forward to their time away, part of him wished he'd chosen a different weekend. Florence would be three tomorrow—another birthday when he wouldn't have the chance to see her, or make a fuss of her, or even talk to her on the phone to wish her a lovely day.

But this was going to be a new start for him, a way of doing something positive on that day instead of brooding and missing his little girl. And he didn't want to spoil Jenna's trip. He wanted her to love Italy and love his family as much as he did.

So he forced himself to smile and chatter about Verona and Lake Garda on the plane. Plus he'd arranged to pick up a hire car at the airport that he knew he'd love driving, and hoped Jenna would find it fun, too.

Jenna stepped out of the plane at Verona and the heat hit her like a wall.

She stumbled slightly and Lorenzo asked, 'Are you OK?'

'Ye-es. I just wasn't expecting it to be quite this hot, quite this early in the day,' she admitted.

'Apparently there's a heatwave sweeping across the whole of Italy, so it's a good ten degrees hotter than it usually is at this time of year,' he said.

'Just as well I brought really light clothing,' she said with a smile. 'And I think we're going to need a lot of ice cream.'

He laughed. 'Great idea. Let's go and pick up the car.'

'Oh, now that's seriously flashy,' she said when she saw the bright red two-seater car, with its shiny wire wheels and soft top.

'This part of the world is made for cars like this, and today is the perfect day to have the roof down,' he said. 'Do you have a headscarf? Because you'll need to protect your head from the sun, and your floppy hat isn't going to work.'

'No, I don't.'

'That's easily fixed.' He shepherded her back to the shops in the airport and bought a headscarf for her. Once she was sitting in the passenger seat with the headscarf and her sunglasses in place, he smiled at her. 'You look like Grace Kelly.'

She laughed. 'Hardly, but thank you for the compliment. She's gorgeous.'

'So are you.'

'You're not so bad yourself, Dr Conti,' she said. But Jenna's heart gave a leap of excitement. She was happier with Lorenzo than she could ever remember. And being out here in the sunshine, with the roof of the car down and the wind in their faces and the gorgeous scenery, was just perfect.

He plugged his phone into the car and put on some bright, summery pop songs, then drove them away from the city and through narrow roads flanked by olive groves, lemon groves and rows of vines. It felt like being in the middle of a painting, and Jenna loved every second of it. Danny would've chosen a car like this because it was expensive; Lorenzo had clearly chosen it because he liked the design of the car and enjoyed driving it. And that made all the difference for her: substance over style.

Lorenzo definitely had substance.

Finally he pulled on to a very long track; at the end was a massive villa.

'That's your grandparents' house?' Jenna asked.

'It's the family house,' Lorenzo explained. 'My aunts, uncles and cousins have apartments on the top two floors, and Nonna and Nonno have an apartment downstairs in the centre, along with the family rooms everyone uses.'

Nerves flooded through her, but she didn't have time to ask Lorenzo for any kind of reassurance because people were pulling out of the front door. Lots of people.

'Jenna, how lovely to meet you,' Lorenzo's grandmother said, greeting her with a hug.

'And you, Signora Conti.' Jenna diffidently handed her the flowers she'd bought at the airport that morning and the chocolates she'd bought in London. 'I, um… These are for you.'

'That's so kind! Thank you.' Nonna smiled. 'You're just like Luisa said you were. Now, you must call me Nonna, and this is Nonno.'

Jenna was introduced to so many people that she could barely remember everyone's name. But everyone welcomed her warmly, with a hug and a kiss on both cheeks, and she was swept into the kitchen.

'Coffee,' Nonna said decisively. 'And *torta di mela*. Apple cake. You'll have a big piece because you've been travelling, and travelling makes everyone hungry.'

Jenna glanced at Lorenzo, who spread his hands in resignation.

Go with it, then, she thought.

The coffee was excellent. And the cake… 'This has to be the best apple cake I've ever eaten,' she said. It was still warm, and the cinnamon and apple topping complemented the fluffy sponge base perfectly.

'I made it for you this morning,' Nonna said. 'With our own apples.'

After cake, Nonno showed her round the garden—including his prized roses—and part of the vineyard while Lorenzo stayed in his grandmother's kitchen for what looked like a serious chat, though Jenna wasn't sure what they were saying as the old lady had switched to Italian. She just hoped that she hadn't done or said anything to make the Contis disapprove of her, because Nonna looked concerned.

'You must come back for the *vendemmia* in September—the harvest,' Nonno said when he took her back to the house.

To her relief, whatever Nonna and Lorenzo had

been talking about while she and Nonno had been on a walkabout, they both looked relaxed now.

'It's hard work and a long day, but there's nothing more satisfying than picking the grapes when they're perfectly ripe and knowing that in years to come you're still going to enjoy the wine.'

'Lorenzo's introduced me to your award-winning wine,' Jenna said. 'And it's fabulous.'

Nonno looked pleased. 'My children and grandchildren are carrying on the family traditions. Though some have branched out. Enrico with his architecture and Renzo being a doctor.'

'And I get to meet Matteo tomorrow,' Jenna said. 'I've heard so much about his food.'

'He deserves that Michelin star.' Nonno smiled. 'And he'll be the first to tell you, he started learning in the kitchen at his grandmother's knee.'

'I remember teaching him how to tell when pasta is cooked, and how to make a simple tomato sauce of butter, tomatoes and onions,' Nonna said. 'He always wanted to know, why does this herb taste different from this herb, and what happens if you swap one ingredient for another. And he paid attention to how you present food to make it look as good as it tastes. I knew he'd go far.'

By the end of the afternoon, Jenna felt very much part of this warm, noisy, happy family; even more so in the evening, when she helped to set a massive table in the garden and carry large dishes of food to place in the centre, and everyone sat down to share bread, pasta, salad and wine. Lorenzo was right in the middle, the youngest members of the family were climbing over their Tio Renzo and chattering away to him, and he looked really happy. A family man.

Lorenzo loved having all the little ones chattering to him and wanting him to tell them jokes and stories, to see the drawings they'd made and hear all about their favourite cat or dog. But at the same time he was so aware of how much he missed his little girl. She'd be one of the youngest here, but she'd be right in the middle of them, chattering away and laughing and playing. So his happiness here was bittersweet; he was glad he'd brought Jenna to meet his family, but at the same time he couldn't help feeling how much Florence was missing out on.

Would the shadows ever go away?

Seeing Lorenzo here in Italy with his extended family made Jenna realise how much she'd fallen in love with him. Lorenzo Conti was a kind, gentle man with an enormous heart—a heart he'd kept guarded, though now he'd let her see exactly who he was and where he belonged. And she really wanted to be with him.

It was a real wrench to leave the villa, the next morning.

'Enjoy Verona, and tell Matteo we love him,' Nonno said, giving her a hug.

'And thank you, *cara mia*,' Nonna said, holding her close. 'Because of you, our Renzo is smiling again. That's so good to see.'

'Lorenzo's special,' Jenna said simply. 'And he's changed my life, too.'

'Good. Now, you promise me you'll come back for the harvest, even if it's only for one day,' Nonna insisted.

'We will,' Jenna promised.

'And you remember what I said, Renzo,' Nonna added.

'*Sì*, Nonna.' He kissed her.

Whatever it was, Lorenzo hadn't chosen to share it with her, and Jenna didn't want to push the subject. Maybe it was her imagination, or were there shadows in Lorenzo's eyes again? But then he put on a pair of sunglasses and shepherded her to the soft-top car.

'Let's go,' he said.

When Lorenzo had driven them to Verona, on roads flanked by more vineyards and olive groves, it was still too early to check into the hotel, so they left their luggage in the hotel's store-room for later and went exploring.

'You took me to see the remains of a bath house in London,' Lorenzo said. 'Now I'm taking you to see the remains of the third biggest arena in Italy.'

And it was stunning: two storeys high with perfect arches outside, and massive pink and white marble tiered seats inside, along with a huge stage that was clearly set up for a production. 'This is amazing,' Jenna said. 'When I went to Rome as a student with my parents, I thought the Colosseum was incredible, but this... You really can imagine the audience sitting here and being entertained, because they still actually sit here in front of the stage.'

'We don't have time to come here tonight, because we have a table booked at Matteo's restaurant, but maybe we can come back to Verona another time and see the opera,' Lorenzo said.

'I'd really like that,' she said.

'And now,' he said, 'I have to take you to the most romantic place in Italy.'

He led her through the streets to an unassuming archway, which led into a small cobbled courtyard. Inside, the walls were completely covered with scribbles of names and labels and sticky notes and sticking plasters.

'This is La Casa di Giulietta,' he said. 'Juliet's house.'

She glanced up at the protecting rectangle built of brick and white stone. 'And the famous balcony, I presume—where Juliet declaimed "Oh, Romeo, Romeo, wherefore art thou, Romeo?"'

'The house itself is fourteenth century, but the authorities made the balcony from a seventeenth-century sarcophagus and installed it on the house less than a century ago,' he said with a grin. 'And obviously Juliet was fictional, but the house belonged to the Capello family, which is about as close as you can get to Capulet. It's still a nice thought, though. Celebrating love.'

Some of the courtyard was covered in ivy, and in one corner there were locks inscribed with lovers' initials. 'It's to seal their love,' Lorenzo told her. 'And if you put a note on the wall here, they say your love will last for ever.'

She shared a glance with him, and her heart felt as if it had done a somersault.

He hadn't said the three little words—and neither had she—but she was pretty sure that they both felt the same. That over the last few weeks they'd learned to trust each other, to trust themselves, and to trust to love again. There were still moments where she could sense the sadness in him, but maybe in time she'd help to heal that.

'Maybe we should follow the tradition,' Jenna said.

'We should,' he agreed, and took a pack of sticky notes and a pen from his pocket.

She blinked, not quite believing this. 'Are you telling me you came prepared?'

'Of course I came prepared.' He stole a kiss. 'And I've never done this with anyone else, not even Georgia. I never brought her to Verona.' He drew a heart shape on the sticky note, and wrote their initials inside it before handing the note to Jenna.

'Are we supposed to do this together?' she asked.

'We are indeed.' Ceremoniously, they each took a corner of the note and stuck it to the wall.

'And we have to do something else important,' he said, gesturing to the bronze statue of Juliet. 'Legend has it that if you touch the right breast of her statue, your love will last for life.'

Jenna could see that Juliet's right breast was much shinier and brighter than the rest of the statue. 'Then let's join the queue and do it,' she said.

'Do you want me to take your picture?' a middle-aged woman standing behind them in the queue asked as they reached the front.

'Thank you—that's very kind,' Lorenzo said, handing his phone over.

They duly posed for the photograph with the statue, and thanked the kind tourist.

'So now it's just the last thing—the kiss on the balcony,' he said with a smile. 'Even though our families aren't like the Montagues and Capulets.'

'I'm very glad they're not,' Jenna said. They'd had a family barbecue, the previous weekend, and their families had got on really well. Ava had loved playing with Jack and Emily, toddling after them and letting Emily boss her about. All she'd talked about ever since was 'Emmy and Dak'. All three generations had liked each other, and Jenna had started to think that this was what she really wanted. A large, noisy, happy family.

And a child of her own.

But did Lorenzo want that, too?

The way he'd been with his family, right in the middle, made her think maybe he did. Now, among the crowd of tourists, wasn't really the right place to bring up the subject. But she'd talk to him later.

They wandered through the old house, looking at the exhibition, and then waited their turn to kiss on the famed balcony.

And he kissed her as if he really meant it. As if he was telling her without words, here in the most romantic place in Verona, that he loved her. That their love would last for all time, like that of the star-crossed lovers...

Jenna enjoyed wandering hand in hand with Lorenzo through Verona, exploring the city; the old buildings were beautiful, with the plaster on the walls painted all shades of cream, saffron, deep red, pink and apricot. Some had arched loggias; others had wrought iron balconies stuffed with terracotta pots of deep red geraniums which she couldn't resist photographing; and a tall stripy tower loomed up above the roofs in the old market place.

'This is so beautiful,' she said.

'There's something special about the city,' he agreed.

And when they finally went back to the hotel to shower and change, Jenna loved the view from the rooftop terrace: the red roofs of Verona spread out before them, with the sun setting in the background.

Nerves swooped in her stomach as they walked to Matteo's restaurant. She'd got on well with Lorenzo's grandparents and his family at the villa. Would she get on as well with his famous chef cousin? Celebrity chefs always seemed to have volatile tempers which they lost easily; although Lorenzo had said that Matteo was down to earth—warm and sweet, like the rest of his family—she worried. Lorenzo was close to his family. If any of them didn't like her...

'OK?' Lorenzo asked, his fingers tightening round hers.

'OK,' she fibbed.

'It's fine. He and Patrizia will love you,' he said, as if guessing at her worries. 'Mum's already texted me to say that Nonna called her and told how much everyone loved you at the villa.'

Matteo's wife Patrizia greeted them at the door and showed them to their table. 'We're so glad to meet you, Jenna,' she said. 'Matteo will be out to see you with dessert and Alessia—our daughter—is your waitress tonight.'

'Thank you,' Jenna said. 'It's lovely to meet you, too. And the restaurant is gorgeous.' It was very plain, with soft wall lighting; the tables all had plain cream damask cloths and a single bright red gerbera, teamed with dark wood chairs with cream padded seats.

'Matteo wanted the customers' attention on the food, not the decor,' Patrizia said, following her gaze.

And how, Jenna thought when she tasted it. Lorenzo had ordered the tasting menu, so there was an *amuse-bouche* of a scallop in foamed anchovy butter, followed by courgette flowers stuffed with ricotta, taleggio and thyme.

'This is amazing,' she said when Alessia came to collect their plates. 'I can see exactly why your father has a Michelin star.'

The angel-hair pasta with butter and truffles was equally gorgeous, followed by cod with a sesame crust, spinach, creamed beans and wasabi mayonnaise.

And then finally Matteo came out to see them, bringing them the panna cotta with passion fruit.

'It's been too long, Renzo,' he said, enveloping Lorenzo in a bear hug. 'Welcome to Verona, Jenna. I hope you're enjoying our city.' He kissed her on both cheeks.

'Your food is utterly amazing,' she said.

He grinned. 'Thank you. Renzo says you have a good palate but you're hopeless in the kitchen and even I couldn't teach you how to boil water.'

'That's about right,' she said, smiling back. 'Washing up I can do, though. Or pouring a bowl of cereal and mixing in some yogurt and berries.'

Matteo laughed and hugged her. 'Well, as long as you enjoy eating. That's what matters.'

'Oh, I do,' she said with a smile.

'See. I told you. Flashy dabs of sauce,' Lorenzo said, pointing to the plate.

'That's coulis, to you, Lorenzo Conti. Dabs, indeed. I'll have you know it's *artfully* done,' Matteo said, but he was laughing rather than appearing offended. 'How do you like the city, Jenna?'

'It's a beautiful place,' Jenna said.

'And yesterday you met Nonna, Nonno and the rest of the family?'

She nodded. 'At the vineyard.'

'It's a good place. Happy,' he said. 'I'm needed in the kitchen, but maybe Renzo will bring you back for a longer visit, next time, so Patrizia and I can spend some proper time with you.'

'I'd like that,' Jenna said.

'I will,' Lorenzo promised.

When they'd finished their coffee and petits fours, they said goodbye to Patrizia and Alessia, then walked along the river before finally heading back to the hotel. They sat on the wrought-iron chairs on the hotel's rooftop terrace, sipping Prosecco and chilling out under the stars. And when they finally went back to their room, Lorenzo made love to Jenna so tenderly that she thought her heart would burst with happiness.

'Thank you for bringing me here to meet your family,' she said. 'I know your parents pretty much pushed you into it.'

'That's par for the course in an Italian family,' he said. 'But their hearts were in the right place. They adored you and they wanted the rest of the family to meet you and adore you, too.'

'I like your family. And I like the fact that you're all so close.' She rested her head on his shoulder. 'I've been thinking. You know you asked me how hard it was to give up Ava, and I said to you it wasn't that difficult because I always knew she was Lucy's and I knew most of my feelings were due to pregnancy hormones? I don't think I was entirely honest with you—or with myself. I always did think of Ava as Lucy's baby rather than mine, and that hasn't changed; but now I know I want something like that for myself. A partner I love and who loves me all the way back, and a baby to make our family complete.'

Lorenzo had been thinking along similar lines, particularly when he and Jenna had stuck the note with their initials onto the wall at Juliet's house. But now she was actually saying it out loud, a rush of panic flooded through him.

Jenna wasn't like Georgia. She'd been open about

the difficulties with her ex and he knew she'd been the one to walk away. He knew that Jenna would never, ever take a baby away from anyone. For pity's sake, she'd given her twin the most precious gift of all— she'd carried Ava for Lucy.

But the panic just wouldn't go away. The last time he'd committed to a family life, it was suddenly pulled out from beneath him.

And today was the toughest day of the year for him. Florence's birthday. He'd hoped that this year wouldn't be as bad as last year, that if he filled his time thoroughly and spent it with people he loved it would stop him brooding. Yet now it all slammed back. The loss. The sadness. The lack of closure. Not knowing how she was and if she was happy.

He wanted to move on, he really did. But today was the one day of the year he found really hard. A day when he didn't want to think about anything too monumental and taxing—something as massive as the idea of starting another family.

Everything was suddenly so overwhelming that he couldn't think straight and he couldn't think how to explain it.

He was silent for so long that she twisted round to look up at him. 'Lorenzo? Are you OK?'

'I… I can't do this,' he said. 'I'm sorry. I thought I could. But I can't.'

He hated himself for the surge of misery that welled up in her eyes.

'It's not you,' he said, wanting to make it better. 'It's

me.' And he knew he owed her a proper explanation. He raked his hand through his hair. 'It's Florence's birthday today.'

Florence's birthday.

Lorenzo's little girl. The child he didn't get to see.

Maybe that was what his grandmother had talked to him about.

And Jenna had just talked to him about starting a family, on the day he'd clearly been upset about but had been trying to hide it. It was the worst possible time she could've chosen to talk about wanting children, and she wouldn't have said a word if she'd known what today was. She felt absolutely horrible, as if she'd just rubbed the top off all his scars—though she really hadn't intended to hurt him. 'Why didn't you tell me before?' she asked.

'Because I…' He shook his head, looking lost. 'I guess I wanted to try and do something positive today. I wanted you to have a good time here in Italy.'

'I did. But…' She bit her lip. 'You haven't.'

'It's not you. It's me,' he said.

And that was the problem, she realised. That hurt would never, ever go away. That aching sense of loss. She would always be part of Ava's life; but Lorenzo wasn't part of Florence's and never could be. And until he could come to terms with that—and she wasn't sure he ever could—he was just too hurt to be able to open his heart fully to someone else.

She simply wasn't going to be enough for him.

'I'm so sor—' he began.

'Please don't,' she said. 'Please don't say anything else, Lorenzo. I get it. I wish I could fix everything for you, but I can't. And I'm not going to make things worse by trying and failing over and over again.'

Jenna turned her back to him, lying right on the edge of the mattress, clearly putting as much distance as she could between them. How Lorenzo wanted to pull her into his arms and tell her he hadn't meant it like that. But he was pretty sure that she'd push him away physically, just as he'd pushed her away emotionally. Hating this whole situation and not having a clue how to fix it, he turned his back to her.

So much for this being the romantic weekend away he'd planned.

What the hell was wrong with him? His family adored her, and she adored them.

Why couldn't he break away from his past and move on properly, the way he wanted to?

He still didn't have an answer, the next morning. From the shadows under Jenna's eyes, she'd slept as badly as he had.

And things were more awkward between them this morning than he'd ever thought possible. She could barely look him in the eye.

'You have the shower first,' he said. 'Do you want me to arrange room service for breakfast?'

She shook her head. 'No, it's OK. I'm not hungry.'

'You need to eat, Jenna—or at least have some coffee,' he said.

'Coffee, then.'

He had pastries sent up as well. She crumbled a corner of one of them onto a plate but didn't eat. He didn't feel like eating, either, and the coffee didn't help much.

'I know we were supposed to be going to the lake today,' she said, 'but I'd rather not. I'm not feeling so great.'

And he knew why. Because he'd hurt her. 'I'm s—'

'Please don't, Renzo,' she cut in, and the pain in her voice slashed at him. 'I just want to go home.'

'OK. Give me half an hour to change our flights and sort everything out,' he said.

'Thank you. I'll go for a walk to clear my head,' she said. 'Alone.'

'But—'

'I'm a grown-up, Renzo. If I lose my way, I'll use the app on my phone to get my bearings and direct me back to the hotel.'

He couldn't argue with that. 'I'll see you later, then.'

What had she done wrong? Jenna wondered.

Or maybe it wasn't something she had or hadn't done. Maybe it was simply who she was.

Danny had rejected her, too.

She didn't think Lorenzo had rejected her because of the surrogacy; he'd seemed absolutely fine when he'd met her family. And he'd even said how much his family liked her. His grandparents wanted her to come back, his cousin had teased her but in a way that made her feel she was part of the family...

But Lorenzo himself clearly wasn't ready for this.

He might never be. She'd been the one to push it, last night. Buoyed by the way he'd looked at her at Juliet's house, the way he'd put a note with their initials on the wall, she'd told him straight out that she wanted a family. Too much, too soon; OK she hadn't known that it was Florence's birthday yesterday, but she'd known how much he missed his little girl and how hard he found it to let go of the past. She'd been carried away by the romance of the city, opened up to him about what was in her heart when maybe she should have waited. She'd fallen too hard and too fast for him—and this was the result. Utter misery.

Now she knew her mistake. And she'd keep things professional between them in future.

Lorenzo drove them to the airport, glad that having the roof of the car down meant it was too noisy to talk to each other. It was the best excuse he could come up with.

Jenna had completely backed off from him.

It was his own fault, and he knew it: he'd been the one to push her away. Then again, she knew his situation. If she'd really wanted to be with him, she wouldn't have let him push her away. So maybe taking things back to a professional relationship only was the best thing for both of them.

CHAPTER TEN

WORKING TOGETHER ON the ward was awful.

Lorenzo was perfectly polite and professional towards Jenna at the hospital; but she knew a whole other side of him, and she found it hard to reconcile the warm, sexy, gentle man she'd dated with the cool, closed-off doctor she worked with now.

She was pretty sure everyone else on the ward had noticed the coolness between them, though thankfully nobody seemed to be gossiping about them.

And of course Lucy had wanted to know how everything had gone in Verona, as had Jenna's parents. Jenna deliberately hadn't told them that she'd come back to London a day early, and because she wasn't supposed to be home on the Monday night she managed to avoid her usual dinner with Lucy on the grounds that she was in Italy. Being busy with work and her exercise classes during the rest of the week meant she'd got a breathing space until the weekend before she saw her family face to face, so she was able to fudge things and talk happily on the phone to them about how nice Lorenzo's grandparents were and how beautiful Verona and the area around it was.

She was telling them the truth: just not the whole truth.

The truth that she and Lorenzo weren't a couple any more.

The truth that she'd blown it.

She still hadn't found the words to explain to her family by the middle of the week, when she was rostered onto the Paediatric Assessment Unit. Thankfully, Lorenzo had ward rounds and clinic, so she knew she wouldn't have to work with him and face the awkwardness between them that day.

'Florence Reynolds?' Jenna asked.

A worried-looking woman stood up, carrying a toddler.

'Please come and sit down,' Jenna said, ushering her over to the cubicle. 'Obviously I've seen the note from your family doctor, but I always like to hear what my patients' parents have to say, so can you tell me how Florence has been, Mrs Reynolds?'

'She's always been healthy, apart from the odd cold that everyone gets. But a month ago she went off her food, started sleeping more than usual, and she seems to be breathing really fast.' She stroked the little girl's hair. 'I took her to our family doctor—he said he thought it was a bug, but she didn't get any better so I went back. He referred Florence for tests.'

'You said she's sleeping more than usual. I know she's only nineteen months old, but does she say she's tired, or do you just notice her getting more tired than usual when she does everyday things?'

'She doesn't seem to have as much energy at toddler group as she used to, and she seems to get out of breath quickly,' Mrs Reynolds said. 'We do one of those baby gym classes, and she's been a bit clingy with me there, wanting to sit on my lap rather than doing what the others do.'

Jenna made a note. Breathless, tired... 'Can I examine Florence?'

'Of course.'

Jenna noticed a slight dilation around Florence's ankles and abdomen. The little girl's pulse was slower than she would like; and the number of breaths Florence took per minute was more than average, too.

This was starting to look very much like a heart problem.

'I'm going to check the oxygen levels in her blood—what happens is that I put this little clip over her finger, and there's a beam of light to measure the oxygen levels,' Jenna explained. 'It won't hurt her.'

She wasn't happy with the oxygen saturation levels, either; and, when she listened with the stethoscope, Florence's heart sounded much too slow.

'I'm going to send Florence for a chest X-ray,' she said.

'You think there's a problem with her chest?' Mrs Reynolds asked.

'I think there might be a problem with her heart, but I want to do some more tests to be sure,' Jenna said. 'You can go with her to the X-ray department and be with her, and if you've got any questions at any point then please ask, because that's what we're all here for.'

When the chest X-ray results came in, they really worried Jenna; Florence's heart looked big. Before seeing the Reynoldses again, she wanted a second opinion. But, when she went to find one of the senior doctors, of course the only one available *would* have to be Lorenzo.

Well, her patient came first. Even though she'd rather work with someone else, she'd just have to put her feelings aside and talk to him. Be professional and cool, the way he was with her. And she did at least respect him as a doctor. He was quick and knowledgeable; and he was kind to the patients and their parents, putting them at their ease so they could ask questions instead of looking things up on the Internet and worrying themselves even more.

She took a deep breath and rapped on his open door. 'Sorry to interrupt, but there isn't anyone else around. I need a second opinion on one of my patients, Florence.'

The colour drained from his face. 'Florence?'

Of course—she should have thought he'd react like that to the child's name. 'Don't worry, this isn't your Florence,' Jenna said. 'This is Florence Reynolds. She's nineteen months old, and I think she has cardiomyopathy.' Lorenzo seemed to shake himself mentally, and she ran through the symptoms. 'Can I show you the X-ray?'

He nodded, and she called up the file.

'I agree—it looks and sounds like a cardiac issue. OK. I'll come and see her,' he said.

She walked back to the cubicles with him—for once not talking on the way—called the Reynoldses in, and introduced Lorenzo to them.

'I agree with Dr Harris that we need to check the way Florence's heart is working,' Lorenzo said. 'I'd like to give Florence an ECG—it checks the electrical activity of the heart, and won't hurt her,' he explained.

The results backed up Jenna's suspicions.

'Dilated cardiomyopathy?' she asked Lorenzo.

He nodded. 'It's going to be a lot for Florence's mother to take in. I'll stay and back you up.'

'Thank you.' They might have personal issues, but Jenna respected his clinical judgement.

She called Mrs Reynolds in again.

'So did the ECG show what was wrong?' Mrs Reynolds asked.

'Yes. Florence has a condition called dilated cardiomyopathy,' Jenna said. 'It means her heart muscle has become enlarged and weakened, so it can't pump blood efficiently to her lungs and her body. That's why she's breathless and tired, and fluid has built up in her body.'

'But—how can that happen?' Mrs Reynolds asked. 'She's only nineteen months.'

'It can happen at any age,' Lorenzo said. 'Sometimes it's an inherited condition, or sometimes it develops after a virus.'

'She had a bug, a few weeks back—that's what our family doctor thought it was, but she just never seemed to get better.' Mrs Reynolds bit her lip. 'Can it be cured?'

'We can give her some medication to help with the tiredness and help her heart pump blood round her body a bit better, but because her heart beat is too slow she'll need a pacemaker as well,' Jenna said.

'What's a pacemaker?' Mrs Reynolds asked.

'It's a small metal box containing batteries and electronic circuits. It has wires which carry electrical impulses to Florence's heart to regulate her heartbeat,' Lorenzo explained.

'A metal box?' Mrs Reynolds looked horrified.

'It's not that big—it's about the size of a matchbox, and it weighs less than fifty grams,' Jenna reassured her. 'Because Florence is so small, you might see a raised bump on her skin where the pacemaker sits, but when she's older you won't know it's there.'

'It's programmed to a certain number of beats per minute, so if the gap between two of Florence's heartbeats is longer than it should be, the pacemaker will send an impulse through the wire into Florence's heart to make it contract and produce a beat,' Lorenzo added.

'And when the wire sends something into her heart, it doesn't hurt?' Mrs Reynolds asked.

'It doesn't hurt,' Jenna confirmed.

'But Florence will need an operation to insert the box into her chest,' Lorenzo said.

'An operation.' Mrs Reynolds looked petrified. 'But she's only nineteen months old.'

'If she doesn't have the pacemaker,' Jenna said gently, 'she won't get better and she might end up needing a heart transplant, which is a much bigger operation.'

Mrs Reynolds bit her lip. 'This is a lot to get my head round.'

'Of course it is, and of course you're worried.' Lorenzo squeezed her hand. 'But a pacemaker is the best way to help Florence get better.'

'Can you do the operation here?' Mrs Reynolds asked.

'Yes. We have a special operating room called a catheter lab, and one of the cardiac surgeons will do the operation,' Jenna told her. 'I'll book an appointment so you get to meet the cardiac team before the operation, and then after the operation we'll look after Florence here on the ward.'

'How long does the operation take?' Mrs Reynolds asked.

'About an hour. She'll need to come in the day before, so we can do tests to prepare her for the operation. She won't be able to have anything to eat or drink for about six hours before the operation, because she'll have a general anaesthetic—she'll be asleep during the operation,' Lorenzo explained. 'But you can stay with her right until she's had the anaesthetic and she's asleep.'

'Can't I go in with her?' Mrs Reynolds asked.

Jenna shook her head. 'We only allow doctors, nurses and technicians into the catheter lab, to help us stop any infections. But as soon as Florence is awake in the recovery room after the operation, you can be with her again.'

'But a metal box.' Mrs Reynolds looked anguished. 'You're going to cut her chest wide open?'

Lorenzo shook his head. 'The surgeon will make a small cut—not even as long as your thumb—under her collar bone on her left-hand side, so he can make a pocket for the pacemaker box and thread an electrode lead into a vein. He'll use an X-ray to help him put the lead in the right place in Florence's heart, then connect it to the box and fit it in the pocket.'

'They use dissolvable stitches when they close the cut,' Jenna said, 'so she won't have to have any stitches removed. And, when you see the surgeon, he'll show you what the pacemaker looks like and I think that'll reassure you.'

'Once she's awake again, she'll go back onto our ward, and the team here will check her wound dressing and give her antibiotics to make sure she doesn't get an infection,' Lorenzo said.

'Florence will have another X-ray, the next day, to make sure the pacemaker lead is in the right place,' Jenna said. 'We recommend she doesn't do any really active things like the toddler gym club for about three weeks after the operation, and during that time it's a good idea not to let her make big movements with her arm on the side where the pacemaker's fitted, to make sure the leads don't move.'

'Will it hurt, after the operation?' Mrs Reynolds asked.

'It might be a little bit sore,' Lorenzo said. 'We can give her some infant paracetamol to help with that, but it's important she doesn't pick at the wound or scratch it, or it might get infected.'

'And then after that she'll be better?' Mrs Reynolds asked.

'She should be better,' Jenna said, 'and she can live a normal life—though we would advise that you don't let her take up contact sports like karate.'

'The pacemaker will set off any alarm detector at the airport,' Lorenzo said, 'but we'll give you a card you can show to security staff. She won't be able to have an MRI scan with a pacemaker, and if you've got an induction hob in your kitchen she needs to stay away from it, because the magnets will interfere with the settings of her pacemaker.'

'And if she does look at things on your mobile phone, make sure the phone's in the opposite hand to where the pacemaker's fitted,' Jenna said.

'Will she have a pacemaker for the rest of her life, and will she need a different pacemaker when she's bigger?' Mrs Reynolds asked.

'To the first, we don't know—it depends how she responds to treatment. The pacemaker will last for about four or five years,' Jenna said, 'and then she'll need it to be replaced.'

'It's a lot to take in,' Lorenzo said. 'We can give you some leaflets about Florence's heart condition and about the pacemaker, and you'll probably have more questions over the next few days. Come and see us or give us a call, and we'll do our best to answer.'

'Thank you,' Mrs Reynolds said. 'I'm still trying to get my head round the fact she's so ill.'

'We can put you in touch with a support group, too,' Jenna said. 'It'll help to talk to other mums who've already been through this. But I would advise not reading too much on the Internet. You tend to get the really scary stuff there.'

'I guess it's like when you're pregnant,' Mrs Reynolds said, 'and you hear about all the really awful labours people have been through and not the ones that just went normally.'

'Pretty much,' Lorenzo said with a smile. 'Pacemakers have been around now for around fifty years, and about five hundred people in Britain get a pacemaker fitted every week.'

Mrs Reynolds looked surprised. 'As many as that?'

Jenna nodded. 'So our cardiac team is really used to doing the procedure. Florence will be in excellent hands.'

Mrs Reynolds blew out a breath. 'Thank you for that. I feel a bit better about it.'

Jenna smiled at her. 'We'll have Florence feeling better soon. And then you'll be less worried.'

'Jenna will sort everything out for you—I'm afraid I'm due in clinic shortly and there are some things I need to do before I see my patients,' Lorenzo said.

'Thank you, Doctor,' Mrs Reynolds said.

'Yes—thank you, Dr Conti,' Jenna added.

'It's what I'm here for,' Lorenzo said, but his smile was solely directed towards Mrs Reynolds and her daughter. He didn't even look Jenna in the eye.

At least he too had put their patients first, she

thought. And things would get easier between them on the ward. Eventually. It would just take a bit of time.

And as for how long it would take her to get over him…

She'd just have to focus on her job.

Lorenzo was checking through some files at his desk before clinic when his phone beeped. He took it out of his pocket and glanced at the screen; when he saw the notification, he nearly dropped the phone in shock.

Why would Georgia be emailing him?

And it looked as if there was an attachment to her email. Maybe it was a mistake, then, and someone had hacked into her account and sent a message to everyone who'd ever been in her contact list.

He went into his email account to delete the message unread, but accidentally clicked on the message.

When he saw the photograph attached to the file he caught his breath. It was a photograph of Florence, wearing a blue dress and holding a pink balloon bearing the slogan '3 Today' in glittery silver writing.

His little girl, on the birthday he'd missed.

He had to blink away the tears.

Why had Georgia sent this now?

The words of the email blurred before his eyes, and he had to read it three times before the message sank in. Georgia was moving back to London with Scott, who had a new job. They were happy; they'd got married and they'd had a little boy, a brother for Florence, the previous month. She realised she'd been unfair to him, so if he'd like to see Florence once they'd settled in he'd be very welcome to come round.

If he'd like to see Florence?

His heart felt as if it had just cracked.

She added the caveat, We probably need to talk first and agree what we tell her about you. Maybe you could be her Uncle Renzo.

Not Dada. Not the man who'd held her when she was only a few seconds old, who'd brought her up as his little girl. That stung. But the important thing was that he'd still be part of her life: the thing he'd wanted so desperately and missed so much.

He looked at the photo again. Florence had changed so much in the last eighteen months; then again, he knew from his niece and nephew that toddlers changed very swiftly. He wondered if she'd become a total chatterbox, if she still loved having stories read to her, if she liked singing or dancing or messy play. Right now he didn't have a clue.

But what hadn't changed was the brightness of her smile. She looked happy.

And that was what he'd wanted to know more than anything: that his little girl was happy.

Once Jenna had booked the appointment for Mrs Reynolds and Florence with the cardiac team, reassured Mrs Reynolds further and given her all the information leaflets and information about support groups, she went in search of Lorenzo. Hopefully she'd catch him before his clinic and she could talk to him, thank him for his help and maybe try to bridge the gap between them. If nothing else, it would make things easier at work.

When she rapped on his door, he looked up. The expression on his face was slightly dazed. Was he OK?

He beckoned her in, and she closed the door behind her. Close up, she could see that he had wet eyes.

Something was definitely wrong.

'Right—start talking,' she said.

'I...' His voice tailed off and he shook his head.

For him to have tears in his eyes, something serious must have happened. Was someone in his family seriously ill—or, worse, had there been an accident? She couldn't just switch off her feelings or ignore it. He was clearly hurting and her first instinct was to make it better. 'Renzo, I know we're not exactly getting on right now, and you're the King of Clamming Up, but I do care about you and I'm here. Something's obviously happened, or your eyes wouldn't be wet.'

'Florence,' he said helplessly.

Oh, no. Worse than she'd thought. 'Something's happened to her?' she asked carefully.

'I... Oh, it'll be easier for you to see it yourself.' He handed her his phone with the email open.

She could see that the message was from Georgia, and there was a picture attached of a little girl that she assumed was Florence. On her third birthday, by the look of it. The day she and Lorenzo had been in Verona.

'Renzo, this is personal,' she said warily.

'Read it,' he said.

She scanned it swiftly, and she felt her eyes widen in surprise. 'She's actually going to let you see Florence?'

He nodded. 'I can't believe it, either. But it's there in black and white. She's even given me her new phone number so I can call her and arrange to meet.'

'What made her change her mind?'

'I have no idea. Maybe it's because they're coming back to London, and maybe her parents talked to her.' He shrugged. 'Maybe now they've had another baby, it's made Scott realise what they took from me and he's talked to her about it. But the main thing is she's actually going to let me see Florence.'

'That's good. I'm glad for you.'

He rubbed his eyes. 'Jenna, I have to go to clinic— it's not fair to my patients to be late—but maybe... Can we perhaps talk afterwards?'

'After our shift,' she said. 'Sure. I'll meet you at the main entrance.'

'Thank you.' He looked at her. 'Was there something you needed?'

Yes, but she wasn't going to ask and risk being rejected again. 'I just came to let you know that Florence Reynolds is booked in with the cardio team, and to say thanks for your help.'

'It's my job,' he said.

And their job was all they had together now. She got it. 'OK.'

'I'll see you later,' he said. 'We'll talk.'

Just as long as he didn't make it a Dear Jane talk. Then she'd have to stop him and walk away.

After his shift, Lorenzo waited by the main entrance to the hospital. And waited. And waited.

He glanced at his watch. He knew Jenna wasn't the

sort to be deliberately late and he didn't think she'd just not turn up, so she was probably still with a patient. She was meticulous at work, kind and caring.

She was kind and caring outside work, too.

Even though they weren't getting on right now, she'd still noticed that something was wrong and still offered to let him talk to her, unload whatever was upsetting him.

Right now he had a lot to say. Starting with a massive apology. He just hoped that she'd listen to him and not shut him out—even though he knew he was being a massive hypocrite because he'd shut her out.

Eventually she came rushing up to him. 'Sorry, sorry. I was—'

'Patients come first,' he cut in gently. 'It's not like a job where you can close a file for the evening and come back to it tomorrow.'

'No. I just hoped you didn't think I'd...' She grimaced.

Just abandoned him? That wasn't Jenna. 'Of course I didn't. Thank you for meeting me.' He took a deep breath. 'Shall we go somewhere a bit quieter?'

'Good idea.'

They headed out to Alexandra Park, and found a quiet bench in a corner.

'First of all,' he said, 'I owe you a massive apology for what happened in Verona. I know I hurt you, and I'm sorry for that. That really wasn't my intention.'

She winced. 'It was my own fault. I expected too much. I shouldn't have said anything.'

He shook his head. Of course it wasn't her fault,

and of course she hadn't expected too much. 'It's not that at all.' He grimaced. 'I should've told you it was Florence's birthday before we went. Actually, I probably should've arranged our weekend away for another date, one where my head wouldn't have been in the wrong place. Stupidly, I thought that being with you and my family, and keeping myself busy, would mean I wouldn't brood about not seeing my little girl on her birthday for the second year running—and I was wrong.'

'I wouldn't have said what I did if I'd known it was her birthday,' Jenna said. 'I know it's hard for you to deal with what happened.'

He nodded. 'I find it hard to talk about Florence, about what a black hole it was when Georgia left. I could just about accept that she loved Scott so much, it overtook her feelings for me, and that was why she cheated on me. That hurt, but I came to terms with it. But I couldn't accept not having my family any more. Not being a dad, when I'd loved it so much. And when you talked about having a family, all I could think about was how it felt to have that all ripped away from me.'

'I'm not Georgia,' she said softly.

'I know, and you'd never take a child away from someone. I know you're not like that. You've got a huge, huge heart and you're an amazing woman.'

'But I'm not the woman for you. It's OK. You don't have to say any more. I get it.' Her face was filled with sadness. 'I hope you find the right one for you, Renzo, because I'd hate you to spend the rest of your life feeling lonely. Even though Georgia said in that email she'd let you see Florence, she also made it clear that Florence isn't your daughter—that maybe you'll be like an uncle or a godfather or something, but Florence already has a dad and she doesn't need another one.'

Hard words, but he knew he needed to hear them. And he also knew that Jenna was right. 'All I wanted to know is that she's happy, that Scott's being a good dad to her and bringing her up with as much love as I did,' he said. 'And you're right. I'm not Florence's dad. Maybe one day she'll know that I was her dad for a little while, while Scott wasn't there. But just knowing she's happy, seeing her from time to time—that'll be enough for me. And I realise now that's what's been missing from my life. What's kept me stuck and unable to move on with anyone else.'

'OK. Well, if you want some moral support when you meet up with Georgia, you know where to find me.'

He was amazed at how generous she was being. 'You'd do that for me, even though I pushed you away?' Even though she thought he'd rejected her?

'Of course.'

'It's like I said. You've got a huge, huge heart and you're an amazing woman.'

She sighed. 'You don't have to over-egg it, Renzo.'

'I'm not. I'm trying to tell you that you're wrong about something.'

She frowned. 'What?'

'About you not being the right one for me. I meant what we did in Verona. Before I was really stupid in the evening, I mean,' he said. 'When we put our names on

the wall of Juliet's house and we kissed on the balcony.'
He hadn't actually said the three little words, but he'd
made it as clear as it could be.

'But then you rejected me.'

And the pain in her eyes made him suddenly
realise. It wasn't just that he'd backed away; it was
that he'd backed away from *her*. 'I'm not Danny. I'm not
rejecting you because you don't meet some ridiculous
notion of what my partner ought to be.'

'You rejected me,' she repeated.

'No. It wasn't you. I panicked. And I couldn't find
the right words to explain what was wrong and why I
was being such an idiot. You'd think that, growing up
in a massive Italian family where everyone talks a lot,
I'd be good at that sort of thing—but I'm not. After
Georgia, I went kind of inward on myself and stopped
knowing how to talk about my feelings. I spent all the
time smiling and telling everyone I was absolutely fine,
when actually I wasn't.'

He reached over and took her hand. 'I should've told
you that, although I was finding it hard to get my head
round it, what you said you wanted was exactly what
I want, too. And now I know that Florence is happy,
that I can see her from time to time, it's released me
from being stuck in one place. Given me closure. And
now I can move forward and I know what I want. A
partner I love, one who loves me all the way back, and
a baby to make our family complete. I admit it scares
me, even though I know it's what I want, because I've
been there before and it went wrong—and I don't want
it to go wrong with you.'

'It went wrong for me, too,' she said. 'Not the baby part—I don't ever regret having Ava for my sister and I never will.' She lifted her chin. 'But I understand where you're coming from about telling everyone you were OK when you weren't.'

'Because you did it, too?' he guessed.

She nodded.

'I'm not Danny,' he said. 'I'm proud of you. Your priorities are in exactly the right place. And I know you're not Georgia.'

'But how do I know you're not going to close off to me in future?' she asked. 'That next time you're upset about something, instead of talking it over with me you're going to brood and push me away?'

It was a fair question, and she deserved an honest answer. 'Because,' he said, 'it's different now. My head isn't in the same place that it was when we were in Verona. I've really missed being with you, and I've been miserable without you.' Right now, he could see in her expression that she felt vulnerable. So maybe he needed to take a risk. Say the words. Show her that he meant it. 'I love you, Jenna, and with you the world's a much better place. It's a place where I want to make a family. Where I can see us growing old together, watching our children grow up, and then having our home filled with grandchildren. Though I'll be the one making cakes in the kitchen, and you'll be the one teaching the little ones how to salsa.'

She looked at him, her blue eyes filled with worry. 'I love you, too, but it scares me.'

'I'm not going to let you down again,' he said.

'Before today, I didn't have closure, and that was what got in the way in Verona. Now things have changed. Georgia's actually going to let me be part of Florence's life. Not a huge part, but enough so I can see her grow up and know she's happy.' He looked at her. 'I want to be a family with you, Jenna. It'll be a blended family, but one full of love.' He paused. 'And I want a baby with you. Not a replacement for Florence, but someone for us both to love and help grow up.'

A partner she loved, one who loved her all the way back, and a baby to make their family complete. Everything that she'd seen make her sister so happy, and what she'd only recently realised was what she wanted, too.

'Be a family with you,' she said.

Her doubts still clearly showed on her face, because his fingers tightened round hers. 'I know this is a risk. I know that worries you. But I have your back, just as I know you have mine. So I'm going to ask you the question that makes me vulnerable, because I trust you and I know we can face anything together.' He shifted slightly so he could drop down on one knee, and took a deep breath. 'I love you, Jenna. I want to grow old with you and love you until my very last breath. Will you marry me?'

She could see the sincerity in his eyes. He knew this was a risk for her—just as it was a risk for him. But it was one he was prepared to take. Did she have the courage to join him?

He said he'd learned from the past. That shutting her out was a mistake.

So she could continue to put a wall between them in the hope of keeping her heart safe, and stay lonely; or she could give him the second chance he was asking for and look forward to the future—together.

And he'd said it first. That he loved her. And he loved her for herself, not for her position as a doctor or her salary. He'd said she was an amazing woman with a huge, huge heart—the same way she felt about him.

And that made the decision easy. She smiled. 'Yes.'

He whooped, pulled her to her feet, spun her round in a circle—and then kissed her until she was dizzy.

'I won't let you down,' he said when he finally broke the kiss. 'I love you. And even when life hits a sticky patch, we're going to be all right—because we have each other.'

EPILOGUE

Six months later

JENNA STOPPED TO catch her breath for a moment and grabbed a glass of water. Nearly everyone at the wedding was on the dance floor—their family, their colleagues, their friends outside work. The hospital band, Maybe Baby, was playing and really doing them proud. And the fast salsa she'd just done with her friends from her dance class had left her almost as breathless as her new husband did.

Lorenzo looked incredibly handsome in his wedding outfit. But, more importantly for Jenna, he looked relaxed and happy. And he was dancing with all the bridesmaids at once: his sister, her sister, Ava, Emily—and Florence.

'Look at them. They're all having such a good time,' Georgia said, coming up to her. 'Thank you so much for asking Florence to be a bridesmaid. That's so kind of you—I don't have a sister and neither does Scott, so I never thought she'd have the chance to be a bridesmaid for anyone.'

'We wanted her, because she's part of our family,' Jenna said with a smile. At the slight worry in Georgia's eyes, she said, 'Families come in all shapes and sizes, nowadays. And I'm so glad you're able to let Renzo be part of Florence's life now.'

Georgia seemed to relax again. 'I panicked when we moved to Birmingham. I guess I was scared I might've made the wrong choice, and...' She looked over at Scott, who was rocking their little boy on his shoulder and talking to Will.

Jenna understood exactly where she was coming from: scared that Scott would go back to his old ways. It wasn't fear for herself, but fear for their daughter and that she'd chosen the wrong role model. But being a dad had clearly been the making of Scott.

'We all make mistakes and wrong choices,' Jenna said. 'But if we learn from them and we can get a chance to do it right second time round, like your Scott has—well, it makes life better.'

'You're amazing.' Georgia hugged her. 'I hope you and Renzo are really, really happy.'

Jenna hugged her back. 'Thank you. And I'm so glad you all came to the wedding today.'

'I wouldn't have missed it,' Georgia said. 'I know I hurt him really badly and I'm sorry for that. But he looks happy now. Thanks to you.'

'And to Florence. He's really enjoying being Uncle Renzo to her—and to baby Ollie.'

'That was Scott's idea,' Georgia said, confirming what Jenna knew Lorenzo had guessed a while back.

'And it was an excellent one,' Jenna said. 'Now go

and dance with your husband, while I reclaim mine from the bridesmaids.'

She made a detour via the stage and asked Maybe Baby for a slow song; Keely gave her the thumbs-up. Then she walked over to Lorenzo. 'Might I have this dance, Dr Conti?'

'I'd be delighted, Dr Conti,' he said with a grin, and drew her into his arms. 'Happy?' he asked, holding her close.

She smiled. 'Very happy. You?'

'I've got a partner I love, and who loves me all the way back,' he said. 'Of course I'm happy. And I saw you just now with Georgia.'

'We were talking about Florence. And how families are all different shapes and sizes. You were right, by the way. The uncle bit was Scott's idea.'

'Just like I said—you have an enormous heart.'

She smiled. 'Funnily enough, so has my husband.' She paused. 'There was something that I wanted to talk to you about.'

She could see the faint worry in his eyes. 'Oh?' he asked carefully.

'What you just said. You missed something off the list.'

He went very still. 'Are you telling me...?'

'It's why I only had the tiniest sips of Prosecco during the toasts. I did a test yesterday morning. In secret—which isn't exactly easy when everyone's around helping with wedding preparations. Our mums, our sisters, our grandmothers, our aunts...' She smiled. 'I almost told you yesterday—but I thought today would be better.' Even though part of her worried, because this could be an opportunity for him to brood, the way he'd done in Verona. But hopefully he'd make the connection: Georgia hadn't wanted to get married while she was pregnant, but Jenna most definitely had.

'How long?'

'It's very early days. Six weeks, maybe. But we're going to have a baby, Lorenzo.'

She could see him doing the maths in his head. 'An Italian baby, conceived on the shores of Lake Garda on New Year's Eve.'

'The night we watched the sun set,' she said, 'and you showed me that mountain that looked like a face and told me that story about Lady Gardenia.'

'The immortal who fell in love with a mortal man, and when he died, she was so broken-hearted that she lay down and cried so much that her tears became the lake—Garda, which was named after her.'

'That's too sad a story to tell on our wedding day,' she said.

He kissed her again. 'Ah, but, unlike Lady Gardenia, we have a happy ending in front of us. A baby. And that's the best wedding present of all.'

And finally Jenna could relax, knowing that Lorenzo had at last put his past behind him. And now they could really look forward to the future. As a family.

* * * * *

SAVING THE
SINGLE DAD DOC

LOUISA HEATON

MILLS & BOON

To Nan and Grandad,
whom we lost within weeks of each other.

It was way too soon and no one was ready.

This is for you.

CHAPTER ONE

'So…you're going after all, then?'

Dr Bethan Monroe didn't need to look at her grandmother to know she was disappointed. She'd heard it in her voice. But what was she to do?

'I have to, Nanna.'

'No, you don't. Not with him. Not with a *Brodie*.'

Bethan groaned out loud. It really was quite childish, this feud her nanna had against that family. Okay, maybe not the *whole* family, but most definitely against one of them in particular. Thankfully the one she was seeing today was *not* her nanna's arch-nemesis—rather, he was his grandson.

'I do!' She stepped over to the kitchen table, snatched up the not insignificant pile of final demands in her fist and waved them about. 'Because if I don't then you lose the house. We had the phone cut off last week for a whole day!'

Her exasperation wore off instantly when she noted the discomfort on her beloved grandmother's face.

She softened her tone. 'Grace is in school now. I can work again and pay my way.'

She'd missed it. Incredibly so. Being a doctor was her calling and, though she'd loved being a stay-at-home mum whilst her daughter grew to school age, she felt a real yearning to get back into the consulting room. It had always been the plan that she would take this break, but she'd not known how difficult it would be alone.

'But surely there must be other posts you could apply for? Somewhere further afield? In Glencoe or Fort William?'

Perhaps there were. But they lived *here* now. In Gilloch. And she didn't want to be that far away from her loved ones. Not any more. Grace was growing up fast, and she didn't want her nanna to miss any of it. Commuting for hours each day simply wasn't on her agenda.

Living in Cornwall had been wonderful, but that was in the past now. She'd returned to her proper home three years after Ashley had died. Back to the place she had been born. And it felt right. Coming home.

'This job—right here in the village—it's a gift in itself! I'll be able to get home whenever I'm needed. Say, if there was an emergency.'

She couldn't help but feel guilty once again as she thought back to when Ashley had died. For weeks she'd sat by his bed—keeping him company, holding his hand, reading to him, never missing a minute—and then one day she'd been called into work. There'd been an emergency—a train derailment—and all hands had been needed on deck.

And Ashley had died alone. She'd received the call at work, from a neighbour who'd had a key and had promised to keep an eye out. She'd not been able to get home quickly enough. Had got caught in endless traffic jams, delayed by lights and drivers who hadn't seemed to know which pedal the accelerator was.

She'd just wanted to get back to Grace. Pick her up from the childminder and hold her close against her heart before making that final walk into their bedroom, where Ashley had lain. She'd vowed never to be that far away ever again.

'It'll be okay, Nanna.'

Mhairi sank shakily into a seat by the table, adjusting the woven scarf at her neck. 'You have more faith than I. What that Angus Brodie put me through...'

'I know.'

'He ruined my life. I don't want to see another Brodie man ruin yours.'

'I might not even get the job.'

But she hoped she would. 'Brodie man' or not. They *needed* this! She'd only been back a few months and their financial situation was getting more dire. They couldn't live off Ashley's life insurance for ever.

This was about a job. Employment. That was all. It was a business transaction—not an affair of the heart. It wasn't going to be anything like what had happened between her nanna and Angus Brodie. Those had been different times back then. It was the past. And Bethan didn't feel she was ready for another relationship yet. She was over the raw pain of Ashley's death, yes, and she worried something rotten about raising Grace without a father figure around, but did that mean her heart was on the open market?

No. Not yet.

She kissed her nanna's soft, downy cheek and sat beside her at the kitchen table, one eye on the clock. 'We'll be okay.'

Nanna covered Bethan's hand with her own, more gnarly, liver-spotted one. 'I'm just so used to having you here now. I worry he'll hurt you, like Angus did me. But I'm just being a worry-wart, that's all.'

'It's in the past. Where it should belong. Let's look positively to the future. I'm a strong woman. I can handle myself and any Brodie male who even *tries* to cause me trouble.'

'Even handsome ones? That grandson of his… I've seen him about. I've seen how the young women of this village look at him. Like they could eat him alive!' Nanna smiled with reluctance.

'Even the good-looking ones.' She held her nanna's hand and squeezed it reassuringly.

Her grandmother smiled. 'I suppose I can't persuade you to become a sheep farmer instead?'

Bethan pretended to consider it. 'I'm not sure I'm an open-air kind of girl. Besides, wouldn't that be a waste of all my education?'

Nanna mock-doffed her cap. 'I don't know where you get it from. Your father loved to fish before he became a stablehand, and your mother enjoyed to sew…'

Bethan nodded. 'I *do* enjoy suturing.'

'Och, it's not the same and you know it!'

She got up from the table again and took the red bills from where Bethan had left them and went to switch on the kettle. She let out a heavy sigh, as if resigning herself to the fact that she was going to lose this battle of wills today.

'Okay…let's take a look at you.'

Bethan stood up, straightening her navy trouser suit

and making sure her cream blouse was crease-free. 'Will I do?'

'He'd be a dunderheid to turn you down, lass.'

'Good.' She checked her watch. 'I'll be late. Will you be all right?'

''Course I will. I've looked after myself for nearly twenty years—I think I can probably manage the next hour or so. Besides, I've had a few orders come in for the shop, so I need to get those bagged up.'

'Okay. Well...wish me luck?'

'Good luck, lassie.'

Bethan gave her a quick hug and one last look that she hoped conveyed that everything would be all right, and then she picked up her briefcase and headed out of the door.

Nanna wasn't the only one who was doubtful about expecting a Brodie to take her on. She'd probably been the most surprised when a letter had arrived, inviting her for an interview with a Dr Cameron Brodie. But the past was the past and she herself had no argument with the Brodies. Clearly Dr Cameron Brodie didn't have a grudge either, or she wouldn't have been invited for the interview.

Nanna's part-time job—dying her own rare wool skeins to sell in an online shop—barely covered the bills, and in the last three months sales hadn't been good. They'd struggled—and struggled hard. But now, with Grace having started school full-time, Bethan had become free to get herself a proper job again.

She'd really missed work. She'd come home to start their lives afresh, and nothing could beat being a mother, but her whole heart had always wanted to care for others. There was something about being a GP that spoke to her. The way you could build a relationship with patients over years, so they wouldn't be strangers. It was a privilege to be a friend as well as a doctor, and although sometimes that was a difficult line to walk she did it anyway.

Helping people—healing them, curing them of their ailments—was a magical thing and something that she treasured. But the most she'd done over the last few years with Grace had been to patch scuffed knees, wipe snotty noses and nurse Grace through a particularly scratchy episode of chicken pox. The closest she'd got to medication was calamine lotion.

And what she'd been through prior to that, with Ashley, that had been... *Well, I don't regret a day of that.*

But he'd not been a patient, nor a friend. He'd been her husband. Grace's father. Their relationship had been all-consuming in that last year, and she'd been bereft when he'd died. Quite unable to believe that she would still be able to get up and carry on each day without him.

But I did. For Grace.

She'd made the decision to move away from Cornwall three years afterwards, and coming back to Gilloch—to Nanna—had seemed the right thing. Mhairi was alone, too. She knew what the pain of losing a husband—and, sadly, a child—felt like. They were comrades in grief to start with.

But that was the past and now the future beckoned— and with it a fresh sense of purpose for Bethan. She felt it in her bones. This job—this interview—was the way forward for all of them.

As she strode through the streets of Gilloch, her

head high and the strong breeze blowing her hair from her shoulders, she remembered Ashley's last words— *'You'll go on without me and you'll be absolutely fine.'*

She'd doubted it back then. That she would get through life without him. But time, as they said, was a great healer, and now she often found herself yearning for that kind of closeness again.

But she was absolutely sure—no matter how good-looking Dr Cameron Brodie was—that she would keep her work relationships on a different level from her personal ones.

Dr Cameron Brodie swallowed the tablets with a glass of water and hoped that his headache would pass. He'd woken with it pounding away in his skull and it had been a real struggle to open his eyes to the bright light of the early morning, to get up and get dressed to face the day. If it hadn't been for Rosie then he would no doubt have pulled the quilt over his head and gone back to sleep.

But it wasn't just Rosie. He had someone to interview today. Someone he hoped would take his place permanently at the Gilloch surgery. Not that she would realise that at first. He'd advertised it as a year's post. Twelve months—start to finish. But he knew that before those twelve months were up the people he left behind would have to rearrange their aspirations.

He had a ticking time bomb in his head. An inoperable glioma. And Dr Bethan Monroe had been the only applicant for the post. *Beggars can't be choosers.* Wasn't that what they said?

He made it to the surgery and opened up, having driven there wearing the strongest pair of sunglasses he owned. Sometimes in the early mornings the sunlight in Scotland could be so bright, so fierce, it would make your eyes water. The sun so low in the sky, its light reflecting off the wet road, was almost blinding.

The headache would ease soon. He knew that. The tablets his consultant had prescribed were excellent at doing their job.

And they allowed him to do his.

For a little while longer anyway.

He hoped that this Bethan character was a strong applicant. Her CV was impressive.

By all accounts in her last post she had started up a support group for people with anxiety and panic attacks. Somewhere for them to get together and share stories and ideas in the hope that they could learn that they were not alone in the fight. She had also put together a volunteer 'buddy system', for older people who were lonely to be paired up with a younger person who could be a friend and check in on them whenever it was needed.

Her references were glowing. Her previous colleagues and partners all sang her praises and had been sad to see her go. For 'personal reasons', whatever that meant.

He checked the time. If she was as punctual as she said she was in her CV, no doubt she would be arriving in the next ten minutes.

There was a small mirror above the sink in his room, and he quickly checked his reflection to make sure that he didn't look too rough—that there was some colour in his normally pale cheeks. That was the problem with being a redhead—he had such pale skin that when he was actually sick he looked deathly.

He rubbed his jawline, ruffling the short red bristles, and figured he'd have to do. There were some dark shadows beneath his eyes, but there was nothing he could do about those.

Cameron sat down in his chair and his gaze fell upon the one small picture of his daughter Rosie which he allowed on his desk. In it she sat on a beach, with the sun setting behind her and her long red hair over one shoulder as she smiled at him behind the camera. She'd put a flower behind her ear and begged him to take a picture.

She'd looked so much like her mother at that moment he'd almost been unable to do so. For a moment it had been as if Holly was looking back at him, smiling. She had simply taken his breath away that day. He had almost put the camera down.

'Daddy! Take my picture!'

He was doing this for *her.* It was all for Rosie now. They didn't have long left together and he wanted whatever time they had to be spent together, having fun and making memories, so that she remembered him long after he was gone. His voice, his laughter, how much he'd loved her, how much he'd wanted to spend time with her. He wanted her to know that she had been cherished and adored.

So it didn't matter if this Dr Bethan Monroe was a three-headed monster from Mars—he needed someone to take his place at the surgery and *soon*. If she was qualified, and didn't have a death sentence of her own, then she was going to be perfect for the job.

His phone buzzed. Janet from Reception. 'Aye?'

'Dr Bethan Monroe is here to see you.' Janet had put on her 'customer service' voice. It always made him smile when he heard it, because she somehow lost most of her Scottish brogue and sounded more English than anything.

'Thank you. Could you send her through?'

'Certainly, Doctor.'

He sucked in a breath and closed his eyes. Everything seemed so much easier when he took a moment to do that. Took a moment to meditate. To calm the body. Concentrate on his breathing.

Perhaps I ought to take up yoga? he thought with amusement.

There was a slight tap at the door.

He opened his eyes and stood up. 'Come in!'

Janet came in first, smiling, her bonny cheeks rosy-red. 'Dr Bethan Monroe for you. Can I get you both a pot of tea? Or coffee?'

He lifted his hand to demur, but then he caught sight of the tall, willowy woman who had walked into his room behind his receptionist, her long, chocolatey locks of wavy hair flowing either side of her beautiful face, and he found himself unable to speak any words.

She was beautiful. Elegant. Elfin bone structure.

For a moment she looked startled, then she gathered her composure after seeing his no doubt deathly pale face and walked towards him and held out her hand. 'Very pleased to meet you.'

Now, she *did* have an English accent. A real one.

He suddenly became aware of his throat. His tongue. Had the temperature of the room increased? He felt hot, his mouth dry, but so he didn't give Janet too much fodder for the village grapevine he managed to force a smile himself and shake her hand. 'Hello, there.'

'Did you want tea, Doctors?' Janet persisted, looking from one to the other with wry amusement.

He hadn't wanted any before, but with his mouth this dry it might be a good idea. 'Er...aye...thank you, that would be great.'

Bethan Monroe nodded agreement. 'Thank you.'

'I'll be back in a moment, then.' And Janet hurried from the room, closing the door behind her.

He couldn't get over Bethan's eyes. As chocolate-brown as her hair, if not more so. She also had beautiful, creamy skin, with a hint of the English rose on her cheekbones and a wide, full-lipped mouth. She looked nothing like her grandmother, whom he knew well—even though she'd refused to be his patient for years and saw Dr McKellen instead, over in the next village.

You couldn't help but see the same faces out and about in Gilloch, and her grandmother, Mhairi, was well-known to him because of the upset between her and his grandfather years back, that probably no one except them ever talked about any more. He often saw her. She took long walks down to the wool mill, or along the front of the bay to sit outside the coffee shop, wrapped up in swathes of knitted garments and watching the fishermen come in with their catch.

'I'm Cameron. Very pleased to meet you.'

'Bethan. Likewise.'

'Please take a seat.'

She was long-limbed but graceful as she sank into the seat opposite and laid her briefcase neatly against her chair. 'Thank you.'

'You found us all right?'

Clearly, or she wouldn't be here, idiot!

'I did. It's not far from my nanna's house. Well, *my* house, too, now, I guess.'

'You've been back in the area for a short while?'

'A few months, yes. I moved here from Cornwall.'

He nodded. Good. That was all good.

You're staring.

Cameron cleared his throat and stared down at her paperwork. The *only* application on his desk.

'So, we're here to discuss the vacancy of general practitioner here in Gilloch.'

He needed time to think. Time to reorganise his thoughts. He picked up her CV and read it through as if it were the first time.

'You're looking for a full-time post?'

'Yes.'

'And you've spent the last few years as a full-time mother? That's correct?'

'Yes.'

'You're aware that this post is very demanding? Long hours—frequently past school pick-up time—sometimes evening work, call-outs, home visits, that kind of thing?'

Are you trying to scare her away?

She seemed to bristle slightly. Had he implied that she wouldn't be able to cope because she had a child? He hadn't meant to.

'What I mean is, it'll be an abrupt change from what you're used to.'

'I don't think so at all. Being a mother is about having demands made on you all the time—all day long and sometimes through the night. There are no days off. You can't go sick or take a holiday. You're always on call.' She smiled.

He nodded, seemingly unable to tear his gaze away from her. There was something so vibrant about her. So intriguing.

'You're absolutely right. I have a child myself. Same age as…' he quickly scanned her personal statement again '…Grace, is it?'

Bethan smiled. 'Yes. She's just started at Gilloch Infants' School.'

'So has Rosie. My daughter.'

She looked surprised. 'Which teacher does she have?'

'Mrs Carlisle.'

'Oh! They're in the same class, then.'

'I'm sure they'll become good friends.'

She smiled at him—a beautiful smile. 'Let's hope so.'

He considered her, enjoying her optimistic outlook. It had been a long time since he'd felt optimistic about anything, and it was just fascinating to see someone who shone so brightly with it. Surely there had to be shadows somewhere?

'It says here that you left your last post for personal reasons?'

'That's right.'

'Not because of the job itself?'

'No. I loved working as a GP, but my husband got sick and needed someone to look after him.'

'Oh. I'm very sorry to hear that. I hope he's better now?'

She looked down at the ground for a brief moment, her smile faltering, before she met his gaze again. 'He died. Of pancreatic cancer.'

He was shocked. And a little embarrassed at having pushed her to explain. 'I'm very sorry.'

'You weren't to know.'

'I lost my wife when Rosie was born. It's difficult being a single parent, isn't it?'

'I'm sorry, too. It can be, if you're truly on your own. That's why it's good to have family around.'

'Is that why you moved to Gilloch?'

'Yes, I was born here. Lived here in Gilloch until about the age of three or four, when my parents moved to Cornwall. My father was looking for better job prospects—my mother for better weather!'

She laughed at the personal memory and he loved the way her eyes lit up as she spoke of her parents.

'It was in Cornwall that I met my husband. He was a doctor, too. When he died I felt incredibly alone. My parents were gone by then, and I just felt a yearning to be with family. It's important, that connection. More than any other. We'd always kept in touch with my grandmother, speaking online and on the phone, and I wanted Grace to know her properly instead of just being a voice…an image. So I decided to move back here so we could look after each other.'

'Mhairi?'

She nodded.

Cameron put down her paperwork. 'Tell me what you think you can bring to this post.'

But at that moment there was another knock on the door and Janet was there, carefully balancing a tray with cups, saucers, a teapot and a small plate of biscuits.

'Thank you, Janet.' He dismissed her and waited

for her to leave the room before turning his attention back to Bethan.

'I'm punctual, committed, hard-working. I'm good with patients and I know how to build a rapport with them. I believe myself to be very efficient, and I have a good talent for hearing what people *aren't* saying.'

Is that right?

'What would you say are your weaknesses?'

She shifted in her seat. 'I get attached. I care too much, too quickly, and don't always control my emotions.'

He frowned. That was a red flag. He didn't need anyone getting attached to *him*! Even if it was just as a friend or a trusted colleague. He didn't need anyone to be hurt by his passing. It was going to be bad enough for Rosie. He needed strong people around to be there for her, not crying a river for their own pain.

'How do you mean?'

'It's the human element. I find it hard to create a professional distance sometimes. Especially with people that I feel I know well. I care for them. Feel for them. When they're hurting, so am I.'

She leaned forward, planted her elbows on his desk.

'What I mean is, if I've been looking after someone and then I have to deliver a shocking diagnosis that's going to affect their lives then I'm going to feel that pain with them. It will make me cry. Not whilst I'm *with* them,' she clarified. 'I'm not that unprofessional. But sometimes it can get a little bit too much.'

She looked at him with concern, as if she were worried she'd said too much.

'Actually, I'm not sure if that *is* a weakness.' She

smiled. 'I think it just makes me human, and I think people *like* having doctors who aren't made of steel.'

She jutted out her chin, but didn't meet his gaze.

He suspected she thought she'd blown it.

She hadn't. Not at all. But she didn't know she was the only applicant, and she didn't know just how much he needed her. He *had* to employ her. No matter what. His time was running out. He would just keep his distance. As much as he could.

'I need someone who can take over my role completely. I'm leaving the practice for a year's sabbatical, to spend time with my wee girl, but obviously there will be a short transition period during which I will sit in with the new doctor and observe until they feel able to fly solo. How would you feel about that? Me looking over your shoulder?'

She nodded, smiling. 'That sounds fine.' Then she frowned. 'You're leaving? Completely?'

Cameron smiled. 'Completely. For a year,' he lied.

'Oh.'

Was she using that special skill of hers right now? Trying to work out what it was that he *wasn't* saying? Perhaps she was. He watched her observing him, looking for clues, trying to work out why a fully trained doctor would just leave like this, but he knew she wouldn't find the answer.

There were no outward signs of his death sentence. Just paleness and bags under his eyes, which lots of people had, and a slowly fading headache that she couldn't see. No one else knew either. Except family. He'd *had* to tell them. But everyone else just thought he'd been sick for a while and was now over it.

Cameron leaned forward and poured them both a cup of tea, standing up to pass her a cup and saucer.

'Thank you.'

'This practice has always worked well. There's a good team here. How would you make sure you'd fit in?'

She sipped from the teacup. 'I'm a local girl who's come home. I'm sure there will be lots of questions, which I'll do my best to answer honestly. You can't be a GP without having good people skills.'

He smiled. *Good.* 'Do you have any questions you'd like to ask me?'

Surely there had to be. All good interviewees were taught to ask something at this stage. To sound interested in the post, if nothing else.

Bethan stirred her drink and he noticed what fine hands she had. Lithe fingers, short nails with clear polish. He was struck by a sense of admiration for this woman. Her husband had died and she was a widow. A single parent like himself.

'There is one.'

'Aye?' He sipped his own tea, wincing at the heat of it upon his tongue.

'I'd like to know if I'd have full autonomy from day one? I know you'd be observing, but how long would you observe me for?'

He smiled. He *liked* this woman. She had spirit. And enthusiasm. And that mattered to him most of all. He was going to be leaving his patients in the care of someone else. Patients he had looked after for a good few years. He needed to know they were in good hands. She seemed a steady, comforting individual. Someone who—if he hadn't had this death sentence hanging over him—he could imagine becoming great friends with.

And for that reason he'd have to keep her at arm's length whilst they worked together. Keep everything brief and to the point.

'You'll have autonomy. And I'd like to observe for two weeks.'

We won't get close.

'Two weeks…'

'Two weeks of me sitting in the corner and saying nothing. Unless you need me to, of course.'

She nodded. Smiled. 'That's okay by me.'

'Good.'

He decided to shock her. See how she dealt with surprises.

'When would you like to start?'

She stood outside in the bright morning sun, a little stunned.

I got the job!

Her first job application after a long break away!

Dr Brodie had seemed a very likeable man. Handsome, tall, broad-shouldered… A typical Scot, if there was one, with that beautiful head of red hair. And his eyes… Such a piercing blue against those dark shadows that lurked beneath them.

Clearly he had not been sleeping well recently. Or he was worried about something. Was it his decision to take a year off? Was he concerned about leaving his patients with someone he didn't know? Perhaps there was something else. Something she didn't know yet.

It's none of my business.

What *was* her business, though, was the fact that

she could start her new job next Monday! Cameron had said that Mondays were appointment days at the surgery. Tuesdays were for home visits, Wednesday was procedure day, when they'd perform small surgeries such as skin tag removal, wound care, that sort of thing, and Thursdays were for more appointments, as were Fridays.

Weekends and evenings were usually spent on call, but they shared the on-call with the practice over in the next village, so that they did actually get some time off on alternate weekends, and he'd said they didn't often get lots of call-outs.

Gilloch was a small coastal village in the Highlands. She could smell the brine in the air from wherever she stood. No more than a thousand people lived here and they were of sturdy stock. And now *she* would be their doctor.

Smiling, she set off back to her nanna's, to tell her the good news. She had no doubt at all that her grandmother would be suspicious about Cameron Brodie's motives, but Bethan was determined not to be!

I'm going to make this work. I'm going to make Cameron Brodie see that I am a brilliant doctor and that I will be able to care for all his patients as if he were still doing it himself! If not better!

She needed this. *Wanted* this.

And now it was in her grasp.

Life was changing now that she was back.

Just as she'd hoped it would.

CHAPTER TWO

'YOU'VE GOT YOUR phone in case I need you?'

'Yes, Nanna.'

'Your purse?'

'Of course.'

'You'll call me if anything goes wrong?'

Bethan laughed at her nanna's fussing. 'Why would anything go wrong?'

Nanna fiddled with the pendant at her neck. 'I don't know. I just have a bad feeling about this.'

Bethan held out her arms and scooped her grandmother into a hug. She needed one. She'd been nervous these last few days as her starting day had got closer. And Nanna was still utterly convinced it was all a great big trick to humiliate her further.

'It'll be okay. Dr Brodie is a very nice man.'

'Impossible! Brodie men are the *worst*.'

'Not this one. He's different.'

Nanna pulled back to look at her. 'You believe that?'

She smiled. 'I do. What happened between you and old Angus Brodie is ancient news.'

'Maybe to *you*.'

Bethan picked up her briefcase. 'You're all right getting Grace to school?'

Nanna smiled. 'Of course.'

'And picking her up at three?'

'Aye. I've a few orders to dye up today, but I'll remember. I'm not senile, you know.'

'I've told the school you'll be picking her up from now on.'

Nanna leaned against the kitchen sink. 'You're stalling.'

'I'm nervous.'

'You'll be absolutely fine. You're a wonderful doctor, lassie. The people here in Gilloch are lucky to have you.' She reached into her pocket and pulled out a small box tied with ribbon. 'I want you to have this.'

'What is it?'

'They were your mother's.'

Bethan opened the lid of the box and found inside a small pair of diamond earrings, sitting on a bed of red velvet. 'They're beautiful!'

'Your father gave them to your mother after she had you. I should have given them to you long ago, after you had Grace, but they're yours now.'

Bethan was touched. Such a wonderful gesture! She put them in and went to look in the mirror. Perfect.

'Thank you, Nanna.'

Mhairi smiled. 'Now, you go and show that Brodie boy who's boss!'

Bethan felt a little odd, knowing that she was in *his* seat and he was in a smaller chair right next to her as he showed her the ins and outs of the computer system.

She'd not said much to her nanna over the weekend, but Dr Brodie had been in her thoughts more than she'd let on.

Nanna was right. He *was* a handsome man, and when she'd first walked into that interview room she'd almost stalled, her mouth drying upon her first sight of him—this tall Scottish hunk, unfolding his long, rangy figure from behind the desk and stretching out a hand for her to shake. She'd felt sure he would notice the tremble that had begun in her body in response to him.

And now he kept reaching across the desk to point things out on the computer and he smelt *so* good! It had been a long time since she had felt aware of another man, and having one who smelt so great sitting right beside her was throwing her concentration slightly. Irritating her as she tried to fight it.

'So, if you want to print off some information about a condition, click on this box here, next to the diagnosis, and it links to a medical database. You see?'

He brought up an information sheet on scoliosis as an example.

She snapped back into professional mode. 'Perfect. And if I want to look up information on medication…?'

'Well, we have books, but if you click on that question mark next to the prescription box you can usually find what you need regarding the pharmacology.'

'That's wonderful. Thank you. It's pretty similar to the last system I used.'

'Any telephone calls with patients, any advice or queries, you mark them down in the patient notes—no matter how trivial. See the notepad icon? It all has to be logged. I find that helps with any possible discrepancies down the line, if they query anything.'

'Well, I hope there won't be any discrepancies. Not from me.'

'Excellent. Well, I think you're ready! Feel like meeting your first patient?'

She turned to look into his face, at those warm crystal-blue eyes of his that twinkled in his pale face, and felt a rush of heat hit her in the solar plexus.

Oh, boy, I'm in trouble!

'I am.'

'Well, just push that button there to call her in. Her name will come up on the screen in the waiting room.'

Bethan smiled, nervousness suddenly flooding her system. She adjusted her chair and let out a breath. Then pushed the button.

Mrs Percy was a sweet old lady who used a walker that she'd jazzed up with some fake flowers and pretty ribbons. She shuffled her way into the room and sat down with a satisfied sigh and a smile as she took in the two doctors facing her.

'Two for the price of one, eh? Lucky me.'

Bethan smiled. She liked her already. 'What can I do for you, Mrs Percy?'

She'd already checked her screen and observed that apart from some arthritis in her hips and knees, Mrs Percy didn't have much wrong with her. Blood pressure had been good on her last check and her cholesterol levels were low.

'I want to do the Edinburgh Half-Marathon,' she said, giving one firm nod as she delivered her surprising statement.

'You do?' Nothing could have surprised Bethan more. She'd maybe expected *My knees are giving me some gip* or *I'm not sleeping well at night*. Anything but what she'd actually said.

'Aye, I do. And they tell you, don't they—on the television and whatnot—that if you're about to embark on a new training regime or exercise you should consult your doctor? So that's why I'm here. Thought you'd better check me out so I don't drop dead halfway around.'

Cameron laughed beside her. 'Mrs Percy is our resident adrenaline junkie.'

Mrs Percy winked at him. 'Well, adrenaline keeps you going, doesn't it? I've seen those medical shows on TV, when someone's about to cork it and they give them a shot of adrenaline. *Brenda*, I tell myself, *you need some of that every day.*'

Bethan nodded. Fair enough! 'Okay…well, I guess we need to check you over, then. We'll need to take your blood pressure, listen to your heart, take your pulse. All right?'

'Aye, dear. You go for it.' Mrs Percy rolled up the sleeve of her vast knitted cardigan to reveal a scrawny arm. 'But I want a good answer, mind. I've got lots more living in me, and I haven't abseiled down a building yet—or swam with sharks.'

'You want to swim with sharks?'

'Great white sharks! The meanest buggers of them all! Oh, aye!'

Mrs Percy's blood pressure was normal. Which was impressive, seeing as she was talking about one of the greatest predators of all time and being stuck in a tiny cage next to one.

'Well, you're braver than me, Mrs Percy. I'm quite happy to keep my feet on solid ground.'

'Och, that's no way to live, dear. You have to be scared every day. Keeps you fresh. Keeps the blood pumping! You know what I'm talking about, don't you, Dr Brodie? What with your little foray into illness?'

Cameron gave a polite smile and nodded.

'Illness is a mean old beast—we all know that—but it's also the biggest wake-up call.'

'Well, your BP and heart-rate are good. I think as long as you train sensibly and take your time there's no reason why you shouldn't enter the half-marathon if it's really what you want to do.'

'Och, that's brilliant, Doctor. Thank you very much. This your first day, is it?'

Bethan glanced at Cameron and smiled. 'It is. And you're my first patient.'

'Och, really? Do I get a prize?'

'Just the prize of continued good health, Mrs Percy.'

Mrs Percy nodded. 'Aye. 'tis a gift not given to all, but I'm taking full advantage of mine whilst I've got it. How are *you* feeling now, Dr Brodie?'

Cameron's face seemed to flush slightly before he answered, and he wasn't even looking at Bethan. 'Much better, thank you.'

Bethan wondered what Cameron had been ill with. Probably a cold, or something. Maybe the flu? If he was back after a brief illness that might explain the dark circles.

She got up to walk Mrs Percy to the door and held it open for her.

Mrs Percy thanked her. 'Reckon I'll get myself a gold medal one day. Beat the clock.'

'You win if you cross the line at the end, Mrs Percy. That should be your goal. Don't worry about the clock.'

'But the clock's the whole *point*, Doctor. Time's always against us.'

Bethan closed the door and turned to look at Cameron.

He smiled at her casually, guilelessly, as if he had nothing to hide, and she shrugged her worries away.

It had probably just been man-flu.

Nothing to worry about at all.

How many of his patients might give the game away?

That had been a close-run thing with Mrs Percy. She liked to talk…liked to gossip. Oddly, the people who talked non-stop never seemed to come to his surgery with sore throats or laryngitis. But a lot of people in Gilloch knew he'd had a run-in with cancer. They didn't know all the details—he'd only shared those with direct family—but gossip and rumour were rife in a small place such as this.

He'd told everyone else it was over. He'd beaten it. Why upset them? Why put himself in a position of having everyone look at him with sympathy and pity? A dead man walking. They'd be throwing flowers at him before he was six feet under, and who wanted that?

His father had not taken the news of his prognosis well. Why would he? No one wanted to hear things like that. No parent wanted to hear that they would outlive their child, and that was exactly what he'd had to tell his own father.

'They estimate I maybe have a year left.'

He'd almost not told him. The very idea of sitting down in the living room and having to utter those words had made him feel physically sick. He didn't ever want to remind himself of the look on his father's face when he had, silently wiping away his tears, his mouth grim as he looked away and gave one solitary sniff.

'I'm going to leave the practice. I'm going to spend my time with Rosie and you, as much as I can.'

He could appreciate Mrs Percy's outlook on life. You *did* have to grab every second of it. You didn't realise how precious it was until someone told you there wasn't as much left as you thought there was.

Everyone has a limited time. It's just that some have more sand in their hourglass than others.

Bethan sat beside him, typing in the notes about Mrs Percy's consultation, oblivious to his torment and secrets. Her fine fingers were flitting across the keyboard, and he noticed the way she gently bit her lower lip as she concentrated.

She's pretty.

There was no point in telling anyone else the bad news. Sitting down and telling his family had been bad enough—he didn't want to have to keep on repeating it. Seeing people he cared about breaking down and crying and having to be the one to comfort *them*. He needed his strength for himself.

So he'd lied. Told them the chemo had worked. The tumour was gone. It was all over. Life could carry on. Except he'd quite like a year's sabbatical. Just to spend some time with Rosie. It had been a hard few months for her, watching her dad lose his hair and his strength.

Everyone at the practice had understood. They thought it was a marvellous idea, though they'd be sad not to see him every day.

He cleared the dark thoughts from his head. He didn't need to linger on the thought of everyone else's pain. He had a new mantra—*make it all about Rosie.* He wasn't being mean. He wasn't being selfish. But he needed to create distance from people now. They were all too close, all too friendly. He knew what it felt like to lose someone close, and it was horrible. Best to make it easier for everyone by being a little standoffish.

He liked what he'd seen of Bethan so far and she'd been right. But she did exude warmth and an easy-going nature, and he had no doubt he would have a problem keeping her away if she knew the truth. Bethan's ease at being able to chat with her patient as if she'd known her for a long time took skill. If she found out about his glioma he just knew she wouldn't let it go.

And hadn't she been through this before? With her husband? What kind of cruel person would put someone as nice as her through that again?

He hated lying, but he needed to. It was self-preservation.

Cameron thought of all those people in his waiting room—all those familiar faces, all those people he had come to care for. People who would still be here after his time had come and gone.

Part of him didn't want to go. Part of him was still rebelling at his diagnosis—*physician, heal thyself*—and part of him just wanted to lie down and have it all be done with.

He knew that was the depressive side of things. He had tablets for that. For the depression. His consultant had said they would help him come to terms with it. Be less of a shock to the system.

He wasn't sure they were working. He spent far more time than he should wallowing in dark thoughts.

But who wouldn't with a terminal diagnosis?

And why put other people through it when they didn't have to?

It was best to just go quietly.

Let them sort it out after he was gone.

Her first morning of seeing patients was the usual kind of mix. Some were simply curious. Some turned up to see her about some spurious sore throat or trifling cough, just so they could go home and tell everyone else that they'd met Mhairi's prodigal granddaughter.

She treated housemaid's knee, an actual chest infection that needed antibiotics, a suspected urine infection and a clear case of pompholyx—which was an itchy, painful rash that appeared on the hands and feet. She examined two men complaining of bad backs— one with a shoulder injury after a fall in the garden onto a wooden picnic bench—and diagnosed a case of cellulitis.

She was enjoying herself immensely. Back in the job she loved. Seeing new people—people who would come to mean a lot to her.

She felt Cam's presence behind her like a guardian angel, and he was being as good as his word, letting her be autonomous and get on with everything herself, only butting in when he had to—when there was something she wasn't sure of on the computer, or to tell her where various equipment was stored in the consulting room.

At lunchtime, they stopped for something to eat.

'Well, I think that was a successful morning!' she said, smiling, happy at what she'd achieved. Happy at having been able to help people.

It had been so long since she'd had the experience of feeling she was actually *curing* someone instead of just obscuring their pain. She felt as if she was exactly where she needed to be.

'Aye. You did well,' Cameron said, before gathering up his jacket and bits and pieces.

Bethan followed him through to the staffroom. It wasn't overly large. They were, after all, a small community with a tiny doctor surgery, but it was enough for everyone there. Cosy, comfortable. Apart from Janet, there was an office manager and two nurses. It was enough.

Someone had made a cake—coffee and walnut—and they each took a small slice.

'So, how are you finding it, Doctor?' asked Sarah, the senior nurse.

'It's been good, thank you. Everyone's been so nice. And it's good to feel useful again. Like I'm actually *doing* something. It's great being a mum and staying at home, but after years of watching children's television I was really beginning to feel like my brain was turning into mush.'

There was an odd silence then, and she wasn't sure why. The staff seemed to look at Cameron, then at each other, before looking away and suddenly finding their cake extremely interesting, or sipping from a mug of tea.

What had she said? Was it what she'd said about staying at home to be a parent? Did they think she was implying that it wouldn't be good for Cameron to do it? That he'd somehow stagnate at being at home? Perhaps they didn't agree with his choice to leave them?

Okay. Tough crowd. But loyal to their boss, which I guess is nice.

'You're from Cornwall—is that right?' asked Sarah, changing the subject.

Bethan smiled, thankful to the nurse for breaking

the weird, awkward silence. 'Yes, but I was born here in Gilloch. We moved away when I was a child.'

'What's it like to return home?'

It was odd. Because she hadn't been able to return with her parents. They'd passed away just before her husband had. Being dealt three deaths in quick succession had almost destroyed her. But she'd had to remain strong after her parents had died because Ashley had been sick and deteriorating fast. He'd needed her, needed her strength. She wasn't sure she'd ever grieved properly for her mum and dad. And then there'd been Grace to look after, too.

She'd become a 'coper' because there'd been no other way to be. These last few years it had been like living on autopilot—locked into her routine with Grace each day, because routine was secure and familiar. It made her feel safe. But then, when her grandmother Mhairi had got in touch, she'd realised just how lonely her grandmother was. Nanna had lost her only son, and Bethan and Grace were all she had left.

That yearning for family had increased with every passing day, so Bethan had sold her home in St Austell and moved back to live in Gilloch just a few short months ago. She hadn't resented doing so. Hadn't resented being needed again. It had been so good to see Nanna and Grace's relationship flourish. And she hadn't realised just how much she'd missed having someone love her back. Someone watching out for *her*.

'It's good to be back with family. You never know how long you have left with someone, do you?'

'No.' Sarah smiled at her and bit into her cake.

Being reminded of family made her think of Nanna. She'd no doubt be busy dyeing her wool, but she would be worrying about Bethan's first day at work and would probably appreciate an update.

'Excuse me—I need to make a phone call.' She put down her cake and grabbed her mobile from her handbag, then headed outside.

As she stood outside the surgery, shivering slightly in the cool breeze, she found a bright smile filling her face. She was pleased with how well everything was going. Cameron Brodie was not the tyrant her grandmother believed. In fact he was quite polite. Reserved... Kept his distance...

Smelt great...

'Hey, it's me.'

'Hello, my lovely, how's your first day going?'

Mhairi sounded genuinely interested. Also concerned and fretful. Here, at last, was someone who was worried about *her* feelings.

'It's good.'

'Really? Och, I'm so pleased for you.'

'How's Ye Olde Dyeworks?' That was the name of Nanna's wool business.

'I'm up to my armpits in aubergine and turquoise dye, but it's coming out well. What about you? Had to lance any boils today?'

'No, not yet. They're probably saving that for procedure day. They don't want to scare me off too soon.'

'Well, of course they don't. I was thinking of making your old favourite—custard tarts—for dessert tonight. Fancy that?'

Bethan smiled, remembering the small round tarts her nanna had made for her when she was a little girl.

Sprinkled with nutmeg and melting in the mouth with soft, buttery pastry.

'I haven't had those since I was little. They sound great. Thank you.'

'Anything for you, lassie.'

'I'd do anything for *you*, too.'

Cameron helped clear up the lunch mess, put a cover over the rest of the cake and then headed back to his room to await afternoon surgery.

He was surprised to see Bethan already there. 'I didn't know you'd come back in. Have you had time to eat?'

'I'm not that hungry. Running on adrenaline.'

He wanted to make a comment about her looking after herself better, but held it in. She wasn't his concern. He had his own health to worry about. But he felt awkward enough to say *something*.

'Everything all right?'

She smiled brightly. 'Of course!'

'Good. I'm glad to hear that.'

His mind raced to think about who she might have called. Mhairi? Her daughter's school?

'Gilloch Infants' School is very good.'

She seemed puzzled by his comment, so he guessed she hadn't called the school, after all.

'Yes, it seemed to be when we did the tour.'

He nodded, studying her. Then he looked away. She was one of those beautiful women men couldn't help but stare at. But she was *so* beautiful it was difficult to tear his eyes away. He could easily get lost in the soft curves of her face. Her lips, her cheekbones, the downward slope of her nose. The way her hair fell in waves.

Everything about her said *soft*.

His headache began to return—probably because he was allowing himself to become irritated by the track of his thought-processes.

She looks soft, but she had to be strong, right?

She'd nursed her husband through terminal cancer. This was a new start in her life. A new chapter. She looked capable, bright and optimistic. Where had she found that strength?

She told me in her interview that she gets attached quickly, that she gets emotional, but that to her it's a strength, not a weakness.

Perhaps she turned *all* her supposed weaknesses into strengths? Put a positive spin on everything?

He knew it would be best if he just oversaw these next two weeks and then slipped away quietly to live the rest of his life with Rosie. That was what he wanted now. An uncomplicated life. Living with his daughter and bringing her joy whilst he still could. That was who should be his focus. *Rosie.* Not Bethan.

'Ready for the afternoon?' he asked.

She nodded, her eyes bright and gleaming. 'I am!'

Her beauty struck him again. How noble-looking she was. Even though she'd been through some terrible times, had lost her parents and her husband, she still managed to emit kindness and positivity.

Cam looked out through the window, seeing the heather-covered hills behind the surgery, the dark mountains beyond those. In the slightly grey sky he saw birds circling, their wings buffeted by the wind. Life was beautiful. He should take a page out of Bethan's book and remain optimistic. See the good stuff in life rather than focusing on the bad.

The headaches weren't too bad right now—the painkillers controlled them—and he was able to sleep. The tumour hadn't yet encroached into his optic nerve, so he still had time to *see* that beauty. To remember it for when the time came that his sight was taken from him towards the end.

He sat in his chair as the next patient came in. Caitriona MacDonald. She'd been born deaf and had learnt how to lip-read.

He sat back and observed Bethan checking out Caitriona. She did everything he would have done. She was thorough, and caring, and once again it made him see that even though she had been his only candidate for the post Bethan was absolutely the one he would have chosen even if there'd been a choice of hundreds.

She *was* a people person and, yes, everyone did matter to her. She wanted to do her very best for everyone she saw. Leaving no stone unturned, she checked everything she needed to. There was no slacking. No shortcuts. She did it all.

He felt a sudden need to tell her everything. To just blurt it all out.

To have her look at me like that—the way she's looking and listening to Caitriona.

But then she'd treat him as a patient, wouldn't she? And he didn't want to be the weak one here.

He shifted in his seat, suddenly uncomfortable.

He didn't want her to care for him as he slowly deteriorated. He didn't want her to feel that she was failing again—because doctors always hoped to cheat death if they could.

She'd had enough death in her short life, and she had real patients to care for. Patients who could be cured. Let her concentrate all her efforts on them. She could actually *do* something for them.

Bethan was concluding that Caitriona might have an inner ear infection, and she prescribed some antibiotics and got a promise that Caitriona would return in three weeks to let her know how she'd got on.

They waved their patient goodbye and he watched, fascinated, as Bethan inputted her notes and observations. Her head was bent over the keyboard, her brow furrowed in concentration, her lips gently parted as she bit her bottom lip.

He smiled at the already familiar gesture and felt a pang. Of something. As he looked at her, studied her whilst he could, he realised something else that was disturbing.

I'm attracted to her.

The thought made him smile. He almost chuckled.

The human body was an amazing thing.

The laws of attraction never stopped working. Not until the heart itself ceased beating.

CHAPTER THREE

CAMERON LEFT FOR home exhausted. He'd had no idea just how tiring it was to sit in a chair all day and do nothing except observe someone. And, because he knew how specifically aware he was to Bethan's presence, he'd been determined not to observe her *too* closely. Noticing her beautiful eyes and her smile was *not* the kind of observation he wanted to make.

He was glad to make it to the end of the day and go and collect Rosie from her after-school club. His daughter brought joy into his heart every time he saw her, and renewed his strength and determination.

'How was school?'

'Great! I played with my new friend Grace today.'

Bethan's daughter.

'Really?'

'And, look—I made a caterpillar!'

She ran to fetch her creation from the Art Corner. She had indeed made a caterpillar, from the remains of green cardboard egg cartons, stuck together in a line and painted garish colours.

'Wow! That's fabulous!'

'We're learning about bugs.'

'I can see that.'

'Not the bugs that you have to heal people from.'

He smiled. 'Ah…'

They went home and he made her some dinner. And once she'd had a bath he settled into his favourite part of the day with his daughter. Storytime.

There was nothing he loved more than being able to sit and read with her, making up silly voices and discussing the characters and what they thought was going to happen. Rosie never ceased to amaze him with the insight she had for such a young girl. And his time with her was precious.

How many more stories would he get to read for her? Would they even finish this long book? What if the tumour damaged his optic nerve soon and he could no longer read? Would she sit upstairs alone? Trying to read by herself?

She'll be alone someday.

That thought almost did him in daily. Rosie was so young. She'd already lost her mother, and now she was going to lose her father, too. Life wasn't fair. But he knew he couldn't allow himself to get lost in the injustice of it all. That way madness lay. His time was short—he couldn't waste it on self-pity. It wasn't how he wanted his daughter to remember him.

He knew that at some point he would have to start letting her stay with his father a bit more, in preparation for when she'd have to live there permanently—after he was gone.

His dad was already trying to make up a room for her to stay in. His old bedroom was being converted from his father's home office. The walls had recently been stripped of the old blue wallpaper and Rosie had picked out a pretty peaches-and-cream pattern she wanted.

He wasn't sure that Rosie understood what was going to happen eventually. Talking to his child about his death was impossible. How much could she truly understand? And was it right to burden her in advance? Instead he'd pretended that he was going to 'go away'. They were trying to make the transition as easy for her as they could, making her new room at his father's a fun thing.

He pointed at the book they were reading. 'You know how in the story Harry lives with his aunt and uncle?'

Rosie nodded.

'Because his own parents aren't around any more?'

Another nod. 'They're dead,' said Rosie.

'Well, you'll be doing that one day. Living with Grandpa Doug?'

She seemed to think about it. 'But I won't be in the cupboard under the stairs, will I? I'm having my own room.'

'That's right.' He smiled.

'And Grandpa Doug is *nice* to me. Not like Harry's family.'

'Grandpa Doug is *very* nice. And he loves you loads.'

'And you'll be gone away?'

He swallowed hard. 'That's right. I won't be able to come back, but you'll be able to see me in here.' He touched the side of her head. 'And in here.' He pointed at where her heart was.

Rosie seemed to think about this for a while. Then, 'Who'll read to me at night?'

'Grandpa Doug will.'

'But he doesn't do the voices.'

Cameron kissed the top of her head and smiled to himself, loving it that her greatest concern was the right voices for her story. If that was her greatest worry, then it would be fine. He was happy with that. He could carry all the other worries by himself.

That was how it should be anyway. She was too young to be burdened by the world. And he didn't want to tell his daughter he was going to die. How could he?

'Right—hush, now. One more chapter and then it's sleepy time, okay?'

'Okay, Daddy.'

And she snuggled into his side and listened until she fell fast asleep.

It was raining, and the roads were slick with water and puddles. Beneath the endless grey sky Bethan parked her car, right outside the surgery door, ready to do a day of home visits after she'd collected the medical files and any equipment she might need.

She liked it that the practice had a whole day to do home visits. Not every practice offered this service any more, but she'd always enjoyed doing them. You didn't always get to understand a person's home-life and true situation from an eight-minute consultation in the surgery, so it was good to see people in their own environment. And there were quite a few people who couldn't get to the surgery, so it was a worthwhile opportunity for them all.

She merrily chirped a hello to Janet on Reception.

'Good morning, Dr Monroe! How are you today?'

'Good, thank you. How are you?'

'Bonny, Doctor, always bonny.'

She smiled and passed on through to the office to collect her schedule.

Cameron was already there, checking the files off against a list. He looked up when he saw her and she was struck by how pale he looked today. He was pale anyway—the standard complexion for someone with such beautiful red hair—but today that paleness had an ashen quality to it. And the shadows beneath his eyes looked darker than they had before.

Had he had a bad night's sleep? Was he still recovering from that bout of flu?

'Morning, Dr Brodie.'

'Cam, please.' He smiled. 'We've got time for a brief cuppa before we head out. Can I make you one?'

'Oh, thank you. That would be lovely.'

She'd managed to make a cup of tea first thing that morning, but she'd only had a couple of sips, in her rush to get Grace ready for school, and then her nanna had asked her to help bring down some wool skeins from the spare room she used as a dye room—she needed to get them off in the post. She'd spent so much time running around her tea had gone cold and there hadn't been time to make a fresh one.

She sighed with delight as he passed her a hot, steaming mug. 'Perfect.'

'We've got twelve house calls to make today—which doesn't sound much, but a lot of these patients can talk for ever, so we'll need to keep an eye on the time.'

'All right. Anything in particular I should know about?'

He raised an eyebrow and looked uncomfortable.

'Well, one of the patients is my grandfather, Angus Brodie. He can be a bit of a…a curmudgeon.'

His grandfather? The infamous Angus?

'Okay.'

'He can get a bit…grumpy.'

Cam was looking as if 'grumpy' was the most polite word he could come up with for his grandfather, so she smiled in sympathy. Did Angus know who she was? Mhairi's granddaughter? Would he be biased against her, the way Nanna was against him?

Cam looked exhausted. Was he fit to do a full day of home visits?

'And are you okay? You look a little…washed out.'

He stared right back at her, his face set in a stern frown that brooked no argument. 'I'm bonny.'

Yes, you look it, she thought with wry amusement. Clearly he was not a man who admitted weakness.

He was a good man. A strong man. Handsome, too. But she was trying her best not to notice *that* part.

She'd spoken to Nanna about him the previous night.

'He was very sweet all day.'

'He can afford to be. He's your boss.'

'It wasn't like that, Nanna. He was charming and considerate and kind.'

'Easy on the eye, too, I bet? Don't you blush like that, young Bethan. I've seen him.'

'He's a widower, Nanna. And devoted to his daughter. I don't think he's looking for love.'

'*All* men look for love—at least until they nail down the coffin lid.'

Bethan had gone to bed that night understanding why the young women of Gilloch might all look twice at Cameron Brodie. Why wouldn't they? *She* had. All day. Stealing looks when she'd thought he wouldn't see. He was handsome, tall, rugged and broad, clearly intelligent and a dedicated father. Who *wouldn't* want to be noticed and cared for by a man like that?

It had made her think about her own love-life as she'd lain in bed alone. She hadn't given it much thought after Ashley died. She'd been concentrating on Grace. Getting them both through. Getting them through the trauma and out the other side in one piece. Men had not been on her radar because she'd given her all to Ashley—especially in those last few weeks. It had been all she'd thought about—getting through each day. She'd not given any thought to dating again. Not back then.

But now...?

Cameron Brodie was hot, no doubt about it, but they'd both had loss in their lives and that did something to a person. It marked them. Sometimes it made people afraid to talk to you, as if they didn't quite know what to say. It was a lonely experience, but it was one that united them. They'd both lost a spouse. They were both single parents with girls the same age. She felt a connection to him. An understanding. She might be on the lookout for romance, but would she find it with a colleague?

'You must be looking forward to the time you're going to have with Rosie. No more long days spent at work or rushing out in the middle of the night on call!'

He settled into the chair opposite her, looking rugged in dark jeans and a red plaid shirt. He looked as if he was going to go and chop some wood.

'I am. But I'll miss this, too. My job. All my life I

wanted to be a doctor. Never changed my mind once. And yet here I am—giving it up.'

'But only for a year!' She smiled, trying to imply that a year wasn't that long and he'd be back before he knew it. 'When you come back you'll be raring to go again.'

He nodded. Looked away. Sipped his tea. 'Sure.'

Bethan frowned. There seemed to be something more to this situation, but he clearly wasn't going to tell her about it. And why would he?

Cam got up out of his chair and started packing the items they might need. Clearly, for him, the subject was closed, and she was puzzled by the abrupt change from polite conversation to something that had touched a nerve.

What am I not seeing? Or perhaps I am seeing it, but not understanding it?

He was pale. And those shadows beneath his eyes…

Was he suffering from stress? Being a GP *could* be incredibly stressful—listening to people complaining all day about their ailments, bringing you their problems for you to solve. It heaped a whole lot of responsibility on a doctor's shoulders and not everyone could bear that easily.

She watched him pack, his large, capable hands, quickly gathering all the equipment, methodical as he ticked off a checklist, clearly back in the world of work and not listening to probing questions.

Perhaps it was best if she gave him his personal space. Clearly he didn't want her asking anything more, and she had only known him a day. It wasn't her place. Not yet.

There's still time to find out. We have nine more days of working together.

But she couldn't help but worry about him. She packed her own medical kit, stealing glances at him as he worked. She frowned.

Had the loss of his wife changed him?

Losing Ashley had deeply affected *her*.

She followed him out of the room, out of the surgery and to her car. She pressed the key fob, allowing him into the passenger side, and decided that at the end of the day, when their list was over, she would offer him a listening ear.

Perhaps all he needed was a friend who understood?

The first patient on their list was a Mrs Cromarty. Seventy-nine years old and unable to get around much because of a bad case of cellulitis in her left leg and an open wound on her foot that never seemed to heal properly. Mrs Cromarty had apparently developed the infection after a fall in her back garden, when she'd tripped over a crooked paving slab as she tended to her runner beans.

Bethan parked outside an old stone cottage that sat in a small terrace of four and grabbed her bag from the back seat. She rapped her knuckles on the front door, which was painted a pale duck-egg-blue, and smiled when she saw a small sign that said, *Only come knocking when this place ain't a rocking.*

Cam smiled at her reaction. 'Mrs Cromarty has a delicious sense of humour—despite her situation.'

It took some time for Mrs Cromarty to make it to the door, and when she did Bethan was confronted by a tiny woman who couldn't be more than five feet tall, walking with the aid of a stick.

'You must be the new doctor?' She peered around Bethan. 'Hello, Dr Brodie.'

'Morning, Vera, how are you today?' he asked.

'Still alive, so I can't complain.'

They followed Vera Cromarty—very slowly—back into her living room. It was a cosy room, with crocheted blankets draped over chairs and pristine white antimacassars on the arms for extra protection. Every conceivable surface was filled with little knick-knacks—mostly small animals—and in the middle of the sofa, curled into a tight ball, was a very large, very fat, ginger cat.

'Don't mind Moriarty. He won't mind you.' Vera settled back into a chair with a heavy sigh, slightly out of breath. 'I'd offer you tea, but it takes me so long to walk it'd be cold by the time you got it.'

'Don't worry, Mrs Cromarty, we had tea just before we left. Now, how are you today?'

'Not bad, Doctor, not bad. Can't complain.'

Bethan raised an eyebrow. 'But if you *were* to complain, what would you say?'

Vera sighed. 'Well, the leg is slowing me down, I can't move it much because it's swollen so badly. It means all my friends have to come here to see me and I don't get out. Your grandmother was here just the other day. She's a lovely woman, Mhairi. Very kind.'

Bethan smiled. So Nanna and Vera Cromarty were friends…

'She was so excited you were coming back to live with her here in Gilloch. She's been terribly lonely… so alone since she lost your grandad…and then when your poor father died, too...' Vera crossed herself. 'She had nobody. Absolutely nobody! I thought she'd die of a broken heart—I really did, poor wee thing. But look at you now—all grown up! I remember when you were a wee bairn. You were just the sweetest thing. Not that you aren't now, of course. You're beautiful! You've got your father's eyes and—' She suddenly seemed to remember something. 'I'm *so* sorry. You lost your husband, didn't you? Just terrible! *Terrible!*'

Bethan looked briefly at Cam and smiled.

'Cancer, wasn't it? You must have had an awful time. Thank the Lord that you had your own wee bairn to get you through. Grace, isn't it? Do you have a picture?'

'Er...not on me, no.' She did have a picture. It was in her purse. But she didn't feel it was appropriate to share personal details with a patient. Even if that patient already seemed to know so much about her.

'I lost my Seamus to cancer. Brutal disease. *Brutal!*'

Out of the corner of her eye she saw Cam check his watch. He looked a little antsy.

'He had it in his lungs... Mind you, he'd been a smoker all his life, so we shouldn't have been surprised, but there was no dignity in it. None at all. He suffered at the end—he truly did. If I could have put him out of his misery, then I would have done, God rest his soul. I know we shouldn't say things like that, but it's the honest truth. We wouldn't let dogs suffer the way they let my Seamus suffer. If he'd have been a wee terrier the vet would have put him down. Dr Brodie here prescribed morphine for him, but it was never enough.' She wiped her eyes and sniffed. 'Never enough...'

Bethan stared at Vera Cromarty, not sure what to

say. There had been some tough days with Ashley. Days when he'd seemed in so much pain and the Oramorph had barely touched it. Days when she'd become frustrated with her own skills as a doctor, unsure of what she could do to help him.

But there'd also been days when she'd sat by his bedside, holding his hand, and they'd just talked. Talked about everything. Silly stuff. Deep and meaningful stuff. Those were the moments she treasured. Laughing with him. Reminiscing. Remembering the good times. It had been a long time since they'd just sat together and talked. They'd always been so busy, before, both of them...

'I'm sorry for your loss, Mrs Cromarty.'

'Vera, pet.'

Bethan nodded, mindful of the time. 'Vera. Well, let me check you out, see how that wound's getting along. Are you still taking your antibiotics?'

She'd run out, she said, but when Bethan unwrapped the leg and saw that the wound still looked as if it wasn't healing, she wondered if Vera was on the *correct* antibiotics?

She checked her patient's file, to see what she'd been given so far, and saw they'd been pretty broad-spectrum.

'I'm going to take a swab of the wound, Vera. See if we can culture whatever it is that's keeping it open and get you some focused medication.'

'And that should make it better, should it?'

'Hopefully, yes.'

Bethan redressed the wound, and all the time Vera chatted non-stop about how Bethan had once played in Vera's front garden, and how she had come in with mud all over her face, having tried to eat a mud pie.

She laughed so much, trying to describe the look on the face of Bethan's mum, that Bethan was soon laughing, too, at her childhood antics.

It seemed that Vera had an endless supply of stories, and Cam eventually interrupted her by standing up. 'I'm sorry, Vera, but we must go.'

Bethan was surprised by his terse manner, but chose not to say anything. He was still technically her boss, and he *had* told her that some of their patients could talk for Scotland.

Vera nodded solemnly, clearly sad to be losing her audience. 'You tell that grandmother of yours I've got that book she was after. She can come round anytime to get it.'

'I will. Thank you. Now, you take care of yourself, and I'll call you when the results of the swab come in.'

'All right, pet. We'll speak again soon.'

'Don't get up. We'll see ourselves out.'

Bethan and Cam hurried outside, back to the car, keen to get on their way.

'I never thought we'd get away,' Cam said, sounding irritated.

'She's probably lonely if she's not getting out much.'

'Believe you me—Vera Cromarty could talk your ears off *before* she got housebound.'

Bethan smiled. 'Where to next?'

'Wide Way Farm. It's on the outskirts of the village.'

'Direct me?' She started the engine and began to drive.

There was silence in the car for a while, almost as if they were both enjoying the rest their ears were receiving, and then Cameron broke it to ask her a surprising question.

'How does Grace cope without her father?'

A flurry of thoughts and emotions swirled around her for a moment in a blizzard of uncertainty. Uncomfortably so.

She kept her gaze on the road ahead as she answered, surprised that he'd asked. 'She was a baby when he died. She never really knew him. I don't think she has any memories, and if she does it's because of the stories I've told her about him.'

He seemed to think about this. 'But she's happy?'

That question was easier. 'Yes, she is. I'm sure it will get a little more difficult when she's older. Perhaps when she's a teenager?' A thought occurred to her. 'You must have similar concerns? Because Rosie doesn't have a mother? Are you worried about her not having a maternal influence?'

He looked out of the window, away across the open fields to the gentle hues of heather and gorse, greens and purples and greys, that swept away from them off to the horizon. There was a brown partridge pecking at the ground that held his attention for a moment.

'A little.' He sounded gruff.

'Children are very resilient. We have to give them more credit.'

He didn't say anything.

'But you wouldn't be a good parent if you didn't worry. I think it's part of the job description.'

'Take the next right here.' He pointed to an upcoming lane.

She gave him a quick sideways glance. Some of his colour had returned. He looked a lot healthier than he had done this morning. But clearly he had things on his mind.

'Things get better when you get a decent night's sleep,' she said.

He turned to look at her. 'What makes you think I'm not sleeping?'

'Well, no offence, but you look like you haven't had a decent night's sleep in weeks. Have you been worrying about things? Giving up work? The changes that are coming? I can imagine it's very stressful.'

She could sense him staring at her. Considering her. She gave him a quick smile—one that she hoped conveyed friendship and not interference. She was a doctor. She couldn't help but notice the signs that his body was under stress and that he was trying to power through whatever was ailing him.

'I'm fine.'

And even though it was clear he didn't want to discuss it, she couldn't help babbling. 'It's intense, being a single parent. We have no one to share our worries and fears with, so we end up all alone with our thoughts and we carry those concerns like burdens. Sometimes we have to let go of them—even if it's just for half an hour. Have you tried doing something to reduce stress? Yoga, perhaps? Or meditation?'

She knew a lot of people who swore by these solutions. Taking some time out to just breathe and concentrate on the body and relaxation. Sometimes it could be enough to make things bearable.

Cameron laughed, but it wasn't a pleasant sound. It seemed bitter.

'Yoga? I think I'm past the point of needing the Downward Dog as a cure-all.'

'A *real* dog, then? Pets are known as great stress-relievers! Unless you already have one, of course?'

She glanced at him, saw his brow was lined with a deep frown, and suddenly wondered if she was overstepping the mark. Getting into his personal business. Trying to fix him when he was a doctor himself. And weren't medics the worst kind of patient?

'I'm sorry, Cam. This is none of my business.'

'You're right. It's not.'

I've upset him.

She wanted him to leave the practice knowing he had left it in the most capable hands. She wanted him to feel good. She *cared*. He was a fellow single parent in the trenches, for one thing!

The lane they were on took them through a gorgeous tree tunnel. It was as if Mother Nature was trying to embrace them as they drove through, and when they emerged on the other side she spotted a lone farmhouse, surrounded by flocks of woolly sheep.

'Is that Wide Way?'

'Mmm. Just follow the road and then take the left-hand turning when it comes up. And watch out for Robbie.'

'Robbie?'

'The sheepdog. He's often roaming the grounds.'

'All right... You know this patient well?'

He sighed. 'I should do. This is my grandfather's farm.'

A sense of foreboding went through her. Anticipation? Fear? She'd heard many tales about Angus Brodie. He was a formidable man, by all accounts. True, most of her knowledge about him came from her grandmother, but...

Never trust a Brodie.

And here she sat. Beside one whom she liked and respected and about to treat one she hadn't met, but who was causing her great anticipation.

Nanna had said the man had ruined her life and reputation. Cam had said he was a grumpy curmudgeon. Would he be as terrible as everyone made out?

Her hands trembled slightly as she turned into the farm's long driveway, and she hoped that Cameron didn't notice as her car rumbled along the pitted and potholed drive. She saw no dog running loose, which was good, because she didn't think they'd get off to a good start if she ran over the family sheepdog.

'What am I seeing him for?'

She should have asked earlier. If she had then she would have had time to consider everything she knew about his condition.

She wanted to walk into Wide Way Farm as a solid professional with whom Angus Brodie would find no fault. He would think of her as a good, friendly doctor whom he could trust.

He was her patient now. Not just her nanna's ex-beau. Best to set the tone for the rest of their relationship on a positive footing.

'He's developed a rash. Told me he thinks it's shingles.'

'You haven't seen him yourself?'

'No. He only rang me last night, so I made him an appointment. I told him he'd be seeing you. It's not good to treat your own family. He…er…wasn't too impressed when he found out who you were.'

'Right.'

She pulled the car to a stop and just sat there for

a moment to steady her breathing. To try and calm herself so that she could present the illusion of being a professional who was in control.

'You okay?' Cam was looking at her.

'Fine!' She tried to sound breezy, but she'd have been lying if she hadn't admitted she was nervous.

All the stories she'd heard about Angus Brodie but she'd never met him. And now here she was. Quaking in her boots. Trying to seem brave. If he'd already taken against her, he might be a difficult patient.

'We…er…we'd better go inside. He doesn't like to be kept waiting.'

The farmhouse door opened and a round woman with a huge bosom and wiry grey hair tied back in a low bun emerged, her arms open in greeting.

This was it. The lion's den.

She was trying to joke away her fear, but it was real and palpable. Nanna had made this man out to be the devil himself.

Swallowing hard, she opened the car door, her legs trembling as she grabbed her doctor's bag from the back seat. A border collie was suddenly sniffing at her trouser legs, and she held out her hand for it to sniff. The dog licked her fingertips and then ran away to smell something else.

She stood up, straightening her spine, trying to find the courage inside that she knew she'd need to get her through the next few minutes. She did have it inside her. She had got through the deaths of her parents and the death of her husband, she was raising a child alone and she was doing a great job!

Buoyed up, she walked with determination across

to where Cameron stood with the woman who could only be his grandmother.

'Mrs Brodie? Dr Bethan Monroe.' She held out her hand for the woman to shake.

Cam's grandmother beamed a smile at her. 'Hello, lass. He's in the bedroom. Hasn't got up today. I guess I ought to take you through.'

'Lead the way.'

Bethan swallowed a very tiny amount of saliva as she followed Cam and his grandmother up the stairs.

At least she's *friendly!*

Cam's grandmother led them into a large bedroom, and the first thing Bethan saw was a beautiful bedspread in shades of purple. It looked hand-quilted and stitched. And there, at the head of the bed, propped up by a vast mountain of pillows, sat an old man, with a balding pate and a white beard. Circular reading glasses were perched on the end of his nose.

'Cameron!' Angus looked pleased to see his grandson. A broad smile broke across his face, but it quickly disappeared as Bethan appeared from behind him.

Cam's grandfather looked startled. Then angry. His eyes darkened and a withered hand pointed at her. '*You*... You're the new doctor?'

She smiled, determined to make him like her. 'Yes, I—'

'You ought to be ashamed of yourself! How *dare* you come to my house? How dare you walk in here, bold as you like, treading in a dead man's shoes!'

Wait? What?

Angus pointed at Cam emphatically. 'He is *dying*! Dying! And you think you can replace him? Get out of here. I don't want to see you. *Get out!*' he raged, his voice a throaty roar.

Bethan was confused as she stared at the angry old man in the bed. His face was red with fury and rage, and Cam was doing his best to calm the old man down, but the most puzzling thing was the words that were swirling around in her brain.

'He is dying! And you think you can replace him?'

Who was dying?

The only person she was replacing was Cam, and that was just for a year...

Her eyes met Cam's and instantly she knew the truth. In his blue eyes she saw the reality of his situation. The guilt. The admission as he looked down and away.

Cam had been sick. She knew that.

But clearly whatever it was that ailed him had not gone away.

He was not going on a year's sabbatical.

He was going to die.

And he'd lied to everyone.

Including her.

She swallowed back her tears and squared her shoulders.

Bethan looked pale and shaken, but somehow she steadied her voice and met the senior Brodie's eyes.

'Mr Brodie,' she began. 'I am your doctor and you have an appointment. I am here to help you. Now, if you *do* have shingles, and you want to get better, I need to examine your rash and decide on an appropriate treatment regime.'

Her chin lifted. Clearly she was determined to stare him down if necessary.

Her courage, her bravery, astounded Cam. And it made him like her even more than he already did. No one had ever stood up against his grandfather like this. The grumpy old man had a temper bad enough to scare off rabid dogs.

And now she knows about me.

He looked down at the floor as he sucked in a breath of his own. She was persistent. She was strong. She was not the type of person to let this news go without a fight. And it irked him that he was going to have to let her get involved.

Angus stared back at her, clearly taken aback that she was not going to be cowed by him. There was a pregnant pause, an atmosphere so thick nobody could move. They all stood like statues, waiting for Angus Brodie's approval.

The old man curled his lip and looked away. 'Do what you have to.'

Cam looked at Bethan.

A small smile of triumph powered her forward to stand by his grandfather's bed.

'Okay. Let's see what we can do for you.'

CHAPTER FOUR

SHE STEPPED TOWARDS his bed. 'May I sit down?'

He looked at the chair beside his bed. 'Suit yourself.'

She pulled it closer and looked him square in the face. Her heart was racing like mad, and she felt sure there were rivulets of sweat running down her back and beneath her arms, but she forged onwards anyway.

It had taken a lot to stand up to him, but she was damned if he was going to intimidate her. She was not of her grandmother's generation. Women did not have to be cowed by patriarchal men any more.

He's dying. Cam's dying.

Her brain wanted to focus on that. The thought kept echoing around her skull. But she couldn't give it any time right now. She had to concentrate on Angus and treat him. Cameron's health would have to be touched upon later. Maybe when they were back in the car, or after they'd finished the home visits. People were depending on them to see them. To keep it together and not be distracted.

But what could it be? What was wrong with him?

Don't be cancer. Please, don't let it be cancer.

'You have a rash? Would you like to show me where?'

Angus glared at her, but slowly began to unbutton

his pyjama top, opening it to reveal an angry red, blistering rash that curved under his chest and slightly around to his back, beneath his right shoulder blade. It looked very sore and painful.

'It does look like shingles. How long have you had it?'

'A couple of days.'

She nodded and reached into her bag for a prescription pad. 'I'll write you up for some acyclovir. It won't kill the virus, but it will help stop it multiplying. You could also take paracetamol for the pain you're experiencing.'

'Right.' Angus redid the buttons on his top.

'Keep the area as clean and dry as you can, and wear loose-fitting tops like the one you have on now.'

She turned to look at Cam's grandmother.

'You can use calamine for any itching, and if any of the blisters begin to weep at all you could use a cool compress—a flannel wrung out with cool water will do. And don't share his towels with anyone else in the house.'

'Yes, Doctor,' she said.

'Anything else?' Angus asked, clearly resentful of her orders.

'If it gets any worse please call the surgery and I'll come out to see you again. See how you're doing. Is there anything else I can help you with whilst I'm here?'

Normally she wouldn't be so curt with a patient. It wasn't her style at all. But she figured that today she would keep it simple and to the point and then, over time, they might expand their trust and friendliness towards each other.

'No. I'm fine. Thank you.'

She nodded and stood up, packing away her things, snapping her bag shut and going to leave the room. In the doorway she stopped, had a thought and turned around.

'I'm a good doctor, Mr Brodie. A good person. But I'm here to be me. I'm not trying to replace anyone.'

He said nothing, so she turned to go down the stairs, but as she went she heard Angus Brodie clear his throat and speak once more.

'You're Mhairi's granddaughter.'

It wasn't a question.

She turned, wondering where this was leading. 'I am.'

He nodded, clearly uncomfortable making conversation with her. 'Your father... Mhairi's son... he's passed away?'

She gave a curt nod, not sure whether or not Angus was about to rain down insults against her dead father. If he was, she was going to stop him in his tracks! She would *not* have her father bad-mouthed.

But he didn't. He simply nodded in understanding, his eyes darkening with sadness. 'You tell her I'm sorry for her loss.' He looked up. 'And for yours.'

Bethan stood there shocked. Sympathy was the *last* thing she would have expected from Angus Brodie!

'Thank you. I'll pass that on.'

She followed Cam and Mrs Brodie down the stairs, still a little on the back foot as to what had just happened. Was that Angus's way of holding out an olive branch? Or was he seeing similarities between himself and Mhairi? Nanna had lost her son and he foresaw himself losing Cam?

They walked outside and congregated by the car.

Cam hugged his grandmother and told her he'd see her soon and Bethan studied him, looking for clues, for signs that he was dying. Could it be true? She'd seen him take painkillers a few times, but he'd always brushed it off as a headache. He was pale... And those dark circles under his eyes—were they a sign?

'I'm leaving to spend time with my daughter.'

Life didn't seem fair. He was a good man. A father. She'd hoped he would be a good friend. For some reason she didn't understand she felt a small sting of tears at the backs of her eyes—which was weird, because she barely knew him. It had to be because she liked him. Liked him a lot. She'd hoped she was making a new friend, and now she was going to lose him before they could create that friendship.

And, as she'd told him in that interview, which seemed so long ago now, she got attached quickly. She got attached and emotionally involved. She couldn't help it. It was her nature. She cared for her fellow human beings and she'd seen enough suffering in her life already.

Would she have to watch him suffer, too?

And what about Rosie?

If she knew *she* were dying, leaving Grace as an orphan...

Bethan blinked back tears and got inside the car.

As they drove away from Wide Way Farm, Cameron found himself biting down on his lip, not sure what to say.

How could he explain all that Bethan had heard and

learnt inside the farmhouse with his grandfather? Was it best to say nothing? To pretend that she'd misheard?

He shook his head, not enjoying the idea of outright lying to her. But he was angry that she was now involved. Of all the people in the world he *didn't* want to lay this on, she was the foremost. Because of what had happened with her husband. She'd already done this. She'd lost someone, and so had he, and he damn well knew how painful that was.

But he wasn't sure what to say. He'd kept her out of it for a day. Just a day! He hadn't known his grandfather would react to her so vehemently.

Now she knew, would she tell everyone else?

'I'd appreciate it if you kept what you've learnt to yourself.'

She kept her eyes on the road, her hands steady on the wheel. 'Well, it falls under patient confidentiality, doesn't it?'

She sounded hurt. Betrayed. But how could that be? They hadn't known each other long. Was it his lying that caused her to sound like that?

'I'm not your patient, but…thank you.'

She continued to drive, her eyes on the road, not once glancing at him. 'We need to talk about it, though. We can't not. Not now that I know.'

'I know.'

He looked out of the window at the low grey sky, at the dark clouds overhead threatening later rainfall. The sky was grey…the mountains were grey. Even the heathers that were normally so bright and full of colour looked dull today. Muted.

He didn't want to lay any of this at her door, but he knew he would have to tell her the full truth now.

'Why don't you come to my house after work today? Bring Grace. The girls can play and we can talk in another room.'

She was frowning. But she nodded. 'Okay. Tonight, then.'

She indicated to take a left turn and let out a long, low breath.

He glanced at her. At the small divot between her dark eyebrows, the determined set of her jaw. This was a woman who would not let him get away with any excuses. She *did* get attached and emotionally involved. Exactly as she'd warned him she would.

Cam pulled up the next patient's file. 'All right. Back to work, then. We're off to number seventeen, Hudson Road. Mrs Davina McClane.'

'Work. Yes. Absolutely.'

But he could tell the atmosphere between them had changed. No longer were they just employer and employee. No longer was it all about two colleagues working together. Now it was about two people who shared a terrible secret. It was a secret that he had no doubt would spread throughout their small community as his condition deteriorated, but for now it was theirs.

Bethan knew about death. About people dying from cancer. She'd lived through it—was a survivor of that war.

He was a soldier, fighting a losing battle.

Knowing that he was not going to win.

Bethan walked through the front door and Grace ran straight into her arms. 'Mummy!'

She scooped up her daughter and squeezed her tight, cherishing the love and comfort that her daughter gave her, inhaling her scent, enjoying the feel of her little body, relishing the moment of holding someone she loved.

Here was a pure relationship. A relationship with no secrets.

It had been a long, difficult day, and the atmosphere in the car had been strained after their visit to Angus Brodie, the friendship that they had only just begun to cultivate, already under strain.

She hoped that when she went to his home later and heard the truth—the full story—they could go back a few steps and start again. But this time from a stronger place, because this time she would know everything. But apprehension and fear filled her heart. She wasn't sure she was ready to hear such a story yet again. Such dreadful news…

'Mummy, I drew a ladybird! Come and look!'

Grace slithered from her arms and ran into the kitchen, from which delicious smells emanated. Slow-cooked beef, if she wasn't mistaken.

'Okay, I'm coming.' She hung up her coat and bag and went into the kitchen to admire her daughter's drawing. Nanna was there, seated at the kitchen table preparing vegetables. 'Hello, Nanna. Something smells nice.'

'Beef hotpot. I'm just about to steam some broccoli and carrots to go with it.' Nanna looked up at her and frowned. 'How was your day? You look done in.'

'It was long.'

She took a moment to tell Grace how beautiful her picture was, stuck to the fridge by a magnet from the Isle of Mull, and then sat down for a moment.

Grace skipped from the room and Bethan turned back to her grandmother. 'I had to see Angus Brodie today.'

Mhairi stiffened and put down her knife. 'Oh. How did that wee delight go?'

Bethan sighed. 'Horribly. He was on our list of home visits.'

'And he let you treat him? Wonders will never cease.' She picked her knife up again and continued to peel carrots.

'He told me something. Something that I...' The words choked in her throat and she knew she couldn't continue. It was not her secret to tell.

'Something?'

She decided to change the subject. 'He asked after you.'

Mhairi coloured, her lined cheeks flushing a rosy red. 'Me? Whatever for?'

Bethan shrugged. 'He just asked after you. Told me to tell you that he was sorry for the loss of Dad.'

Mhairi got up from the table, deliberately keeping her back to Bethan as she messed around by the kettle, noisily preparing two cups of tea.

'He must have heard about it and he offered his condolences.'

Mhairi slammed shut the cupboard door from which she'd got the mugs. 'Well, it was a few years ago now. He's a bit late.'

Bethan shrugged. 'I'm just passing on the message. I was surprised he even said it—I mean, I didn't think he was meant to care about you.'

'He doesn't. He was probably just being polite

because he had to be. Though that would have been a world first for Angus Brodie.'

'He wasn't polite to start with.'

'I bet!'

'He yelled at me.'

Mhairi turned, came back to the table and grabbed Bethan's hand within her own, squeezing it tight. 'Och, that *horrible* man! Are you all right?'

She nodded. 'It was okay. I told him that I was his doctor and he ought to treat me with some respect.'

Mhairi cackled. 'Och, I wish I could have been there to see that!'

Bethan smiled, then looked down at the table. 'I've been invited to Cam's tonight, but we'll eat here before we go.'

Mhairi stared. 'Why do you have to go there?'

'We have some things to discuss about today. Work stuff. I'm going to take Grace to play with Rosie— they're in the same class.'

'Och, I'm not sure I'm comfortable with all this.'

'We're just talking, Nanna. It's not like it's a *date*!'

She laughed, to relieve the tension, but Mhairi didn't laugh with her as she'd expected.

Mhairi just stared at her. 'It had better not be. Be careful, lass.' She laid a hand on hers. 'You can't trust them.'

'It's not like it's a date!'

So why was she upstairs in her bedroom, choosing what clothes to wear when she went to Cam's house?

She'd spent the entire day with him. Working. Tending to patients. All of whom had been delightful with the exception of Angus Brodie. There'd been a few tentative enquiries about her life from one or two others who knew her grandmother, but that had been it.

Some of the patients had wanted to know about her time in Cornwall. About how she'd met Ashley, about Grace, and then the horrible twists of fate that had driven her back to Gilloch, to the only family she had left.

It had made her think about Ashley's parents. About how they must be missing seeing Grace every day. They lived in Cornwall, too. In Polperro—a small fishing village on the south coast.

She'd felt guilty about leaving them behind, knowing she was taking Grace—their one connection to their son. But they'd had the first few years of Grace's life and Nanna had only ever seen her online or talked to her on the phone!

Besides, she'd had to do what she'd felt was right. She was Grace's mother and she would make the decision that was best.

I ought to call them. Maybe send one or two photos so they don't feel out of the loop.

Her wardrobe was open before her. She was *not* choosing fancy clothes to look nice for Cameron.

What did you wear to hear a confession? They were going to be talking. He was going to explain everything. Probably tell her something horrible.

She was choosing different clothes because she'd been working in these all day and she wanted to feel fresh. So she picked out an aquamarine dress and a cropped cream cardigan and lay them on her bed, before taking a shower to wash away the cares of the day. To prepare herself mentally for what lay ahead.

This time she'd got a warning.

As she stood under the spray she thought about what she would be discussing with Cam. His illness. His sickness. What could it be?

She'd been through cancer with Ashley, so she fervently hoped it wasn't that. It was such a cruel disease, and she wasn't sure she could watch someone go through that again. Which she would have to do—as a doctor, if nothing else. She would be the one caring for him, making his days as comfortable as she could.

It could be Huntington's... Motor Neurone Disease?

He was so young! To be struck down in the prime of life and with a small child to worry about...

She felt for him. In one way she'd had it easy, with Grace being a baby. She'd not had to explain to a small child what was happening to her daddy, because Grace had only just been learning to sit up and make tentative attempts to crawl when Ashley had died.

Rosie would *know*. She knew who her father was. She loved him. He was her everything.

Bethan wiped away tears at the thought of being in a similar situation, having to find the words to explain such a thing to Grace.

She wrapped her hair in a towel and went through to her bedroom, to find Nanna standing in the doorway, looking at the dress.

'Everything okay?'

She nodded, then pointed at the dress. 'That's pretty.'

'Oh, thanks. I got it ages ago.'

'It'll bring out the colour of your eyes.'

'Will it? That's not why I'm wearing it,' she said irritably, meeting her nanna's gaze. She didn't want her worrying, but Nanna knew nothing about Cam's news just yet, and she didn't feel right telling her that she was going to Cameron's house to hear about his diagnosis.

'You'll look very pretty. But then, why wouldn't you? You're a beautiful young woman. I'm very proud.'

'Thanks.'

Nanna sank onto the bed. 'Can I ask...when you met Angus today...was he really sick?'

Bethan smiled to herself. Beneath all that bluster, all that hot air, there was still a little nuance of concern for Angus Brodie.

'I can't tell you that, Nanna. Patient confidentiality.'

'Och, I know, but... He's not at death's door, or anything?'

'No. No, he's not.'

Nanna nodded, somewhat mollified. 'Good. That's good. Well, I'll let you get on with it, then. Will you be back late?'

'I shouldn't think so. I'll have Grace back for her bedtime.'

Nanna seemed happy with that, and left Bethan to get dressed.

Cam lived in a very picturesque cottage that she found instantly charming and quaint. It was made of old Highland stone, with a low thatched roof and a pistachio-green door, and the front garden contained a small blue rowing boat that was being used as a garden planter, overflowing with flowers in bright, cerise pinks and rich, heathery purples. By the front door was an old pair of wellington boots that tumbled dark green ivy onto the stepping stone path. It was whimsical, with a nod to the fishing traditions that this village had been made from. She liked it. Could almost imagine herself working in this garden herself.

'Mummy, look—a boat!' said Grace.

'Yes, I see it.'

She walked up to the front door, the nerves in her stomach chasing each other around like children playing tag, and rapped the lion's head knocker.

A few seconds passed and then Cameron was there, opening up, and a little girl with long red locks was appearing behind him. This had to be Rosie—she was the spitting image of her father.

'Hi.'

'Hey. Come on in.'

He stepped back and Rosie grabbed Grace's hand to rush her off to her bedroom to play.

Bethan had hoped that the girls would stay with them for a while, to keep the conversation and the atmosphere pleasant, but with the girls gone she rubbed at her arms and looked about the place, surprised to see such a homely home.

'This is beautiful.'

'Thanks. Can I get you a drink? Tea? Coffee? Something a wee bit stronger?'

Something a bit stronger would be perfect. To settle her nerves. A wee dram of whisky knocked back in one gulp, perhaps?

'Er...tea, please.'

'Milk and one sugar, right?'

'Yes, thank you.'

She followed him through to the kitchen. Every room she entered made her wish she had a home like this one. There was an inglenook fireplace with an old Aga, and copper pots and pans hanging from a rack on the ceiling along with sprays of dried flowers. There was even a tray of freshly baked cookies on the side, cooling under a white-netted cloche.

He bakes?

She wanted to tell him that she thought the place was amazing. That *he* was amazing. But the words stayed clogged up in her throat, refusing to come out.

'Take a seat. I won't be long.'

She sat and watched him bustle about the kitchen. He knew his way around it perfectly, and served them a tray of tea with a side plate of the freshly baked biscuits.

'Apple and cinnamon.' He offered her one.

'Thanks.' She took one and tucked it in beside her cup. 'I never imagined you as the kind of man who dons an apron.' She smiled at him.

Cam laughed and pointed at what looked like a yellow apron hanging on the back of a door. 'If it makes you feel any better, I didn't actually put it on.'

'Shame. I bet yellow is your colour.'

'With *this* hair? No.' He smiled.

She took a bite of the biscuit. It was soft and crumbly, with chunks of soft apple and a hint of spice to warm the palate afterwards. 'They're good.'

'I've had time to practise.'

'You'll have even more when you leave work.'

He nodded, looking uncomfortable.

She put the cookie down. 'This seems very odd.'

'Yeah.' He smiled ruefully.

Neither of them spoke for a moment, and the tension between them hung in the air like a thick fog. Neither of them was sure how to make a start in the conversation.

When it became clear that Cam couldn't start it off, she decided to take a step.

'So...your grandfather said some pretty startling things today.'

A nod. 'He did.'

'He accused me of stepping into a dead man's shoes. Said that you were...dying.'

She said it quietly, pausing for a moment to study his face—the weariness that was now in his eyes, the dark shadows beneath. He looked like a pale Scottish vampire.

'What did he mean? I need to know if I'm to help you.'

Death was not a new thing to Bethan. She was accustomed to hearing about it. About hearing diagnoses, delivering them herself. She just hadn't expected to hear it from him.

'I don't want to be a burden to anyone. I know you've had enough of that in your life already. I wasn't going to tell you anything.'

'You were going to try and keep this secret?'

He nodded again. 'It seemed the best way.' He sounded resigned to his fate. 'When you told me about your husband, I knew I couldn't let you know about me.'

'So it's true?'

'Yes.'

'What is it?' She felt a churning deep in her stomach.

He sighed and gazed back at her, considering his answer. 'It's a high grade-four glioma, near my optic nerve. They say it's near impossible to operate on. That I have probably less than a year left. A year I want to spend with Rosie.'

A glioma. Brain cancer. *Dammit.*

Her face flushed hot. Her mind flooded with knowledge about the condition, all that she knew rushing to the forefront as if a dam had burst. This wasn't fair! A surge of anger almost overwhelmed her, but as her mind raced she remained calm outwardly, like a swan on the surface of the water.

'What symptoms do you have?'

'I get headaches and nausea. Mood swings. They tell me I might lose my sight, if it invades the optic nerve—which it probably will do, seeing as it's fast-growing and aggressive.'

Cancer. Damn!

'Cameron...' She reached out to lay her hand on his. An instinctive gesture. She needed to make contact, to give comfort. She wasn't worrying about it being misunderstood—she just needed to touch him. To make him know that he wasn't alone. And it felt good. It felt *right.*

She met his gaze and saw that he was staring at her hand on his. As if he wasn't used to it. As if she'd done the oddest thing possible. Had she made him uncomfortable? She withdrew it.

Cameron cleared his throat and got to his feet and began to pace the kitchen. 'Before you ask, I've had chemo and radiotherapy. There's nothing more to be done.'

'I can't believe this. It seems so unfair.'

'Life isn't fair—as *you* know all too well.'

'They can't operate? Not at all? Surely they could remove *some* of it?'

'It would just keep growing back. And the trauma on my body of countless operations—'

'But if it gave you more time—'

'What would be the quality of that extra time if it was spent in a hospital bed? What's the point of all that if it just gives me more time hooked up to a drip, feeling like I'm at death's door anyway? I don't want Rosie seeing me like that.'

'No...of course not.'

But her mind was racing, thinking of who she knew—who might be able to help. Friends of friends... colleagues of colleagues. Someone must know *something* to give this man more time with his child. To give Rosie more time to make memories with her father. To give *her* more time with him.

She liked him. Liked this man. Her colleague. Her employer. She sensed that he would be a good friend if they had the time to develop their friendship. He was a decent man. Kind and caring. She didn't want to lose him. She'd just met him.

I'm staring at him.

She looked away. Away from those blue eyes of his. Eyes that held such intelligence and yet also sorrow and resignation and regret. They were haunting. One look saw far too much.

'Don't be sad for me, Bethan. I don't need pity.'

'How can I not be sad when this doesn't seem fair?'

From the other room, they heard the delightful sounds of laughter from the two girls. Two girls enjoying life and having fun.

'Many things aren't fair. But we make the best of them because of those we love. Right now my daughter is in the other room and she doesn't know—fully— what's coming. I tried to tell her. To prepare her. But I couldn't say the words. I just said I was ill and I would have to go away. For ever. Do you know what she said? She said, *"Daddy, you're a doctor. You can make yourself better."* When I told her that I couldn't, that it didn't work that way and that I wasn't the indestructible superhero she'd always imagined me to be, she got angry. And I had to let her be angry, so she could process it.'

He sighed again. 'Now *you* need to process it. I know it stinks—*I know this*—and so do you. But we need to make the best of it. For our own peace of mind.'

She knew he was right. But that didn't make it any better. More than anything she wanted to get on her computer and start researching this. There had to be something they could do. A medical trial? Some new research?

But, more than anyone, she knew the poisonous touch of hope. Hope made you think you could escape something bad. Hope made you an optimist. Made you think anything was possible. And when you finally realised that there was no point in hope... That was the crash. The deep, agonising roar of pain and depression as hope receded and reality punched its way into your life.

People thought they could cheat death. They always tried. Especially doctors.

'Let me help you, Cam.'

'I don't need you to be my doctor. Just my friend.'

She leaned forward, emphatic. '*I am* your friend.'

He sat down again and he reached for *her* hand this time. Squeezed her fingers in a thank-you gesture. *Thanks for saying that. I appreciate it.*

That was all it was.
Right?
So why was her heart beating so fast?

CHAPTER FIVE

THEY WERE A week into working together. Bethan found herself concentrating hard on work, but also concentrating hard on keeping an eye on Cam. Each morning he arrived to work with her she would ask him the same question.

'How are you feeling today?'

To begin with he'd borne her concern well, but by the third day he'd begun to lose patience.

'You don't have to check on me every day, you know!'

'I'm sorry. I'm just concerned about you, that's all. How could I not be?'

He'd looked a little abashed then. Rubbed his face with his hands. 'I'm sorry, too. I shouldn't have bitten your head off like that. Can we start again?'

And she had smiled, nodded. Keen for them to be on good terms.

In between patients she would turn to him and engage him in conversation, trying to keep their conversation bright and chirpy.

She'd found during the time she'd spent with Ashley that keeping a positive mental attitude had helped a lot—for both of them—so she was applying it to this situation. It was better than dwelling on the alternative.

Plus, she was feeling on edge. Finding herself in such a situation again. She wanted to help. To do something. But Cam seemed resigned to his fate, so she wasn't sure what was best to do. His moods swung wildly from day to day. Sometimes he was short of temper, and at other times he was the sweetest guy ever!

As he had been with what had happened with Andy Glen.

Andy had come in with a severe cough that he'd had for at least two weeks.

Bethan had listened to his chest, taken his temperature, but everything had seemed normal enough. There had been no extraneous sounds in his lungs…his chest had seemed clear.

'It's just a virus, Mr Glen. I know it's miserable, but you're just going to have to wait for it to clear on its own.'

Mr Glen had not looked happy with that response. 'You what? I've been coughing my guts up for a bloody fortnight—you think I'm going to keep on doing that? Give me some antibiotics!' His voice had risen with irritation and anger.

'Antibiotics won't make the slightest bit of difference to you, Mr Glen. In fact, they could even make you worse.'

'Don't give me that old rubbish! I've been watching the news. I've seen you doctors, trying to cut back on how many you give out. It's all about the money, ain't it? Rather than people!'

'I can assure you, Mr Glen—'

Mr Glen had stood up, his face a mask of anger, ready to rain down a storm of abuse and bile.

Bethan had shrunk back in her chair, but before

she'd been able to do anything Cameron had leapt to his feet and taken Mr Glen by the arm.

'You need to calm down, Andy!' he'd said. His voice firm and brooking no nonsense.

'Calm down? Why should I?'

'Because I won't tolerate abuse in this surgery, and your treatment of a doctor who is doing her best to care for you in the correct manner is rude and threatening.'

Andy had blustered for a moment, his cheeks reddening, before he had to cough again, covering his mouth with his sleeve. 'Do you hear that? All that phlegm? I can't get rid of it!'

'As Dr Monroe stated, very clearly, it will go away of its own accord.'

Andy had looked at Bethan, then back at Cameron. 'I want *you* to check me over.'

'There's no need. Dr Monroe has done a thorough examination.'

Andy had shrugged off Cameron's hand, still on his arm. Then, glaring at the pair of them, he'd stormed out, slamming the door behind him for good measure.

Cameron had turned to her immediately. 'Are you all right?'

She'd nodded, a little shaken.

It was hard sometimes. Patients came to see their doctors determined to come away with pills, or creams, or *something* to make them feel something was being done. But in lots of cases nothing *could* be done, and in the case of most viruses they had to burn out by themselves.

She'd forgotten what it was like to face an angry patient.

'Thank you for that.'

He'd sat back in his chair behind her. 'It's a problem sometimes. I guess the one thing I haven't shown you is the red button.'

She'd raised her eyebrows.

'Look under your desk.'

She'd done so, and spotted a discreet red button situated to the far right.

'It's a silent panic button. I had it installed a while back, for cases such as this. When I was going through chemo, and often felt weak or ill, some patients tried to take advantage and I didn't have the strength to see off the ones who got a little *demonstrative*. Press it and it will bring people running in. In case you need it when I'm no longer here.'

It was thoughtful. And just the kind of thing she'd expect a kind and considerate man like him to do. She hated the fact that people had tried to take advantage of his sickness to better their own interests.

She'd smiled at him. 'Thanks.'

She didn't want to think of him as *no longer here*. That just seemed so terribly final.

She'd put out a few feelers. Contacted other doctors she knew, asked them for their opinions. But they'd come back to her to say that they couldn't really give a definitive answer without seeing Cameron's scans and reports—which she knew were on the system, but she also knew she couldn't share them with anyone without his approval. She'd looked at them herself, of course, and had felt her heart sinking on seeing them.

But she was only a GP. Not a neurosurgeon. What did she know about it for sure?

At the end of morning surgery, before they went into lunch, she turned to him and smiled.

Cameron raised a suspicious eyebrow at her. 'Okay, what's going on?'

'Cam, I've been thinking a lot just lately. About your situation and I've got in touch with a few people...' She saw him roll his eyes and then he sat back in his chair, his arms folded, as he listened out of politeness. 'They're people who might be able to help, but they'd need to see your scans and medical history and I wondered if—'

'No, Bethan.'

'But, if it could help...'

'No one can help me! Do you think I've not tried to find a way out of this situation? Do you think I'm just rolling over and waiting to die? That some quack told me I have a year and I've just gone, *Oh, okay, fine!* I've *looked.* I've *searched.* I've found nothing.'

'But how long ago was that? A month? Two months? You know things can change quickly in medicine— advances are being made all the time! I know a colleague in Edinburgh who's doing amazing deep brain laser surgery. Please let me show him your scans.'

'I don't see the point.'

'Well, I do!'

A small smidgen of anger entered her tone and she blushed at hearing it. Shouting at her boss? She took a breath. And another. Allowing herself a moment to get that back under control.

'If they say they can't help, then you haven't lost anything, have you? But if they say there might be something, then...' She let Cameron fill in the blanks in his own head. The implication was there. A chance. Maybe. Who knew, if they didn't try? She knew she was walking him down that road of hope again, but it might be worth it.

Cameron sighed and got up out of his chair to pace the small room.

She watched him and waited, hoping desperately that he would say yes. He was such a wonderful man. She really liked him and he had a wicked sense of humour. Some of the jokes he had told her over the past few days!

And he'd kept her buoyed up when she'd had to treat old Jenna Jackson and her advanced Motor Neurone Disease; he'd passed her tissues when she'd cried after spending an hour with a woman who'd recently miscarried.

'It's going to be okay,' he'd said. 'Are you all right?'

She'd sniffed, dabbing at her nose. 'It's just so *sad*. She really wanted that baby. To see her break down like that…'

Just remembering the woman weeping in front of her had set Bethan off again. It had reminded her of the time she'd thought she was miscarrying Grace, having an early bleed. She'd never felt so much fear. Never felt so much terror. She'd been lucky. She hadn't lost her baby. But her poor patient had.

She'd leaned into Cameron in that brief moment, appreciating his strength and warmth, his arm around her shoulder as he'd waited for her to gather herself, the truly strange feeling of having someone support *her* for a change.

So why wouldn't he let her do the same for him?

'Fine. Go ahead,' he said now.

'Really?' A smile broke out across her features and

she jumped from her chair like an excited schoolgirl and pulled him to her for a hug.

It was just meant to be a thank-you. She stood there, wrapped in his arms as he laughed with her, and then the laughter stopped and she realised. *I don't want to let him go.* She was pressed up against his body and how good that felt.

Guilt rushed through her with the strength and power of a tsunami and she quickly let him go. Blushing. Hot. Unable to meet his gaze, which she could feel upon her.

I've overstepped the mark.

She glanced up at him. Once. Her Princess Diana look, Nanna had once called it. Tucked her hair behind her ear. 'Thanks.'

He swallowed, staring at her, seemingly just as shocked as she was. 'It's okay.'

Bethan sank back down into her chair and for the want of nothing else to do powered down the computer so they could go to lunch.

Being up against Cameron had felt so good! The feel of a strong, powerful man in her arms again had been… She couldn't think of the words. All she knew was that it had felt good. He had *smelt* good. She had felt his hands upon her—one on her shoulder blade, the other in the small of her back—and it had suddenly felt as if his hands were made of blazing fire and her skin was being seared by his touch, even through her clothes.

Awareness of this man… Cameron Brodie…

Am I falling for him? Forget all that. That's not why you're here. Concentrate on the fact that you've got his permission.

'Right… I…er… I guess we ought to go for lunch.'

'Aye, we ought to.'

He seemed just as unsure as she did. Awkward. Uncomfortable. She'd practically thrown herself at him—he must have wondered what the hell was going on.

It was embarrassing. She didn't know what had got into her. But she felt a fire inside her. A fire that needed feeding in her pursuit to help Cam fight his condition. Because she wasn't ready to let him go. She felt there was a chance with him. A chance she and Ashley had never had. There was time.

I really like him.

They'd just met. She was only just getting to know him. And it wasn't fair that someone so lovely could possibly be taken from her.

Again.

Was that it? Was her psyche, her heart, fed up with being robbed? Life had taken her parents from her. It had taken Ashley. And she had returned to Gilloch to start anew. A fresh beginning, away from all that trauma and pain. And now life was trying it on again. By threatening to take Cam. By threatening to make her play out the same role in the same horrifying nightmare.

She wanted to fight it. She wanted to win! Surely it was her turn? Because death wasn't supposed to be here in Gilloch for her. This place was about life and love. The open, loving arms of her grandmother. Her birthplace. New friends.

Cameron Brodie.

She had to admit, even if only to herself, that she felt something for him. She knew it was true—there was no point in denying it. Maybe if it had been different circumstances, then...

But the way he looked at her. Those sparkling blue eyes. The way he laughed—so open and warm. Genuine. He was a gentleman. Kind. A good listener. A great doctor.

And she wanted more time with him.

A year would not be enough.

She had to fight for him.

It was what a friend would do.

He knew she was just trying to help. Just doing her job in the best interests of a patient. Only he *wasn't* her patient. He was her colleague. Her boss. Her...*what?*

It felt like something more.

She had been right. Absolutely right when she'd told him at her interview that she got attached quickly. Emotionally involved. He could see that in her eyes. A fiery determination to beat his diagnosis, as if she was some crazy magician who had one last rabbit to draw out of the hat.

But he was disturbed. More disturbed than he had been in a long time. And he was a man who had heard he only had a year to live recently.

Something was happening between them. He could feel it. A small flame of something, burning quietly in the background. They were both studiously trying to ignore it—because he was *dying*, and what was the point in getting involved with someone? Especially someone who'd lost her own husband to cancer?

He couldn't put her through all that again, though he felt instinctively that she was prepared to do it. He knew what it was like to stand by a graveside and weep.

He knew what it was like to miss someone so much you often felt as if you couldn't breathe.

He had to keep a distance between them. So sudden hugs when they were alone together were not a good idea! The way she'd felt in his arms had been... He shook his head to try and clear the image. She'd felt so good! He'd leaned his head on top of hers and inhaled the scent of her hair, and his eyes had closed in delight as he'd squeezed her tighter against him.

It had been a subconscious response, he hadn't realised he was doing it, and she had jumped out of his arms so fast!

He missed holding a woman. He missed having someone to lean on. To share things with. And, although she'd only been with him for a week, he'd found himself telling her things he hadn't expected.

Bethan was so easy to talk to—she invited confidences. Just last week he'd told her about some of the things he had on his Bucket List. He'd looked at her sheepishly.

'It's not daredevil stuff. It's nothing amazingly brilliant, like some people want. It's more the simple things, small pleasures—watching the sunrise; learning how to play the piano; falling in love one last time...'

He'd blushed at that last one. He hadn't meant to share it. It was an intensely private wish that he'd thought he would never admit out loud. But he missed what he'd had with his wife, and this diagnosis made him feel so alone—even though he had Rosie and his family. He was lonely. Separate from everyone else. He yearned for those heady days of falling in love, but knew it would never happen again—because who would fall for a man with a death sentence?

And who said you had to fall in love with a person? You could fall in love with a language, with food, with music. It could be anything! He just hadn't explained it properly.

Blushing, he'd found himself tongue-tied when he'd seen the look on her face.

She'd smiled at him. 'I think those things sound wonderful. And you never know...'

'Well, I know about that last one.'

'Why not? Why couldn't you fall in love again?'

'It would be unfair to the other person. I couldn't allow it. No matter how much I wanted it.'

He'd liked sitting with Bethan, chatting easily to her, seeing her beautiful smile and hearing her gentle laughter, aware of her caring nature, her ability to invite people to talk and confess their inner secrets...

But he felt bare in front of her now. A wee bit exposed. He wasn't ungrateful for her help, the fact that she was still trying, but he'd done that part—denial. He had raged against his diagnosis, had been determined that *somehow* he would find someone to help him.

He hadn't.

And that had been the difficult part. Having every specialist he'd asked tell him that they were very sorry, but there was nothing they could do. That he had to accept it and live his life the best way he could. Let go of hope.

So, he might not allow himself to fall in love, but it did look as if he would bow out of this life with one amazing brand-new friend at his side...and the idea of that pleased him.

He'd been so determined to keep everyone out. To put up fences, barriers. To keep his distance, make his passing less painful for those who worked with him or knew him.

It would be different for his family, of course. For his father, burying his only son. For Rosie, losing her father. He could not make it better for them, but he could damn well make it better for everyone else.

And now he had Bethan. She was different, somehow. She understood. She *knew* what he was going through without him having to say.

He hadn't realised how much he'd needed that. How much he needed *her*.

He wanted to embrace it so badly!

But he was terrified of what it might ultimately mean...

Cameron kissed his grandmother on the cheek. 'How is the old monster?'

'Itchy. And grumpy. As per usual.'

He smiled. 'Thought I'd come and check on him. See how he's doing with the antibiotics Bethan prescribed.'

'He's doing well. And the rash hasn't got any worse.' His grandmother began to brew a new pot of tea.

'I thought she was very nice, Dr Monroe. 'tis a shame your grandfather bit her head off the way he did. If he hadn't been so ill I would have given him a clout. Shameful behaviour, it was.'

'You won't hear me disagreeing with you.'

He settled onto a kitchen chair, feeling weary after a long day at the surgery. Bethan was doing very well now. She knew her way through the practice computer like a hacker. He even suspected she knew how to make it do a few things that even *he* didn't know about! And everyone was warming to her charm, her ready smile and listening ear. He'd made a very good choice.

'And how are *you* doing, laddie?'

'Not bad, considering.'

'Where's Rosie?'

'She's at Bethan's. Play date.'

She smiled. 'Let's not mention that wee bit of info to your granda'.'

He laughed. 'No.'

His grandmother studied him as she set down the tea before him. 'She's a bonny lass.'

'Rosie?'

'Dr Monroe.'

'Is she? I hadn't noticed,' he lied, sipping from his hot drink and hoping that his grandmother would change the subject and not notice the flare of heat he felt in his cheeks. Hopefully she would put it down to the steaming tea.

'Mhairi must be very pleased to have her back in the fold.'

'I know.'

And then, as was the way with some people of the older generation, even though they'd already told you a story once, they wanted to tell it again.

'They used to go out together. Your granda' and Mhairi. They were quite the lovebirds, by all accounts.'

'I remember him saying.'

His grandmother looked rueful. 'They always say you never forget your first love, don't they?'

Did she think her husband still had a thing for Bethan's nanna? Had she been upset that his grandfather had asked after Mhairi after all these years?

He peered at her closely. 'He's *your* first love, though, isn't he?'

She smiled and nodded, her cheeks flushed. 'Aye. He is.'

Cameron felt the need to reassure her. 'He does love you, you know. Just because you weren't his first love, it doesn't mean he loves you any less.'

'I know.' She patted his hand and looked at him. 'And just because you've had one great love, it doesn't mean you can't have another.'

Cam frowned. 'What do you mean?'

She laughed. 'You'll work it out, laddie.'

He looked down at the old kitchen table, ingrained and scored by decades of wear and tear. Was she saying he could still have a chance to fall in love? Despite the ticking of the clock? Who would be foolish enough to give him that?

'So…do you want to go upstairs and say hello to the old stick-in-the-mud?'

He looked up, laughed and nodded. 'Why not?'

Bethan was drinking pretend tea out of a small pink plastic tea cup with Grace and Rosie in her daughter's bedroom.

The two girls had been merrily playing outside in Nanna's back garden for a while, but the already overcast skies had started to darken and grumble and so they'd come indoors, looking for something to do. Now they all sat around a small table, sipping their 'tea' with dolls and teddies in attendance.

'Mummy, do we have any cake?' asked Grace.

'I'm not sure. Shall I go and check?'

'Yes, please.'

She hurried downstairs, glad for the chance to stretch her legs and her back, aching from being seated on the floor. There wasn't any cake downstairs, but she did find a half-packet of biscuits, so decided to take those upstairs.

As she got closer to her daughter's room she could hear the two girls chatting, and she slowed to listen when she heard Rosie's voice.

'I don't have a mummy like you do.'

'You don't have a mummy?'

'No. Just a daddy.'

She heard Grace sigh. 'I don't have a daddy.'

'My daddy is going to go away soon.'

'On holiday?'

'No. Just away. And he won't be coming back.'

'Who will be your daddy, then?'

'Grandpa Doug. I'm going to live with him. I like it there, he has dogs.'

'I wish we had a dog. I love animals.'

'Me, too.'

Bethan could feel her heart pounding in her chest. She hadn't known how much Rosie knew, but clearly Cameron had tried to talk with her about the future. It was heartbreaking, listening to the two girls chat about something so huge and life-changing, and she had to fight her instinct to rush inside Grace's bedroom and pull both girls into her arms and hug them.

'I know,' Grace said. 'You could come and live with us!'

Bethan chose that moment to head back in, before *that* conversation could develop.

'I've got biscuits!' she declared, waving the packet

before her, hoping that the promise of a sugary snack would steer the conversation back onto safer ground.

'Mummy? Could Grace come and live with us when her daddy goes away?'

'Oh, I'm not sure, honey…'

'Or you could marry Rosie's daddy and then we'd both have a mummy and a daddy.'

Oh, dear. The biscuit thing clearly hadn't worked.

She felt her cheeks flush and her jaw work as she fumbled for the right thing to say. She sighed with relief when, downstairs, the doorbell rang. *Saved by the bell.*

'Let me see who that is,' she said.

Nanna was out. She'd popped round to see Vera Cromarty to pick up a book, and had no doubt stopped for a tea and natter. Gratefully, she ran down the stairs to see who it was.

She pulled open the door. 'Cameron! Hi, come on in.'

'Thanks. How's it gone?'

Bethan hadn't realised how quickly the time had passed. A quick glance at the clock in the hallway showed that it was seven p.m.—the time he'd said he'd pick up Rosie.

'Good! The girls have loved it. They really are very good friends. Rosie's been no bother at all. I hardly noticed she was here.'

Which was a lie, because of course she'd noticed. Wanting to make sure the little girl had a good time, she'd hovered in the background to keep an eye on both of them. She hadn't been able to help it, knowing she was responsible for Cameron's little girl.

She had watched Rosie play, marvelling at that gloriously long red hair of hers, at her bright blue eyes so like her father's. She'd studied her, looking for signs of her mother, wondering which of her traits had been passed down.

'That's great. Thanks for having her over.'

'Are you kidding? Grace wouldn't stop asking me. I hope you've had a pleasant couple of hours in peace?'

'Kind of. I went to see my grandparents.'

She nodded. 'Oh. How is Angus? Coping okay?'

'He is. As well as can be expected.'

Bethan ushered him through to the kitchen rather than have him standing in the hallway. She proffered a chair and sat opposite.

'Does he need me to pop in again?' She would do it if she had to, no matter what. If her patient needed her…

'No, he's doing okay.'

'That's good. I might give him a ring at some point, then. Just to check in.'

'He'd probably like that.'

Cam smiled and she knew he meant the opposite. Some people just didn't like doctors, but Angus Brodie was a different fish-filled kettle!

Behind them, they both heard a key in the front door. Nanna was back.

Bethan smiled. 'I'll get the kettle on.'

'That'll be lovely, lassie. Vera can't half chat, and she makes a lousy brew.' Nanna bustled into the kitchen and smiled at Cameron. 'Och, hello, pet.'

'Hello, Mhairi.' He stood and smiled at her.

Nanna looked at both of them, a smile on her face. 'So what have you two lovebirds been chatting about, then?'

'Nanna!'

Mhairi chuckled to herself. 'Och, don't mind me, I'm just playing with you.'

Cameron smiled at them both, the ultimate gentleman, politeness personified. 'I'd better get going. See if I can tear my wee lass away.'

Bethan stood up, too. 'They're in Grace's room.' She followed him to the bottom of the stairs. 'Girls? Rosie? Your dad's here to take you home.'

'I want to stay here!' Rosie called down.

'Come on, Rosie. We must be off, if you're to have a bath before bed.'

There were some gentle grumbling noises from Grace's bedroom and then the two girls came trotting down the stairs, both smiling.

Rosie threw herself into her daddy's arms. Bethan smiled at the two of them. Their easy nature with each other. It was clear to anyone that they had a great relationship. One that would soon be soured when Cam's health deteriorated.

'Thanks once again for having her over.'

'It was no trouble.'

'Perhaps I could cook you dinner as a thank-you, one night? Maybe this Friday? After my last day at work? You can celebrate getting rid of me.'

Dinner. With Cameron. At his place.

Her heart thudded. She knew Nanna would be listening and putting two and two together and coming up with four hundred.

'Oh...er...'

'It's just a thank-you. For everything, really. Come on—say yes. I promise I can cook as well as bake. I'm not going to give you a ready meal from the microwave.'

She didn't know what to say to this sudden surge of friendliness. She wanted to say yes, but she knew if she spent an hour or two staring at this man across a table her feelings for him would intensify. But if she said no that would be rude and would make their time together awkward.

'All right. That would be lovely, thank you.'

'Okay. Say seven o clock?'

'Perfect.' She waved them both goodbye from the front doorstep, watching as Cam opened the car door for his daughter and made sure she was strapped in properly before getting into the driver's seat. He was such a good father. And a great doctor. An amazing man. He was so brave in what he was facing.

She'd spent hours each night, sitting up in bed with her laptop on her lap, scrolling through websites and published medical papers on gliomas, surgeries and morbidity rates. She would always fall asleep exhausted, her mind running through tables of figures and trial data.

Easy bedtime reading it was not. But she was determined to find something that would help him. Even if it was just some extra time with his daughter. Rosie deserved it. *He* deserved it.

Cam gave her one last wave and a cheery smile as he drove away, and Bethan became aware of her nanna standing close behind. 'I suppose you heard that.'

'Heard what, lass?' Nanna asked.

'Hmm…' Bethan closed the front door and raised an eyebrow as she turned to face her. 'Really?'

Nanna's face was the perfect mask of innocence.

Except for her all-knowing smile.

She couldn't quite believe it. Her two weeks with Cam were nearly up. This was to be their last day working together. One last day of appointments in the surgery.

Two weeks ago she'd yearned to be at the stage when she would work unaccompanied. Had ached for the moment when she would take over fully, flying solo as the only doctor in Gilloch.

Now she had other thoughts. Other feelings. Perhaps some she didn't want to examine too closely.

She felt a responsibility for Cam's wellbeing. Was watching over him. Perhaps it was because that had been her role with Ashley—who knew?—but she felt the need to keep an eye on him. And with him not being around after today she was beginning to feel a little anxiety creeping in.

Time had gone so quickly. She'd enjoyed sharing his workspace, his patients, working together with him, talking with each other, discussing patients, breaking down their method of approach to each case.

Alone, they had made each other smile and laugh, and she had been bowled over by his kindness, his commitment to his work. And that was made even more evident now, when he arrived in the surgery with a sheaf of papers—detailed lists of what he had to do each day, each week, each month and each year, so that she wouldn't miss anything.

'In case there's something I've forgotten, Janet should be able to point you in the right direction—or the office manager, of course.'

'Thank you for these, Cam, they're great.'

He looked pale again today. More so than he had before. She didn't want to start her day with the same question she asked him every day, but his pallor, forced it from her lips.

'How are you doing today?'

He shrugged. 'So-so.'

'If you're not well you could go home and get some rest, whilst Rosie is at school, and we could do dinner another day.'

She was trying to make it easier for him. Trying to lighten the load. She remembered what it had been like for Ashley when he'd forced himself into doing activities when he'd felt poorly, simply exhausting himself and making himself worse.

'It's all right. I promised you two weeks and two weeks I will do. Besides, I'm just going to be sitting in that chair. It's not as if I'm operating on someone. I've taken my painkillers—they'll kick in soon.'

'Well, if you're sure?'

'I'm sure.'

'Let me at least check your blood pressure.' She bent to pick up the cuff.

'No!' he snapped, instantly looking aghast at the way he'd raised his voice to her. 'Sorry. I'm fine. You don't need to check on me.'

Was it simply anger? Irritation? Or was it a sign of the mood swings that gliomas could cause? She'd read about those—that as the glioma grew it could cause uncharacteristic behaviour and mood swings. It could cause patients to be reckless—and fearless, too.

He'd never raised his voice to her before. He had always been gently spoken. Wonderfully so, with that soft Scottish burr.

He looked appalled with himself. 'I'm sorry, I...'

'It's okay.'

'No, it's not. I...' He let out a sigh. 'It was appalling behaviour. I guess there's a bit of Angus in me after all?' He tried a smile to lighten the joke, but it fell flat.

She was worried about him. Incredibly so.

He sank into his chair by the window and the light from the weak sunshine increased the shadows upon his face. He looked a haunted man.

She had to fight the urge to go to him and drape her arms around him, pull him close. Just to give him a hug, to show him that it was all right, that she was here, that she would help him through this. That he didn't have to fight this alone.

But she didn't.

Instead she awkwardly sank into her seat and pressed the buzzer for their first patient of their last day.

She gave him one last look, but he didn't see. He was rubbing at his face, as if weary and tired, and she had to look away again as their patient arrived.

In walked Mrs McConnell, her step determined, her face meaning business.

'I'm not here about me, Doctor, I'm here about my husband, Don.'

'Oh? What appears to be the trouble?'

'He's driving me mad, I tell you. Every time I speak to him I have to repeat myself three times, four times, because the daft old beggar can't hear me! He's gone deaf. But will he come to see you to have it checked out? Will he heck!'

Bethan smiled. She could imagine it would drive someone batty if they had to keep repeating themselves.

'Well, he really needs to make an appointment, Mrs McConnell. I can't check him out like this. Would he let me visit him at home? He might just need his ears syringed.'

Mrs McConnell sighed. 'Would you do that? Visit him at home? I wouldn't tell him in advance, though—

he'd go out and leave me in the lurch. We'll keep it a surprise from him.'

Bethan understood, but she wasn't fond of surprising someone at home. 'It might be best if he *does* know, Mrs McConnell. I'd hate him to think we were ganging up on him.'

'Ganging up on him is much better than me whacking him over the head with a frying pan, lassie! Which I'm sorely tempted to do right now!'

Bethan made an appointment on the system and put Don McConnell on her home visit list.

Her first home visits without Cam.

Mrs McConnell took a closer glance at Cam. 'Perhaps you ought to put this one on your list, too. He looks a wee bit peaky again.'

'Oh, don't you worry, Mrs McConnell. I'll be keeping a good firm eye on him.'

Her patient nodded glumly. 'What would these men do without us, huh?'

CHAPTER SIX

THE QUESTION WAS, what to wear for dinner at Cam's house?

It was a thank-you dinner, a goodbye dinner, a handing-over-the-reins dinner, and she wanted to look as if she'd made an effort—but she didn't want to look as if she was dressing up for a man. Nanna would spot it a mile off, for a start, and—as she kept telling herself—she was not trying to date Cam. She was not trying to attract him in any way.

So why was she standing in front of her wardrobe, yet again, wondering what to wear? She had plenty of smart casual clothes that she wore for work and every day, but hardly any *going out* clothes.

There had never been any reason to go out for years—she'd just looked after Grace and stayed at home. Occasionally she'd go to a friend's house, but that had always been a girlfriend's house and that was different.

There was one dress in her wardrobe that was smart enough for dinner, but she didn't know whether she should wear it…

'Just wear the damn dress, Bethan,' she muttered to herself, grabbing at the hanger and slipping into it, pulling up the side zipper and twisting and turning in front of the mirror to make sure it still looked okay.

She'd lost some weight. Stress, probably.

By the time she made it downstairs she was wearing make-up and heels and dangly earrings, and she stood awkwardly in front of Mhairi, waiting for some acerbic comment.

'You look very nice, lass.'

'That's it? *Nice?*'

Nanna nodded. 'Aye.'

'You don't think it's too...flirty?'

'Well, what do *you* think?'

Bethan lifted her chin, determined to stand her ground. 'I think it strikes the right balance of professional, smart and feminine. It's a dress that I'm wearing because it suits me and nobody else.' She gave one firm nod of her head. 'And it's not *for* anyone else.'

'Okay, then.'

'Right, well... I'll be off. You'll call me if I'm needed? If Grace doesn't settle?' Bethan picked up her mobile and slipped it into her bag.

'She'll be fine. *We'll* be fine. Now, get off with you. Time's a-ticking.'

It was. And she still hadn't told Nanna that Cameron was sick.

'I'll see you later, then.'

The lamb shanks were roasting nicely in the oven, filling the cottage with a delicious aroma. The steamer was quietly cooking the baby potatoes and assorted veggies, and in the fridge sat a tiramisu that had been made with a few wee drams of the Scotch his granda' had given him.

He'd almost given in and got a shop-bought dessert. He felt so exhausted today. So tired. The pain in his head had been quietly hammering away all day, with the painkillers not really doing much to touch it. He hoped he would improve tomorrow. He hoped that this was not going to be the state of affairs for the rest of his time left on this earth.

He'd snapped at not just Bethan today, but also Janet, when she'd asked him to sign off on some prescriptions as he was on his way out of the door. And then at Rosie, when she'd nagged him over and over about getting a puppy, because a friend at school had just got one and it was, *'The only thing she wanted in the whole, wide world, ever. Pleeeease?'*

She'd just not let it go! And he'd turned on her like an ogre, roaring at her to go to her room.

Afterwards he'd felt so guilty. He'd knocked on her bedroom door and asked if he was allowed in, and when she had let him come in he'd found her cross-legged on her bed, her face stained with tears.

That had almost broken his heart.

But not enough to grant her wish of having a puppy. Puppies took commitment and time, and time wasn't on his side. Having a puppy wasn't his decision to make any more. He'd need to ask his father, because he'd be the one looking after Rosie when he was gone. He'd be the one to do the dog's toilet training and feed it and pay any vet's bills. He couldn't lump that on him—it wasn't fair.

Afterwards he'd got Rosie to help him in the kitchen and they'd made the tiramisu together. It had earned him a few Brownie points with his daughter and she'd eventually gone up to her room to read alone, knowing he was having Bethan over for dinner.

'Is Grace coming, too? Could she have a sleepover?'

'No, it's just Bethan. Maybe another time?'

He'd taken some more of his painkillers and had a bit of a tidy-up, showered and put on some dark trousers and a white shirt. He couldn't remember the last time he'd dressed up for a woman and the thought gave him pause. Was he trying too hard? Was he going to too much trouble?

This was meant to be a thank-you, a goodbye, and an it's-all-in-your-hands-now kind of thing. The last woman he'd got dressed up for had been his wife, which seemed such a long time ago. Years. Much too long a time of being alone.

Why did it feel as if he was getting ready for a date? With those same nervous butterflies in his stomach? That same adrenaline flooding his veins? The same anticipation?

He removed the tie he'd selected and hung it back up. Took off the shoes he'd meticulously polished. *I'll do it in my socks.* Men didn't flirt that way, did they? In their socks? Besides, Bethan would probably just turn up in some old work clothes, or something. They were colleagues, and that was all.

His doorbell rang, and with it his nerves jumped into overdrive. Trotting down the stairs, he gave his reflection one last check in the hall mirror and then opened the door.

And gasped.

He hoped afterwards that he hadn't looked like a landed fish, but Bethan looked absolutely amazing. Stunning was the word. In a beautiful bright dress with one side of her lush brown hair held back by a diamond slide. Her features were accentuated by dark eyeliner and mascara, there was a faint hint of blusher on her creamy cheeks, and her lips were highlighted by a dark red slash of lipstick.

I'm in trouble.

His capacity for forming words seemed to disappear, and he wasn't entirely sure he could blame that on the glioma. Eventually he managed to close his mouth and smile, before uttering, 'You look amazing. Come on in.'

'Thanks.'

She stepped past him and he inhaled her perfume as she landed a brief kiss of greeting on his cheek. Something light and fruity, almost citrus. It did strange things to his insides and he had to take a deep breath of air to stop himself from turning her to face him, just so he could take her in with his eyes all over again.

He didn't know how much longer he had left to enjoy beautiful things, and Bethan was certainly one of those! But what was he doing? It was ridiculous.

I'm dying. I have a year left, maybe less—who knows? And what? Suddenly I'm like a horny teenager?

Perhaps it was the fact that he had so little time left? Time in which he wanted to live! To enjoy the simple things in life. The natural beauty in the world. And what was more natural than love? His internal Bucket List had it as his last hope: *to fall in love one last time.* He'd thought it impossible. He might want it, because it would feel great, but was it ethical? To do that to someone knowing he would leave them in such grief? He knew what that felt like…to lose the love of your life.

And so did Bethan.

He shook his head to try and clear it of such romantic thoughts. 'Why don't you go through to the kitchen? Can I get you a drink?'

'Oh, that reminds me…' She reached into the bag at her side and pulled from it a bottle of red wine that she handed to him. 'I didn't know what we were having, but I know this is good, so…'

He thanked her and let her lead the way, following behind her, breathing in the hints of her perfume and silently telling himself to pull it together. To get a grip!

In the kitchen, he pulled out a chair for her. 'So… drink?'

'I'll have a glass of wine, please—whatever you're having. Seeing as I'm not on call this weekend.'

He already had a bottle of red open, so he poured her a nice glass of shiraz. Then he grabbed his own glass and proposed a toast. 'To good friends and friendship. However long it may last.'

She raised her glass and took a sip of wine. 'Something smells delicious. What are we having?'

'Lamb shanks.'

'Marvellous. Is there anything I can help you with?'

He made a mock pretence of looking around him. 'Er…no, I don't think so. It all seems under control. So…how does it feel to know you're on your own from next week?'

He saw her smile, the way it lit up her eyes, the slight dimple to her right cheek. 'I'm used to being on my own.'

Idiot, Cam!

'Oh, I didn't mean—'

She held up her hands. 'It's okay—really. I know you didn't mean it like that. And neither did I. What I meant was it's how we usually work, isn't it? On our own? I have enjoyed our two weeks, though. It's been great. I shall miss you sitting beside me.'

I'll miss you, too.

But he didn't say it out loud. Before he knew her he'd been dreading these last two weeks of hand-over. Imagining days during which he'd just want to be at home with Rosie now that he'd made the decision to retire. But then he'd met Bethan, and she was delightful and charming and *interesting*, and there was so much more he wanted to know about her.

But would he ever get to have that chance? He wouldn't be spending every day with her any more. He'd be at home. The only time he'd see her would be out and about, the odd hello in the village.

He'd already decided he didn't want her as his doctor. Not because he didn't like her—far from it! He liked her *too much*, and he didn't want her having to care for him in his final days the way she'd had to with her husband.

He wanted to spare her that. He wanted her to remember him as a vital young man. One still in full control. Almost healthy. He didn't want her to see him slowly deteriorate. He wanted her final memories of him to be good ones. Of their days together at work— the jokes they'd laughed at, the moments that only they had shared.

'I'll…er…just check the veg.' He turned to poke a knife into the broccoli and baby sweetcorn. They were just about done. 'They're good. Okay, I'll just make up some gravy.'

'Should I…er…lay the table?'

What?

He turned and looked around.

Of course! The table! How on earth did I forget to do that?

He flushed bright red and let out a sigh. 'I can't believe I forgot that.'

That *was* ridiculous, wasn't it? He'd been forgetting a few things just lately—the table setting; the ketchup that Rosie preferred; her *bedtime!* Last night he'd forgotten that she always had a bath before bed, and when he'd sent her up to get into her pyjamas she'd looked at him strangely and started running her *own* bath. When he'd gone upstairs to ask her what she was doing she'd had to remind him...

The glioma. Was it affecting him? He knew it could affect mood and impulse control, but memory?

Bethan politely dismissed his lapse and asked him where everything was, and before he knew it she'd laid a beautiful table for both of them, even finding matches to light the candle she'd set in the middle. He was impressed.

He pulled the lamb shanks from the oven in their crockpot and set them to one side to rest for a moment whilst he dished up the vegetables and potatoes. He set some home-made mint sauce on the table and then served the shanks. The food sat before them, issuing clouds of steam full of delicious aroma.

'Bon appetit.'

He was smiling, realising that for the first time today his headache had gone.

He waited for her to try the food first, and when he was convinced she was eating it because she was enjoying it he tucked into his own, feeling a little more relaxed.

'This is delicious. I had no idea you were such a good cook.'

'Originally I wasn't. But when I lost my wife, Holly, I had to learn. Porridge and beans on toast just wasn't going to cut it any more. Not with a growing bairn.'

She smiled and nodded. 'I know what you mean. I was never the greatest of cooks either. Ashley loved to be in the kitchen, but in those final days I had to take over and try to make him delicious things he thought he might eat. The cancer affected his appetite, and the chemo practically ruined his taste buds.' She looked up at him. 'Did it have the same effect on you? The chemo?'

'To start with. Everything tasted metallic—even water. But it's got better since I've stopped having it.'

It was a reminder that he hadn't stopped through choice but rather because his consultants had said there was no longer any point. It wasn't working, and would only make his remaining time on this earth more unpleasant.

He dabbed at his mouth and considered her from across the table. She truly was beautiful. He'd noticed it the second she'd entered his room for her interview just a couple of weeks ago. And he was so pleased that he had met her and employed her as his replacement. She was perfect.

But it was making him confused. He hadn't expected this.

'Can I ask about Ashley? What he was like?'

She met his gaze and nodded. 'Sure. He was...' She paused to think. 'He was kind and considerate—a Scorpio.' She laughed. 'He loved to play the piano, and I used to tell him that he could've been a professional pianist. He had such a delicate touch—a real ear for music and sound. He taught me how to play. He composed a piece once, and every time he played it I got goosebumps...'

Her gaze drifted off to one side. Was she hearing that music once again?

'I wish I could have known him. Heard him play.'

His response seemed to drag her back into the present. 'Tell me about Holly,' she said, spearing a floret of broccoli with her fork.

'Okay. She was a farm girl when I met her, helping out on her parents' farm, and the first time we met I pulled a stray piece of straw from her hair. She had hair like Rosie's, long and red, and a fiery temper to match, but we hit it off straight away. We got married, and then we found out she was expecting Rosie. We didn't think our lives could get any better.'

She was watching him, listening to him. Taking in every word. 'Can I ask...?'

'Amniotic embolism.'

Bethan closed her eyes, as if in pain, and looked down at her plate.

It was a terrible, sudden way to die. Almost without warning and too late to do anything about it. It was a rare event. Nothing that could be predicted in advance. Some of the amniotic fluid would enter the bloodstream of the mother, triggering a serious reaction that resulted in a cardio-respiratory collapse and massive bleeding.

He'd gone from being elated at the birth of his daughter to experiencing sudden pain and fear as Holly had collapsed, having not yet held her child. Cam had thought it was cruel enough to have his wife taken from him so soon. To have his daughter's mother stolen away. And then, when he'd received his own diagnosis, nothing had made much sense any more. What was the point of it all?

He'd been depressed—had even briefly entertained thoughts of just getting it over and done with himself. But he had Rosie, and knew he couldn't do that to her, so he'd soldiered on. Doing his best to fight it until he knew it was time to enjoy his last few days rather than suffer them. Hence his decision to leave work and spend time with his loved ones.

'I'm so sorry, Cameron. That must have been a terrible shock.'

'You get through it. You know that as well as I do.'

She nodded. 'I do.'

They stared into each other's eyes for a moment, two souls connecting on an intimate level. Each one bared and open to show its scars. And then the rest of the world seemed to return—the ticking of the kitchen clock, a thud from upstairs.

Cameron looked up at the ceiling. 'I'd better go and check she's all right. Help yourself to more wine if you need it.'

Rosie was fine. She'd been building with some wooden blocks and knocked the tower down. She asked for a goodnight kiss and a hug.

'Is Bethan downstairs?'

'Yes.'

'Can I go downstairs and say hello?'

'No, but you can get into bed, like I asked you to, and go to sleep.' He kissed her on the forehead, tucked her in and closed her door behind him before going back downstairs.

Bethan was waiting for him and she'd refilled both their glasses.

'Thanks.'

'No problem.' She drew a breath. 'Are we destined to talk about death and dying, do you think? Because we've both been through so much of it?'

He smiled and nodded. 'Probably. It's common ground, if nothing else.'

'But we have something else in common.'

He frowned. 'What?'

She raised her glass in a silent toast and smiled at him. 'Surviving.'

She meant it. Surviving was more important than death. But being a survivor left you with a certain amount of guilt. A feeling of responsibility to carry on and to carry on *well*.

Like this evening, for example. Here she was with her colleague, her friend, enjoying a lovely meal. He was a great cook. And she loved being here in his home, appreciating the warmth of it, the welcome, his friendship.

He'd cooked the shanks perfectly, in a rich sauce, and the meat was just sliding off the bone and melting in her mouth. Simple things like this were to be enjoyed, because life for those left behind didn't always have to be filled with enormous things. Amazement and enjoyment could come from a sunrise, or a smile. Or a friend.

'I thought I'd call on your grandfather next week— see how he is.'

'He's doing well. I spoke to him on the phone just this morning.'

'That's good to hear.' She put down her knife and fork. 'He's very proud of you, isn't he?'

Cam smiled and nodded. 'Don't you mean *fiercely protective*?'

She laughed. 'That, too.'

'I was the first of our family to go to university. To become a doctor. My whole family had been fishermen and trawlermen. At first he didn't understand when I went away, leaving the old traditions behind, but when I came back here to Gilloch as a GP there couldn't have been anyone prouder.'

Bethan smiled at his story. 'My mother worked as a seamstress. She helped make wedding dresses. Growing up, I remember her teaching me how to sew, convinced I would work in the family shop in St Austell. But when I told her I wanted something different she supported me—as did Dad. And when I became a doctor that was how she kept introducing me to people— "This is my daughter, Bethan. *The doctor.*"' She smiled at the memory.

'I wish I could have met them.'

'They would have liked you, Cam.'

He smiled. 'It must have been hard for you to lose them both. I can't imagine losing my father...and I guess I won't have to. He'll lose me.'

She reached for his hand and squeezed it. 'You're going to fight it, aren't you? Every step of the way?'

He swept his thumb over her knuckles, looking down at their entwined hands. 'I already have. And I'm going to fight for every extra day I can spend with Rosie.'

'What about the rest of us? Don't you want to stick around for the rest of us, too?'

Cam nodded, then glanced at her plate. 'Have you finished?'

'Yes.' Was he changing the subject?

'I'll clear the table, then.' He made to get up.

'I'll help you.'

But as she got up with him she slipped on something on the floor. Spilt water, perhaps? Something… Before she knew it she was going head over heels and grabbing onto anything that might prevent her fall.

She grabbed Cameron.

And pulled him down with her.

She hit the floor, felt a whoosh as he landed somewhat heavily upon her—the air gone from her lungs. Her first instinct was to blush and laugh and be embarrassed at having fallen. Hoping she hadn't hurt either of them. She laughed long and hard, feeling the weight of him upon her. The weight of him against her body.

And then the laughter stopped.

The flush of embarrassment filled her cheeks, and Cam's face was so close to hers. He was staring into her eyes. His eyes were so blue, so intense, as he lay on top of her. Her hands were on his chest, but not pushing him away, just feeling its rise and fall, the accelerated beat of his heart.

'Are you okay?' she asked, her voice shaky and uncertain.

'Aye… I'm…'

And then his gaze dropped to her lips and she knew.

Knew he would kiss her. Felt her own lips part as her breathing rapidly increased.

He lowered his head.

What are you doing? You shouldn't be kissing him!

A thousand different voices in her head were telling that this would end in tears. That this was not good. That this was not a good idea. The voices were loud. Screaming at her. Fuelled by doubts that came from her past.

But there was one lone voice. One pure voice in her head that was louder. And it told her she wanted this. Needed this. The feel of his lips on hers, the weight of his body upon hers.

She had not been kissed for a long time and she'd forgotten what it felt like. What it felt like to be desired. What it felt like to be seen as *a woman* and not just as a care-giver—someone who mopped a sweaty brow, controlled the medication. Someone who made the pain go away.

She sank into the kiss and a throaty murmur escaped her—she couldn't help it. The kiss was so unexpected, the feelings she was experiencing so intense and amazing. A flurry—no, a whirlwind of emotions was pulling her this way and that. Giving her what she needed in that moment.

You're kissing Cam. You shouldn't be doing that.

Oh, but it feels so good. I don't want to stop! I love how this feels. I don't want to regret something so good. We both need this.

Her fingers sank into the softness of his hair as her body thrummed at the joy of his hard, lean body against the length of hers. He'd taken his weight from her, so that she could breathe, but there was still contact between them. As if he didn't want to part from her. As if he needed this as much as she did.

The kiss intensified, became deeper, and she felt parts of her body coming alive that had been dormant for far too long. Nerve-endings were awakening, and her body was yearning for his caress, his touch, experiencing its own need to reach out and touch and explore, to find this man who had built up walls around himself for far too long.

Two lonely, hurt souls were finding solace in each other.

And then they both came up for air.

She stared into his intense blue eyes, not knowing what to say. She hoped he didn't regret it. *She* didn't. And she didn't want him to bolt. He hadn't taken advantage of her and she didn't want him to feel guilty about this.

Bethan smiled at him. 'Was that dessert?'

The corners of his mouth curved upwards. Relief?

He stood up and held out his hand for her, pulling her to her feet and then pulling her back towards him, back into his embrace, reaching up to tuck a stray strand of her hair back behind her hair.

'I don't know what that was. But I enjoyed it.'

Her cheeks flushed with heat. *Good.* So had she.

She stroked his cheek, then pulled him towards her and kissed him again.

Someone was knocking at his front door. Cam blinked hard and tried to focus on the digital clock by his bedside—five forty-eight a.m. *What the...?*

He pulled on a tee shirt and some joggers and tiptoed quietly down the stairs to unlock the door.

Perhaps someone was sick? Perhaps they were calling to ask for help?

But when he opened the door he realised it wasn't anything like that.

It was Bethan, grinning like a loon, and behind her, rubbing their hands in the chill morning air, were Mhairi and Grace.

'Is everything all right?'

'Everything's perfect. The sun rises in half an hour, so get dressed—we're going out to watch it happen. Nanna will stay to look after the girls.'

He peered at Mhairi, standing behind her grand-daughter, and received a smile and a nod. 'And it's brass monkeys out here, so if you could let us in we'd be most grateful!' the older woman said.

He couldn't quite believe it. She'd *remembered*? She didn't have to do this for him.

'I don't know what to say.'

Mhairi stepped forward into his house. 'You say, *Thank you very much and come on in*!'

She stalked down the hallway, Grace following her with a sleepy smile, wrapped in a blanket and clutching a teddy.

Bethan stood beside him. 'Is this okay?'

Of course it was okay. It was more than okay! Since they'd kissed a week ago his world had changed its axis. He felt brighter. More alive. More positive than he had felt in ages! Having Bethan beside him had changed things in ways he had never suspected they could.

Oh, he had doubts. Of course he did.

What am I doing? I shouldn't be doing this to her,

getting her involved with me. What can I offer her but my death?

But his need to be close to her had overridden his doubts. Just that brief taste of her that night had fired his desire to be intimate with someone again. Why *shouldn't* he live life to the full? He didn't have much time left!

I'm dying!

He was hungry to soak up every experience he could. He'd thought that keeping everyone at a distance was working, but hadn't realised just how much he actually needed.

And he needed Bethan. He was still alive for now, and life—no matter how short—needed love in it. He loved his daughter and had thought that was enough. But, no. He needed *love*, too. Not for one minute did he imagine that Bethan loved him already! But she cared for him. She had feelings for him—he could see that.

And I have feelings for her.

He'd felt her need. It matched his own. The desire to be seen as something more than what they were. These last few weeks he'd felt as if everywhere he went he had a big neon sign flashing over his head that said *Dead Man Walking!* Even though no one outside of his family and Bethan could possibly know about his death sentence. He felt it. Keenly. And his need to feel something else—something better, something *real*— was a hunger that had made him feel hollow.

With Bethan he felt full again. Fully human. A man. A man with something to give. Something to offer. Someone with value and presence.

People saw a widow and a widower and it marked

out him and Bethan as characters of pity. Maybe it was all in his imagination, but…

But what people forgot was that they still had feelings. They still had thoughts and hopes for the future and their hearts still bled with pain.

We don't need pity. We need love.

That was why he'd reached out. Well, part of the reason. He was attracted to Bethan. Knew he really liked her. And quite clearly his libido still thought it was alive!

Kissing her—the feel of her, the scent of her in his arms—had almost driven him wild, and he felt sure she'd pretty much felt the same. He'd heard the sound of need, of hunger, of desire from her, and it was like a wake-up call in his head. Like a military trumpeter sounding a bugle call. A call to arms.

There'd been many more kisses since. Kisses he'd wanted to take further. He wanted to be intimate with her, but he was worried about Rosie walking in on them. Or Grace. Or Mhairi! And he also knew that if they took that extra step in their relationship there would be no going back. No putting on the brakes, no keeping her at arm's length. It would mean something more to them both.

Right now, it was still casual. He could pretend that everything was fine. Only it wasn't fine, was it? Because they were here fulfilling his Bucket List. And Bucket Lists were for people running out of time.

Bethan drove them up Mount Gillochrie to a lay-by halfway up the mountain. She had blankets for them, and a flask of hot tea, and they opened up the large boot of her car and sat in the back, looking to the east, where the dark blue sky was beginning to fill with warmer colours.

'Thank you for this. I probably never would have done it on my own.'

'It's no problem.'

'I can't believe I'm in my thirties and I've never seen the sun rise before. Not in real life anyway. There might have been times when I was out on call and it happened, but I was always too busy to notice.'

'Life frequently makes us too busy to notice the simple things.'

He sipped at his tea. 'I guess once I've done this there are only two things left for me to do.'

She smiled. 'Learn to play the piano.'

'And fall in love again.'

Bethan flushed and looked away, smiling. She was so beautiful. Inside and out. What she had given him in this short amount of time she would never understand. Right now, he found it hard to believe he was terminally ill. He didn't *feel* that way. He felt full of life. And he wanted to celebrate it.

The sun crept into view, filling the vast skies with hues of orange and yellow and pink, diluting the clouds with its warmth and bright rays. It was magnificent!

They watched in awe as it slowly crept upwards in the sky, and he suddenly found himself staring at Bethan, rather than the sun.

She turned her face towards him. 'Thank you.'

She smiled. Then kissed him.

And the kiss deepened, becoming something so much more…

CHAPTER SEVEN

'WHAT ON EARTH is that?'

They lay together beneath the blankets in the back of the car, snug and warm, her body wrapped in his. Making love to Cam had been so unexpected! She'd certainly not brought him out here to seduce him or anything. She'd brought him out here to see the sun rise, just as he'd wanted, but watching such beauty form before their eyes had caused them to create their own beauty, so swept up had they been in what they were seeing and feeling.

She'd watched as Cam had stared at the glowing sun, had seen how he had taken in all the colours of the sky. How his face had lit up with a yellow hue as the sun rose. She'd watched him absorb it all, trying to etch it into his memory so that he would always know what it had looked like if he were to lose his eyesight.

It had been such a moving moment, but she'd imagined that once they had seen the sun rise she would bring out her next surprise—the electronic keyboard she had stashed in the back.

She wasn't an expert at the piano by any means—that had been Ashley's forte—but she knew enough to teach Cam something basic. She'd pictured in her mind teaching him the piano as the sun warmed their faces and hands, high on the mountainside above Gilloch.

She flushed. 'Oh, it's surprise number two.'

She watched as he pulled the cover off the keyboard and then laughed at the surprise on his face.

'It's a keyboard,' he said.

She laughed. 'Yes! Well, I could hardly get a grand piano in the back of the car, could I?'

He smiled at her. 'You don't have to give me everything, you know. It doesn't have to be your responsibility.'

'It's not. I'm doing it because I want to.'

He stared back at her, considering her explanation. 'I don't want to use you, Bethan. I don't want you to feel used after all this, when I...when I die.'

'You're not using me... I'm using *you*.'

He gazed at her, confused. 'For what?'

How could she explain? How could she tell him that she was testing herself? Seeing how she felt about getting involved with this man above any other.

She could have had anyone she wanted in this world. A man who wasn't dying. A man who didn't have a time limit, the way Ashley had. A man who wouldn't hurt her by dying and leaving her behind to pick up the pieces.

But she had picked *him*. Because it felt right and because she couldn't imagine being with anyone else. The more she got involved with him, the stronger she knew she was. Even if she was facing death again, having only had him for such a short time.

Perhaps it was the wrong thing to do? She didn't know. But what she *did* know, and what she knew felt *right*, was being in his arms. Being in his embrace and letting her heart have free rein to…*to love him?*

'I need to be with you, Cam. It's as simple as that, right now. I want to give you my all. To show you that love is worth it, even if it is for a short time. Neither of us knows how much time we have, but we know it's limited. Let's embrace every second. Let's enjoy every moment as if it's a sunrise. Let's just be together. I promise you, you won't regret it.'

'But will *you*? Regret it?'

She stroked his face and smiled. 'Never.'

They drove back in silence, occasionally glancing at each other and smiling. Not needing to say anything.

Bethan was right. She did get involved—maybe a bit too quickly—but it wasn't her weakness. It was her strength. She had a resolve and a determination that was unlike most people's.

There were so many people in this world who wouldn't have the strength to care for one dying person, never mind two. Nurses, doctors, first responders— they all had a little extra-special something in their hearts. Caring for those in need was more than just a job. It was a calling. Something they could not turn away from even if it was to the detriment of themselves. They would always make sure their patient was okay. More than okay, if they could make that happen.

And, even though he hadn't known he wanted it this much, he was extremely glad that she was in his corner. She was a support he hadn't known was missing, and he felt closer to her now than he'd ever believed possible at that first moment she had walked into his surgery.

The sun was rising high now, warming the land, and outside the world was coming to life. No doubt the birds were singing already, and he saw one or two rabbits getting in their last mouthfuls of grass before the car shot past them. He stared at one as they neared it, its little grey furry body curled up as it nibbled at the grass.

As he stared at the rabbit he felt something inside him shift and a hot fork of pain pierced his skull. His hands rushed up to clutch his head. He gasped, the keening sound gushing out of him. Unaware of much except the feel of the hurt deep within his skull, he felt sick, as if he might vomit. A cold sweat beaded his skin, and then he began to hear her voice.

'Cameron? *Cameron!* What's happening? Speak to me! Please. Tell me what's going on!'

He knew the car had come to a halt, but he couldn't speak. He hurt too much. He was nothing but white-hot pain as the world began to fade out...

'I'm all right now. I feel better.'

Bethan stared at him from the end of his bed, her arms crossed tightly over her body. 'I don't care. You need to stay in bed. Doctor's orders.'

'But I feel fine now. It's gone. It's passed.'

She shone a light into his eyes, checking his pupil reflex. 'Maybe, but you have a little girl in the next room, full of excitement and energy, and you're in no fit state to look after her.'

'I disagree.' He threw back the blankets to get out of bed.

'Don't you *dare* get out of bed, Cameron! Seriously! I'm not joking.' She sounded afraid.

Cameron stopped, his feet on the ground, looking up at her. 'Seriously?'

'Yes. I need to check you over properly.'

'Look, Bethan, I appreciate you're trying to help, but I can call Dr McKellen. I'm sure he can check me over later.'

'What's the point of that when you have a qualified physician in your bedroom already?'

He pulled a face and it made her smile. It was like treating a petulant child. Doctors really did make the worst patients.

'Now, lie back and let me examine you.'

His blood pressure was slightly high—no doubt from the stress—and his pulse was high, too. But nothing that unduly concerned her.

'You really scared me, Cam.'

He looked up at her. 'It scared me, too.'

'Has that happened before? Pain like that out of nowhere?'

'No. It could mean that...' He trailed off, not wanting to finish the thought.

'You think the tumour is advancing? Growing? Possibly. We'd need a scan to confirm. But you can still see? No blurriness?'

'My sight's fine.'

'Honestly?'

He smiled and laid his hand on hers. 'Honestly.'

Bethan looked down at his hand upon hers and she ached for him. Physically felt her heart ache for him. The incident in the car had terrified her. She'd thought she was losing him then and there. When he'd slumped, groaning, clutching his skull as if he wanted to tear off his own head because it hurt so much, she had fought to keep it together. To stay professional and distant when all she'd wanted to scream was, *Don't you die on me, Cameron Brodie! I need you!*

She'd not thought about that again until now. Now that he was no longer in pain and was sitting up in bed, safe in his own home and holding her hand in his.

I need him.

This was so hard! Why was life such a challenge? Just when you thought you had it under control, another crisis would rumble along and tear the ground out from under your feet.

What was she supposed to do? She felt as if she could sit there with his hand on hers for ever, but the idea of seeing him in that much pain again... That was hard. Ashley had been in pain, but he'd had morphine, and it hadn't been in his head—hadn't been as terrifying as what she'd just witnessed with Cam.

The urge to lie down beside him, rest her head upon his chest and just hold him overwhelmed her. She wanted to comfort him. She wanted to feel him against her, to let him know that she would protect him.

Bethan stood up, pulling her hand free from his, her cheeks burning as she went to the window, taking a moment to breathe again.

He's still here. I didn't lose him.

It was a stark reminder of what it had felt like to lose someone she had strong feelings for. Begging for just one more day. One more moment. Not knowing if life would grant her that wish.

Looking out, she saw a vehicle pull up outside. An older man got out, his red hair shot through with grey. This had to be Cam's father.

'Your father's here.'

'I ought to go down and say hi.'

'Stay there. I'll let him know you're up here. He can come to you.'

'Bethan—'

'Please, Cam…do this for me?'

She hurried downstairs and opened the door.

Dougal Brodie gave her a smile. 'The famous Bethan, I take it?'

She smiled. 'How do you do, Mr Brodie?'

He gave her a broad smile and she could see so much of Cam in his father's face. 'I do very well, lass. Even more so since you put my da' in his place.'

Oh. That. Of course. It seems such a long time ago now.

Her cheeks coloured once again.

He laughed—a big, whole-hearted laugh—and stepped forward and gave her a bear hug. 'I've never laughed so much in my entire life hearing him tell the tale!' He let go and looked around. 'How's Cam doing?'

Bethan checked to make sure Rosie wasn't in earshot. 'He's not well.'

The smile disappeared. 'How bad?'

'It was bad.'

She told him in a subdued voice what had happened, and that she was making him rest now, despite his son's protests.

'You're a good 'un, lassie. Need *me* to go up there and tell him to stay in bed, too?'

'If you like—though I think he'll behave.'

'I'll just pop up and see him.'

Bethan waited downstairs and got Rosie a drink and a biscuit from the tin she'd found in the kitchen. Then she put on the television, found a cartoon channel and left it on low in the background while Rosie got out a jigsaw puzzle to solve.

Bethan went into the hall as footsteps came trotting down the stairs once again.

'He's staying put. He knows what's good for him.' Dougal looked at her, his head cocked to one side. 'You're good for this entire family. You put my da' in his place, you're helping Cam and wee Rosie. You're good for us all. You care. I can see it in your eyes. Maybe a bit more than that.'

Bethan wasn't sure what he meant, but she smiled anyway, glad that this Brodie man was happy to see her. Dougal was not her enemy. None of the Brodies had ever been that. It was just a figment of the past, held in the memory of Angus and Mhairi, who had never quite got over their enforced separation.

'I'll always do my best to look after my patients, Mr Brodie.'

Dougal nodded and opened the front door, ready to go. 'Aye. But he isn't just another patient, though, is he? Bye, Rosie! I'll see you later, lass.' And he waved a goodbye and strolled down the path.

Bethan watched him go, her brain muddled and confused by all that had happened in the last few hours.

As she closed the door she heard her mobile phone ring in the kitchen and she rushed to answer it. Picking it up and glancing at the screen, she saw *Private Number Calling.*

She frowned. Who could it be?

Pressing *Answer*, she lifted the phone to her ear. 'Hello?'

'Bethan? Bethan Monroe? It's Keir MacIntyre.'

Keir. She'd sent him Cameron's scans and reports.

He'd been a friend since a long time ago. She'd even had the privilege of watching him operate once, and it had been amazing to watch him work a miracle on a neuroblastoma. The delicateness of his work, the skill involved… He had always seriously impressed her, and she had felt that if there was anyone in the world who could help Cam, it was him.

'Hi. Thanks for getting back to me. Have you had a chance to look at those scans?'

'I have. I'm sorry for the delay in getting back to you, but I wanted to be thorough before I got in touch.'

'And what do you think? Can you help? Is there anything you can do? Anything at all?'

'It's a very difficult tumour, and I'd need a current scan to confirm it hasn't grown too much since this last one, but…yes, I think I can help him.'

She heard the smile in his voice. Heard his confidence. His knowledge and belief in his own skills.

She almost dropped the phone. 'You think you could…' She almost didn't want to jinx things by saying the word *cure*, but that was what he'd suggested. *Right?* 'You could get rid of it? *All* of it?'

'It's an extreme chance. But if the patient is willing to give it a go then so am I—depending upon the current scan, of course.'

She thought she might faint. She felt hot and dizzy. Her legs weak. She sat down on one of the kitchen chairs, clutching the phone. Cam could *live*! Here was his opportunity to escape his terminal diagnosis!

'When could you do it?'

'As soon as possible. If Mr Brodie is willing to come to Edinburgh, I can dedicate my time to getting him sorted out immediately. We can't wait with this tumour.

It's already aggressive. I'm assuming the patient has had no eye infiltration yet?'

'No. He can still see well.'

'That's good to hear. When can you get him to Edinburgh?'

'I don't know. I'll have to tell him first. Can you give me a day or so? So we can organise childcare and travel arrangements?'

'Two days. But no more than that, Bethan. We're risking it as it is.'

'I'll tell him right now. We'll be there.'

'I'll schedule him into my diary.'

'I'm not doing it.' Cam sat in his bed, staring at her, the muscle in his jaw twitching as he stared straight ahead.

She stared at him, incredulous. 'Did you not hear what I said? He thinks he can get it all out! It would *cure* you!'

'Or kill me. I could die on the table if it goes wrong, or he fails, and I've not had my time with Rosie yet. I promised her I'd be around for a while.'

'But your time with her will not be as you imagine it will. You'll be getting sicker. The tumour will blind you. Does she need to see that happen to you? Do you want to have to explain why you can't see her face any more?'

'That's not fair.'

'Nothing about this *is*! The tumour will make you into a different person, Cam. It's in your *brain*. You'll have mood swings—you might become violent, angry, lash out. I don't mean physically, but verbally. Do you want to put Rosie through that?'

'I would never do that to her. She's not ready for me to die.'

'No child is ever ready when they lose a parent. Even if they know it's coming. Even if they think they've prepared. Even if they're a grown-up themselves. She'll never be ready. Take it from me, Cam, there will never be a *good time* for this. So why not give her a chance to have you for a lot longer? To see her grow up? To see her go off to college, or walk her down the aisle, or introduce you to your grandchildren? You could *have* that.'

'*If* I take the risk.'

'If you take the risk.'

'The window of success is so small... I know nothing about this Keir MacIntyre—he could be a risk-taker.'

'Of *course* he's a risk-taker! He's taking on a tumour that everyone else has said no to. But that's what he does. He gives people who are willing to take the chance an opportunity.'

'To die.'

'To *live*. You're going to die anyway—why not take the chance to stick around for longer than you had ever dreamed?'

Cam shook his head. 'You don't understand...'

Was he *kidding*? He thought she didn't understand how scary this was for him? Or how scary it was for her? She didn't want to lose him either.

'I've just got to have you as my friend, Cam. A truly blessed and great friend. I don't want to lose you. And I don't have to. You've been given a chance to stay, to live—to beat this and stick two fingers up to cancer and gliomas. I need you to be brave enough to do it.'

'Why?'

She didn't want to say why. Didn't want to admit it out loud. But this was life and death, and everything she said here could matter. He needed to know the truth, if he was to make an informed decision.

'Because I care for you. I have feelings for you. And…and I think we could have something amazing if you'll just give it a chance. Give Keir a chance. Look him up on the internet. Research him. Say yes. You'll have to have more scans, but if they're bad, then you won't have lost anything—'

'I *will* lose something.' He looked up at her with tears in his eyes. 'I'll lose hope. I've accepted my fate. My lot in life, however short it may be. But if I do this it'll make me hope, and I'm not sure I'm strong enough to lose it again. To go all that way? To Edinburgh? With hope in my heart? Do you know how cruel it would be to get turned down when the scan shows the tumour has grown out of control?'

'We don't know that will happen.'

'I know what I felt today. Something's changed. Something bad.'

She nodded and went to sit beside him on the bed, grabbed his hand in hers. 'Yes, something's changed. *We've* changed. What I feel for you—I shouldn't be feeling it, it's too big, it's too scary, but I do.'

Cam gripped her hand and made her look at him. 'I have feelings for you, too. I'd be a terrible liar to deny it. But this—this situation—it's cruel. To give you hope, too. To let you watch me go into surgery, knowing I might die…'

'I'm going to lose you anyway if you don't try. Is *that* fair on me?'

He looked into her eyes with such sadness. 'No. It's not.'

'Nor is it fair on Rosie. But it will happen, Cam. It will. If you don't do something *now* to change it. Please change it. Take action. *Please.*'

Tears ran freely down her cheeks but she didn't care if she had panda eyes—didn't care if she looked awful. He had to know how much this meant. Not just to him, but to her and Rosie and all his family. Everyone who loved him.

Oh...

She gazed into his eyes through blurry tears and he pulled her towards him and kissed her. Just once. A strong, determined kiss.

Then he held her quivering body tight against his, stroking her back. 'Okay. Okay, we'll go.'

CHAPTER EIGHT

'*I THINK WE could have something amazing...*'

That was what kept going round and round in his mind as they drove to Edinburgh. Alongside the look on his daughter's face as she'd tearfully kissed him goodbye, broken-hearted, hiding behind her grandfather's legs as they drove away.

He knew he should never have turned around for one last look at his family. He'd seen the look in the eyes of his father, seen quite clearly his question—*Is this the last time I'll see my son?*

It had almost been enough to make him turn around and tell Bethan they weren't going.

Almost.

As much as he hated to admit it, since Keir's call he'd thought of nothing else—the possibility that this thing in his head could be taken away completely. That he could be cured...that he could have a life again. A future! With Rosie and those whom he loved.

Bethan.

'*I think we could have something amazing.*'

So did he. Their connection was strong. Probably because they'd both fought it so much, trying to keep it contained, trying to *deny* it.

When you're told not to think of the elephant in the room, it's all you can do.

Trying not to acknowledge his feelings for Bethan had simply forced him to think of almost nothing else—wondering what might have been, what kind of future they might have had, if only…

And now he had his *if only*. And it was terrifying. Because his chances of dying on the table were high. He could have a rupture, a brain-bleed. He could die. Or wake up in an even worse state, with disabilities he'd never had before *and* a life sentence.

But what if you don't? the voices in his head kept saying. *What if you wake up cured? What if you wake up and it's all gone and you can have everything you've ever wanted?*

This wasn't a fairy tale. There wasn't an imagined pot of gold at the end of the rainbow. This was reality. Keir MacIntyre believed he could do this, so it was possible—no matter how slim the chance.

'How are you feeling?' Bethan asked as she drove them onto the main road out of Gilloch.

'Nauseated. Terrified. You?'

'The same, but hopeful.'

He laid his hand on hers and squeezed. 'Let's not get hopeful yet. I've still got to have the scans, remember? We might see those and then just drive straight back home again.'

She nodded. 'Or they just might give you a bed.'

Cam looked out of the window and let out a big sigh. He hoped so. He hoped that what he'd felt the other day had just been a bad migraine attack and not signs of the tumour encroaching into places he didn't want. It couldn't have grown much—he could still see, after all. His sight had not yet been affected and he'd always assumed the first sign of everything going downhill would be a blurriness of vision, or losing his peripheral vision—something like that.

But for now he could look out at the wondrous landscape that was Scotland. Its high grey mountains, its sweeping valleys filled with gorse and heathers. A pheasant plodded through a field as crows soared high overhead.

Would this be the last time he'd see his beloved country? Were these sights the last things he would ever see? If so, he wanted to soak them up completely. The rich colours—purples, greys, greens. The beautiful blue sky above, with soft, wispy white clouds. The trees in rich brown and chocolate, their silver bark, the shadows beneath them. The broken remains of an old grey stone castle, high on a hilltop.

This was what he wanted to see. Not hospital walls. Not the stark white of an ICU.

'Stop the car.'

'What?'

'Stop the car.'

'Why? You haven't changed your mind, have you? Oh, Cam, please—'

'I haven't changed my mind—just stop the car. I need to do something.'

She checked her mirrors and indicated, pulled over into a small lay-by. She turned to look at him. 'What is it?'

'Get out for a moment.'

He opened his car door and got out, stretching his legs and sucking in a long lungful of air, his gaze on

the mountains, aware that Bethan was coming round
to his side of the vehicle.

'Do you feel okay?'

He turned to look at her. Beautiful Bethan. *His*
beautiful Bethan. He wouldn't be doing any of this if
it wasn't for her. He wouldn't have known about this
chance to live if it hadn't been for her. He owed it all
to her.

'I feel fine. But this could be my last chance to
do anything, for all I know, and there's one last thing
I want to do before we get embroiled in tests and
procedures.'

'What?'

He smiled and took a step towards her, cupping her
face with his hands and marvelling at the softness of
her skin before bringing her lips to his and kissing her.
Just one last time.

Who knew? After this operation he could be dead.
He might wake disabled. And if there was one good
thing he wanted to lie in bed and remember it was
kissing Bethan. Being a man. He might never get the
chance to kiss anyone ever again, so right now he
wanted to celebrate life.

He'd make love to her if he could, but they were on
a main road, not an abandoned mountainside track, and
if he was going to make love to this woman again then
he wanted it to be wonderful. For both of them. Satin
sheets and a four-poster bed. A roaring fire.

He might never get that wish, but he could kiss her.
And he was going to kiss her until neither of them
could breathe or think of anything else. He wanted
everything else in the world to go away, and the only

way he could do that was by losing himself. Kissing Bethan was making that happen.

It was all going—the tumour, the possibility of death, the look on Rosie's face as they'd driven away...

Bethan sank into his embrace, kissed him back, and he only stopped when he felt her tears touch his face.

'Hey, you okay?' He touched his forehead to hers and stared deeply into her eyes.

Traffic roared past beside them, but that didn't matter. All that mattered was her.

'I'm sad.'

'Don't be.'

'I can't help it. Every time you kiss me it makes me think of what we could have.'

He sucked in a breath. 'You think it's going to fail. You think I'm going to die on that table.'

She shook her head. '*No*. I don't want to think that. Not at all. I want this. I want you to have the operation, and I want it to be a success, but the closer we get to Edinburgh, the closer I am to sitting at the bedside of the man that I... I don't want to lose.'

Love. She'd been going to say love.

He'd seen it in her eyes. Her heart. Her soul.

He realised, with a pang, just how emotionally involved she had got with him. How much he meant to her. And he felt guilt. Guilt for putting her in this position. The one thing he'd hoped never to do.

He let out a low sigh and let her go.

She hadn't really known what she was getting into when she'd started all this. Sending off emails to old colleagues, people she'd thought might help. She'd done it once before, when Ashley had got sick, but no one had been able to help him.

This—what was happening now—was all new territory, and she didn't know how to feel. Getting Keir's telephone call had completely thrown her.

She'd hoped so much that someone would be able to help her husband. She'd avidly checked her emails every day. Made secret telephone calls late at night, trying to contact colleagues of colleagues, patiently explaining the situation. And finally she'd had to accept the fact that Ashley was going to die. It had been a weird process of acceptance, of resignation—despite her desire to yell and scream at the world about it being unfair.

Cam was getting a chance. There was hope. And she didn't know how to feel about that. He could have his scans, go under the knife and die. Within the week!

Am I ready for that?

She had allowed her feelings—*their* feelings—free rein, relishing their connection, the taste and feel of him, drowning in the glory of it, the joy of it, the excitement of it. Finally allowing herself happiness at last—only for it to be threatened like this.

Am I crazy for letting this happen? What's the point if it's all going to end under a surgeon's knife?

Fate was being cruel. Making her go through this again? But it was going to be worth it if he survived! He had a *chance* here. The only way she was going to get through the next few days was to believe in that. With all her heart. Because she had to. There was no other choice.

I love him.

Both families were waiting back home. Waiting for

news and updates. She was the one here to support him. The one who would do the hand-holding. The calm, assertive force in the background, the person who had managed this whole event. She would be the one to pace the floor during surgery. She would be the one jumping to her feet every time someone in scrubs walked towards her. She would be the one to make the phone calls home.

Unhelpfully, her mind provided her with a re-run of those moments just after Ashley's death. How she had felt. That empty ache in her heart. The feeling that she couldn't breathe, as if someone had punched her in the gut. The knowledge that she would never see, hear, speak to or hold her loved one ever again. That he'd left her behind.

She'd sworn to never do this again. To get so attached to someone that their death would rip apart her heart. Grace was meant to be her world. And yet here she sat, beside another man with a terminal diagnosis, driving him to a hospital where he might either die on the table or die a few months later, most probably blind and in pain, lashing out at those who cared for him.

The chance of him surviving, of the operation being successful, had to be slim. But it was a chance she believed was worth taking. Because the prize for being brave, the prize for pulling through, would be worth more to her than anything. Because that prize would be love. And a future together.

But what if it all goes wrong? I'm the one who persuaded him to do this. What if he dies? Will his death be on my conscience?

Of course it would. She was playing God when she

ought not to be. Trying to save Cam. Pushing her own agenda when it should be his.

A wave of guilt washed over her and she could barely look at him. She felt a wave of heat over her face and let the driver's window down to cool her skin.

'Are you okay?'

She tried to nod enthusiastically. To force a smile. 'Sure!'

If he chose to go ahead it was *his* choice, right? The onus of responsibility was on *him*. Not on her. She couldn't carry guilt about Cam as well as guilt about Ashley. It would be too much.

She risked a glance at him, wishing more than anything that they were in a situation where she could turn this car around and forget everything. Go and watch another sunrise.

'I never did get the chance to teach you the piano.'

'No.'

'Maybe they'll have one in the hospital somewhere.'

'You think teaching me "Chopsticks" will improve my last few days?'

She smiled. 'You never know.'

'Well, we still might get sent home, once Keir has seen the scans. Perhaps you can teach me then?'

She didn't want to blurt out, *But what if you don't get sent home? What if you stay and they operate and it all goes wrong?*

'Let's just get there and do the scans. See what they say. Whatever you decide, I'll back you one hundred per cent.'

But even as she said it she knew she was lying. She was trying to make *him* make the decision—the final decision—because then it would be off her shoulders. The responsibility would be his.

But if Keir thought he could operate and Cam walked away she had no idea how she'd feel. She would always wonder in the days to follow, as she watched Cam deteriorate and then pass away, if he might have survived? If he might have had a life. She would feel so much anger towards him if he walked away from that chance.

She didn't want to hate him.

She wanted to love him. So very much!

And that was what made everything so difficult.

The Royal Livingston Hospital sat atop a hill—a crowning glory of glass and steel, looking down upon the city below.

Bethan drove around the car park twice before they found a parking spot, and Cameron couldn't help but fear that this was some kind of omen—*There's no space for you here. Go home.*

Once they were parked, they headed inside and got directions up to Keir's office in the neurosurgical department. A prim receptionist with thickly curled silver hair asked them to take a seat and they sat nervously in the waiting room, staring at an abstract painting of a brain that was actually made out of carefully folded naked people.

They didn't speak. Neither seemed to have anything to say. He knew that they were both waiting to see what Keir said. What the scans said. There was nothing else either of them could do. As doctors, they wanted the science and the evidence before them. It seemed silly to talk over hypotheticals now.

Cam felt sick. Nervous. He wished he was back home in Gilloch with Rosie, reading her a story or doing something that was absolutely nothing to do with life or death. Looking out of his cottage window at the moorland beyond, trying to spot a partridge or a pheasant or a deer. He'd never liked big cities. Had never liked their impersonal touch—

'Dr Brodie?'

A man stood facing him, dressed in a suit, shirt and tie, a stethoscope draped casually around his neck and an ID card clipped to his belt. This had to be Keir MacIntyre, and Cam was briefly reassured that he looked to be in his mid-forties, experienced and knowledgeable, rather than like someone fresh out of medical school.

He managed a smile and shook Keir's hand, then he and Bethan followed him into his consulting room.

'Please, take a seat. Bethan, it's good to see you—you're looking well.'

He watched, detached, as Keir kissed Bethan's cheek and briefly considered what a handsome couple they would make after his death.

'Thank you for seeing us, Keir.'

'No problem. I had a good long look at those scans you sent me—and the medical history. That's one hell of a glioma you've got here, Dr Brodie.'

'Cam, please. And, yes, it is. But you think you can do something about it?'

Keir nodded. 'As long as the scans are good, and it hasn't grown past its margins from the last one, I think so. I think there's a chance.'

'How much of a chance?' Cam asked, needing to know numbers. Percentages. Risk levels.

'I couldn't possibly say until we get you scanned.

I've blocked some time on the scanner for eleven o'clock, if you're all ready to go?'

This was it, then. Cam nodded, not trusting himself to speak. Being back inside these hospital walls reminded him of having chemo. He'd always hated being a patient, and he hated it even more now. It was such a surreal conversation—discussing whether you'd live out the week or not.

Keir smiled. 'First things first, though...'

He ran Cam through some of the finer details of his medical history—first sign of symptoms, type of symptoms, medication he was on, family medical history—all the things he already had in front of him on his computer, but he was clearly double-checking.

'Any recent new symptoms?'

'No, nothing—'

'He had a head pain,' interrupted Bethan. 'The day you called us. Just before your call, actually. He seemed fine. We were in the car, driving home, and then he screamed and bent double, clutching his head.'

'But I was fine afterwards. It only lasted a few seconds,' Cam explained.

'But it happened.' Bethan's face was serious. She was determined to make sure Keir had all the facts. Was she trying to jeopardise the operation? Perhaps *she* was having second thoughts about the operation? Despite being the one to push for it? He felt a frisson of irritation.

'And, yes, it did pass—but it was the worst I'd seen him.'

'Okay, that's good to know. Well, if you're ready, then, Cam, I'll call a nurse to take you down to the Imaging Centre and we'll get straight to work.'

'Okay.'

This was it. This moment—or rather, the next hour or so—would determine whether he lived a long and happy life, or whether he died, as expected, in his own bed in just a few months.

He almost couldn't feel his legs. Would they work at all? His stomach was working overtime—his acid production seemed to be in overdrive, churning up his guts. He pushed up from the chair and found he could stand, and walk, too.

A nurse met him at the door and he followed her to the Imaging Centre, got dressed in a blue hospital gown and lay down on the machine's bed.

She passed him the panic button, popped a pillow under his knees and then clamped down the cage over his face. There was a small mirror inside it, so that he could see the technicians in another room.

He felt incredibly alone. And insignificant. Not worth all this trouble. Surely the scan would just show that his glioma—his *aggressive* glioma—had done nothing but grow. Invading his brain... Tendrils of tumour snaking through so many areas it would be impossible to contain it...

Keir would take a look and see an impossible job. He would send Cameron and Bethan home. One to die and one to cry.

Why am I putting everyone through this?

He'd never wanted to involve Bethan. *Ever*. And yet he'd given her permission to send out his scans, his medical history, he'd kissed her, held her in his arms, made love to her and let her drive him here. His only support.

She would be the one to hold his hand as he heard the bad news, and she would have to drive him home to die. Or she would have to sit in a cold, sterile waiting room, staring at the clock for hours, waiting for news. News that would most likely be dire.

He couldn't do this to her. It wasn't fair. On either of them. He'd let her become involved far too much. He had to stop it.

As the machine began to hum all around him he vowed he would send her home as soon as the scans were done. Somehow he would get her to leave.

Let a nurse call home with bad news. Or Keir could do it.

He'd taken this too far with Bethan, and it was only now, as he lay prone in the scanner that hummed and clanked all around him, minutely scanning the layers of his brain, that he could see where all his mistakes lay.

He'd been selfish. He had allowed his need for comfort and love to get in the way of what he knew was the logical thing to do.

'How did it go? The scan?' she asked Cam as he came out of the changing room after getting back into his clothes.

He said nothing. Just shrugged.

'Did the technicians give you any clue?'

She was hungry for news and didn't understand why he wasn't saying anything. Maybe he was just scared.

Cam sat down in the waiting room and stared into space.

This cold shoulder she was feeling from him was unsettling. What was going on?

'Cam?'

Nothing.

'Will you answer me?'

Finally he turned, stared at her with coldness and detachment in his eyes. 'I want you to go back to Gilloch. Just go and…and forget about me.'

She laughed, incredulous. 'Oh, it's that easy, is it? What kind of world do you live in that people can just wash their hands of each other?'

'I'm serious, Bethan. I should never have got you involved in all this. I want you to go.'

She crossed her arms. 'Well, I'm not going.'

'I can tell Keir I don't want you here and he'll make you leave, but I'd rather you did it yourself.'

She watched him as he continued to button up his shirt. The scan was over. He'd been in that machine for almost forty-five minutes and it had been forty-five minutes of hell for her. What would it show? Did he still have a chance? Would Keir take the risk and try to save him?

'I can't leave you alone. You'll have no one here to support you.'

'I don't need support.'

'If you have brain surgery you will.'

And then a thought entered her head. A frightening realisation.

'You're not going to do it, are you? No matter what he says, you're backing out.'

'Oh, I'll do it. If there's a chance for me, then I'm going to do it.'

'I'm glad to hear it. But why do you want me to go?'

He turned, then. Glared at her. 'Because I should never have involved you! I knew it was wrong. From the very first day we met I told myself I wouldn't even *tell* you what was going on and I couldn't even get that part right.'

'Your grandfather let the cat out of the bag. Not you.'

She couldn't believe what she was hearing. He wanted her to go? Did he really think that she could do such a thing?

He turned away. 'After all you've been through…'

'Which is on *my* shoulders, not yours.'

'After all you've been through I need to do this next part right and I need to do it on my own. You shouldn't have to take responsibility for me—this shouldn't be your job.'

She stared at him, not quite believing her ears. 'You don't get it, do you?'

He stared at her.

'You're not a *job*, Cam. You're a person I care about. A great deal. Probably more than I should, yes, but I do so willingly. I'm a grown woman and I'm old enough to make my own choices. I choose to be here to support you, no matter what.'

She saw tears fill his eyes. Tears he tried to blink away.

Bethan took his hand. 'Tell me what you're feeling.'

But he pulled his hand free, sending the pain of hurt and rejection through her chest.

'I just don't think we should ever have got involved with each other. It was a bad idea from the start.'

She shook her head. He was wrong. They were destined to be involved. 'Let me be here for you, Cam. Don't be alone. No one should be alone in something like this.'

He looked up at her, meeting her gaze with tear-filled eyes. He was looking for something—something inside her that only he knew. Whatever it was, he seemed to find it. Or at least he found the answer he was looking for.

She could hardly believe that this was the same man who had made her stop the car so that he could kiss her. That within the space of a few hours he had changed completely.

He turned away from her, crossed his arms, his voice brooking no argument. 'I need you to go.'

He watched her bottom lip begin to tremble.

'I can't…' she whispered.

It was killing him, seeing her like this. So small. So broken. But it had to be done if he was going to save her from having to sit by his bedside. From being the one to hear from Keir whether the operation had been successful.

If he'd thought about this more clearly he would have left her back at Gilloch and had his father drive him in instead.

'I'm going in to see Keir on my own. I'll hear the results alone. Make my decision alone.'

'Make your decision? But you've already said you're going to have the operation if it's possible—'

'If it's possible, I want to do it alone. I won't have you sitting by my bed, waiting for me to wake up. I won't have you nursing me. I won't have you being the one to ring my family if it all goes wrong!'

He wanted her to remember him as a vital, strong man. The man with whom she'd watched a sunrise. The man with whom she'd made love—such a cherished memory for him. The man who had held her in his arms, strong and vibrant, keeping her safe.

'Then why bring me in the first place?' Her voice trembled as tears trickled down her cheeks.

'I made a mistake.'

He had to turn away. Couldn't bear to see the pain in her eyes, the hurt she was feeling at his rejection. But he simply couldn't think of any other way to protect her from what was to come.

He had no idea what the scans would say, but he knew in his heart that he was going to tell Keir to try anyway. Even if he only got *some* of the tumour it would be better than nothing. It might buy him some more time with his daughter. He would have liked more time with Bethan, too, but he could see now how wrong it had been for him to get involved with her. To put her through such a thing when she had already faced it once.

The sand in his hourglass was finite. He had less than everyone else. He should have remembered that. But that desire, that yearning to fall in love, had overwhelmed everything the second she had walked into his life. Given him warmth and brightness. He'd known it back then, on the first day they'd met, that she would be more than just a colleague. More than just a woman to replace him. There'd been a connection from the very first second.

And he'd allowed it to happen—succumbing to its potent force, giving in to its temptation. Unable to fight it because he'd wanted it so much.

And now I love her. And I'm hurting her. But I'm doing it to save her. She'll thank me. One day.

'I can't believe this. That you're saying this now. This isn't you, Cam. It's fear speaking. *I* know it. *You* know it.'

'It doesn't matter. I just know I have to do what's right.' He turned back to face her. 'I don't love you, Bethan. You should go.'

'Is Bethan not joining us?' Keir asked as he invited Cameron back into his office.

Cam had been staring at that image of the human brain for far too long, trying not to let the tears fall, trying to identify the separate bodies, the separate shapes that made up the whole. Because that was the only way he wasn't going to fall apart at suddenly being alone.

'She…er…got called back home,' he lied.

He had no idea if she'd gone home or not. All he'd seen was the way she'd picked up her handbag and run from him, crying.

Keir frowned as he sat down and rubbed his jawline. 'There's no way she can come back?'

No. Definitely not. She's long gone, I made sure of that.

Cam leaned forward. 'Why would she need to come back?'

'Because you'll need someone here when you come round from the operation.'

Cam let out a slow, steady breath as the import of Keir's words sank in. *'Because you'll need someone…'*

All other thoughts, all his guilt, disappeared. 'You can do it?'

The other man smiled. 'I think I can. I'll need another detailed scan to confirm, of course, but the first signs are promising.'

'You can take it out?'

'Clean margins. Yes.'

Cam exhaled, long and steady, once again. 'What's the chance of success?'

'I'm not keen to discuss numbers like those. There are all types of risk factors with deep brain surgery—unexpected bleeding, a rise in pressure, cardiac factors...'

'I need a number.'

Keir looked at him, unblinking. 'I think we're looking at a thirty per cent chance of success.'

Thirty per cent? That was almost nothing. 'So a seventy percent chance of failure?'

'Or the operation could be a success but you may be left with...deficits.'

'Such as?'

'We wouldn't know until you woke up.'

'*If* I woke up.'

Keir nodded. 'This is why you need someone here with you. You need to discuss this with someone you trust before you make such a big decision. I know Bethan. She can handle this.'

'I've already made my decision. I made it before I came here.'

'And that is?'

'To give myself a chance of a life. I have to do it. For my daughter.'

It can't be for Bethan any more. I've ruined that. But I had to do it to save her.

'How old is she?'

'Five.'

'I have a ten-year-old. A boy.'

'So you understand why I have to do this?'

Keir stared at him for a moment. Then nodded. 'I do. I just wish you weren't doing it alone.'

Cam stared back at the consultant. He wouldn't understand why. No matter how much he tried to explain.

They're going to operate. I have a chance. And so does Bethan.

He was in a hospital gown. In a hospital bed. He would have his operation first thing tomorrow.

Around him in the six-bed ward it was visiting time, and he was the only person without a friend or family member at his side. He'd called home already. Told them the operation was a go and that he was going to do it. His father had offered to bring Rosie before he went down to Theatre, but Cam didn't want to think of her waiting for him to come out of surgery.

If he made it out of surgery.

And Bethan? Where was she now? If he died on the table tomorrow all she would remember would be his rejection of her. Telling her he didn't love her.

He'd lied. Of *course* he'd lied! But he was trying to protect her—and if she was angry with him...well, that was better than being desolate with grief, wasn't it?

He hadn't meant it. But he couldn't put her through the waiting game. Couldn't make her be the one to have to drive home and tell his family either that he had died or had woken with deficits.

He could remember driving home to tell everyone that Holly had died. He could remember telephoning Holly's parents with the news of Rosie's birth—giving them the good news first, hoping to give them that one ray of sunshine before telling them the rest—and the silence down the phone that had seemed to last an age.

And then that terrible wailing sound her mother had made. The crying. The anguish.

He'd sat on the other end of the phone, feeling powerless and just as devastated himself, not knowing what to do, knowing that they would remember him only as the man who had told them their daughter had died.

He couldn't allow people to think of Bethan that way. He didn't want her blamed for anything. She had given him this gift. This chance to save his life. This attempt to give him back everything he needed—time.

And what if he woke with deficits? Such a politically correct word. Less frightening than blindness, or the inability to speak or to feed yourself. Less daunting. Smaller somehow. Less frightening.

Or was it?

He hoped the operation would be a success. Of course he did. He'd looked up Keir's record and his results were fifty-fifty. But, then again, he did take on the cases that no one else would, so fifty-fifty was quite impressive when you considered that. Cam trusted Keir's ability in Theatre.

Hopefully Bethan would forgive him. She would realise why he had said what he had. That he'd been doing it to save her. To help her.

If only I could forget the look on her face just before she left...

Cam didn't sleep well, and the night was long and uncomfortable. At last the ward lights were being switched on and everyone was served breakfast except him. He got a pre-med instead. And a blood pressure check.

One last phone call with Rosie... She sounded happy

to hear his voice, and he could picture her at home in his father's kitchen, sat upon his knee as she ate her porridge, topped with honey just as she liked it.

'Have you spoken to Bethan?' he asked his father.

'Bethan? No. Isn't she with you?' his dad asked, sounding confused.

'No, she, er …' and then he ran out of words. Didn't know how he could explain it to his father. What he had done to Bethan. What he had said.

There was another silence then, for a few seconds. 'I love you, son. And I'm so proud of you for doing this. I know the chances are small, but the fact that you're taking that chance… Well, I'm very proud of you.'

He heard the crack in his dad's voice. Normally he was a man so stoic he'd give statues a run for their money.

'Thanks, Dad. I love you, too.'

He wished he'd been brave enough to say that to Bethan.

Bethan stood watching at the far end of the corridor as Cam was prepped and taken to Theatre. She felt sick to her stomach as the nurses began to wheel him out in his bed, wishing she could run up to him one last time and hold him. Kiss him.

She watched, following silently behind them, as they walked down the corridors towards Theatre, then stopped behind the red line as he disappeared through a set of double doors.

Fear kept her silent.

She glanced up at the big wall clock and noted the time. How long would this take? When would she know? When would her heart break?

Keir noticed her and came over. 'It's good to see you. You've got a long wait ahead of you. Why don't you get something to eat? Maybe get some rest?'

'I don't think I could eat a thing.'

He nodded, understanding. 'I'll look after him. I'll do my best for him.'

She braved a smile. 'I know you will.'

Keir gave her a brief hug. 'I ought to go.'

Bethan nodded, feeling tears prick her eyes. 'Do your best work in there. For Cameron.'

'I will.'

Cam lay in Theatre and wondered if this room was the last thing he would ever see in his life. He hoped not.

He'd always imagined that he would die in his bed at home. Surrounded by family. Holding their hands. Looking into the eyes of his daughter. Or Bethan. Either one of those would have been good. But he knew he'd burnt his bridges with Bethan. He'd had to be cruel to be kind—she'd work that out in the end.

The mask was lowered over his face and he began to count back from ten as in his mind's eye he pictured their last kiss. Tried to remember the feel of her in his arms.

If he was going to die now, he wanted to die happy.

CHAPTER NINE

'ANY NEWS?' NANNA asked over the telephone.

Bethan glanced at the clock. Cam had been under the knife for almost five hours so far. An interminable amount of time. Especially since she knew she had gone against his final wishes. If he died...

'No, nothing yet.'

She'd needed to hear a kind voice. A comforting voice. To talk to someone who wouldn't blame her, or try to interpret what she had done. There would be no judgement from Nanna.

'You'd think these doctors would know that people are waiting and worrying. Would it hurt them to come out and tell you occasionally that it's all going okay?'

'I'd rather they were in there worrying about him, not me.'

'Of course. You're right. Grace is here. Do you want to have a quick chat?'

Yes. She did. More than anything right now she wanted to hear her daughter's bright, happy tones. The voice of someone who loved her and valued her.

Cameron had crushed her with his admission that he didn't love her. She'd thought that maybe he did. She'd thought that perhaps he felt the same way as her.

So what if he didn't? It didn't mean that she had to stop caring about him. She could never leave him at a time like this, no matter what he'd said. He could have said *I hate you* and she would not have walked away. What did that say about her? That she was stupid? Stubborn? A glutton for punishment?

She didn't care. She just needed to know in her own heart that she had done the right thing. If the operation worked and Cameron lived through it she would do the decent thing and walk away. Leave him to his life with Rosie. She would be polite, but distant, and only she would know the turmoil that was in her heart. She would not let him see anything.

And if he died…

You won't have died alone.

She almost choked on a sob at the thought, and had to pretend to Grace that she was just clearing her throat. Grace babbled on, utterly unaware of her mother's anguish.

What Keir managed to do in that room would either end everything or give Cameron everything he'd ever wanted. She hoped, for his sake, it was the latter. And if it was successful she would make sure he was okay and *then* she would leave. It would be the right thing to do. She and Grace and Nanna would carry on looking after themselves, keeping their noses out of anything to do with Cameron, and hopefully live in peace together within the confines of Gilloch village.

Grace chattered on about what she'd got up to at school that day, and how Nanna had allowed her to invite Rosie to their house for a playdate and sleepover.

Bethan's heart sank at the thought of the budding friendship between the two girls. If the surgery worked, she would have to decide the best way to deal with it. Maybe let them remain friends, but put the stop on playdates and parties and sleepovers. She didn't want to have to see Cameron if she could help it. It would hurt too much. Or maybe she'd let them happen and Nanna could take Rosie back to her father's house each time. Why should the girls suffer just because their parents couldn't get it together?

But the thought of having to be indifferent almost broke her heart in two. Her feelings for him had grown exponentially. They were unstoppable and he had hurt her unbearably.

When Nanna got back on the phone, Bethan asked, 'How is Rosie? Has she said anything about her father?'

'Just that he's in hospital. She seems to think he'll be coming home soon. I daren't say anything, just in case.'

'No, it's best not to. I'll ring when I have news.'

'Have you eaten? Are you looking after yourself?'

'I've got a sandwich,' she lied, staring at the cold cup of coffee that sat before her on the low table.

'Good. You need to keep your strength up. I hope it's successful for him, I really do, but I'll be a lot happier when you're back home safe and sound with me.'

'Me, too.'

It was the truth. All she wanted was to be surrounded by love once again. To sink into the loving warmth of her nanna's embrace and try to forget that her heart belonged to Cameron.

The next few hours passed slowly. She couldn't eat. Or drink. She just sat and watched the clock tick round and round. And then, after twelve hours and forty-two minutes of surgery, she saw Keir walking towards her.

He still wore scrubs. He looked tired, but beyond

that she wasn't sure of his expression. His face gave nothing away.

It was only when he stood in front of her and she got up from her chair and asked, 'Well…?' that he began to smile. Broadly.

'I got it. I got it all.'

'You got the tumour?' She almost didn't believe it.

'Yes. It's all up to him now. He's got a long future ahead of him with you by his side.'

As Keir walked away she sank back into her chair. Cameron was going to be okay! Well, he'd made it out of surgery, at least. Whether he'd suffered any deficits was yet to be known, but he would *live*.

I can go home now.

But her feet wouldn't move. She knew she couldn't go. She had to be there when he woke up.

'With you by his side…'

Her heart thundered away in her chest.

I have to make sure he's okay.

She sat in the neurological intensive care unit beside his bed, waiting for him to wake. Afraid of his judgement when he did. But she had *some* pride. She would not cry. She would not beg. She would just tell him that he was okay. That it was over. And then she would leave.

The nurse had said he'd briefly come round after the operation, mumbled something she couldn't understand and then gone back to sleep again.

'His body has been through an ordeal. He needs to rest. We'll know more later,' she'd said, hoping to be reassuring.

Bethan didn't need to be reassured. What she needed

was to steel herself for seeing him open his eyes, telling him he'd made it through.

She could not be with him. A man who had told her to her face that he didn't love her. Had he used her? Maybe. She was too confused to know anything for sure right now.

She should never have got involved with Cameron Brodie. She should have listened to Nanna.

Cam stirred and her gaze instantly latched onto his face to see if he was about to open his eyes. His head was wrapped in a bandage, and he looked so pale, but all the machines around him were beeping out a reassuring rhythm. Numbers…measurements that she knew she could trust.

His heart-rate seemed good. His blood pressure was stable. Inter-cranial pressure exactly what it should be. No temperature spikes. He just needed to wake. She just needed to see that he wasn't blind, that he wasn't deaf and that he could talk—that was all she needed to know.

She wanted to give him the comfort of not waking alone and then she would go. It would hurt to walk away, but she would do it. It wasn't safe for her to stay—because if she stayed she would continue to love him, and she couldn't allow herself to do that.

He moaned. Muttered something unintelligible.

She felt her mouth go dry. He looked so helpless in the bed. She yearned to reach out and stroke his brow. Run her fingers along his bearded jaw. Tell him that she loved him. That she wished him all the best. A happy future with Rosie. And that she would no doubt see him out and about in the village, but that would be all.

They would be like strangers. Strangers who might have been something more.

His eyes fluttered open, blinking in the bright lights of the intensive care unit.

He can see.

Light, at least. Could he see anything more? Shapes? Faces? Details?

'Bethan?'

She gasped upon hearing her name spoken from his lips.

He can talk!

And his first word had been her name!

Don't get excited. It doesn't mean anything.

Fighting the urge to rush to his bedside and cover his face with grateful kisses, she stood stiffly, away from the bed, gritting her teeth, determined not to move her feet. Had he the right to ask for her after the way he'd dismissed her before?

'I'm here, Cameron.'

His head turned towards her voice.

He can move. He can hear.

And his eyes were focused upon her face.

'You're here.'

'I had to make sure you were okay.'

His gaze travelled around the room, taking in his surroundings, the machines he was hooked up to, then moved back to her face once again. 'Is it over?'

Yes. It's all over.

'Yes. Keir did it. He got the tumour. You're going to be fine.'

He frowned as he listened to her, but said nothing as he processed the immensity of her news. A ghostly smile lifted the corners of his mouth. 'I'll live?'

'A long time. You have a future, now.'

Without me.

'But I… Does everyone…?'

He was tired. His sentences were falling away before he could complete them. It was understandable—and expected.

'I'll call everyone. Let them know.'

His gaze fell back to her face. Studied her. 'Why do you seem so sad?'

She gazed down upon him, feeling a wearying sadness exhausting her body. They'd both been through so much in the last day or two. She was spent, too. And it was hard work, shutting down her heart. Telling it that it could no longer have feelings for the man she had come to love. She'd done it once before and survived.

I can do it again.

It hurt. And it was terrifyingly familiar. Like a death. Only worse. The man of her heart still lived. He was still here. And she would see him every day. Be reminded of what she had lost every day.

Perhaps it would have been better if she had never returned to Gilloch? Perhaps she should be thinking of moving away again? Only it wasn't that simple. She was a doctor now. She had taken on the post at Gilloch promising that she would stay.

But he won't need me there any more. He's survived. He's going to live. He can be a doctor once again, setting me free.

The thought did not cheer her in the least.

'I have to go now. I just needed to make sure you were okay. You were right, Cameron. I'm walking away because you don't need me any more. Perhaps you never did. I thought you were safe. Can you believe that? That your diagnosis made me safe. I thought I wouldn't be risking my heart with you. Only I did. I'm sorry.'

And she turned on her heel and walked away.

She heard him try to call out. To stop her, perhaps? But all it succeeded in doing was making hot, salty tears fall from her eyes.

Cam had never needed her except as someone to step into his shoes when he'd believed he was on his way out through the exit door of life. Only he'd been given a reprieve. A last-minute chance.

No one except maybe Nanna needed her to stick around any more. Cameron could have his old job back. Everything could return to how it was before.

Perhaps I should stay for Nanna.

But something inside her told her that that was all she ever did. Fitted her life around other people's needs. When had she ever put her own needs first? She hadn't with Ashley. She hadn't with Cam. Not until now. Would Nanna want her to stay because of her? Surely she would see how unhappy she was and tell her to go and make her own life for once?

She'd thought she'd already done it—by returning to Gilloch. But she'd been wrong. So terribly wrong. And it had taken Cameron's second chance at life to make her see that maybe she needed to give *herself* a second chance at a life.

She pressed the button to open the door and walked out, knowing that this time she would drive away. There was no need for her to return.

Every step was a stab in her heart. Every movement away from him, from her heart, her soul, tore her in two. Tears streamed down her face as she fought to breathe, as she fought to keep her back straight and not crumple into a heap on the ground.

Cameron didn't need her. He didn't want her. He didn't love her the way that she loved him.

Now she was putting herself first.

And it was time to go home to her daughter and live.

'It was *so* good to see Dr Brodie!' Janet enthused, clutching her mug of hot, steaming tea. 'Smiling and chatting away like he hadn't a care in the world! It really was quite naughty of him to keep the fact that he was still ill from everyone. Especially when he must have known how concerned we were about him.'

Bethan nodded and smiled. She'd bet he didn't have a care in the world. He was healthy again. No terminal diagnosis any more. A future with his daughter. Which was all that he'd wanted.

The last week for her had been the complete opposite, but no one apart from Nanna had seen it in her eyes.

'I called in on him yesterday morning,' Janet went on. 'He comes home from the hospital late on Monday, by all accounts.'

Bethan smiled. 'That's great.'

Next week? That meant she only had a few more days before she might start seeing him around. That was going to be hard. She wasn't sure she was ready yet. Everything was still so raw.

'I've booked him onto the system so that you can give him a home check.'

Bethan blinked. 'Sorry? What did you say?'

'I've booked him in for a home visit. Early Tuesday morning—he's your first patient.'

'He's not a patient at this surgery—he's booked in under Dr McKellen in the next village.'

'Och, I know, lass, but Dr McKellen is away for two days at a conference, and Dr Brodie has to have a doctor's visit on his return home. It's one of the conditions of his release. I knew you wouldn't mind, what with the two of you being such firm friends.'

Her heart was racing. Thudding away in her chest like a pneumatic drill. Of *course* she minded! Having to see him. Touch him. Speak to him!

She suddenly felt a bit faint and sat down in her chair.

'Are you okay, lass? You've gone awful pale.'

'Oh, just…er…low blood sugar. I'll have something to eat.'

She grabbed a chocolate digestive from the packet on the table, but it was like ash in her mouth. Like chewing wood shavings. She felt sick, but she forced the biscuit down and sipped at her tea to help it on its way.

'I'd better get the day started.' She hurried away before Janet made her explain anything.

Cameron's going to be my patient?

Was it too late to quit? Would people think badly of her if she just turned tail and ran? Of course they would.

And I'm meant to be made of sterner stuff than this! I'll just have to be polite. Quick. Check him over and leave. Hopefully he'll be surrounded by the entire Brodie mob and we won't have any chance to talk.

Her first patient of the day was Malcolm McDowd. He shuffled into the room, looking tired and exhausted, leaning on his walking stick heavily and sinking into the chair with a sigh.

'Morning, Doctor.'

'How can I help you today?' She desperately wanted a conversation that didn't concern Cameron. Just for a short while it would be nice not to have to think about him at all.

Malcolm sighed again. 'I don't know why I'm here, really. I guess I just need someone to talk to. Someone who'll understand.'

Bethan glanced at his medical records on screen. Malcolm suffered from type two diabetes and high blood pressure. He had a bad hip after a car accident many years ago, and he was also a carer for his wife, who had Alzheimer's.

'Things have been a bit difficult lately with Barbara. She doesn't know who she is half the time, or where she is, and she keeps getting scared. Screams half the night. I get no sleep—I have to keep going in to reassure her. And when she's not scared, she's yelling at me. Throwing things. See this mark here?' He pointed at a small cut just above his left eye. 'That was a cup. Nothing hot in it, though, thank God.'

'It must be difficult for you. Do you get any respite?'

He shook his head. 'No. She made me promise. I swore to her that I...' He sniffed and wiped at his nostrils with a proper cotton handkerchief. 'But I guess now she doesn't even know who I am, so getting someone in might help.'

'I can certainly make some arrangements for you to be assessed, Malcolm. Carers today are hugely recognised for the contribution they make, and everyone is aware of how the carers themselves need time off. Perhaps we could get someone in to do the mornings and evenings for you? You know…getting her up and dressed, and then put back into bed again at night?'

'I'd feel so bad about not doing it myself. Like I'm letting her down.'

She knew all about feeling as if she'd let someone down…

'You're not, though. By looking after yourself you're helping her in the long run. Have you any other family that could help? Maybe give you a weekend away occasionally?'

'Our daughter down in Newcastle might—but she's got kiddies of her own to care for.'

'Sometimes people don't realise you need help if you don't ask for it. They assume you're okay because you put on a brave face for them. It's okay to hold your hands up and say you need a break. Some time for *you*.'

'Well, if you could arrange anything, Doctor, that would help me. It'd be nice to get down the bowling green once again—I do miss my games.'

She smiled. 'I bet. I'll send off a letter and I'll also give the respite teams a call. See what they can do at short notice. You're happy for me to give them your contact details—phone number, that kind of thing?'

Malcolm nodded. 'It's a weight off my mind. Thank you, Doctor. I hate to ask. No one likes to show weakness, do they?'

No. They didn't. If *she* ever did she quickly made up for it. She liked to think she used her fear in a positive way—unlike Cameron, who used his in a negative way. At least that was how she was explaining his actions—he'd been scared. But people often revealed their true selves when they were afraid. Saying what they really felt—and Cameron had been blunt and to the point.

'I don't love you, Bethan.'

'Let's check your blood pressure whilst you're here.'

She grabbed the cuff and wrapped it around Malcolm's upper arm, then manually pumped up the sleeve, listening in with her stethoscope, waiting to hear the pulsations that would give her his systolic and diastolic readings.

She released the cuff from his arms and smiled. 'It's a little high, still. One forty-two over ninety-six. But not as bad as it was before, so it's going in the right direction. Are you still taking your medication?'

'Yes, Doctor.'

'And your statins?'

'Every day—regular as clockwork.'

'Good. Barbara needs you to look after yourself.'

'And who's looking after *you*?' he asked, with a slightly cheeky grin. 'Young slip of a thing like you?'

She smiled politely. 'No one. But I like it that way.'

'You must miss it—being married. I heard you were a widow. I'm so sorry, lass. I can't imagine not having my Barbara—even if she doesn't know who I am. I know who *she* is, though.'

There was so much she missed. The easy nature of just being with someone every day. Having someone to hold you tight. Having someone you could talk to. Nanna did her best, but it wasn't the same. And she missed Cameron. Missed feeling loved by him.

I was so convinced he loved me, too! But perhaps it was all just on my side.

Relationships were complicated, and they often caused more pain than you needed.

'I miss some things, but not all.'

Malcolm struggled to his feet. 'No, I understand that, lass. People are hard, but I find that in the end the difficulties are worth it.'

'You think so?' she asked him as he ambled towards the door.

She tried to work out if her difficulties with Cameron had been worth it. She didn't think so. All she'd been left with was hurt and loneliness. She'd felt fine before she got involved with him!

'If you love them, yes. My Barbara doesn't know who I am, but I know who *she* is and that's what matters. Her brain may not recognise me, but my heart recognises her, and no matter how hard you may try you can't just shut those things down. Except maybe with some heavy medication.'

He smiled.

'Thank you, Doctor. For today. For listening. It's been such a long time since anyone's actually heard what I've been saying. I don't get many visitors.'

'You take care of yourself.'

She smiled back at Malcolm as he left, but she was left feeling empty. It had been a long time since anyone had heard *her*, too. She did try to say what she felt, but she always got shot down. Nanna did it sometimes. Grace often did—but she was just a child. And Cameron. Had *he* ever listened to what she had to say? What she felt?

He'd said his piece in the hospital and it had stunned her into silence. But had she ever been given *her* chance to speak? To say what *she* needed to say?

Perhaps that was why she still felt so bad? Because

she hadn't been given any closure? Given her chance, her moment, to say what Cameron had meant to her?

Should she say anything on Tuesday at his home visit? Or would that be unprofessional?

All she knew was that her heart *ached*. It physically hurt in her chest. Every morning since she'd left the hospital in Edinburgh she'd woken with no energy whatsoever. Each day was like wading through molasses.

And as for the idea of seeing him again... She wanted to—so much! But then again she was scared to. Seeing him again would open up the wound.

She could never *un*-hear what he had said to her. Would he remember? Or would he have forgotten it now? Was he concentrating only on his recovery? Thinking only of how he could get back to full strength the quickest? He was surrounded by his family, with his little girl, imagining the future they now had together.

She had provided him with that gift. At least she had contributed to making it happen. Was he headache-free for the first time in a long time? Bethan imagined that he was probably the happiest man on the planet right now...

In the quiet of the nights he remembered how she'd walked away from him. And how he'd wanted to stop her. In what should have been one of the happiest moments of his life she had changed everything, and in his exhaustion, and the fugue after the anaesthetic, chained to the bed by monitoring equipment and IVs, he had felt himself slipping away back into sleep when all he'd wanted to do was run after her.

He dreamt about her often. She would always be

ahead of him, her back turned towards him as she walked away, and no matter how hard he tried he could never quite catch up. Sometimes he dreamt that his fingertips drifted over the fabric of her blouse, but it was never enough. She always slipped away.

And then he'd remember. What he'd said before he went down for surgery—his attempt to make her leave him. He'd been trying to save her. Save her from having to tell everyone the bad news. She'd had to do it for her parents and her husband already—did he really need to put her through that again?

But it had worked. The surgery had been a success. And when he'd woken from his anaesthetic and seen her standing there so stiffly, so far away both physically and emotionally, he'd been in shock. Unable to believe that he wasn't dreaming. That he wasn't in heaven and that the sight of her there wasn't just a cruel trick of his mind.

He'd had a death sentence. A one-way ticket to an early grave. And he'd accepted that future. For it now to be so radically different was confusing and scary, and lying in that hospital bed, staring at the almost too bright white walls, he'd wanted to reach out and hold her hand, tell her he was sorry. But he'd never got the chance.

He'd called her a few times from the hospital in the days that followed. She hadn't answered her mobile, and at the house Mhairi would answer and tell him that he couldn't speak to her. It was like trying to get past a guardian at a gate, or a bouncer at a nightclub—only in this case the bouncer was a little old lady in her seventies, armed with a surprising capacity for swear words.

His father had visited often and brought Rosie. He'd never been so happy to see his daughter. The last time he'd seen her had been at home, waving goodbye, believing that he'd said goodbye for ever, and yet here they were, reunited. And it hadn't mattered that she'd wanted to bounce around on his bed, or that she'd spoken really loudly and begged him to read her a story. It had been his pleasure, and he knew he would never take for granted a single second that he got to spend with her from now on.

No moving in with Grandpa Doug.

He had Keir to thank for that.

And Bethan.

He wanted to say thank you even if she wouldn't allow him anything else. He knew he'd probably broken her heart by saying what he had, but he hadn't meant it! She was angry with him. Hurt by him. But surely she would give him the chance to explain?

And he just might get that chance today. Bethan was scheduled to pay him a home visit in place of Dr McKellen, who was away. He needed his vitals checked. His wound checked and redressed. Though as far as he knew it was healing well.

He missed her. Dreadfully. Every time the hospital door had opened he'd hoped she'd walk through. Every time a nurse had said, 'I have a message for you,' he'd hoped it would be from her. Only it never was.

Perhaps it was time to accept that he'd ruined things? Irrevocably.

He'd wanted to live for a future with his daughter, but he'd also hoped for a future with *her*. There. He could admit it to himself. He wanted Bethan back. But had he hurt her so much she wouldn't be able to see past her anger and hurt?

He missed her smile. The way she determinedly bit her lip when she was thinking hard. The way her eyes twinkled when she found something amusing. Just the way she made him feel. There'd been no future for them before, but there was now, and surely she should give him the benefit of the doubt and allow him time to say he was sorry? To explain it all?

Cameron glanced at the clock. Eight forty-six a.m. She would be here soon. How could he look her in the eye? Would she even turn up?

Yes, of course she will.

Suddenly he felt afraid. Afraid that if he told her everything and she still walked away...

'I want to cancel Bethan,' he told his father in a panic.

'Don't be a dunderheid! You need your wound redressed.'

He'd not told his father the whole story. Why he'd gone into surgery alone.

'She didn't leave me, Dad.'

'Did she not?'

'It was me. I said something to her...'

'What kind of thing?'

'That bit's not important. She wanted to stay with me. She wanted to be with me to the end.'

His father frowned. 'So what happened, then?'

'I got scared. I couldn't bear the idea of her having to give the news of my death to everyone—she'd done that enough times with her own family—so I said something horrible to make her go. She didn't want to leave me, but I made her.'

He looked down at the bedspread, guilty. Ashamed. He could feel the weight of his father's stare upon him. 'Are you telling me that she wanted to be with you but you got *rid* of her?'

Cam nodded.

'You great lump! You don't know how lucky you are sometimes.'

'*Lucky?* I had a death sentence hanging over me.'

'And yet you still managed to find a woman who wanted to be with you! Despite that, you great lummock! Och, I can't understand you young folk these days.'

'I'm sorry.'

His father looked out of the window at the sound of a car door being closed. 'Well, you need to tell *her* that.' He straightened his jumper and turned around. 'Because, she's here.'

Cam felt his heart begin to race in his chest. Bethan was here. He was going to see her again. Words couldn't express how he felt about that. It was so much more than nerves and anticipation and excitement and worry.

There were so many things he wanted to say to her, he wasn't sure what to say first. Start with an apology? Beg for forgiveness? What if she accepted his apology but still didn't want anything to do with him?

That would kill him. Her absence would be worse than any brain tumour.

He tried to sit up straight in his bed. He looked around the room, hoping it didn't look too much of a mess, but who was he fooling? Rosie had practically camped out in his bedroom since he got home, and the floor was covered in her books and toys and dolls.

It would have to do.

He would have to do.

His father was right. He had been a ridiculous fool.

CHAPTER TEN

SHE'D FELT SICK driving over. Her mind had kept coming up with all the different ways she could get out of this appointment—another patient emergency, perhaps, or a flat tyre. She had a migraine and couldn't drive… She had smallpox. Anything, no matter how ridiculous, just so she didn't have to face the man she knew she loved.

How stupid am I? Falling in love with a man who doesn't want me?

She'd spent the whole weekend telling herself how ridiculous it was. Falling for a man who was dying. *Dying!* Who would punish themselves in such a way? There had to be something wrong with her. She *liked* pain. She *liked* grief. Somehow she was attracted to it.

No wonder he'd got rid of her. He must have felt appalled. Thinking of her as some weird ghoul, entranced by sickness and death.

It didn't matter that she didn't really think it was true. The blind could not see.

Cam would hate seeing her today. He would be angry that Dr McKellen wasn't around to do this visit and that he would have to endure her.

Well, she wasn't looking forward to it either!

Now, Bethan glanced at his cottage, then away

again. She felt sick. Shaky. Her legs were weak and wobbly. He would know that she was here. He would know that she was sitting in her car, not wanting to go in, and he would know that she was a coward.

It was enough to force her into movement.

Her mouth dry, she got out of the car and collected her bag from the boot. With dread in her heart she began the slow walk to the cottage's front door—a condemned woman going to the gallows.

Just do this quickly. In. Out. Then it'll all be over.

She hoped he would be congenial. Polite, if nothing else. But it would break her heart if he didn't look at her. Or say anything. This was going to be awkward for both of them.

Bethan knocked on the door, knowing that someone from his family would answer. Cam would be in bed, so who would it be? Rosie would be good. That sweet little girl whom she and Grace adored.

Instead Dougal Brodie opened it, and stood there looking at her.

Bethan looked down and away, before sucking in a breath and looking up again. 'I'm here on Dr McKellen's behalf,' she managed to mutter.

'Aye. Come in, lass.'

She frowned, a little put on the back foot, because this wasn't the greeting she'd expected from him. Hadn't she abandoned his son? Surely he'd be angry?

'He's upstairs. You know the way?'

She'd never been in his bedroom.

'I'll find it.'

She began to head up the stairs, feeling her heart begin to pound faster and faster at the idea of seeing

Cam again. But before she got halfway up Dougal stopped her.

'He told me what happened. Between the two of you.'

Here it comes...

'I think he lost his mind for a moment there.' He shrugged. 'Fear will do strange things to a man...'

Bethan frowned, not sure what he was trying to say. When it became clear that Dougal wasn't going to say anything else, she continued to climb the stairs.

It felt like so long since she'd last seen Cam, but really it had only been a matter of a couple of weeks. She yearned for him still, no matter what he thought of her and that made her feel pathetic.

What kind of an idiot am I? An embarrassing sap.

On the landing at the top of the stairs she saw that only one door was open and sunlight streamed through from the windows inside. Tentatively she took a step forward and Cam, in his bed, moved into her view.

He looks amazing. Despite all that he's been through.

He looked healthy. Vital. Full colour in his cheeks despite the stark white dressing on the front of his head. He was looking at her with eyes filled with sorrow, which she guessed was better than anger, and so, with a slightly stronger resolve than she had felt since waking that morning, she stepped into his room.

'Hello, Cameron.'

'Bethan. You look well.'

'So do you.'

Look at how polite we're being with each other. Let's hope it stays that way and I survive this if I'm to walk away again.

'How have you been?' he asked.

Miserable without you. But how can I tell you that without you thinking I'm pathetic?

'Busy. You?'

Then she cringed, because of course he wouldn't have been busy. He'd been recuperating from the major brain surgery that had saved his life.

'I...er...need to check your dressing—is that all right?'

He nodded, never taking his eyes off her.

Why wouldn't he look away? Why was he watching her so intently? It was unnerving, and she could see that her hands were trembling as she opened up her bag and got out fresh dressings and her BP cuff and all the other paraphernalia she'd need.

'Is there a bathroom available? I need to wash my hands.'

What she actually needed was space to breathe. To gather herself. To get control of the shakes.

'The next room on your left.'

'Thank you.'

She practically raced from the room, shutting herself in the bathroom and leaning back against the door, fighting back the tears threatening to storm down her face—because she just couldn't bear this tense politeness they had going on between them.

It had used to be so *good*! They'd had such an easy manner between them. Had been able to talk about anything. Laugh about anything. And she missed that. Missed *him*. What she wanted more than anything else in the whole wide world right now was to sink into his arms, lay her head against his chest and have him hold her and stroke her hair, tell her everything would be all right between them.

She wiped her eyes and stared at herself in the mirror.

Get a grip!

Bethan washed her hands rigorously, dried them, and then checked her reflection one last time. Were her eyes still red? Or was it just the light in here? She took a deep breath and relaxed her shoulders, and then opened the door to head back to the bedroom.

Cam was still in bed. Waiting for her. Looking at her apprehensively. 'Are you okay?'

'Fine! Right—let's have a look at this wound, shall we?'

It was smaller than she'd imagined it would be. She'd half expected to see staples running in a half-moon over the front of his skull, but the incision was only about five centimetres in length and it was healing well. No redness, no signs of infection.

'These staples can come out now, I think.'

'That's great,' he answered.

She used a small tool that quickly and effectively removed the staples, dropping them into the small cardboard kidney dish she'd brought with her. Then she redressed the wound and removed the gloves she'd put on before beginning the procedure.

'Try and keep it dry for another few days, and then you should be able to wash your hair. Though do it carefully until you're fully healed.'

'Thanks. That'll feel good.'

'I'm sure it will. Do you mind if I do your blood pressure? Check your temperature?'

He nodded.

At least her hands weren't shaking any more. She was feeling emboldened by the fact that he hadn't attacked her verbally, or given her one of those looks, or treated her unkindly at all. And she could lose herself in the business of being a doctor. A place where she felt comfortable and in control.

'Bethan?'

She looked up and met his gaze. 'Yes?'

He looked apprehensive. Anxious. 'I...er... I need to say something.'

Oh. Here it comes.

Nausea hit her like a brick and she swallowed hard in a mouth that was as dry as dust. 'Right...'

His cheeks flushed with colour before he managed to make eye contact with her again. 'I...er...have to apologise. To you. Hugely apologise. If I gathered up every sorry in the world it wouldn't be enough to say just how sorry I am that I hurt you so badly. Appallingly, in fact.'

This was not what she'd been expecting and she stared at him in shock, her heart pounding.

'What I said to you in the hospital—I was scared. Scared not just for my life, and what was about to happen, but also scared for you.'

'Me?'

'Yes.' He let out a breath. 'You'd been through so much. What with your parents dying and then your husband. All I could see was you sitting beside me, knowing I might die, too, and I couldn't make you go through it again.'

His voice broke on the last word.

'It just felt so wrong, knowing that I was putting you through that, and I didn't want you to have to be the one to tell my daughter that I had died on the table. I felt that you would take the blame for putting me in contact with Keir and you would feel guilty for robbing me of my last few months with my daughter and…'

He looked up at her, a tear tumbling down his cheek. Met her gaze intently. 'I couldn't do that to you. I had to make you go. I tried to set you free.'

She stared back at him. Stunned.

'I tried to do it in the most awful way. By telling you I didn't love you. I lied, Bethan. I *lied*.'

Bethan stood up, unable to sit still a moment longer. 'You…' Her words choked in her throat.

He'd lied?

He stared at her, hearing his bedside clock ticking away the seconds that passed in the silence.

'You lied?'

'Yes. I didn't mean it.'

She stared back. She was acutely aware that his father was downstairs, no doubt listening with one ear. Bethan looked away from him. Out of the window, across the lane and to the mountain that rose behind it in the distance. Mount Gillochrie, where they had first made love in the warmth of the early-morning sun.

He'd lied.

'Bethan? Would you look at me, please?'

She couldn't. Her mind was racing. Tumbling through all the confused thoughts she'd begun to have. If he'd lied to her then that meant that he *did* love her, and she loved him, and everything could be all right.

Couldn't it?

But she was scared. Trembling as she stood looking out of the window, her arms hugging her own body.

The tears fell freely and silently. She didn't want him to see that she was crying.

She must have been in a world of her own. Because she didn't hear him get out of bed and pad across the floor to her in bare feet. The first she knew was his hot touch on her arm. She spun so fast, shocked that he'd crept up on her, that he had to grab her to steady her.

'I don't understand…'

'I was trying to protect you. From *me*. From the pain of my passing. That sounds incredibly arrogant, I know, but I thought if we argued, if you thought we weren't as close as we had been, then it would be easier for you, somehow.'

She needed some space to think. She couldn't think clearly with him touching her. Not when she craved his touch.

'Easier?'

'I was trying to protect you, Bethan. Do you want to know why?'

'Because you pitied me?'

'Not pity, no. It was because I love you. And the only thing I could give you was my protection.'

Bethan stared. He loved her. Those were the words she'd dreamt of hearing. But now that he was saying them out loud, in real life, it was terrifying.

Was there the possibility of happiness after all?

'You love me? You're *in* love with me?'

He stared back at her, helpless and vulnerable to anything she might throw at him.

'Yes. I know I went about it the wrong way, but when you're faced with a death sentence and the depths of love at the same time, all you can do is try and protect those you love.'

She did know that. She *did*. 'You put me through hell, Cameron.'

'I know.'

'You hurt me.'

'I know. And I'll be sorry for that every day of my life. But let me make it up to you by being the best Cameron Brodie I can be in the life that you have given me. This gift that you have given me. You gave me everything back, Bethan. You fought for me, gave me life, and a future, and time with my daughter that I thought I would never get to enjoy.'

'Anyone would have done the same thing...'

'No, they wouldn't. You went the extra mile.'

'I *had* to.'

'Thank you.' He reached out and tentatively took her hands in his.

Bethan stared at him. He loved her. He was in love with her! Something she'd thought would never happen! And all that he had said had been a terrible lie. Could she forgive him for that? Could she forget it?

Time was a great healer. Wasn't that what everyone said? And his hands in hers felt amazing. She wanted more—to be back in his arms, where she felt she belonged. But she was afraid to tell him the truth. To tell him that she loved him, too.

'So what happens now?' she asked, looking at him with tears in her eyes and running down her cheeks. She must look a sight, but she really didn't care at that moment.

'It's up to you. It's *all* up to you. I just had to be honest and tell you how I feel—even if you don't feel the same way as me. You deserve my honesty.'

'Right...' She nodded, feeling her heart racing in

her chest like a racehorse thundering down the final straight. 'Only I do.'

He blinked and looked at her. 'What?'

'I do feel the same way.'

'As in…?'

She laughed. And hiccupped. 'As in I love you, too, you idiot! Why do you think I got so upset back then?'

He looked surprised, then a huge smile broke across his face and he pulled her towards him in a great big bear hug, squeezing her tight against his chest. She sank into it. Sank into the feel of him, the smell of him. The *wonder* of him.

She began to laugh, her smile broad against his tee shirt, as she hugged him back.

'Have we been *complete* fools?' she asked, closing her eyes in delight.

She had him back. He loved her and she loved him and they had a future. There was no tumour ready to strike him down in a few short months.

'We may just possibly have been the very worst of them,' Cameron agreed. 'We were scared fools. Terrified fools.'

She looked up at him. 'I don't ever want to be a fool again.'

'Nor me.'

He leaned in to kiss her. The warmth of his lips upon hers made her feel like sighing with contentment. Like purring with happiness. The cat that got the cream. Kissing him was everything she'd hoped it would be and more. She was home at last. And home was *everything*.

He squeezed her tight against him once more. 'I never dared to hope that you might feel the same.'

She laughed and held her finger up to his lips, silencing him. 'What matters is that there is a future for us. Together.'

'Definitely.' He kissed her again.

EPILOGUE

THE LITTLE CHURCH in Gilloch was filled to overflowing, with guests in their finest suits and dresses, hats and fascinators.

From outside, Bethan could hear them all chattering to one another as she organised her two flower girls, Grace and Rosie, into the correct position. Oh, and Hamish—Rosie's new Labrador puppy—who wore a bright red bow around his neck and seemed determined to remove it by prancing around and trying to eat it.

The girls smiled and giggled at his antics and she gave each of them a kiss on the cheek.

It had been a long six months, waiting for this day. But everyone was happy for them. Even old Angus Brodie, Cameron's grandfather, had come around.

Mhairi and Angus had got together at their engagement party and begun talking, putting the world to rights between them for the sake of their grandchildren.

It had taken Bethan some time to get used to the idea that she was going to get married again, but when Cameron had proposed halfway up Mount Gillochrie it had been a wonderful surprise! A memory she would cherish for ever.

Cameron had had a couple of check-ups with Keir and his scans were clear. There were no more cancer markers, so he was considered completely cured. He was just like any other man.

Except that he *wasn't* just any other man.

He was *her* man.

And she loved him more than she would have thought possible.

Bethan lowered her veil over her face and sucked in a deep breath. In a moment she would be Mrs Brodie. Dr Bethan Brodie. Working in the same GP practice as her husband and mother to two little girls.

Or maybe it would be *three*?

She had her suspicions. Something felt different, but it was still too soon to know.

Maybe she'd find out on their honeymoon? They were going to go away to Italy. To a beautiful villa on Lake Como. The idea of telling Cameron she was carrying their child there lit her up inside so much she thought she would explode with light and joy. That so much life could come from so much darkness!

I'm ready.

She nodded to the usher and he opened the door. Inside she heard the music change to the traditional 'Wedding March'.

Grace, Rosie and Hamish stepped forward, perfectly in step, and the girls began to cast their rose petals.

And then Bethan stepped forward, too.

Into her happy and *long* future with the man she loved with all her heart.

* * * * *

COMING SOON!

We really hope you enjoyed reading this book. If you're looking for more romance, be sure to head to the shops when new books are available on

Thursday
28th June

MILLS & BOON

Coming next month

LOCKED DOWN WITH THE ARMY DOC
Scarlet Wilson

Amber gulped. For infectious diseases she was fine. But she wasn't quite as confident as Jack at being thrown in at the deep end. It wasn't that she didn't feel capable. She would always help out in an emergency. She wasn't sure how qualified or equipped she'd be to deal with things. She'd never really worked in an ER setting.

It was almost as if Jack sensed something from her. He leaned over and whispered in her ear. "Don't worry. I've got your back."

Then he did something completely unexpected. He turned her toward him and lowered his forehead onto hers. It was a gesture of security. Of solidarity. Of reassurance.

Warmth spread through her. She looked up and met his gaze. His dark brown eyes were fixed on hers. They were genuine and steady.

She pressed her lips together and took a deep breath, so many thoughts flooding into her mind. Her brain was such a mess. All she could concentrate on was the feel of his hands on the tops of her arms and the gentle way his forehead pressed against hers. His warm breath danced across her skin. Her gaze was naturally lowered and she could see the rise and fall of his chest.

He was a doctor. The type of guy she'd spent most of her life trying to avoid any romantic entanglements with. And this was crazy. She'd already seen a flash of something in him that reminded him of the focused way her father used to be.

So, if she already had alarm bells flashing in her head, why wasn't she running for the hills? She could pretend it was the hurricane. That the only reason she wasn't moving was because she was stuck here.

But that wasn't what was anchoring her feet firmly to the ground.

That wasn't what was letting the heat from the palms of his hands slowly permeate through her jacket and trickle its way through her body. Her last few boyfriends had been as far removed from medicine as possible—a landscape gardener, then a chef. But somehow she hadn't felt this. This connection.

And she couldn't understand it. She'd only met Jack last night. And yes, they'd clicked. There was no doubt the man was attractive. There was no doubt her mind was imagining so many other places they could go.

Continue reading
LOCKED DOWN WITH THE ARMY DOC
Scarlet Wilson

Available next month
www.millsandboon.co.uk